# MY FATHER'S LAND

## GWAMBI TETRALOGY
### BOOK ONE

## A. C. WILSON

WISE PATH
BOOKS

Interior illustrations by Shelby Elizabeth

Cover by Kirk DouPonce

ISBNs:

978-1-959666-00-4 (paperback)

978-1-959666-01-1 (ebook)

Published by:

**Wise Path Books**

a division of To A Finish LLC

12407 N MoPac Expy #250

Austin, TX 78758


www.wisepathbooks.com

*To my many friends and acquaintances who inspired this book. It was your personalities that helped me envision the setting of this story. You are many of the characters within these pages. If you see yourself in this book, it is because you have inspired me with your faith, joy, courage, spirit, and beauty. May God bless you and continue to use you to advance His kingdom.*

# CONTENTS

## GWAMBI TETRALOGY

# GWAMBI TETRALOGY

## BOOK ONE

The Year 1026 KA
Blisa Village, Slyzwir

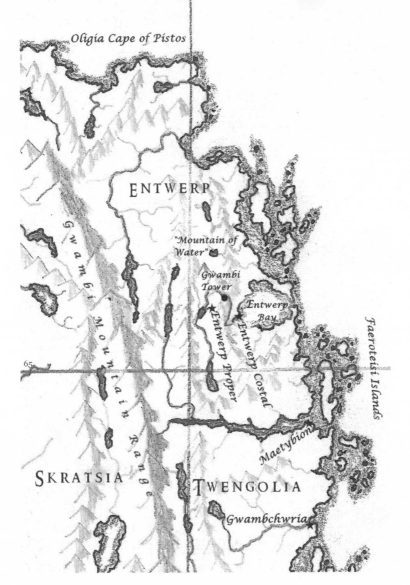

# ENTWERP AND SUROUNDING STATES

Oligia Cape of Pistos

ENTWERP

"Mountain of Water"

Gwambi Tower

Entwerp Bay

Gwambi Mountain Range

Entwerp Proper

Entwerp Costal

Faeroteisi Islands

Maetybion

SKRATSIA

TWENGOLIA

Gwambchwria

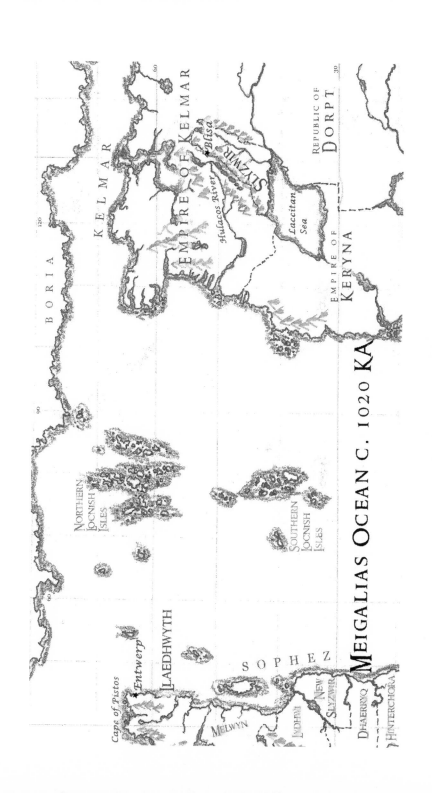

# 1

## THE PRISONER

*A* hand clamped firmly over Ella's mouth. She couldn't scream. She couldn't run. Strong arms seized her and wrapped around her body, holding her down. A sudden terror fell over her. It had come out of nowhere. She felt paralyzed, completely in the power of her captor.

Someone snatched the bread from her arms, casting it into the shadowy alleyway. A face leered above her—little more than a black silhouette against the night-time sky.

"What's this, little petticoat?"

The man was handsome, but his dark-olive features looked branded by some deep mark of evil. He wasn't human, but Ella couldn't tell how she knew. Was he a gnome? Or perhaps a leprechaun?

Even if Ella could respond, she wouldn't have. Her mind was reeling with shock. Nothing seemed to be as it should. Jock wasn't here in the alley, but these men were. Who were they, anyway? And what were they doing in Blisa? They looked like sailors—what were they doing so far into the mountains?

The man gestured to a figure in the shadows. "Well, old man, you've a pretty little friend here coming to give you bread at this time on night. Holgard will be happy for the offering, sure."

There was a groan from the shadows.

Just then, the chapel bells rang out vespers to the village. The sound of their ringing cleared Ella's head. Whoever these men were, they were up to no good, and they were holding her against her will. She had to get help. She needed to scream—that's what any heroine in the books would do.

Jabbing her elbow into her captor's ribs, Ella bit hard into his hand at the same time. The man let out a muffled yell but didn't relax his pressure. Instead, a substantial fist struck her skull. Her vision blurred, and her knees gave way. Yet the man holding her captive kept her upright.

The rogue in front of her laughed, waving his left hand in her face. Ella gasped. It was no hand at all, only two brass hooks; one curved like a shepherd's staff to point back at himself, and the other reached only a semi-circle. Together, they formed a hideous, twisted claw. Ella swallowed hard.

"Don't move, or you can take this in your vitals, sure."

Ella stood stock still.

The man with the hooks motioned to another ruffian. "Bring the old man."

The ruffian lifted the crumpled form of an old beggar from the shadows, letting the moonlight illuminate his face.

Ella caught her breath; it was Jock. The beggar looked more disheveled than usual. He was bleeding and bruised all over. His left eye was swollen and purple. Yet his eyes seemed kindled with the fire of determination.

"Do you know this girl?" the man with the hooks asked.

Jock opened his bloody lips slowly. "There is a stone wall behind ye. Look ye, it should answer ye before I do."

The thug lashed forward with his fist and caught Jock in the stomach. Jock groaned and doubled over. With a savage kick, the ruffian thrust him back into the shadows. Ella gasped in horror at the brutal treatment.

The figure who held Ella now spoke in a deep and powerful voice. "He knows her. I can see it in his eyes."

The man with the hooks turned on Ella. He gripped her chin firmly and looked her in the eye. She could feel his strength in his grip. Her pulse pounded in her throat. What was he going to do to her?

"I'm called Killjelly. Never mind my first name, just Killjelly. I've slayed many a creature with only my hand and hook." He paused. "Tell me: do you know this old man?"

Ella tried to speak, too terrified to worry about her lisp. "I was just twying to give him some b'ead..."

Jock hissed in warning.

Ella stopped. She shouldn't tell these rogues anything; none of the heroes in the books would have talked with malevolent villains. Hopefully, they couldn't understand her through her lisp. She had to be brave. She had to be courageous. They would never make her talk.

One of the ruffians clubbed Jock across the head and back with a large cudgel. Ella tried to turn her head away, but the man with the hooks held her fast. When the other ruffian was done with Jock, the man with the hooks turned back to her. Letting go, he slapped her hard on the cheek.

"You know him?"

Ella whimpered. The man who held her put his hand over her mouth before she recovered the presence of mind to scream.

The man with the hooks looked at her in disgust. "Tie her up, gag her, and then leave her here. You can peel her first, sure."

The man who held her spoke again. "That would be very imprudent."

The man with the hooks shrugged. "Do whatever you want with her, then. Knife her."

*Killjelly*

Ella shivered.

Just then, the other ruffian stepped forward. Ella knew immediately that he was a young dwarf from his square frame and slitted, cat-like eyes. She had met dwarves before. She knew what they looked like. "Why not take her back with us? I'm sure she could be useful to us on the ship."

The man with the hooks snickered. "A woman on a pirate ship?"

"We could sell her if'n we can't use her," the dwarf replied.

The man with the hook laughed again. "Ynwyr, she'll die either way."

The dwarf shrugged.

"He is right," the man who held Ella said, and the tone of his voice ended the argument. "Bring her with us. She may have information."

"If'n we must," the man with the hooks said with a sigh.

Pulling out a rope, they tied her wrists and gagged her. The ruffians forced her out of the alleyway and bundled her down the main road out of Blisa village. Ella only caught one last glimpse of the many homey lights from the windows, winking up and down the streets, before one ruffian pushed her forward, forcing her off into the woods outside the village.

A wagon pulled out of the shadows as they reached the trees. The pirates threw Ella and Jock into the back amidst a few sacks and barrels, and then they mounted horses of their own.

With a lurch, the wagon started careening down the mountain as fast as the horses could pull it. Jock lay still for a few moments as they jostled roughly down the rutted road. Then he leaned across the cart and pulled Ella's gag off, motioning for her to stay quiet.

"Ye should not has come, look ye," he said. "I could has waited on the bread."

"But I felt so bad about fo'getting, I just had to b'ing it tonight..."

Jock looked at her closely. "What did yer parents think av it?"

Ella didn't reply.

Jock sighed. "I has done my bestest, look ye, but I cannot promise ye will survive this. It is prayint to God for safety ye should be. He is our onlyest hope now."

Ella swallowed. "What is all of this about, anyway? Why a'e these men kidnapping us? A'e they piwates? I thought I hea'd them say–"

"The leastest ye know, look ye, and the fartherest away ye are from me, the betterest it will be for ye, whatever," Jock said.

Ella lay motionless, trying to process what had just happened. Suddenly, a thought came to her. "What do you mean you've 'done' you'h best? Don't you mean you will 'do' you'h best?"

Jock grunted as the wagon hit a large bump. "Yer bread made a decent, make-shift envelope."

# 2

# THE GALLEON

*T*he pirates rode down the mountain faster than Ella had thought possible. They continued at this pace across the eastern valleys, avoiding any towns they came to and always making their way down towards the Hulacos River. Ella felt exhausted, but she knew she had better stay awake and keep a careful eye on where these ruffians were taking her—that's what any sensible hero would do in the books.

The great discomfort of the wagon, with its constant jolts and bumps, helped Ella immensely in staying awake, yet she must have eventually dozed off a few hours before sunrise, for she suddenly opened her eyes, and there was the sun, just showing its magnificent rays above the eastern mountains. They must be miles away from Blisa by now, and the pirates were still thundering west along the river road.

At some point during the night, the pirates must have pulled out their muskets; for now, each carried a full assortment of weaponry as if they feared they would have to fight through a line of regulars.

After several hours, much of Ella's paralyzing terror had subsided. Jock had fallen promptly asleep when the sun rose, but Ella couldn't sleep anymore, even if she had wanted to. She was extremely uncomfortable in the back of the cart and was much too nervous for any more repose. What had she missed while she slept? Would she be able to find her way back to Blisa now if she could get away from these pirates? Looking around at the countryside, Ella didn't recognize anything. There was nothing much to see but the great river off to their left and now and then a hamlet or cottage by the side of the road. Had they crossed the border into Kelmar, or were they still in Slyzwir?

With nothing better to do, Ella studied the pirates. She knew enough about the eight intelligent races—the Kin of Man, or anthrogenus—to hazard a guess as to each of her captors. As she had only met humans and dwarves in person, her guesses as to the other races were a shot in the dark; even so, she considered herself educated enough to be confident in her guesswork.

First, there was the dwarf who had spoken up for her—she had already identified him. As for the man driving and the one who first caught her, they were humans like herself. The driver looked like a young man in his late twenties, while the other looked much older. He wore a cloak which disguised most of his face so that all Ella could see of him were locks of very white hair.

As for the other pirate—the one who had brought the cart — after a bit of thought, Ella decided he was a gnome. He was obviously one of the shorter species and was pretty fair-featured. Besides this, he had very large, round ears. That meant that he had to be a gnome or a leprechaun—both of those races had strange ears, but she couldn't remember exactly what they were supposed to look like. What finally made her peg him as a gnome was seeing him turn his head all the way around like an owl. She was pretty sure that only a gnome had the spinal column capable of that much flexibility.

The hooked man—the one who called himself Killjelly—puzzled her. She couldn't figure out what kind of anthrogenus he was. He was shorter than a human, had no beard, and his ears were pointed, like those of a hound. So if the other pirate was a gnome, then this pirate couldn't be one. Then again, this Killjelly could be a leprechaun or a short faerie—after all, height was only relative. Hadn't Master Schultz said that some dwarves were taller than the average human?

Still, wasn't a faerie supposed to have a fatty forehead for his echolocation? After much gazing at this pirate with the hooks, Ella finally decided that he did not have a fatty forehead—though she wasn't entirely sure what a fatty forehead looked like. So Ella guessed he was a leprechaun. Of course, the only way to know for certain would be to starve him for a week and see if he turned green. Or she could feel his pulse when he fell asleep to see if it dropped to almost nothing. Ella noticed something else interesting about the man with the hooks, however. He wore an amulet around his neck. The symbol on the amulet appeared to be something like a circle inside an upside-down triangle. Maybe it was a gift from his lady love?

When she finished scrutinizing the pirates, Ella tried counting the hamlets they passed and the number of bridges, but she soon grew tired of it and sank down in despair and gloom.

The pirates strenuously avoided all towns on their route, sometimes leaving the road and hauling the cart through thorny copses and a few muddy, freshly plowed fields to circumnavigate a village. However, they often passed close enough to a town that Ella could hear the bells of various churches striking out the hour. By this means, Ella could keep track of time as the wagon lurched, bumped, and jolted along through the first hour of the day, then the second, and finally into the third hour.

Ella was certain that any of the heroes she read about in her books would have planned their escape by now and be well on their way to retribution. She, however, hadn't the slightest idea what to do. Here she was, a young woman of twenty–in the flower of youth with a million prospects before her—lying in the bottom of a cart with the town beggar, likely to be murdered by pirates, or worse.

She tried hard to convince herself that there was some hope. Wouldn't her stepfather come looking for her? Then again, how would he know where to look? Surely there was some way out of this. What would those heroes have done? What would they be doing now if they were in her situation? She racked her brain for some kind of answer. Usually, there was a rusty nail, or a forgotten knife, or a loose rope placed conveniently in the hero's way so that he could make his escape. She, however, had no such help. They had the author to look after them, but she had no one. She sobbed quietly, turning her back on Jock's sleeping form to face the wagon's side. Jock stirred a little.

"Ella, my girl?"

Ella sniffed.

"Ye can worry, but do not be afraid. Yer stepfather is a good man, whatever; he will come after ye."

"Do you think?" Ella replied in a choked voice.

Jock sighed. "Pray, my girl. That is all ye can do for certain. God is good—is not that true?"

Ella shrugged, but she felt somewhat better for being talked to.

Around noon, the pirates slowed their pace and turned down a dirt trail that led closer to the river. The trail wound slowly down the cliff until it terminated on a small pier on the river. A skiff sat in the harbor by the pier with two more pirates attending to it. Wordlessly, the pirates unloaded the cart, packing all of their luggage into the skiff before transferring Ella and Jock into the longboat.

This done, the man with the hooks reached into his purse and pulled out a handful of coins, holding them out to the human driver and the gnome. They tipped their hats to him, but as the man with the hooks took a step forward to give them their pay, he stumbled, dropping the coins all over the pier.

"I'm sorry..." the man with the hooks mumbled, shaking his head ruefully.

The human driver and the gnome only grunted as they bent down to pick up the coins. The human stooped directly in front of the gnome, and as they stood up, they both had their backs turned towards the leprechaun with the hooks.

With no warning, the man with the hooks drew a pistol from his belt, aimed, and fired. Both the human driver and the gnome collapsed. Ella jumped, catching her breath. They were *dead*. She had just *seen* that man with the hooks kill them. Blood already stained the pier.

The man with the hooks thrust his pistol back into his belt with a flourish. "Both with one shot! You don't often get *that* lucky, sure!"

The dwarf just shook his head.

"What?" the man with the hooks said, looking back at the dwarf with a smile playing about one side of his mouth. "We couldn't have them ratting us out to anyone, now could we? This is the only way to ensure that no one knows we were here."

The dwarf only shrugged. "I guess. Do what you have to."

Stepping towards the two corpses, the leprechaun with the hooks took his money back from their dead hands. Then, with the toe of his boot, he pitched the corpses into the river.

The man with the hooks smiled again. "You've got to clean up after yourself. That's what my father would say."

"What about the horses?" the dwarf asked.

The man with the hooks pulled out his pistol again, reloading it. "If'n you insist..."

"Oh, no!" the dwarf cried.

The man with the hooks smiled coldly. "They're just animals."

"So they can't rat on us." The dwarf replied, looking at the man with the hooks in disgust.

The man with the hooks just shrugged. "It might not be worth the charges then, sure..."

"I draw the line with the horses," the dwarf said.

The man with the hooks put his pistol back in his belt. "Fine, then."

With that, the man with the hooks got into the skiff. The dwarf cut the horses free from the cart and sent them back up the dirt trail with a slap on the rump. Once the horses had reached the top of the cliff, the dwarf shoved the cart into the river and climbed into the skiff himself. With a deft stroke of the oars, they pushed off.

Ella lay still as the pirates rowed. She could not believe what she had just seen. Had she really just seen that man with the hooks *kill* two people? What might he do to her? Still, they seemed content to leave her alone for now. None of them were playing with their guns or blades—they always did that in the books before they hurt anyone. She looked at the four pirates on board the skiff, then back at the two corpses and the wagon floating down the river. Where was that other man, the mysterious man with the hood, who had caught her initially? Strange, she hadn't seen him leave.

Ella looked the two new pirates over to determine their race—a game to divert her mind from her position and the horror she had just witnessed. The more she could keep her mind on the game, the less her mind could ponder what the pirates might do to her. Unfortunately, she quickly pegged both as gnomes. Ella settled herself down in the luggage and waited.

Finally, the skiff took a turn in the river, and there—hidden in a small cove set about with cliffs—was a large ship. Ella knew little about ships, but she guessed it was a galleon. A flag bearing an auroch's skull on a black field flew from the main mast:

wasn't that a pirate flag? The black flag, at least, was a sure sign of piracy.

Ella swallowed hard. Her limbs felt numb and limp. She was certain her face was white with fear. Didn't the black flag also represent the command for "havoc"? She had read about that in her books; "havoc" meant that no quarter was to be given to your enemies. But if the pirates meant to kill all of their prisoners, would they kill her too?

The shrill blowing of a whistle pierced the air, ropes flew over to the skiff, and heads appeared on the deck, leaning over to look at the skiff, and everyone was talking at once. Questions rained down like hail-stones on the crew of the skiff.

"Do'ed you get the Blowhoarder?" "Are you being followed?" "Who's the little petticoat?" "Is that whiskey in the barrel?"

Ella's head spun with the commotion. The crew quickly hauled aboard the luggage from the skiff, then hauled up Jock. Finally, the dwarf tied a rope around his waist and picked Ella up from the bottom of the skiff. Ella hung limply in his arms as the other pirates hauled the young dwarf aboard. As soon as he stepped on deck, he set Ella down. Her legs buckled, and she fell to her knees, shaking.

The pirates crowded around as if she were a centaur or some other mythical beast. She sank under their intense gaze. There she was with her faded house dress, blonde hair messy and disheveled, and she had left her shawl back at the house.

Besides her fear, she felt miserable. The sleepless night in that jolting wagon left her bruised all over and exhausted. Even had she been in a better state, to have an entire crew of pirates gawking at her at once was mortifying. It was as if she was not a person anymore, but only an object to ogle or discard as the pirates saw fit. The autumn wind blew softly over the deck, and she shivered. Why had she not brought her shawl?

Suddenly, a massive dwarf strode through the ring of pirates. Ella guessed by his demeanor that he was the captain. He grinned at the younger dwarf who had brought Ella on board and embraced him.

"Weel now, son, how'd your first on-shore job treat you?"

Ella blinked. Never would she have guessed that these two were related. The captain may have been a dwarf by race, but he was not a dwarf in size. He towered over others of his race, standing head and shoulders above his son. His shoulders were broad, and his arms were hard as iron. His braided black beard spilled out across his chest, tucked neatly in his belt next to a brace of pistols and a large cutlass. Tattoos of swirling fire and woven designs covered his upper arms, and a small gold ring hung from his nose.

The other was a dwarf, like his father, but there all resemblance stopped. He had bright blue eyes and dark brown hair that hung neatly to his shoulders. He seemed hardly a man with the air of youth still about him. His beard had not grown out to more than a thick, brown fuzz, so that he hardly looked like he had a beard at all. Only the thick, feather-like dwarfine organ above his upper lip gave the impression of a full and mature mustache. His arms were enormous and his shoulders broad. He had a well-rounded chest, but his legs and lower body seemed ridiculously out of proportion to his upper body, being rather small and thin.

Ella shivered again and shrunk down in the shadow of these two dwarfs. The captain then caught sight of her.

"What's this?"

He bent down and yanked Ella to her feet as if she were a shock of barley. He looked her up and down like he was sizing up a dog he planned to buy.

"We bringed her from Blisa," the son said.

"Captain Holgard." It was the man with the hooks who spoke. He tipped his cap to the captain. "She comed upon us after we catched the Blowhoarder. She was going to give him some bread. Our mutual acquaintance suggested that we might find a use for her?"

The captain sized Ella up again and then dropped her to the deck with a grunt. "We might."

He walked away with his hand on his son's shoulder. A burly man with a whistle barked out orders, and the pirates dispersed to do their various tasks. Ella shivered and looked around. Jock wasn't anywhere in sight.

Just then, one of the younger pirates strode up to her. She noted his short, skinny frame and large ears and guessed him to be a gnome. She shrunk away from him, and he stopped, staring at her from a few feet away. He examined her carefully, starting at her feet and scanning up to her head. He first seemed to study her like she was on display at a museum, but his eye softened with pity when he looked her in the face.

"They do'edn't feed you, do'ed they?"

Ella shook her head.

"Well then, come with me." The pirate offered her his hand. "My messmate's the cook, so he can fix that."

Ella slowly gave him her hand, and he lifted her to her feet. She had taken only one step before she collapsed again. The gnome caught her quickly and lifted her up again. "Poor land-rat."

He put her arm over his shoulder, and she moved forward by leaning heavily on him. Although everything she *knew* told her she shouldn't, she felt she could trust *this* pirate. The way he helped her along seemed almost affectionate. She relaxed completely against his side.

"My name's Ernest, if'n you wanted to know," the gnome said as he helped Ella to a steep staircase that led below deck. When they finally reached the bottom of the stairs, Ella found herself in a murky room. Just in front of them sat a long bar that separated one corner from the rest of the room. In this separate section stood a wood stove, a fireplace, and a washbasin, along with several barrels and cabinets and a door that stood open, revealing a pantry.

In the middle of this kitchen, a tall pirate busily scrubbed various bowls and cooking utensils. As they entered the galley, the man looked up. Ella immediately saw that this pirate had a rather large forehead and prominent cheekbones, giving him almost a seal-like look. This man must be a faerie. She remembered studying the faerie with Master Schultz—he liked to call them faeriefolk, or Sheehogue. Seeing the man now took a lot of her mind off her dreadful situation. So this was what a faerie looked like? Master Schultz would be jealous—he had always wanted to see one himself.

She knew that this faerie had a large forehead because of the fat reserve above his frontal sinus. This reserve of fat—Master Schultz called it a 'melon'—could focus the sound waves produced from the sonar gland in the back of the faerie's nasal passages. Ella looked at this man closely. What must it be like to view the world with echolocation? Ella could only imagine that it must be grand and romantic.

"Helen Maria, Ernest!" the faerie said. "Where'd you get this little woman?"

"Killjelly bringed her back with him," Ernest replied as he helped Ella up to the bar and gave her a stool to sit on. "She says she havesn't eaten all day."

"Well, well, well," the faerie cook replied, "we can fix that, now, can't we?"

He snatched up the bowl he had just cleaned and filled it with some colorless stew out of his pot. He handed her the bowl along with a hunk of brown bread. "Gorge yourself on this, girly. It mayn't be hot, but it's food, no doubt."

Ella fell upon the food ravenously. Despite its bland color and consistency, the gruel was perhaps the richest and most flavorful food Ella had ever tasted. She devoured the bowl full of food faster than the faerie could clean his next dish. When she was done, she wiped out the bowl with the bread and then devoured it, too. The bread was also very good, though it was tough and very dense.

"How did you make that? It was delicious," she asked when she finished.

The cook laughed. "It's a bit on a secret, see; I can't tell anyone."

"But su'ely, you can tell me something of what you put in it?"

The cook shook his head. "As I always say, 'good cooking is what people love when they're eating it, and blanch when they hear what was in it.'"

Ella looked at him, unsure of what to think. The cook just grinned and turned back to washing the dishes. Ella sat on her stool for a few moments, staring at her empty bowl. She was still hungry—how could she still be hungry? But she couldn't ask for more. These pirates had already fed her very well.

Ernest apparently noted her position, because he picked up a loaf of bread from the kitchen, tore it in half, and gave a piece to her. Ella accepted it and tried to thank the gnome, but the words caught in her throat, and she choked. Her eyes watered.

"You'h so nice... both of you," Ella finally spluttered.

The cook turned back to her with his bright smile. "Well, well, well, you only think that because you're a helpless woman. If'n you were a man, we would have knifed you on sight."

Ella swallowed a bite of bread. "Yes, but... I've hea'd so many sto'ies... about piwates... I thought... but oh, you a'e *so* nice." She was crying now.

Ernest shifted his weight and cleared his throat, but the faerie cook leaned forward and seriously fixed his eyes on Ella. "I don't know what you've heared about pirates, but it's all true. You've good reason to be mortally afraid on all on us—and you shouldn't trust any on us. If'n you weren't in such awful shape, you probably couldn't trust me or Ernest either. There's hardly a man aboard who would blink twice before doing what I willn't name."

Ella shivered, but she looked the cook straight in the eye.

"That said," the faerie cook resumed, "you are lucky to have come aboard a ship where there are a few on us yet who willn't hurt a girl in your condition. Ernest and I will see that you're treated well—or at least as well as we can reasonably manage. Ynwyr, Captain Holgard's son, will also look out for you. He's too stupid to hurt anything he thinks is weak."

The cook continued to stare Ella in the face for a few seconds, as if trying to impress on her the gravity of his statement. Suddenly, a thought seemed to come to him, and he bent down to loosen a dagger from his leg, handing it to her—straps, scabbard, and all.

"Both Ernest and I will deny I ever gived this to you."

Ella looked at it with alarm.

"It goes on your thigh," the cook said. "You've got enough petticoats on to keep it well hidden, and if'n anyone happens to find it there, they will deserve to get it in their gut—even me or Ernest, mind."

Ella took it, and the cook immediately turned his back on her, washing his dishes as if she didn't exist. Ernest appeared to be concentrating on the cook's work, but Ella felt him watching her out of the corner of his eye. Ella's legs and arms trembled. Hurriedly, she turned her back on Ernest, and as quickly as she could, she lifted her skirts and strapped the dagger to her thigh just above her stockings.

She turned back to see the pirates in the same position they were in before. Ella was shaking, but she still managed to pick up the rest of her bread and start eating again. To tell the truth, she had lost her appetite.

# 3

## CWEEL

$\mathcal{N}$ either Ernest nor the cook seemed to take any more notice of Ella as she finished her bread. After she was done, she simply sat on the stool by the bar, waiting for something to happen. Ernest soon left, trudging back up on deck.

So Ella continued to sit for quite some time while the faerie cook ignored her. Now and then, he would start whistling some hornpipe or sing out a few random phrases of a sea-chanty, but mostly, he was silent. She hardly knew how to compile her thoughts. It almost didn't seem real that she was sitting in the kitchen of a pirate ship. She choked at the thought. What were her mother, stepfather, and siblings doing at the moment? They would know she was missing by now. But what could they do? How were they to know where she was?

"Your bread made a decent, make-shift envelope." Isn't that what Jock had said? But what did that mean? Was there any hope they would find her before the pirates reached the ocean?

Ella's heart sank within her as the thought occurred to her. The ocean—yes, that was her biggest fear. Once the pirates reached the ocean, they could travel anywhere without ever being found. They would most likely dispose of her violated corpse on some abandoned shore, where her mother and step-father would never hear of it. She would disappear from the earth, just like her father.

After nearly half an hour like this, the cook finally finished his last dish and turned to Ella.

"Helen Maria! I almost forgot. Do you need anything to drink?"

She started in surprise, so it took her a few moments to answer. "Yes, please."

The cook whistled merrily, grabbing a tankard from a nail in the wall before he strode over to a keg in the corner to fill the cup. He handed it to her with a grin and then turned back to his kitchen, where he stoked the fire in his stove and began preparing another soup.

Ella took the tankard and looked at it. The contents were a rich brown color. She assumed it was beer. She took a mouthful and nearly spat it back into the cup for surprise. The liquid burned in her mouth and sinuses, sliding down her throat like heated glass. She coughed and gagged, setting the cup away from her. This wasn't beer. It was ugro—grog—the devil's drink. This was the sort of stuff that made people drunk.

Ella looked at the cook, but he apparently hadn't noticed her surprise at the beverage—or if he had, he was purposefully ignoring her. She then looked back at the cup. She dared not swallow any more. Her mother had warned her about such brew. Then again, she couldn't just refuse the drink after the cook had been so nice to her.

Thankfully, a young gnome—somewhere around twelve summers of age—came tramping down the stairs at that moment, saving her from having to decide. Despite his younger age, he was a little thicker than Ernest but more wild-looking.

His shirt was torn open to his stomach, and he wore his hair pulled back with a turban. He seemed to be acting tougher than he actually was.

The gnome stopped at the bottom of the stairs and looked hard at Ella.

"Cap'n wants you." He spoke with an affected roughness to cover up his changing voice.

Ella stood slowly, but the cook spun to face the boy. "Blind prelates, boyo! Let her alone—until she's finished her drink at any rate."

The boy looked hard at the cook. He appeared to be hesitant to disagree with the elder pirate. "Cap'n said."

"What am I supposed to do with the ale, then? I can't just put it back in the keg."

The boy studied the cook for a moment, then strode up to Ella, pushed her roughly aside, and drank the entire contents of the tankard in one gulp. He slammed the tankard down on the counter in a clearly imitative way.

"Anointment," he cursed, swaying slightly. "Now she can come."

Ella followed the boy back up to the deck and then towards the ship's stern. They ascended a couple more flights of stairs as they went further back until they came to the cabin immediately below the aft deck. The boy opened the door and motioned for Ella to enter, but he did not follow her inside.

Ella found herself in a room lighted by a few lanterns, with a large desk in the middle of the room. She noted several barrels by the desk but took in no more of the room, for at that moment her eyes fell on the most fearsome beast she had ever seen.

The creature's body and haunches were like a jaguar's—long and muscular, with dark brown and black splotches on his tan hide. His tail streaked out behind him like a lizard's, though long tail feathers sprouted from its tip. His muscular, golden-colored wings stretched out nearly twenty feet from tip to tip. Owl-like front legs, with two powerful talons in front and two opposite, gripped the barrel the creature perched upon, his claws biting into the wood.

But his head was the most frightening part. Wolf-like ears lay flat against his skull, and his beak-like upper jaw curved down like an osprey's. His lower jaw snapped shut, full of sharp canine teeth and as strong as a lion's maw. Golden feathers covered his neck in a mane and sprinkled his back and shoulders, mingling with his glossy fur. Overall, he was nearly as long as a dwarf is tall, though on all fours he stood only a few feet from the ground.

Ella held her breath. She had only read about beasts like this. She knew what it was all too well, and all too well did she know what feats it could perform. It was an eagle griffin—the fiercest of all the griffin species.

The beast fixed his slitted eyes on her as soon as she entered the room and would not turn them away. Finally, he slid down from the barrel he had been sitting on and scratched his way across the floor to get closer to her. Ella backed away, but she hit the closed door and could go no further.

The griffin stood up on his back legs to look at her more closely. Finally, he opened his mouth and hissed, "*You* are the girl."

Ella gasped in mortal dread. Not only had she run into an eagle griffin, but this was a *talking* eagle griffin.

The beast blinked disdainfully and scuttled back to his barrel. Ella relaxed somewhat, but at that moment, the door opened.

She jumped forward and to the side, and in strode the captain, the captain's son, and the leprechaun with the hooked hand. Ella shivered back against the wall. She remembered what the cook had told her about the captain's son, but she was still terrified of the other two men.

The three took seats around the table, but only the son seemed to note Ella's presence. The captain poured himself a drink from a barrel and sipped it slowly. Meanwhile, the leprechaun tried his hooks on the edge of the table. Now and then, the captain and the leprechaun would glance over at Ella before looking away.

Finally, the captain spoke. "What do you know about the Blowhoarder—Jock, or whatever you call the old man?"

Ella opened her mouth, but no words came. She closed her mouth and tried again, but at that moment, her mind jumped back to the night of the capture, when Jock had hissed to warn her to keep silent. She again heard Jock's words, "The leastest ye know, look ye, and the fartherest away ye are from me, the betterest it will be for ye, whatever."

Ella closed her mouth and shivered.

The leprechaun slammed his hook into the table, and the captain took a long draught of his ale. When he had finished, the captain turned to his son.

"Ynwyr, my boy, might you check out on deck to see that all's still going smoothly?"

"On course." Ynwyr stood up with a broad smile and walked out of the room. As he closed the door behind him, Ella's heart sank. There was no one in the room now to plead her cause. To make matters worse, the eagle griffin still would not take his eyes from her.

As soon as his son was gone, the captain took one last draught of his ale and then fixed his eyes steadily on Ella. "What do you know about Jock?"

Again Ella remembered Jock's warning hiss and didn't answer. Of course, none of the heroes in the books would have answered. They always stood strong through the most dreadful interrogations. Ella tightened her lip. She would not say a word. No matter what they did to her.

The captain turned to the man with the hooks. "You should've killed her already and saved me the trouble."

"She knows Jock," the man with the hooks replied. "I think she may know something that would be hard to get out of him, sure."

The captain leaned back in his chair.

"Make *her* talk," the eagle griffin suddenly said.

The Captain nodded and then stood up, taking a step towards Ella. "If'n that's what you think, Cweel."

Ella cowered back as he approached her. He grabbed her firmly by the shoulders and thrust her into a chair. The color drained from her face. She couldn't speak. She could hardly move. Fear seemed to wrap around her brain, forcing out any rational thoughts. The captain towered over her like a massive wall of limestone, just waiting to fall and crush her.

The captain regarded her for a moment, then grabbed her wrist and slid her sleeve back to bare her arm. With a deft movement, he drew a short knife and held it poised over Ella's arm.

"What do you know about Jock Blowhoarder?"

Ella opened her mouth, but her tongue clung to the roof of her mouth. She would not talk. She would persevere through anything.

The captain waited only a few moments before raising his knife to strike. Ella saw the blade flash, and her tongue came free.

"Wait!" she cried, "I will tell you eve'ything I know about Jock. Please, just don't hu't me!"

The captain held the knife still and stared at her levelly. She could feel the gaze of the griffin on the side of her head. She swallowed.

"Jock came to my village about two months ago—maybe it

was th'ee actually; I'm not su'e. I saw him eve'y now and then, but he was a begga'h, so I didn't talk with him. He also looked like a sailor, so I left him alone. About a month ago, I sta'ted making b'ead for a neighbor and had some left ove'h, so I gave it to Jock since he was a begga'h, and he didn't know his way a'ound the village. Afte'h that I gave him b'ead eve'y week, and sometimes I would talk to him. That's what I was—"

The Captain cut her off, "I asked you what you knowed about him, not how you met him."

Ella gasped in fear. "I don't know anything but that he's a begga'h. I just gave him b'ead that's all. He was a sailor, but now he's a begga'h. That's all I know."

The captain snorted. "Weel, we'll see if'n that's all or not." He slid the knife across her upper arm. Ella cried out in pain, but the captain only sneered. "What do you know about Jock?"

"I told you eve'ything," Ella gasped.

The captain turned to the man with the hooks. "Powder."

The leprechaun lifted a bag of white powder and sprinkled some of it on Ella's wound. Pain like fire passed through Ella's arm. Her vision blurred as the pain throbbed again and again like a battering ram against her skull. The edges of her vision went black and her head slumped forward. The captain caught her by the hair and yanked her head back up before she could faint completely.

"Weel?"

Ella gasped, but she couldn't speak.

"Shall I get the needles?" the leprechaun offered.

Just then, the griffin spoke. "Holgard, step *aside* and let go of *her* arm."

The captain dropped Ella's wrist and stepped to the side. Ella could see the griffin leaning over the table at her. Suddenly he sprang forward, with his wings stretched wide. His talons gripped her shoulder, and the chair fell backward, throwing her to the ground. Her head hit the deck hard, and she stared into the golden eyes of the griffin. He held her shoulders so tightly in his claws that she was bleeding. His beak nearly touched her nose as he glared at her. He was so close that Ella could smell his musty breath and taste it in her mouth as drops of saliva fell on her cheeks. Pain coursed through her head, her shoulders, her arm, her whole body. Pain seemed to epitomize her very existence. She couldn't think for the pain, she could hardly breathe.

"I am *Cweel*, fear *me*."

She lay motionless, practically hypnotized by the griffin's bright, slitted eyes.

"What do *you* know about Jock?"

Her mouth seemed to open of its own accord. "I've told you al'eady, Jock's a begga'h. That's all I know."

The griffin stepped off of her and scratched his way back to the table.

"She has told *us* everything."

The Captain snorted in disgust. "Weel, that was a waste on time."

Ella's heart was pounding at twice its normal rate. She laid her head on the floor and closed her eyes, praying that the nightmare was over. The pirates must have thought she had fainted, for they suddenly talked more freely.

"Shall I kill her?" the captain asked.

"*No*," the Griffin, Cweel, replied.

The Captain snorted again. "She's a waste on food and time. I say kill her now or give her to the crew and then kill her in the morning if'n she's not dead already."

"I say do *not* kill *her*," Cweel said authoritatively.

The Captain growled, "I'm the captain."

"*You* swore fealty to Captain Longfinch," Cweel replied. "*I* am here to see *you* do his orders, and *I* say that you do *not* kill *her* until Longfinch has examined *her*."

The captain murmured something under his breath and snorted.

The man with the hooks tapped his hooks on the table. "I agree with Cweel, sure."

The Griffin made a purring noise.

"Why?" the captain asked.

"If'n we want to get the Gwambi treasure," the man with the hooks replied, "we must seize every opportunity we have. At the very least, this girl may be of some use to us later on. When the Blowhoarder tells us where the treasure is, she may be useful as a decoy."

"Supposing we *don't* use her, though," the captain said. "Then, after we've split the treasure, what do we do with her?"

"Longfinch could *counsel* you then," Cweel answered.

"She is *our* captive, Cweel." The captain said with another snort.

"And Longfinch is *your* lord," Cweel said, "but *I* will not argue. You can *do* whatever you want with *her* then, but not before. Besides, Longfinch will want to question *her*, too."

The captain paused, and Ella thought she could hear him filling his tankard and then taking a long swig. "Alright then," he finally said. "Throw her in with Jock, and we will give her to Longfinch when we meet him."

Ella heard a chair push back, and then a brawny hand grabbed her arm. She gasped in pain as it jerked her to her feet, her wound throbbing like fire. She opened her eyes and looked at her arm. Blood had already run down from her wound and soaked the side of her dress. She felt faint, though from fear or blood loss she couldn't tell.

Ella stumbled along as best she could as the man with the hooks dragged her from the room. The door opened as if by magic, and Ella found herself out on deck again with the sun beating down on her. The cliff faces of the Hulacos river were speeding past on both sides, and the galleon rocked gently as it passed down the river. Her head spun, and she doubled over, vomiting on the deck.

Ella tried to take a step forward, but stumbled and fell hard on the deck. As she caught herself, pain coursed up her arm. Again, her vision narrowed and started turning black. Rough hands grabbed her by the waist and jerked her back to her feet.

"Steady now, girly," Ernest said.

She relaxed somewhat and staggered forward.

"I will tell Lewis about your arm, and he will find a bandage for it." Was he laughing at her?

Somehow, Ella made it down to the next level of decking, where Ernest turned her aside to a small door. He opened it and helped her into a small room. She collapsed on a pile of straw as soon as she was inside.

She heard someone else nearby. It was Jock. "Ella, my girl, what have they done to ye?"

"It's all ove'h now, Jock. They'e done," she shuddered.

Jock examined her arm. "He used the acid, did not he?"

She shuddered again. "The cook's going to get a bandage." After a pause, she said, "They want you to tell them something —something about the Gwambi t'easu'e. That's what the man with the hooks said. Is that what they'h looking fo'h? The Gwambi t'easu'e? Isn't that the City of Gold? Whe'e they made whole coats and petticoats out of diamond mail? And wubies the size of ho'ses?"

Jock snorted disdainfully as he looked up from her arm. "Who told ye, look ye, about the Gwambi Treasure?"

Ella looked down. "My Papa was looking fo' it."

Jock eyed her cautiously. "Ye're Papa?"

Ella shrugged. "He was looking fo' it when he died. He said that he'd make us wich. He said–"

Jock stiffened. "Do not say inything more about it. Ye do not want to know inything else, look ye, because if ye know more, they will get it out av ye."

Ella shuddered yet again.

Jock let out his breath slowly, a look of intense grief spreading over his face. He looked at her arm again. "Ay-eigh! It should heal, but ye might should expect another before this is over, whatever."

4

## THE INQUISITION

*E*lla lay curled up on the mildewed hay of her prison. Her arm bandaged arm had nearly healed, but she was still no better off than when she was first captured four weeks ago. To think, it had already been four weeks in this dirty, vomit-covered cabin. Even when it wasn't storming, she could hardly shake the seasickness.

They had crossed the great sea and were now by the coast of Sophez, near the country of Llaedhwyth and the Cape of Pistos —that's what Jock said at any rate. It was now well into the night, and she should have been sleeping, but she couldn't.

A bright lantern lit the room, held by a long-armed gnome. Jock knelt in the light with two burly pirates holding him down. The beggar's shirt lay to the side, torn to rags, showing his bruised, bloody, and burnt chest. The man with the hooks, Killjelly, stood before Jock with a red-hot iron in his hand. They had been torturing Jock for hours already, but he had said nothing.

For all of that, Killjelly was still remarkably cool. He did not seem angry at the beggar, only calculatingly cruel.

Killjelly jabbed the iron forward onto Jock's bruised chest.

Jock groaned. Ella tried to bury herself in the hay, praying for this nightmare to end. Her stomach writhed inside her, but she had already vomited all she could. She could only wait.

"God, God, God!" she repeatedly whimpered, unable to contrive a more coherent prayer under the circumstances.

One pirate kicked Jock hard on the jaw. "Talk, you baptized land-rat, talk!"

Jock spit blood. "Try askint a dead dog, look ye, and see if ye have iny better luck."

The pirate hit Jock again, but Killjelly stopped him from going any further. "Calm down, Tell, we will loosen his tongue yet."

"Ooh," the long-armed gnome said, "why don't you brand his tongue next?"

"I will brand you if'n you don't stop using it, sure," Killjelly replied.

The gnome mumbled sulkily under his breath.

Killjelly thrust the brand back into the heat of the lantern and then produced a long, thin needle from his coat. Ella trembled. Why did he have to bring out the needles again?

"Do you know what a nerve is?" Killjelly bent over Jock, taking hold of his arm. There was something almost clinical about the way he worked.

Jock only snickered. "I do not think I have any nerve."

"Then this will be an interesting experiment to find out." As Killjelly placed the needle near Jock's elbow, Ella turned away and whimpered. Jock let out a muffled yell.

"Now then," Killjelly said softly, leaving the needle in place, "since you are having so much trouble remembering, let me give you some help. The Gwambi Treasure is in Entwerp?"

Jock forced a wry smile, even as his eyes watered. "Do ye think so?"

Killjelly laughed. "A little birdie told me."

"Well then," Jock said, "it looks like that birdie has told ye more than ye will iver get outta me, whatever."

Killjelly's lip curled in anger, and he kicked Jock in the face. Jock slumped back, bleeding, but a smile of triumph rested on his face.

Killjelly paced back and forth in front of his victim before finally pulling the needle out of Jock's arm. "I know you have a weak point, Jock. You may as well speak now before I find it."

"You could give him the thumbscrew," one pirate suggested.

"Or the rack,"

"Or the boot."

The long-armed gnome shivered in delight.

Just then, Killjelly's eye fell on Ella. She froze and stared back at him. A smile crept over his face.

"Bill, get me the thumbscrew."

The gnome hissed with pleasure. "Blind baptism! Can I give it to her?"

"Just get me the thumbscrew!" Killjelly yelled.

The gnome slunk out the door, mumbling again.

Killjelly smiled. "Jock, talk now if'n you care anything for your little petticoat, sure."

Ella sat rigid with fear. The pirates seemed to have forgotten all about Jock; instead, they all looked closely at her. Their eyes seemed filled with lust and malice. She blanched before their gaze and looked away. Her eyes met Jock's.

He was staring at her just as intensely as the others, but with a greater sense of urgency. He kept her gaze for a few moments and then motioned with his eyes towards the door. Ella followed his gaze to see that the gnome had left the door open.

No sooner had this thought registered then Jock sprang to his feet with a howl of an injured she-wolf. Lashing out with his fists, he laid out both pirates who held him. Killjelly turned on him, but Ella didn't wait to see what would happen. She leapt to her feet in an instant and darted out the door.

Bursting out on deck, a light rain greeted her. Though fog obscured her vision, she could see a guard leaning against the wall—sheltered by the deck above—smoking his pipe. He saw her dart out of the prison and started up.

"Whattaya..."

He snatched at her, throwing her off balance. She fell to the deck on her bad arm and rolled, crashing against the gunwale. The guard threw his pipe down and rushed at her, but just then, Jock charged out of the open door and slammed into the guard.

Jock grabbed the guard by the neck and smashed his head against the wall. "Run, Ella, my girl, run!"

Ella jumped to her feet, her heart pounding against her brain as she looked around desperately.

"Whe'e to?" She was sure the other pirates would hear them soon enough and recapture them. She was not too far wrong, for at that moment, the long-armed gnome strode up, thumbscrew in hand. His mouth dropped open the moment he saw Jock.

Jock jumped at him, but the gnome had the sense to knock him hard over the head with his thumbscrew. Jock reeled backward and fell to the deck. The gnome stepped backward in surprise.

"The Blowhoarder's loose! He's trying to escape!"

Then the gnome saw Ella. With a cry, he leapt at her. She tried to back away, but the gnome caught her by the arm. She kicked at him and screamed, frantically trying to get at her dagger with the other hand.

Jock staggered to his feet and snatched a marlinspike from the deck. Just as Jock came to his feet, Killjelly burst from the prison door. He now had a black eye and a burn across his forehead. Jock spared no time on Killjelly but rushed at the gnome.

The gnome turned a few seconds too late as Jock bashed him across the head with the marlinspike. The gnome went limp and fell to the ground, knocking Ella backward. She stumbled, but her back struck the gunwales with such force that her feet left the deck, and she pitched over into mid-air.

She screamed and thrashed about wildly with her arms. Her fingers caught something—probably a gun port—and she hung suspended for a moment. On deck, she could hear more feet running around. Several pirates were yelling all at once, and she couldn't make out anything they said. Then she heard Killjelly's voice above the noise.

"Throw the Blowhoarder back in quickly, but we must find the girl. Get lines and ropes; she fell overboard, sure."

Ella felt her grip slipping as the waves rocked the boat up and down. She kicked with her legs hoping to find something else to support her, but they swung in mid-air.

The rough voice of the captain suddenly joined in. "What's going on?"

"Cweel, find the girl. She fell overboard, sure," Killjelly cried.

"*I* would, but the fog will hide *her* from me."

Ella desperately clung to the gun port, trying to pull herself up to get a better grip. The waves rocked the boat back, and spray soaked her whole body. Just then, claws scratched the gunwale above her. That must be Cweel. Mortal dread stole over her, and she fought harder than ever to keep her grip.

Killjelly was speaking now, in a lower tone. Most of the other pirates must have either stopped talking or left since Ella couldn't hear anyone else now.

"I feel sure that I could break Jock if'n I haved the girl. She is his weak point."

"Longfinch will not be *happy* if you lose *her* the day before you meet him."

"Then find her," the Captain barked.

Just then, Ella's right hand slipped. She grasped for another hold, but her other hand slipped as well. For a moment, she seemed to float in a great bubble of mist. Then she plunged into icy waters.

# 5

# THE HAWK

*E*lla's pudgy toddler fists gripped her Papa's trousers. She had to be brave. She wouldn't cry. Papa shouldn't see her cry. Yet as she screwed up her face in the bravest expression she could make, moisture gathered on her chubby cheeks.

"Papa, when will you come back?"

Papa laughed and then grinned from ear to ear. "I'll be back by next year—at least." He turned to look down into the valley. Mama and Mr. Donne followed Papa's gaze.

Ella looked, too, wiping her eyes and sniffing. It was miles and miles away. It might take Papa all day to get down from the mountains and reach the little village in the valley. Ella could just make out the small cottages, smoke wafting up from their distant chimneys like so many tiny teapots on to boil.

But she knew Papa wasn't looking at the houses. He was looking at the river. It looked like one of her hair ribbons—so small—from this distance. But Ella knew it was big and wide. Papa had said she wouldn't even be able to throw a stone across that river.

It was *the* big river. It would lead to the sea.

"Papa, do you pwomise?"

Papa turned to her again. "What was that?"

"Do you pwomise you'll come back?"

Now Mama put her hand on Ella's shoulder. "Dear, you needn't press Papa." Her voice trembled ever so slightly.

Papa bent down to Ella's level and looked at her steadily, a smile still peeking out from the corner of his twinkling blue eyes. "Ella, the sea is a queer animal. When it throws a tantrum, there's no one that can stop it—not even me. So, if I'm not back in a year, it will not be because I forgot about you."

He poked her playfully on the nose.

Ella put out her hand and twirled her fingers in Papa's beard. "But you *will* be back?"

"I'll be back for your fifth birthday," Papa grinned. "And when I come back, I'll have jewels and gold and pearls, and I will buy you a silk dress, and I'll buy Mama a gold ring."

Mama sobbed, and Ella started crying.

"Don't you want a silk dress?"

Ella threw her arms around Papa's neck. "I would, Papa, if *you* give it to me."

"Don't cry, girl. Be strong." He sounded stern, even harsh. But then Papa kissed her and held her at arm's length. "Well, Ella, I've left you all my books, except that one. Promise me you'll read them all before I come back."

"I pwomise I will. Papa, I'll wead all the books in Blisa if you want. I'll wead all the books in Slyzwi'h."

Papa laughed. "You needn't do that. But you can talk to all the sailors who come through here—and they will tell you what it is like to be at sea—and then you will know what I've done, and it will be like you were there with me."

Then Papa took Mama and kissed her.

"You will be safe, Silas?"

Papa laughed and kissed her again. "Of course."

Mama sobbed again. "Oh, Silas..."

"Not here," Papa said harshly, his smile fading.

Mama put her hand over her mouth, but she couldn't hold back the sobs. "But you *will* come back to me, won't you, Silas?"

Papa turned away from Mama and nodded to his companion, Titus Donne. He was smiling again.

"Well then, daylight's wasting."

Mr. Donne looked between Mama and Papa slowly. Mama was still sobbing, and Papa wouldn't look at her.

Mr. Donne let out a long sigh. "Very well then...eh...I guess we should be off?"

"Quite," Papa said crisply.

"Silas?" Mama said again.

But Papa must not have heard her. Picking up his rucksack, he turned his back and walked down the road, leaving Blisa village without a second glance. The church bells rang out dolefully—was that the call for Vespers already?

Mr. Donne cast one last sympathetic look on Mama, then picked up his own rucksack and hurriedly followed Papa.

"Goodbye, Papa, I'll pway fo'h you evewy night!" Ella cried, but Papa did not turn and look at her as she waved her little hand. He must not have heard her call.

He never said goodbye.

Mr. Donne returned a week later to say that Papa was safe on his voyage.

Two weeks later, another man knocked at the door of the cottage. Ella put down the speller she was struggling over and looked up as Mama opened the door.

He was a very tall man, dressed in the smart blue-coated uniform of a soldier.

"Mrs. Silas Pickering?"

"Yes," Mama said, wiping her hands on her apron, "that is me. Though Silas is not here."

The man tipped his military cap briskly. "I'm afraid he's dead, ma'am. Pirates sunk the ship and killed everyone on board."

Ella's body racked with convulsions, trying to rid itself of the sea water. Her stomach churned as she coughed and sputtered, lucky to pull in a good breath before she fell to coughing again. She could have been in this state for three hours for all she knew, before she collapsed, exhausted, on the sand. Now and then, a wave would wash over her, but she didn't care; even if she could have moved, she didn't feel like doing so. Her stomach rumbled. She was miserable. Sand and seaweed covered her pitiful frame.

It was in this condition that the morning sunbeams found Ella as they streamed across the eastern ocean.

Her dress clung to her like an overgrown barnacle. The slimy sea-weed and salt filth had turned her skirt from a mellow blue to a revolting brown. Her stockings, too, once white, were nearly black, and torn in several places. The dagger clung to her thigh, though now the leather was stiff and bit into her leg painfully.

The long hours of exposure in the ocean, struggling for air, left her skin wrinkled, her energy drained, her eyes gritty with sand, her mouth tasting like salt and bile, and her hair laying in a tangled, matted mess across her back; that was probably the worst of it.

She hadn't really liked her curly, blonde hair when she was younger—she wanted brown and straight hair—but now she hated it more fiercely than ever. It had been a curse aboard a flea and rat-infested ship, nor was it an asset when floating past rocks, reefs, and driftwood.

Ella reached up and pulled some stray twigs and seaweed from her hair. As she did so, a lock fell in front of her eyes, and she recoiled. The sand and algae had done their work, leaving it filthy and full of slime. Ella groaned. *Well, you have your wish; it's brown now.*

*Ella on the beach*

She rolled on to her back in frustration, blinking in the morning light. Black shapes caught her eye as she peered upward. Ella squinted at them. They were carrion-eaters, mainly sea gulls and crows, but there was a large hawk with them.

"I'm not dead! And I don't plan on it eithe'!" she croaked.

Her voice cracked into a harsh whisper, which only seemed to make the birds curious. A few of the gulls swooped down to the beach where they stood, peering at her. Ella groaned and rolled back over, covering her head with her arms. Why did her life have to be like this? She never should have gone out to give Jock his bread after dark. She had been so stupid. But did she really have to suffer like this for such a minor oversight? How was she to know there would be a wicked, hook-handed leprechaun waiting to capture her?

There seemed to be some kind of perverse irony in her situation. Sixteen years ago, when her father had left her, pirates captured him and killed him. Now here she was on the other side of the ocean with pirates on her trail as well. Her father, of course, had gone willingly to sea, but not Ella. Was this some kind of family curse?

Yet as she lay stretched out on that beach—sore and battered from the night fighting with the malicious ocean for her life—she could remember exactly how she felt when her father died. It was that same numbed feeling that oppressed her now, as if there was nothing left to feel. Even when her mother had sobbed night and day for weeks, Ella had felt nothing. It was only when they ran out of money and started starving that she started feeling again.

That was before Mr. Donne had married Mama. It had gotten better, then. Nevertheless, Papa was gone. There was always that numb feeling tucked away in the corner of her heart, and now—after the battle of the previous night—that feeling had gotten out again and eaten up the part of her heart that could feel.

She lay like this for a couple of moments until she felt a sharp pain on her back. She whacked at it with her hand, knocking a large gull from her back. The bird wriggled awkwardly in the sand with a startled "Yuk!" before regaining its feet and peering at Ella again. Ella could see that it had a small red dot at the end of its beak, and that made her mad.

"Go away, you!" she hissed, waving at the gull.

"Hiyak!" the bird shrieked in response.

Ella grabbed a handful of wet sand and flung it at the bird. It hit with a solid *plop,* and the gull took to the air with a harsh, "Gah-gah-gah!"

Ella lay down again, satisfied with the gull's rout when she again heard a harsh "Hiyak!" She raised her head to see that more gulls had landed around her, along with several of the crows.

"Leave me alone! You can wait on the cliffs if you want to see me die. Just go away!"

Her voice seemed not to affect the birds in the least. Several of the gulls hopped forward to peck at her sea-worn dress. Ella lashed out with her feet and hands, walloping those near enough, but this only temporarily deterred the birds, who were back at her the moment she stopped moving.

Suddenly, a weak, nasal whistle echoed off the cliffs surrounding the secluded beach. The birds stopped and looked around anxiously. Ella took this opportunity to whack a large gull across the head.

Just then, a large hawk swooped to the ground and landed just above Ella's head, its wings spread wide and eyes dark and menacing. The gulls quickly backed away as the hawk jumped this way and that, pecking at any bird that dared try to get between it and Ella. After a few minutes of this, the gulls stood still and watched the hawk strut up and down on the sand as if daring the gulls to try touching the bedraggled girl.

Finally, one of the smaller crows broke rank and fluttered onto Ella's back. The hawk whistled in indignation and, with a few flaps of its wings, attacked the hapless crow. Seizing the culprit in its talons, the hawk rapped the crow sharply on the head with its beak. The crow cawed with pain and took off, followed by the other birds, fluttering to their coastal haunts and leaving the victorious hawk with its prize.

The hawk turned on Ella with satisfaction and surveyed her all around, hopping this way and that as if it might see something new and interesting by viewing her from different angles. Ella groaned again and buried her head in the sand, hoping the bird would lose interest and fly away. After staying in this position for about ten minutes, she raised her head again to spit out some sand, only to see that the hawk was now standing in front of her with its head cocked inquisitively to one side.

"Leave me alone," she growled.

The hawk cackled—something that resembled clearing its throat.

"Fine, I'm glad you chased all the otha'h bi'ds away, but can't you leave me to die in peace?"

The hawk gave out a sharp whistle as if to laugh.

This rankled Ella. In an instant, her apathy fell off of her, replaced by pure rage—rage at the pirates, at herself, and at where she was—somehow it all seemed to be the hawk's fault. She snatched up a handful of sand and threw it as hard as she could at the bird. The hawk hopped nimbly to the side and then squawked in defiance.

Hatred surged through Ella's weak body, and the hawk bounced from one leg to another as if in challenge. Ella lurched to her feet and charged the hawk, who flapped a few feet in the air before alighting on a large rock and whistling again. Ella was up now and wasn't about to lie down again until the hawk was gone or dead.

She scooped up a stone and threw it at the bird, but again the hawk dodged, fluttering to another rock farther away. Again Ella ran at the bird, swinging at it with her hands, and again the hawk alighted on the beach just out of her reach.

Ella glared at the hawk in frustration, and the hawk glanced back at her as if enjoying the fun. Ella snatched up a stick and swung it at the bird with all her strength. The hawk fluttered just out of reach once more, winging its way to a large belt of trees before looking back and whistling, daring Ella to come further.

She growled and charged into the forest after the hawk, waving her stick like a maniac. The bird quickly flew deeper into the forest until Ella, dashing aside a large bush, lost sight of it. She slumped to the ground in exhaustion. It was nearly five minutes before she looked around.

She was in a small clearing covered with sweet-smelling grass, hemmed in all around by aspens and here and there, an evergreen of some kind. The clear dew tingled on Ella's legs and made her mouth run dry. There, in the middle of the glade, ran a clear stream, merry and laughing, as it followed its course from the high cliffs and mountains.

This sight nearly brought tears to Ella's eyes—suddenly feeling she had passed all suffering and life would be good to her from here on. With an effort, Ella got back to her feet and staggered into a shallow pool, throwing herself onto her back and letting the water rush over her.

The frigid water revived Ella somewhat. Grabbing a handful of gritty sand, she scrubbed out her hair and dress as best she could, a little disappointed at how brown it made the virgin waters. Ella shivered out of the water and pranced upstream a few paces, wringing out her dress and petticoats. Coming to a calm eddy in the stream, she halted and looked at herself. To her relief, the image that peered back at her was not a withered hag or half-starved crone, but Ella. Plain, simple Ella—if a little thinner than usual. She glanced at her hair, noting with satisfaction that it was blonde again and already full of curls.

Ella's teeth chattered, and her stomach rumbled. She curled up in the dry moss by the stream, squirming against the autumn chill. Why had she been so foolish as to leave her shawl behind when she started this mad adventure? Perhaps a better question would be why she had left at all. She might now be curled up on her mother's old chair in front of the fire, with the alpine weather barred outside.

She sat up suddenly. Hadn't the old mountaineers said that if you were freezing to death, the worst thing to do was sit still? She jumped to her feet and dashed madly about the clearing, skipping up and down and shaking all over, spinning, twirling, somersaulting...and sliding to an abrupt halt. The birds were not singing anymore, and she felt distinctly ludicrous. She wrapped her arms tightly around herself. Her stomach growled.

Just then, she heard a weak, nasal whistle from not far away. She jerked her head towards the sound and saw the hawk peering at her from the branches of a nearby tree. Ella was no longer angry at the bird. Her rage seemed almost childish to her now—instead, the bird sparked her fascination. The hawk seemed equally fascinated with her, so the two simply stood, looking at each other for a moment. Ella had seen a few hawks in her life, but none this close, and her knowledge of them was very slim, anyway. As far as she could tell, this was a fairly normal bird, just rather large and brown. One thing she found peculiar about this hawk was that it had facial disks similar to an owl's.

*I haven't studied hawks before,* she thought, a little apprehensive. *I'll have to read the next book on hawks that I can find.*

After a bit of consideration, Ella took a step forward. The hawk whistled and turned her back on Ella, displaying a white rump-patch as she flashed her tail. Ella came forward as quietly as possible until she finally came beneath the tree where the hawk perched. The hawk then turned back towards Ella and peered at her again. Ella froze.

The hawk hopped to a branch just above her head, but as it did so, it dislodged a large fruit, which nearly hit Ella. Ella picked up the fruit with a twinge of joy; it was a pear. She looked back at the tree and mentally berated herself. *I will have to study botany before I let myself get captured like this again.*

She bit into the pear ravenously and finished it in seconds, then grabbed another from the tree. No sooner had she finished this one than she heard a heavy wing-stroke above her. It sounded far too large to be the hawk's, so she looked up. The hawk was nowhere to be seen, but a large black shape soared past just above the clearing.

With a gasp, Ella jumped back to the tree trunk and laid herself flat against it. She took cover none too soon, for the shape was back in seconds. With a stroke of his mighty wings, Cweel alighted on the pear tree above Ella and gazed intently around the clearing. Ella held her breath; it was all she could do not to gasp in terror of this beast. Her thoughts spun in a turmoil. Why hadn't she been more careful? She should have known that the pirates would send Cweel to look for her. Why hadn't she thought about it? More relevant to her current position: how would she get away from Cweel now?

Just as she was thinking this, there came a low rustling from the other side of the clearing. Cweel's eye immediately alighted on the spot. The movement stopped for a moment, and for that moment, Ella thought she could see a human-like shape through the underbrush. Cweel seemed to have seen the same thing, only much better than Ella had, for he immediately gave a hiss of disgust and launched back into the sky, apparently annoyed he had mistaken the person in the forest for Ella.

Ella lay as motionless as possible, unsure whether to be more frightened of the Griffin or this new person. With a shudder, she remembered stories she had heard of the savages of Sophez, many of whom she knew were cannibals. Might this be one of them? If so, would she rather risk being caught—and possibly boiled—by him, or flee, risking being caught by Cweel?

She didn't have to choose, however, for at that moment, the figure strode out of the trees and stood in full sunlight.

# 6

## THE SAVAGE

*E*lla sat as still as she could, though she was quite certain she was painfully visible under the pear tree. The newcomer was definitely one of the savages of these Pistosian coasts—and also definitely not human. His little, round head stood only about two-and-a-half feet off the ground and had the air of childhood about it. He wore only a small loincloth, displaying his oily, brown skin shamelessly and letting his pudgy belly hang slightly over the waist-string. His fists were chubby and round, holding a small javelin and sling tightly in their grip. His hair was dark-black and tied back from his face with a rawhide strap.

Ella could hardly take her eyes off this strange person when, to her mortification, the savage turned and looked straight at her. She held her breath.

A wide grin spread across the boy's face. With a sudden bound, he darted across the clearing towards her. Ella jumped to her feet, unable to think of anything else to do. For a moment, she considered running, but she knew that would be futile. This child of the forest would undoubtedly catch her in the end. Besides, she knew nothing of the land, and the Pistosian mountains were treacherous; the last thing she wanted was to fall off some cliff.

The savage stopped abruptly about four feet away and stared at her. With nothing else to do, she studied him with a critical eye. The first thing she noted was the head of his spear, which was all wooden but still razor-sharp. She had read enough about savages to respect and fear their spears. Looking quickly away from the spear, she looked at the boy as a whole. What sort of beast was he?

Master Schultz had laughed at her when she brought home her second book on anthrogenusology—a large book by Dr. Timothias Aersophelis that was liberally filled with diagrams and sketches and bore the judicious title of *A Comprehensive Catalog of the Various Differences and Similarities of the Physiology and the Anatomy of the Eight Anthrogenus Races (or in Layman's Terms, the Races of Man)*. She could still remember the expression on Master Schultz's face when she told him she had finished the book in a week.

"Why did you read it?"

"If I find some othe'h human-like c'eatu'h some day, I want to know what it is," she had said.

Now she was putting her knowledge to use. Her eyes rested on the savage's hands, where she saw with some satisfaction that thin webbing connected each of his fingers. Next she noted his smooth skin and then peered at his nostrils, which seemed to take in breath once for every ten times she breathed.

Nymph—or morrdin in the Helfenic language.

She mentally congratulated herself for identifying the creature. At least now she would know what race of anthrogenus was boiling her up for dinner, if this savage should take that fancy. She ran through her mind everything she knew about nymphs. Their skin was their primary organ of breathing, rather like an amphibian. Their skeleton was composed of noncalcified bones, like a shark. They had double the canines of humans, and regularly ate raw meat. Those were the only details that seemed important to her at the moment. She smiled with pride, remembering that she hadn't missed a single question on the Test of Nymph Anatomy.

Just then, the nymph smiled again and pointed his spear at Ella, spouting off a long sentence of gibberish.

This was not so much Ella's expertise. She had studied many foreign languages but never for long enough to build up much of a vocabulary in any of them. Still, she knew the Pistosian savages spoke a Tylweni language. Therefore, she reached into the back of her mind to pull out as many words as she could remember from Kerynian Tylwen.

*Perhaps I should let him know I know what he is.* Ella pointed back at the savage and spoke as clearly as she could, working her tongue carefully to produce the 'r's.

"Morwyr."

The savage peered at her blankly.

But Ella wasn't done. Next, she pointed to herself and said, "Wmwyr."

The savage blinked, and then let out another string of gibberish. Well, this was getting nowhere.

Pointing to herself again, Ella said, "Ella. Ella."

The savage seemed to understand this new game just fine. He pointed to himself. "Nōlistrw-kagwyr."

Ella gasped. "Noliswoo..."

The savage grinned. "Nōlistrw-kagwyr."

*I might have guessed it would have an 'r' in it*, Ella thought. After a moment of consideration, she pointed at the savage. "Nōli."

The savage's grin widened.

Ella pointed to herself and said, "Ella." Then she pointed to the savage. "Nōli."

The savage gave a small giggle and mimicked her, "Ela. Nōli."

The two looked at each other for a while. Ella shifted her weight awkwardly. Nōli grinned.

With nothing else to do, and this little savage staring at her so expectantly, Ella decided to talk. It was ludicrously pointless, as this little savage could not understand her, but she wasn't talking for *his* sake; she was talking for *her* sake. Somehow, just talking to another person—even someone who couldn't understand her—made her feel better.

"You a'e p'obably wonde'ing how I knew you we'e a nymph, a'en't you? Well, it was easy; see, I've wead seve'al books about anthrogenusology. Fou'h, I think. Maste'h Schultz gave me the fi'st book, but I found the othe'h ones on my own."

Ella paused for a moment. "You p'obably don't even know what anthrogenusology is, anyway, do you? Well, I'll tell you. anthrogenusology is the study of anthrogenuses, and an anthrogenus is an intelligent human-like c'eatu'e. As Doct'h Aersophelis said, 'beasts with the weasoning, b'eath, and image of God.' I liked that definition."

Nōli was still staring at Ella, enthralled. "The'e a'e eight species of anthrogenus," Ella said. "Eight," she held up her fingers with both thumbs tucked in.

Nōli suddenly broke in. "Wcd?"

"What?" Ella asked.

Nōli held up his fingers one at a time while he counted, "Is, dhwa, dri, della, fenda, ecs, ecda, wcd."

"Wcd?" Ella repeated.

Nōli nodded and held up his fingers sans thumbs. "Wcd."

"So there are eight—wcd—races of anthrogenus." She counted them out on her fingers to help Nōli see. "Nymphs, dwa'fs, saty's, elves, lep'echauns, gnomes, fae'iefolk, and humans." Ella wiggled the fingers she had used for nymph and human to give extra emphasis to what she said.

Nōli smiled broadly, saying something under his breath in a humorous tone.

Ella sized him up for a moment. Why was he here, and what was he doing? Did he just enjoy listening to her talk? She couldn't think of any reason to be talking to him in the first place, come to think of it. Then again, she couldn't think of any good reason to be doing anything else. She may as well talk to this savage. Whether or not he could understand her, at least it made her feel better. "You p'obably haven't been to school, have you?"

Nōli sat down at the foot of the pear tree, but continued to look up at her.

"That's fine," Ella said. "I don't go to school myself—not anymore, since I can't get into a university. I used to, but Jon Thompson would always make fun of me fo'h how I talked. So then Maste'h Schultz taught me at home. He's a good teache'h, so I'm glad he helped me. Mama helped me, too, sometimes, and so did my father. Still, I enjoy studying, so I don't think I will eve'h stop, even if I'm done with school. Gove'no'h Theudoclias lets me bo'ow whateve'h book f'om his lib'a'y, and then Maste'h Schultz will discuss it with me..."

Ella stopped abruptly as a sob came involuntarily to her throat. An image of home appeared before her. There was her cozy home, with the Slyzwir mountains rising behind it. Outside, her step-father chopped wood, his breath hovering about in the cool air like ghosts. Her mother cooked supper over the stove, the warm gush of the fire on her cheeks. Her siblings crawled about on the floor, their rosy cheeks flushed with excitement. There was her corner, with her chair and her books—just waiting to be read—and her shawl hanging on the wall as if ready to banish the cold world forever. The image was so clear that she could even hear her mother talking to her.

"Don't worry about your hair, darling. It looks lovely. Blonde is a very nice color. And Ella, don't fret about the curls! Many a young woman would sell her right arm to get curls like yours," then her mother paused. "You look just like your father," which meant her first husband, not the one she had now.

Ella nearly spoke back, but as she opened her mouth, the vision of home vanished, and she was again in the desolate Pistosian wilderness. The chill hit her like a stone wall, and her stomach rumbled. Ella collapsed against the pear tree and sobbed. She forgot all about the savage who sat next to her. She forgot all about the hawk that had brought her to the clearing. She forgot all about Killjelly, Cweel, the pirates, and Jock... everything. All she had left was longing and pain. So she wept.

When she finally dried her tears, the shadows of evening had fallen, and she was slightly ashamed of herself, but she felt better for the crying. She wrapped her arms tightly around herself to stave off the cold. What was she going to do now? She couldn't stay here forever. She needed a plan. What was her goal? Before she had pondered the question very long, she remembered the savage. Turning about, she saw him leaning against the tree, fast asleep, with his broad smile still on his face. Ella sighed. If only she could forget her problems like that little savage.

She directed herself back to the original question. To begin with, she reviewed her position. She was stranded somewhere on the coast of the Pistosian cape, probably in the primitive, newly formed country of Llaedhwyth, possibly miles from any real civilization. Besides this, she had no food, no provisions, and no knowledge of how to obtain either. A vicious eagle griffin was hunting her, and he planned to turn her over to a bunch of blood-thirsty pirates, the worst of whom was that hook-handed leprechaun Killjelly, though Captain Holgard was probably just as evil. The only anthrogenus nearby who could— that is, might—help her were savages and probably cannibals at that. Her only friend—or the closest she had to a friend—lay in prison onboard the pirate ship, possibly dead from torture by now; torture directed by the aforementioned Killjelly.

Ella sighed in frustration and laid her head in her hands hopelessly. She had to make this simpler. What were the issues she needed to fix for her life to return to normal? Ella thought on this for a moment, nodding her head slowly. As far as she saw it, there were two: first, there was an ocean between where she was and where she should be; second, Jock was in the bowels of a pirate ship, not in the little alley in Blisa village.

To return to normal, she would have to conceive of a way not only to find passage for herself across the Great Ocean and then find transport across Kelmar until she reached Slyzwir and her little village, but she would also have to free Jock from Killjelly and Captain Holgard and get him back to Blisa village as well. She could think of no way to achieve these goals.

In frustration, she picked two more pears and gnawed on them while she thought. After swallowing down the last of the fruit, she threw the cores away from herself and leaned her head against the tree, closing her eyes in thought. She racked her brain repeatedly, but still, no solution presented itself. She could not consider any plan of action for long before the ominous figure of Killjelly appeared in her imagination and slashed the plan to pieces with a single swipe of his double-hooked hand.

She didn't know exactly when she fell asleep.

She dreamed she was standing in a narrow hallway. Behind her lay a vast hoard of wealth: gold, diamonds, rubies, silver, and jewels of all shapes and sizes. In the bodice of her dress, she could feel the lumps of diamonds she had hidden. In front of her stood the pirates—Killjelly first, then Captain Holgard and Cweel, then all the rest. Gone were their leering faces and cruel features. Now they just stared at her dumbfounded, their eyes wide and mouths agape. All were well-armed, but all were too afraid to come any closer.

They were whispering to one another, "The Gwambi Treasure!" "She's found it!" "She owns it!"

"Give me Jock," she said with startling severity and power.

Then they were gone: the pirates, the treasure, and the hall. It was just her, Jock, and the diamonds stashed in her bodice. The sea was before them, and Blisa, Slyzwir beyond that.

# 7

# A FOREST TREK

*E*lla suddenly realized that she was awake. She might have been awake for the last ten minutes, or then again, she might have just woken up. She didn't know. Even so, she refused to open her eyes for fear of being confronted with the reality of still being aboard the pirate ship. She had a vague memory of being tossed about at sea, coming to shore, and meeting a savage, but it was all so tangled up with her dreams that she feared that was a dream too.

A light breeze played across her face, but she refused to open her eyes. It was probably just wind blowing in through the window of Jock's cell. Then she heard a shrill, nasal whistle. Her eyes flashed open of their own accord, and she beheld the clearing again in the light of early dawn. There was the stream she had bathed in, the pear tree she was leaning against, and the savage still fast asleep by her side. Then she heard the whistle again.

Looking up, she saw the hawk looking down at her from the tree branches. She was first startled, then relieved, but then confused. It almost seemed like this bird was following her. The hawk turned its head on its side as it looked at her. Ella got to her feet and looked back at the hawk.

"A'e you following me?"

The hawk simply whistled in return. This time, the whistle seemed harsher than usual, with almost a hint of warning in it. Was it warning her to stay back? Was her nest somewhere nearby, and she was just making sure Ella didn't meddle with it?

Ella thought for a moment. Then another thought came to her. No sooner had it occurred to her than she dashed over to the nearest tree she thought she could climb. Up she scampered as high as she could. She had no trouble reaching so near the top of the tree that the branches bowed slightly under her weight. The foliage would conceal her.

Ella scanned the sky anxiously. There was the full moon dipping below the horizon, the daystar well up into the sky, and the golden rays of the sun just peeping out of the eastern sea. Then she saw what she had dreaded. A dark shadow passed over the sky to the south, skimming just over the level of the trees. Cweel was hunting for her again.

Just then, Ella remembered the savage. She cupped her hands to her mouth and spoke as loudly as she dared. "Nōli! Nōli, wake up! Hide you'self!"

Nōli jumped to his feet—as if he had never been asleep—and his smile never dimmed. He looked around in surprise. Just then, the dark shape dropped out of the sky, passing within ten feet of Ella's head as it descended into the clearing.

Ella shivered with fear and slid down to a limb further in where she was better concealed. Peering out from between the branches, she could see Nōli standing motionless in the clearing below. In front of him stood the ominous shape of Cweel, towering over the tiny frame of the savage.

Cweel looked the savage all over before he spoke. To Ella's horror, he spoke in Kerynian Tylwen. She had learned enough of that language to know what he asked.

"*Gwsquey tyshy-se korirshwyr?* Do *you* know where a *girl* is?"

Ella held her breath while she waited for Nōli to answer, but he didn't appear to understand.

Cweel hissed in disgust and lunged at the boy. Quick as a wildcat, the savage darted to the side and snatched up his spear. As Cweel spun to face him, Nōli brandished the weapon in Cweel's face. Cweel ducked his head to the side and swatted the spear aside with his talon. Then he snatched the spear from Nōli's hand and bit it in half.

Cweel threw the two pieces of Nōli's spear to the ground and knocked him off his feet before launching into the sky with an audible hiss of disgust.

As soon as Ella was sure the Griffin was gone, she scrambled down from the tree and ran over to Nōli. The savage was squatting over his broken spear, staring at it with tears in his eyes.

"Oh, Nōli," Ella cried, "that was so b'ave of you! You we'e amazing. Oh, thank you fo'h not answe'ing him, thank you." Then she stopped herself and said the only thing she could think to say in Kerynian Tylwen. "Merthi, Nōli, thank you."

Nōli smiled through his tears, but it was obvious that he did not know what Ella was saying. It was then that she realized that Nōli probably didn't speak Kerynian Tylwen, but some other form of Tylwen which was mutually unintelligible to the Kerynian varieties.

Nōli turned back to his spear. Ella crouched next to him and put her arm over his shoulder. "It's al'ight Nōli; you can get anothe'h. Just be glad that Cweel didn't t'y to kill you."

Nōli stood up and walked over to the pear tree, where he picked himself a pear and then sat to eat it and lament his poor luck. Ella's stomach growled, and so she joined him. She walked over to the tree, but as she stood on her tiptoes to grab a pear, her eyes fell on the hawk, who still perched in the tree. It eyed her critically.

"Thank you," Ella said. Then as an afterthought, she added, "Merthi," just in case the hawk spoke Tylweni.

The hawk whistled and flew off, as if that was all it had been waiting to hear.

Ella watched the hawk fly away in some wonder. What was this hawk? She knew that the bishop back in Blisa had said that angels sometimes come in the form of men, but did they ever come in the form of beasts? Could this hawk be her guardian angel?

As the sun rose above the trees, Ella finished her fifth pear and was now ready to implement the first step in her plan. She didn't remember exactly how she had devised her plan—it had just sort of come to her during the night. First, she would have to find some civilization. Then, she would have to find the Gwambi Treasure before the pirates did. That done, she could barter with Killjelly and Captain Holgard for Jock's life, keeping back just enough of the treasure to pay for passage for Jock and herself back to Slyzwir. The only difficulty would be in finding the Gwambi Treasure. Once that was done, she and Jock would practically be back in Blisa.

Ella threw her pear core away and got up to wash in the stream. As she bent over—letting the water play with her hands—she asked, "Nōli, do you know whe'e Entwe'p is?"

Nōli looked up at her in surprise. "Entwerp?"

"Do you know what that is?"

"*Entwerp Ffolwyn?*"

"I don't know," Ella replied. "All I know is Entwe'p. Do you know whe'e that is?"

Nōli looked at her quizzically, then jumped to his feet and pointed to the north, spouting off another stream of gibberish ending with the words "*Entwerp Ffolwyn.*"

Ella bit her lip as she studied Nōli. "Do you know anything about the Gwambi T'easu'e?"

Nōli stared at her blankly, still pointing to the north.

Ella stood up straight and walked over to Nōli. "Well, take me to this Entwe'p Ffolwyn."

With no further bidding, Nōli picked up his sling and walked into the forest, leaving his broken spear behind him. Ella followed, but quickly fell behind. Nōli seemed to know every-thing there was to know about walking through this thick forest, and besides this, he was so short that very few vines and tree limbs impeded his way, and he wore no clothes for the thorns to snag on. For Ella, it was a different story. Now a thorn would catch in her dress, and then her hair would get tangled in a tree branch.

Finally, she broke free from a thorn bush and stepped into a break in the underbrush to see Nōli standing still and grinning at her.

"Go on and laugh, then."

Nōli turned and was about to keep walking when Ella stopped him.

"Wait a moment; I can solve this."

Nōli halted, so Ella tore off a strip of cloth from the hem of one of her petticoats. Next, she folded up her hair as many times as she could and then tied it back with the strip.

Nōli grinned at her.

"You should be glad that you don't have cu'ly hai'h." Ella said. "Besides, you'h hai'h is black, and tho'ns probably like blonde hai'h bette'h."

Nōli turned and kept walking.

---

The way was very strenuous for Ella. Nōli seemed to keep a course that ran straight across the edge of several mountains. Every so often, he would have to hike up the mountainside a little way to avoid coming to a cliff. In this way, they steadily gained altitude.

For most of the way, the mountainside was very steep both up and down, so Ella had to be very careful not to miss her footing, lest she go tumbling down the slope. This she did very well as she was quite used to climbing the peaks around her village. It was extracting herself from the foliage and underbrush that was her real difficulty. The forests around Blisa were nowhere near as thick as this primeval Pistosian forest.

Now and again, they would break out of the trees into a meadow, and Ella would catch a view of the stunning scenery. To the west stood the peaks of the Sophez Mountains, snow-capped and rugged. To the east, the sea stretched as far as the eye could see. The mountains themselves fell steeply away into the sea, their sheer faces broken now and then, with cliffs, gullies, and valleys. These valleys came down to the sea in a gentler slope and reached the sea as wide beaches or cypress swamps, which contrasted sharply with the sheer cliffs of the mountains.

After several hours of walking, Ella and Nōli descended into a small valley. By noon, they reached the bottom of the valley, where a river blocked their way. The water was pure and clear, but it rushed down to the sea at a terrific speed. It didn't seem angry, only dangerous. The water roared in sheer ecstasy of speed. It burst upon the rocks and curled around them in eddies and whirlpools. It leaped the rough ground in small waterfalls and shook the earth in the wild and raucous contour of its course.

Ella was too terrified of the water to think of swimming across it. Instead, she flopped down on a rock and breathed deeply of the damp air. She knew well the dangers in a fast-flowing mountain stream. Her mother had told her many stories of hidden whirlpools sucking full-grown men to their deaths. And after her most recent fight with the sea, she had no inclination to get into the water again.

Nōli had no such qualms. As soon as he saw the stream, he

dashed to its side and sat down, trailing his toes in the water. Suddenly, he stood up and, glancing at Ella with a broad grin, dove into a small eddy.

Ella gasped in horror, but would not dare get any nearer to the water. Instead, she strained her neck to see as much as she could of the little savage. He appeared to be enjoying himself very much as he darted about in the eddy like a little otter.

Ella leaned back, and her stomach rumbled. It was about lunchtime, but there was no lunch anywhere in sight. She could see no pear trees—or any fruit trees at all. Until this point in her life, she had simply taken lunch for granted. It was like a physical law of the universe that every day at noon, lunch was served. Even on the pirate ship, they had kept strictly to this law. But here, by the side of that river, Ella suddenly realized that lunch was only a hypothesis and not a physical law.

Finally, Nōli's head came above the water, and he grinned at Ella. As quick as he could, he scrambled out of the stream and stood on the bank with his webbed hands stretched wide and his brown skin glistening with water.

"Nōli," Ella shouted over the thunder of rushing water, "I think it's time to eat."

Nōli stared at her blankly.

Ella made signs as if she were putting food into her mouth and then chewing it up. "Eat. It's time to eat."

Nōli laughed and spouted off a long line of unintelligible words.

"But a'en't you hung'y?" Ella replied, a little annoyed. "Isn't you'h stomach bothe'ing you?"

Nōli only laughed again and turned back to the water, motioning Ella to follow him. With much hesitation, Ella stood up and came a pace or two closer to the edge of the stream.

As soon as Nōli saw Ella was following him, he jumped back into the water, but this time he did not stay in the eddy. With a few deft strokes of his webbed hands, he darted out into the current and soon reached a large rock about halfway across the stream. Pausing in the lee of this rock for a moment, Nōli sped on, first to the lee of another rock and then to the other side of the stream. Jumping merrily out of the water, Nōli turned back as if expecting to see Ella following him.

Ella stood stock still on the other side of the stream. She thought she could hear cannon-fire way off in the distance, but certainly she was just imagining it.

Nōli motioned to her and called out another nonsense sentence, as if trying to reassure her. Ella took one look at the water rushing past in torrents and swallowed. Wasn't there any other way she could get over? Couldn't she swim across at some other place where the water was calmer? Just then, she thought of the sea. Surely this stream would be much gentler when it reached the sea. She would simply walk down to where the stream ended and swim across.

She turned quickly and was about to march downstream, when Nōli called to her, and she halted. She turned back to see Nōli motioning to her as if he was swimming. Nōli then pointed to the stream, then her, pretended to swim again, and then grinned. Ella swallowed and looked back at the river. Looking up and down its length, she saw—several yards upstream—a chain of large rocks that she thought were close enough together for her to jump between.

Rushing to these rocks, she climbed onto the first one before her mind had time to catch up with what she was doing. She refused to look at the water and braced herself to jump to the next rock. She stared levelly at the rock and counted slowly to three before jumping. For one hair-raising moment, there was nothing beneath her except the tumult of the waters, then her feet touched the next rock. She bent her knees as she landed and grabbed at the slimy rock with her hands. Her feet slipped out from under her, and her knees slammed hard against the rock, but she did not slide into the water.

Once she was sure of her balance, she looked up and stood slowly to her feet. On the other side of the river, she could see Nōli laughing at her. Now and then he would say something, but even had he been speaking the Common Tongue, she never would have been able to understand him over the noise of the current. It seemed rather cruel of him to mock her when he was safe and far away from danger, and she was in the thick of it.

Her eyes strayed momentarily to the rushing water, but she quickly brought them to the next rock and focused there. She bent her knees and prepared to spring. *One... two... three...* and she leaped.

Again, her feet struck the rock, and she tried to steady herself with her hands, but her feet slipped forward, and she plunged into the icy water. The current enveloped her and dragged her downstream at a frightening pace. Ella flailed about and grabbed at whatever she could. She could feel a stone swat her hard across the arm and then another on her leg. She wondered if it was more painful to die of drowning or to die by having her head cracked open on a rock.

Suddenly, she felt two little arms seize about her waist. She relaxed somewhat, and then the current seemed to come to an abrupt halt. Her head broke the water's surface, and she found herself in a little eddy on the other side of the stream. Dragging herself out of the water, she stretched herself out on the bank. She was sure she could hear Nōli laughing over the sound of the water. She lay in the mud by the side of the stream for nearly ten minutes, breathing deeply and thanking God she had survived her second foray into angry waters.

Finally, she sat up to see Nōli grinning at her. "Can we leave this place?"

Nōli grinned, but seemed to understand her question. With a quick turn, he walked north again. Ella got to her feet, suddenly realizing that she had lost both of her shoes in the river. Her thin stockings were all that protected her feet now. With a groan, she followed after Nōli. She felt at her thigh, a little comforted to find her dagger still there. This stretch of the journey was much more miserable than the trek this morning. She was starving. Now, she had to add the blisters and sores on her shoeless feet to the constant tangling and untangling of herself with the underbrush.

Slowly, they made their way up again onto the side of a mountain. They did again pass through many a large meadow with scenic views all around, but Ella seemed blind to their beauty. She kept her eyes focused on her feet as she constantly dodged thorns and sharp rocks. Understandably, her pace was much slower, and Nōli had to wait for her more often.

After several hours of this miserable hike, Ella looked up to see how far ahead Nōli was, and she stepped on a large thorn. She jumped back with a cry of pain and struck her back against a tree trunk, tangling her hair tightly in a tree branch. She felt very much like weeping.

"Nōli!" she cried. "Wait, please, wait!"

She carefully reached behind her head and—after some untwisting—pulled her hair free. She then retied the strip of cloth about her hair in hopes she wouldn't get tangled again. Lifting her foot, she found the offending thorn protruding through her stockings; it was quite large, at least in diameter. Ella quickly seized the thorn and pulled at it. She expected it to slide out right away, but instead it held fast, and pain coursed up her leg. Gritting her teeth and whimpering a little, Ella yanked hard at the thorn. At once it came free in Ella's hand. Seeing the size of the thorn, Ella's gut twisted. It was so long and wicked looking; it was a wonder it hadn't gone clean through her foot. Ella had only ever seen thorns like this on honey locust trees in Blisa.

Her foot throbbed with pain, but there was nothing else she could do for it. She made a mental note to read the next book she found on wild medicinal plants. She finally spit on her foot to clean the wound somewhat through her stocking, and then she held the puncture tightly with her hand to ease the pain. When she pressed too hard, it felt like the thorn was still embedded in her, and there wasn't any blood on her stockings; was that a good sign, or a bad sign? For a moment, she considered taking her stocking off to examine the injury, but she immediately thought better of it. She was not about to show her ankle to Nōli. What would her mother say?

Just then, Nōli strode up and looked at Ella with a beaming countenance. Ella felt like throttling him. How could he be happy all the time?

"Nōli, I can't keep going like this. Is Entwe'p ve'y fa'h away? I don't think I can keep walking."

Nōli just grinned and said something else about "Entwerp Ffolwyn."

"I can't keep going!" Tears rolled down Ella's cheeks. "I can't. I can't. Don't you unde'stand me?"

Nōli's face seemed to soften a little as if he did indeed understand. He dashed off, but was back in a moment with a few leaves. He crushed them in his hands, chewed them up, and then spit them onto Ella's foot. Ella thought the pain seemed to decrease a little. After massaging her foot for a moment, Nōli reached forward, took Ella by the hand, and continued his hike through the woods. Ella limped along after him, warding off branches and underbrush with her other hand. While she was a bit relieved that Nōli seemed to take a much slower pace, it was all she could do to keep up with him. Every time her weight bore down on her injured foot, pain coursed up her entire leg. More than once, she feared she would swoon.

Over and over, she begged Nōli to stop for a bit, but he didn't seem to hear her. Ella did not know how long Nōli dragged her along, but after what felt like a decade, they suddenly burst out of the forest and came to an abrupt halt. Ella sank to her knees on a wide road. It was raining now, more of a dim drizzle. It must not have been hard enough for Ella to notice it in the forest. Ella let the mud soak all around her, closing her eyes as the rain brushed past her cheeks. At first she was too exhausted to take any note of her surroundings, but when she finally recovered her breath, and the pain in her foot had abated somewhat, she looked around.

The road she was on appeared to run along the top of a cliff that stood right up against a bay. Stretching down to a valley as it skirted along the cliff face of the bay, the road then crossed over a swampy area and ran into a small village.

The cluster of stone and timber houses sat perched between the sea and the rock cliffs of the mountains, with a tall stone dike to keep the tide at bay. A large stone fort stood on the edge of the dike, its back built against a cliff. Below this lay a wide dock where a few merchant vessels bobbed at anchor. Several other ships lay at anchor along the rampart of the dike, each with a gilded red flag flying below the colors of its own country. Just beyond the village was a narrow valley with a wide road that led deeper into the mountains.

Though the village may not have been the most cheery sight in the world, Ella teared up at the sight of civilization. Nōli waved his hands about until Ella looked at him. He pointed at the village.

"Entwerp Ffolwyn."

Without another word, the savage turned and walked off into the forest.

"Thank you, Nōli!" Ella called after him. "Me'thi, Me'thi!"

But he disappeared without even looking back. She strained her eyes after him, even when she was sure he was gone. Finally, she got to her feet and limped off down the road to Entwerp. It was dinnertime now, but there was nothing she could do about it. She had only two miles left to walk before she finally reached Entwerp.

# 8

# THE COOK'S MATE

The fragrant aroma of breakfast wafted through the galley of the pirate ship. Lewis, the faerie cook, had just pulled a massive pot from the stove and now hung it on the hook by the bar. Each pirate filed past, and Lewis served them a heaping scoop of the pot's contents along with a hunk of brown bread. Ernest stood by and watched, filling tankards with grog as the pirates shuffled by. It was always loud in the galley at mealtimes, and Ernest's large gnome ears simply accentuated the noise. Still, he was pretty well used to it by now.

The smell of the soup intrigued the gnome. Lewis would never share his cooking secrets with anyone, even his messmate. It fell to slim little Ernest to figure it out on his own. Ernest peered closely into the ladle every time it turned. It was hard to see much in the thick gruel. Now and then there was the tip of a dumpling peering out into the light, and here and there, he caught glimpses of unidentified meat, but nothing to satisfy his curiosity.

Finally, the last pirate shuffled past Ernest. He filled the man's tankard and then stepped over to the bar to receive his food. Lewis grinned at him broadly and handed him his bowl of soup.

"Have at it, Ernest, boyo!"

Ernest drew up a three-legged stool and sat down by the bar. He held his bowl in one hand and scooped out his food with his bread.

Lewis served himself a bowl of soup, grinning at Ernest across the bar while he ate it. Ernest stopped after about three bites and turned to Lewis.

"How do you make this?"

Lewis laughed.

"You must tell somebody."

Lewis laughed again. "Or not."

Ernest banged his fist on the table passionately. "You cook too well not to tell anyone at all, at all!"

Lewis bowed. "Thank you, thank you, thank you... but no."

But Lewis could not put Ernest off so easily. "If'n you were to die tomorrow, no one could cook, and it would be your fault because you wouldn't tell us. *I* would have to cook then, and the other pirates would keelhaul me if'n they compared my cooking with yours."

Lewis grinned. "You know my motto, don't you?"

Ernest sighed.

"Good food," Lewis said, standing straight like an orator at a royal convention, "is what people love when they taste it, but blanch when they know what you put in it."

"But *I* willn't blanch," Ernest said. "I need to know so I can cook when you pass away."

Lewis laughed. "Good cooks tend to outlive their messmates on pirate ships."

"But you've outlived two already," Ernest replied.

Lewis shrugged. "Doesn't make a difference."

"I bet I could give you one ingredient at any rate!" Ernest cried.

Lewis grinned. "It can't be flour, water, salt, or fish."

Ernest stuck his nose into his soup and took a deep, melodramatic whiff. With eyes closed, he straightened up and snapped his eyes open to stare Lewis right in the face.

"Cumin."

Lewis jumped visibly, but recovered himself quickly. "Helen Maria! I know you are a gnome on many talents, but I believe I see something new on you every day, Ernest."

Ernest grinned slyly.

"No, no, there's something else at work here, boyo. How'd you know cumin?"

"I smelled through your spice cabinet last night," Ernest said without losing his grin.

Lewis clicked his tongue. "Oh, ho, ho! Well, it's a good thing I removed the labels from all on the other spices, then. Cumin's all you can know."

Ernest wriggled his eyebrows mysteriously as he took a bite of his bread.

Lewis looked at him closely. "By prelates, Ernest, I've never haved a mate actually *worry* me before, but I declare you've done it. Why, I suppose all my previous messmates were faeriefolk like myself, but you gnomes are another matter entirely."

Ernest swallowed before replying. "I think you puted some of that red spice in there, too."

"Aha! Now I see yet another side on you. You can operate without the name on the spice. Well, I will have to guard my cabinet more closely, then. My hat is off to you, sir." Lewis bowed dramatically.

Ernest dipped his bread in for more stew.

"But tell me, Ernest," Lewis continued, "which red spice are you referring to?"

"It's the... er..." Ernest jumped up from his stool. "Let me show you."

"Oh, no need, no need," Lewis replied as he ate his stew nonchalantly.

"What are you trying to tell me?" Ernest asked.

Lewis laughed. "It's just this: I don't *have* a red spice in my spice cabinet."

"What?" Ernest cried. "But I seed it!"

"No, you didn't." Lewis swallowed some soup so that Ernest had to wait for him. "It was just a trick on the light."

Ernest looked at him skeptically.

"You *can* trust me. First, I'm your messmate, and second, because I'm a faerie and can see such things without light."

Ernest waved his finger in protest. "You can't pull that one on me! You've sayed yourself that your sonar can't tell colors!"

Lewis shrugged.

Ernest wasn't about to let up now that he had Lewis in a corner. "I will tell you what I think. I think this whole motto, and 'can't tell you how I maked it,' is just a big show, and you don't even believe it yourself. Now then, give me one good reason I should believe you when you don't believe yourself."

Lewis opened his mouth, but Ernest stopped him.

"And you can't just say because you're my messmate and because you're a faerie."

Lewis took a deep breath. "Well, Ernest, you press me hard. By prelates, I see no way out on this but to tell you something about the ingredients."

Ernest's jaw dropped. This was the farthest he had gotten in five years.

Lewis continued, "I want you to think for a moment about all on the parts on a fish you would never want to eat." After a pause, Lewis looked into his bowl meaningfully, then continued eating.

Ernest was not entirely sure that his face wasn't green. "In truth, Lewis? You aren't lying, are you?"

Lewis just grinned. "And there's no cumin in it, either. You must have gotten that mixed up with one on the other spices."

Ernest looked up at his messmate with suspicion. "You're lying now. I can tell that, sure."

"Come, come, Ernest," Lewis replied more seriously, "you know I don't lie. Helen Maria, I will tell you right now that you were right about the 'red spice'—only that the particular spice is not red. As to the cumin, though, you're completely off. That's not to say that I don't use cumin—liberally—just not in this soup."

Before Ernest could respond, a long-armed gnome came up to the bar with his bowl. Lewis put down his bread and snatched up his ladle smartly. "Step right up, step right up!"

The gnome offered his bowl, turning his head nearly all the way around as if he didn't want to be recognized. All the same, it was impossible to hide the massive purple bruise across the side of his face.

"Well, Bill, how'd the night on deck treat you?" Lewis asked. "Do'ed you dream on marlin spikes and old men?"

Bill snarled. "You wouldn't be joking about it if'n you were the one what he hit."

"I figure you can now attest to Jock Blowhoarder's strength. They say he defeated Killjelly in hand-to-hand combat and even escaped from Longfinch himself. Would you vouch for that?" Ernest added.

"Oh ay," Lewis said. "Let the philosophers quarrel all they want; they will never be able to shake Bill's *firm* belief in the solidarity on marlin spikes."

Bill's face went red. "Holy baptism..."

Lewis banged his ladle on the bar as he glared at Bill. His demeanor completely changed—from merriment to indignation. "If'n you keep swearing with that tongue on yours, I might just hit you with a marlin spike myself."

Bill hissed, "You can't make me stop saying what I want to say."

"Oh, ho, ho!" Lewis brandished his ladle as deftly as if it were a saber. "Don't challenge the cook so rashly, now. We have ways on making people shape up. Blind prelates! All I'd have to do is add one spice and..."

Bill growled again. "You have a nice double-tongued standard. Rebuking me for swearing when you do it yourself with pleasure."

Lewis looked him levelly in the eye. "Oh, really?"

"Ay, really!" Bill replied. "Every second sentence you're saying 'prelates' this, and 'prelates' that."

Lewis grinned and took Bill's bowl. "Well, boyo, I'm afraid I will have to educate you on swearing, then." He filled Bill's bowl but didn't give it back until he finished speaking. He waved his ladle to emphasize each point as he made it.

"Swearing is when you use a holy word as if it were unholy. Often it's done with contempt, but usually, the swearer is simply ignorant. Either way, it's blasphemous. Now, you know nothing about baptism, so it behooves you not to swear about it. I have been baptized, so I know it is a holy rite. But as to prelates... they were conceived on by the devil. Since they are unholy to begin with, it's no blasphemy to call them unholy. Thus, 'prelates' isn't swearing. So next time, dear boyo, say, 'blind prelates,' if'n you must, and instead on lecturing you, I will shake your hand!"

With that, Lewis handed Bill his bowl. Bill slunk off moodily, muttering something under his breath.

Ernest looked up at Lewis, grinning broadly. "Well, 'blind prelates,' Lewis, you should've been a preacher, not a pirate cook."

Lewis bowed. "Thank you, thank you..." Yet there was a flicker in the corner of Lewis' eye, the smallest hint betraying that he was acting. Ernest looked closely. It looked like guilt.

But why would Lewis feel guilty? He was certainly the most likable and friendly member of this crew. Yet as soon as the flicker came, it was gone, and Lewis was his normal self again, beaming from ear to ear.

Just then, Quartermaster Harold's whistle sang out loud and clear, calling all hands to action. The pirates leapt up from where they sat and charged out of the galley, bowls and breakfast forgotten. Lewis gave an apologetic shrug, but Ernest had no more time for conversation as he joined the general surge up the stairs to the deck. Yet he cast one more glance back at Lewis. There was a nagging feeling in his stomach that he had just missed something important.

As soon as the salt air hit his face, Ernest looked around, turning his head nearly all the way around to get a full view of the deck. Killjelly and Holgard were standing on the forecastle with Cweel, but before Ernest got his foot on deck, Cweel turned and launched off. Holgard turned and walked back to his cabin while Killjelly stayed on the forecastle, leaning against the gunwales thoughtfully.

Just then, the quartermaster thrust his way through the new deck hands. "We need this here ship moving this here minute! We're going to Longfinch and have to get there by noon! I want to see every sail out on this here ship! Jibs, staysails, the lot on them, baptize me!"

Ernest dashed off to the mizzenmast, looking up as sailors swarmed the shrouds and ratline before shimmying down the yards to unfurl the sails. Ernest took his stand with a group of sailors hauling at a brace line to turn the spars trim with the wind. Holgard's son, Ynwyr, watched the proceedings from his post at the helm. Ernest turned to him, hauling in time with the other sailors. "What's the hurry? Do you know?"

Ynwyr nodded. "There's a merchant ship."

One of the other pirates hauling on the brace line grinned. "Plunder in sight."

Ynwyr shrugged. "If'n Longfinch doesn't get there first."

---

By noon, the pirate galleon was only a few miles away from Entwerp Bay. They had a strong east wind, allowing them to sail briskly on their way. Ynwyr kept them on course, as close to the coast as he dared, without risking reefs or tides. The ease with which he steered the vessel on its way made Ernest guess it was not Ynwyr's first time to navigate these waters.

No matter how hard he looked, Ernest could not see the entrance to the Bay of Entwerp. No doubt the coast's many cliffs and jagged granite outcroppings obscured his view. For several minutes now, the crew could see a sail. They set to their work with a considerable amount of excitement until Killjelly confirmed it was Longfinch's man-o-war.

Finally, Holgard came out of his cabin and gave an order to the quartermaster and then to his son. The quartermaster blew shrilly on his whistle. "Pull in all sails!"

As the crew obeyed, Ynwyr steered the ship behind a huge rock that rose from the water like a knife's edge. The ship slid smoothly behind it until only the topmost rigging showed over the rock.

At this sudden change, several of the crew grumbled. One caught Quartermaster Harold by the arm and pulled him to the side to talk. Ernest saw this and cocked his large ears to hear what they said. Surely the other pirates knew he could hear almost anything said on deck, didn't they? He wasn't the only gnome, after all.

"What's going on now?" the pirate was asking. "I thought we were getting ourselves a merchant ship."

"We are," the quartermaster said. "We're waiting on it now."

"But what about Longfinch?" the pirate replied. "What if'n he gets it first?"

Quartermaster Harold grunted. "This isn't about Longfinch's catch or our catch; we're going to share it between us. Longfinch is driving the merchant ship to us, anyway."

That was all Ernest wanted to hear. He dashed below deck and back into the galley. Lewis had cleaned the place up by this time and washed all the bowls from breakfast. He was now working on a new pot of soup for lunch. Ernest knew Lewis wasted nothing and that he started this new soup with whatever was left over from breakfast. Even so, it smelled completely different, yet just as delicious as usual.

Ernest walked over to his hammock just next to the kitchen, and unlocked the small sea chest containing all of his earthly possessions. After rummaging around in this briefly, he pulled out a spyglass.

Ernest then dashed back up on deck and climbed the shrouds until he reached the yard of the royal—the uppermost sail. Another pirate stood here, peering over the large rock that blocked the ship from the rest of the ocean. The lookout glanced at him as he swung up. "Afternoon, Ernest."

Ernest tipped his hat and then peered out across the ocean. Still, the only sail he could see was Longfinch's. Ernest pulled out his spyglass to study Longfinch's ship more closely. It was a first-class man-o-war, with more sails and masts than Ernest cared to worry about. From the mainmast a flag flew, bearing an aurochs skull on a black field. Ernest finally decided that Longfinch's ship was on the other side of the bay from them and was also waiting.

Ernest listened closely, hoping to hear a whistle or a bell that would betray the ship's presence. With his large ears, he could hear the harsh cries of gulls mingling with the plaintive notes of birds from the shore and the constant booming of the surf against the rocky shore, but otherwise, the air was still.

Just then, a merchant ship—a full-rigged barque—came around a corner of the coast, presumably leaving Entwerp Bay.

It sailed out, unsuspecting, into the open sea, directly between the two pirate ships. The ship was narrow and loaded low in the water with many sails but few guns. Ernest saw smoke rise from the front of Longfinch's ship, and soon afterward he heard the sharp reports of cannons.

Below him, Ernest heard the quartermaster call clearly on his whistle. "Man the cannons! Pass out the swords and guns!"

# 9

# THE BARQUE

The deck below Ernest was a flurry of commotion, but he paid it no heed. He was concentrating on the merchant ship.

The crew of the barque seemed to hurry about in complete confusion as Longfinch's huge man-o-war descended on them. Ernest could see the pirate's starboard gunports open. Before the pirate ship could reach the barque, the merchants had recovered from their shock, and the barque moved forward, tacking into the heavy east-by-northeast wind to flee into the open sea. The barque wheeled slowly and laboriously. For a full-rigged vessel like this one—with all square sails—tacking was what it was worst at. It could only move a few degrees at a time into the direction of the wind. Longfinch's man-o-war, or Holgard's galleon, could easily run it down if it tried to tack into the open sea.

No, this ship was made to sail full tilt with the winds at its back. Then—even loaded down as it was—it would outpace either of these pirate vessels. Right now it was slow and vulnerable, and no doubt the merchants on board knew it. Longfinch's man-o-war turned abruptly, plowing through the sea to cut off the merchant ship's escape.

The barque swerved again back towards the shore. The turn was too wide, however, for the merchant ship to make it back to Entwerp Bay. If they were trying to return to port, they would have to wear ship, swinging their stern across the direction of the wind. Yet by the time they completed that maneuver, Longfinch would have boarded them. No, there was only one thing they could do. Flying as much sail as possible, they would have to flee straight south. Ernest shivered in delight; they were moving directly into the trap.

Longfinch came close on the tail of the barque, firing a shot now and then just to keep the merchants on their toes, though he slowed his pace considerably. Ernest guessed Longfinch would catch up with the barque soon after they passed the rock behind which the galleon lay.

Ernest swung down to the deck and made his way to the armory. All the other pirates had taken their weapons already, and Quartermaster Harold was just locking it up.

"Hold up just a moment," Ernest cried.

The quartermaster opened the door again. "You should've been here sooner, lad. We can't leave this open all day. Now get your weapons and get out."

Ernest grabbed one of the bayoneted muskets and a rapier and then dashed out again as Quartermaster Harold closed the door and grumbled to himself. Ernest slung the musket over his shoulder and then gave his rapier a few experimental twirls. Yes, he liked the way it felt in his hand. Really, he liked this rapier more than any musket. He felt safer, more at ease, with a rapier, like somehow he could control it in a way that he never could a musket. Maybe this was because the monks had taught him a lesson or two with the rapier in school, but he was still figuring out the musket by trial and error.

This was not all of Ernest's weaponry, however. True, there was his knife, but he always kept that on him. His most prized weapon was not in the armory; in fact, few even knew he owned it.

Ernest dashed back below deck. Where the pirates had shared a quiet breakfast just hours earlier, there was now a melee of activity. The gunners had moved the benches aside and rolled the cannons into place, clearing the entire deck so that the gunning squads could move from one side of the ship to the other without difficulty. As with most ships of the time, the galleon was only big enough to carry enough men to crew one side of the ship's guns at a time.

Gunners yelled at one another. Boys dashed back and forth with barrels of sand and gunpowder. The head gunners brought in the ration of balls for the fight. All was noise and crowded bodies. The smell of sweating men filled the thick air, alleviated only by the slight breeze that worked its way through the opened gun ports. Amid the cacophony, Lewis quietly stirred away at his pot.

Ernest slipped over to where his hammock had been now cleared away for the gunners and unlocked his chest again. After replacing the spyglass, he reached into the back and pulled out a wooden box. He opened the lid to reveal an eight-barreled pepperbox pistol. Looking to either side to ensure no one saw it, he tucked it safely inside his vest. His pepperbox pistol was a well-kept secret; only Lewis and Killjelly knew of it.

As Ernest slipped through the crowd, he caught Lewis' eye and gave him an inquiring look. Lewis waved at him. "After the fight, I willn't need you now."

Ernest nodded and dashed up on deck. There was definitely less commotion, but still a commotion. Besides the gun squads that manned the smaller swivel guns on deck, the boarders were preparing for battle, loading their muskets and sharpening their knives. Several of the crew stood by the masts, waiting for orders. Ernest saw Killjelly and made for him.

"Boatswain, sir, cook's-mate off-duty, sir," Ernest saluted.

Killjelly looked at him. One of his eyes was black, and his forehead was wrapped in a bandage—remnants from his struggle with Jock the night Ella escaped. His eyes seemed to see the nearly imperceptible bulge in Ernest's vest. "Join the boarders, sure."

"Sir." Ernest saluted and took his position by the gunwales, though his heart sank a little. He hated working with the boarders. It felt like the most dangerous and exposed job in a fight.

Just then, the lookout yelled, and Quartermaster Harold's whistle blew out loud and clear, "Get this here ship moving!"

Many boarders dropped their weapons and assisted the sailors in hoisting sails and drawing up the anchor, but Ernest stayed where he was.

The ship slid gently forward. They were making a port tack a few degrees into the wind, so the wind filled the sails slowly. Rounding the rock, they appeared in the open sea, directly in the path of the fleeing merchants. The barque was only about fifty yards away, bearing straight towards the galleon. They were close enough for Ernest to see the expression of panic on the faces of the merchant crew. Ernest raised his musket and sited in on an elderly sailor who stood open-mouthed at the appearance of this new pirate vessel. He fired, but missed.

As he reloaded, the gun decks erupted beneath him. Smoke and steel poured from the galleon, and shell after shell blasted through the sides of the barque. The guns were only twenty-four-pounders, but that was more than enough to cut through the merchant ship's hull at this close range. From Ernest's right, a swivel cannon fired. There was a whirling noise as a charge of bar-shot streaked through the air and struck the barque's foremasts. There was a resounding crack, and the mast sagged forward.

*Firing upon the barque*

Just then, Longfinch's man-o-war came level with the merchant ship. Grapnels sailed through the air and caught the barque by the gunwales. As the man-o-war pulled in closer to the merchant ship—its rigging line tangling with those of its prey—it let loose a full volley of steel. The merchants tried to turn their only cannon to face the boarding ship, but before they could load, a shot from one of Longfinch's swivel guns shattered it.

Ernest could hear the quartermaster's whistle above the din of combat, trilling out orders, but he didn't bother to listen closely enough to understand them. The orders were not for him. The galleon slowly turned and pulled up next to the merchant ship on the other side from the man-o-war. As the side of the barque came into view, Ernest could see the word *Liberty* clearly painted in gold letters.

A boarder to Ernest's left spat. "Baptize these christened ships."

Ernest leveled his gun again and searched the deck for a target. There were several cabin boys, but he ignored them; they might swim ashore and escape yet—they had their whole lives ahead of them. It was the older men he would target. Boarders on either side of him pulled out their grapnels and hurled them at the side of the barque.

Ernest fired his musket, and a gray-haired man fell to the deck. Ernest congratulated himself as he loaded his piece again. One dead already. His record was two in one fight.

The gap between the two ships closed quickly. The tumble-home of the two vessels would prevent the gunwales from actually touching. Even when the ships' hulls touched, the two decks' gunwales would be about six feet apart. Still, that was enough space to jump.

Already several merchants had lined the side of the ship, each with a two-pronged repelling-pike. Several boarders balanced themselves on the gunwales, preparing to jump across onto the merchant ship. Ernest didn't join them. He had seen too many pirates impaled on a repelling-pike to risk it himself. He was the cook's-mate—after all—he didn't have to fight that hard; there was no need to seek promotion.

Just then, the swivel to Ernest's right vomited a barrel-full of grapeshot at the defending merchants. The swarm of smaller shells struck in the center of their line, tearing it to pieces. Now the boarders vaulted across the space between the two ships and lay about with their swords, hatchets, and bayonets, finishing off any merchants who had survived the swivel's murderous volley.

As soon as Ernest felt certain that most of the defense was clear of the gunwale, he too jumped over to the merchant ship. A middle-aged faerie must have seen him, for at that moment he jumped through the fog of gunpowder and swung at Ernest with a marlinspike. Ernest had just enough time to lower his piece and fire. The man gave a hideous scream. Ernest had not killed him, but only shot him in the stomach.

Before Ernest could finish the man off with the bayonet, another pirate lunged forward with his cutlass and cut the merchant to the deck. Ernest sighed and looked around for another opponent. He slung his musket over his shoulder, then drew his rapier in his right hand and his knife in his left. The sword felt natural and fit in his hand comfortably, unlike that awkward musket.

All about him was the carnage of a pirate raid. Shattered wood lay strewn all over the deck amidst the broken bodies of the dead and dying. The ring of steel against steel, reports from guns, and screams of pain filled the air. Though he had seen it all many times before, Ernest could never grow accustomed to it. The sheer noise made his head hurt, and the adrenaline pounding through his veins made his gut feel weak.

He peered across the deck through the gunpowder fog, wondering if he could see anyone from Longfinch's crew. Slowly, he turned his head all the way around, taking in the entire scene carefully. Even as he stared, a loud cry rose above the din of battle. Here and there, combatants stepped back and looked around for the cause of the cry. Slowly, the melee died down as all eyes turned to a figure who stood by the mainmast of the merchant ship. He was obviously a pirate (and a leader among Longfinch's crew, no doubt), but he was not Longfinch himself. Ernest knew this even though he had not seen Longfinch for himself; he had heard Longfinch was an elf, but this man was a human.

The man was dark-haired, with dark-olive skin. His eyes were squat, and his nostrils were wide. He only had a straight saber in his hand, and he carried no other weapon except a short dirk which hung at his side.

"Which is!" the man cried. "Let your captain cross swords with me, and if'n he beats me, then you may all go free, whatever."

The merchants looked at each other, unsure of what to think of this proposal. Ernest looked across the deck. Longfinch's men were grinning at each other.

Just then, a tall man in a tri-cornered hat stepped down from the poop deck and pushed his way through the other merchants toward the man. "Who is this that challenges us?"

The man looked at the captain carefully. "Vania. Vania Bloodrummer."

The captain stood before Vania and drew a basket-hilted back-sword from his side. "We accept yer challenge, Mr. Blood-rummer." He spoke as if signing off on a business transaction, not mortal combat.

Vania nodded and drew his dirk in his left hand. The captain stood poised for a moment, unsure of his opponent. Finally, he flicked his blade forward experimentally. Vania whipped his blade to the side and lashed out with his left hand.

The captain stumbled back with a bloody gash across his chest. He again poised himself for battle and, after waiting for a few moments, struck at Vania again. Vania again lashed out, but this time, the captain blocked the blow.

By the second clash of steel, Ernest lost sight of blades as they slashed this way and that, but he did not lose sight of the combatant's faces. The captain's face grew increasingly grim as the fight went on, but Vania smiled. He moved in a lithe, fluid motion, whereas the captain slashed about frantically.

Suddenly, Vania parried a thrust to one side and struck with his dirk. The dagger caught squarely in the captain's basket-hilt. Vania twisted his wrist and held the captain's sword to one side. The captain yanked at his sword, trying to pull it free, but when he realized it was useless, he grew still. Slowly and deliberately, Vania placed his sword on the captain's vest. The captain was completely pale.

"Very well, then. Ye win."

With a flash of a smile, Vania sliced the brass buttons from the captain's vest. The captain winced.

"Ye tain me at your mercy. Shall I surrender, then?"

Vania only laughed. "And what would I do with a prisoner, whatever?"

Longfinch's crew laughed uproariously.

Vania put the tip of his sword to the captain's chest. The merchant crew stood stock still, too horrified to move. Vania stared the captain directly in the eye and thrust him through with his blade.

The captain struggled and tried to free his sword. His adrenaline must be too high to feel his pain. Vania drew back his blade and slashed the captain across the neck. The captain crumpled over, his lifeblood soaking the deck. Vania raised his bloody sword and pointed it at the merchants.

"Death! Havoc!" The pirates yelled in answer and charged at the merchants again. The merchants fell back in terror. Some leapt overboard to save themselves; the pirates hacked the rest to pieces with their hungry swords.

While the screams of mercy from the merchants rang in the air, Ernest simply stood where he was and watched. At one point, through the smoke, he glimpsed Cweel with the mangled pilot in his claws. Just as Ernest was about to turn back to the galleon and see if Lewis needed help passing out lunch, he saw Captain Longfinch.

He was a tall elf, with the dark, color-shifting skin peculiar to that race. It might have been brown, but in the right light, it almost looked like a deep purple shade. His large, tapir-like nose, stood out prominently on his face, combining with his pointed ears to mark him out as an elf. Longfinch wore no hat, but let his raven hair blow free in the wind. His clothing was also not as ornate as most sea-captains', but was plain and loose-fitting. He wore a thick belt that contained only one pistol and a host of knives and daggers. A dirk handle also protruded from his boot, but Longfinch's choice weapon was a large kukri, which hung on his back. Longfinch held a knife in each hand, and blood smeared his shirt and cheek.

Ernest could not help gasping in awe of this pirate. His very aspect demanded respect, yet there was a strange light in his dark eyes, which looked almost friendly. He smiled lightly, as if enjoying a pleasant outing, and now and then, would taste the air with his long, elfin tongue. As Longfinch glanced about, his eyes briefly passed over Ernest, and in that instant, Ernest wondered if that mighty elfin captain could see what thoughts he was thinking.

Just then, Vania came up to his captain, pulling one of the merchant crew behind him. "Which is, Captain Longfinch, this young man wishes to join our crew, whatever."

Longfinch looked at the lad, tasting the air with his tongue. The lad was rather beat up, blood running down his forehead.

"Can you fight?"

"Yes, sir," the lad said. "I jist killed two o' yer men, if ye'll do no mind me sayin', sir."

Longfinch laughed. "As long as you can make up for it."

Vania led the young man away towards the man-o-war.

Out of the smoke, Captain Holgard walked up to Longfinch. He must have come aboard with the boarders early in the combat, as his beard and coat dripped blood. Holgard saluted Longfinch.

"Weel, we meet again, Captain."

Longfinch smiled. "And so close to our prey, too."

Holgard snorted as he wiped his cutlass on his trousers and sheathed it.

"And how is our dear Jock doing? Has he said anything yet?"

Holgard shook his head. "He's as stubborn as a clam. Boatswain Killjelly haves done all he knows, but Jock willn't talk."

"These things just take time."

Holgard nodded. "Killjelly tried to torture the girl to see if'n he would talk then, but she getted away."

"Cweel told me," Longfinch replied. "He's been searching for her since the fog cleared yesterday, and he'll look for her again as soon as we're done here."

Holgard kicked at a dead merchant. "I think the only way to make Jock talk is to threaten the girl. She is his weak spot."

"Yes, but why?"

Holgard snorted.

Longfinch nodded. "I'll let you try Jock again tonight, but in the morning, hand him over, and we'll have at him. Cweel should have the girl soon."

Holgard nodded.

Longfinch turned away, crying to his men, "Sack the ship and split up the bounty, then sink the boat. Tonight we lay at anchor by Entwerp Bay."

Ernest turned and leapt back over to the galleon. Lewis probably had lunch ready by now.

# 10

# ENTWERP COASTAL

*E*lla limped slowly down the road towards Entwerp—or Entwerp Ffolwyn, as Nōli had called it. The way wasn't difficult—certainly it was much easier than her trek through the forest—but it was slow. Even though she rested every so often and wiped her foot off with her petticoats, her wound was soon black with dirt, and her foot was swelling. There must still be a part of a thorn in her foot—though it was hard to tell while she was wearing her stockings. Still, she was not about to take her stocking off and get a better look, not on a public road. The rain hadn't lasted very long, but it had left the road wet and muddy, which didn't help at all.

As the sun touched the tops of the western mountains, Ella reached the narrow bog, which the road crossed in a series of bridges. She was now only half a mile from the village, and Ella purposed not to stop again until she reached it. Yet as she crossed the bridges, the evening winds caught hold of her skirts from below as if purposefully trying to trip her. Once, she did trip and skinned the palms of her hands on the cobblestone. She advanced slowly, limping awkwardly.

This was even more awkward as she now met with civilized

people. The men were broad-shouldered, of various complexions, and various races—mainly human. They all wore tricornered hats, loose-fitting shirts, great-coats, trousers, and knee-boots. Many of them looked her in the eye and made as if to talk to her, but she turned her head away from them and kept walking.

She also ran into a few women, none of whom were having any trouble with their skirts. These women seemed to have the oddest sense of fashion. Their clothes—mostly—were like Ella's, only their skirts were square, with four corners, each with a thick pin in the end. They also all wore straw hats, which made Ella feel all the more out of place with her bare head, shoeless feet, and round skirt.

But what struck her most about these men and women was their vibrant clothing colors. True, the colors were not bright, and Ella was hard-pressed to find a single article of clothing that was not a homey earth-color—mostly browns and greens. But how vibrant and alive these colors looked! Even the browns that these people wore looked rich with life and texture. And how many shades of brown they wore! Everything from soothing tan to luscious chestnut, to imperial bay, to decadent dun, to vibrant russet, and roan mixes of them all. Ella tried her best not to stare.

Once, when she was about halfway across the bog-bridges, she chanced to look behind her. For a moment, she saw a large, winged beast soaring about the mountains far to the south. She smiled despite herself. Cweel did not know she was here.

Finally, she reached the end of the bridges and came to the first house of Entwerp. As soon as she reached it, she sat down on a fallen log and held her foot in her hands. The dirt had now thoroughly filled her thorn-wound. She sighed, and her stomach growled.

Slowly, she got back to her feet and limped into the village. It was a little larger than Blisa village and was definitely dirtier.

Yet for all that, it reminded Ella somewhat of home—with the small stone houses and the mountains looming up on the one side and alpine trees all around. But then again, there was the sound of the sea always in her ears, the feeling of cobblestones beneath her feet, and the strange accents of villagers, telling Ella all too clearly that she was not at home. She was on the other side of the sea, with two pirate ships, a ferocious Griffin, and an ancient treasure between her and home.

She found herself walking in the middle of the street—not purposefully; it was simply to avoid the villagers who bustled about both sides of the street. She didn't want to talk to anyone. She just needed time to herself to think about what to do.

That morning, it had been so clear to her. All she had to do was find the Gwambi Treasure. Now here she was, with no lunch or dinner inside her, no shoes, and an injured foot, in the middle of a strange village, with night nearly upon her. She stopped where she was and tried to think.

The Gwambi Treasure was her goal, but her *immediate* goal was finding some place to sleep. A bed was a luxury she could forgo. A meal was slightly more necessary, but she would have forgone that too—if only she could have some alley in which to spend the night.

Just then, a horse and wagon approached from behind. She had heard a few of these already on other streets. Now she turned, and there was a small wagon with a horse drawing it, trotting quickly and directly at her from the direction of the bog-bridges. The driver at that moment was staring off absent-mindedly at the mountains and didn't see her.

To her surprise, she did not seem able to take the few steps needed to get out of the way of the wagon. Her legs seemed to be rooted to the cobblestones. She would simply stay there until the driver finally saw her, or until the horse had run her over and saved Cweel the trouble of finding her. It wasn't that she was terrified. She just didn't seem to care. It was as if her life was unimportant. It would be a lot simpler for her if she didn't move, and anyway, *she* didn't have a say in the matter since her legs *wouldn't* move.

Suddenly, someone gripped her shoulder and pulled her to the side of the road, yelling at the driver.

"Laendon! Gard where ye're drivin' now. Ye'll will cause a merri o' harm one o' these days!"

The driver came to himself and pulled hard at the reins. His horse came to an abrupt halt just before Ella and the man who had pulled her aside. The driver doffed his hat apologetically.

"I'm terribly sorry, ma'am, I really oughtta-should be gardin' where I drive."

"Ay," the man who pulled Ella aside said, "ye should; maugre spacin' out like that."

The driver fumbled with his hat. "Terribly sorry, ma'am."

Ella bowed her head in embarrassment. "I'm fine."

She tried to move on, but the man who had pulled her aside wouldn't let go of her shoulder.

"Beg yer pardon, ma'am, but I cen no help but see that ye appear to be in some sort o' fix. Ye do no tain any shoes on yer feet, ye ha' lost yer hat, an' ye're hurt."

"Thank you," Ella mumbled, and she tried to leave again, but the man still held her firmly—though in a friendly way.

"If ye'll do no mind my quirin'," he said, "where are ye from? I'd no be merri o' an gentleman if I'll did no help ye to yer house at least."

Ella hesitated. She knew very little about these two young men, except that they seemed fairly nice. "I'm not f'om he'e," she finally said, wincing slightly at her missing r's.

The two men looked at each other. "I s'pose no," the driver finally said, still holding his hat in his hands.

"Do ye tain a place to stay?" the other man asked.

Ella shook her head. "I just came out of the woods." Seeing as neither of the men had anything to say to this, she unbound her problems to them in a flood of words and emotion. "I washed asho'e yeste'day, and I've spent all day and night in the woods, and I haven't had lunch o'h dinn'h today..." She choked on her words and sobbed.

"Ye washed ashore?" the driver asked in a soft tone of voice. Ella nodded.

The man who was holding Ella looked seriously at the driver. "Ye heard the guns today, did no ye?"

The driver's face became very grim. "Ay."

The man turned back to Ella. "Ye were a pirate captive?"

Ella gasped. "How did you know?"

"It wos a guess," the driver replied.

"Here now, ma'am," the other man said. "If ye'll scend on up into the wagon now, me an' Laendon will bring ye back to our house. Ma will tain a nice meal ready fer us by now, an' ye cen sleep in a bed fer the night."

Ella hesitated, but only for a moment. Food, even hay, would have been reason enough for her to come with these two men as far as she was concerned, but the prospect of sleeping in a bed— a *bed*—was like hearing she had arrived in heaven. Besides, she had her dagger still. The driver offered her his hand, and Ella took it, stepping into the cart.

The other man vaulted lightly up next to the driver, and the wagon lurched forward, heading off towards the other side of the village. As they started, the man who had pulled Ella out of the road turned around to face her.

"I do no believe we ha' traded names yet. They call me Martyn Blaeith, an' this is my brother Laendon Blaeith." he rested his hand on the driver's shoulder.

"They call me Ella."

The man nodded and turned back to his brother. Ella looked at the two men closely from where she sat in the back of the cart. Both were human, that she could tell immediately. The older of the two, Martyn, was a smidge taller, with slightly darker features overall. The younger, Laendon, was a little broader of shoulder and rounder of face. A few acne scars peppered his face, and rectangular spectacles rested on his nose. Both of them were young men. Laendon was not much older than herself, and Ella guessed Martyn was about twenty-five. Both looked energetic, broad-shouldered, and well-built.

Just then, Martyn turned to his brother, "Ye really oughtta-should pay more attention when ye're drivin', ye know."

"But I get my ideas when I'll drive," Laendon replied.

"One o' these days ye'll will clude up murderin' someone, an' then ye'll will be in a merri mess."

Laendon thought this through for a moment. "I do no think ye cen call it murder to run someone over on accident."

"That is as it may be," Martyn said, "but how do ye figure it?"

Laendon slowed his horse ever so much. "If I'll recall correctly, it says in the Law that murder has to be preconceived. Now, in the case o' me spacin' out and runnin' some poor soul over, that would no be preconceived, so it would no be murder."

"To play the devil's advocate," Martyn replied, "I believe that recklessness is also a qualification o' murder, an' ye're certainly bein' reckless."

"I do no think ye're right there."

Martyn looked at Laendon for a moment. "Well, be *that* as it may, what sort o' society would we be in if we'll could never punish someone who recklessly killed someone else?"

"I believe that ye could still *punish* him, just no as a murder-er," Laendon said. "It seems like the Law gives provision to pose him under house arrest, or give him a lesser-outlawry in a City of Refuge."

Ella didn't listen to Martyn's reply, but just sat back in the cart, passively watching the village as it passed by her. She paid no heed to where they headed or what turns the men took. At every bump or jolt of the cart, Ella's stomach growled, and her foot throbbed painfully.

Finally, the wagon pulled to a halt, and Ella looked about her. They had stopped in front of a low stone house with a barn nearby. A fence surrounded what yard there was, containing a few fat chickens. The windows were alight with lanterns, and plant boxes full of herbs hung from each. The chimney lazily sighed smoke into the night air.

Both men hopped down from the wagon seat, and Martyn held out his hand to Ella. She took it and hopped to the ground on her one good foot. Laendon then led the horse and wagon into the barn while Martyn, still holding Ella by the hand, led her into the house.

Inside, the house was bright and homey. The low door opened directly into a large front room which was partially divided in half by a low counter. On the side of the counter that the doorway was on stood a broad fireplace, a few chairs and wooden stools, a low writing table, and a very large bookshelf. On the other side of the counter was a kitchen and dining area with several counters, a large cast-iron stove, and a broad oak table that looked large enough to seat a platoon of dwarves.

Three boys sat in the living area of this room, reading books or writing carefully. A young woman oversaw them from where she sat, knitting by the fireplace. In the kitchen, a sturdy woman of about fifty bustled about, putting the last touches on supper.

Martyn led Ella up to the counter and finally let go of her hand. "Ma, I ha' brought home another poor soul, if you'll do no mind."

The lady turned and smiled at Ella. "Well, God bless ye, Miss..."

"Ella."

Martyn looked at her in mild surprise. "Oh, I thought that Ella wos yer first name."

"It is," Ella replied.

The lady held out her hand to Ella. "My name is Fawn Blaeith. Do ye tain a surname?"

Ella took the lady's hand but didn't answer for a moment. That was a harder question than it appeared. Was she to give her stepfather's surname or her real father's surname? She finally went with her stepfather's.

"Donne."

"It is good to meet ye, Miss Ella Donne." The lady leaned forward and kissed Ella on the cheek. Ella was taken a bit by surprise, but kept her composure, smiling politely.

"Please make yerself at home," Fawn Blaeith continued. "I'll tain some supper ready in a moment here."

"Is Da home yet?" Martyn asked.

"He's collectin' eggs jist now."

Ella turned to find the four occupants of the living area gazing at her. She took a few steps towards a chair, limping badly as she did so. The young woman jumped up from her seat and caught Ella.

"Oh, ye poor dear!" she cried. "What's happened to yer foot?"

Ella leaned gratefully on the woman. She was probably about Martyn's age, though she wasn't human. She was shorter than the average human, with a round face, long arms, straight blonde hair, and tender blue eyes.

She bent down and examined Ella's foot. "What happened here?"

With the rest of her body still facing Ella's foot, she twisted her head nearly all the way around so she was looking at Ella again. So this young lady was a gnome then.

"I stepped on a tho'n while I was walking th'ough the woods," Ella said.

"It gards like it merri well might be infected," the gnome said. "Here, sit down; I will treat that fer ye."

The gnome helped Ella take a seat and then dashed off into a back room. She was back in a moment with a bucket of clean water, a sponge, a bar of soap, a jar of ointment, and some bandaging material. Pulling a stool up to Ella, she propped Ella's foot on it. Before Ella could object, the gnome pulled Ella's stocking off and rubbed soap all over Ella's foot. Ella felt deeply embarrassed, looking around at the boys in the room to see if they were watching, yet they all seemed intent on reading their books. Still, she couldn't think that she had even had her bare ankle visible to any man, not since she was a little girl, at any rate.

Yet then, as she looked down at the gnome, Ella realized with some horror that this young gnome woman was not wearing stockings at all. And neither was the older woman in the kitchen. Ella blushed deeply. What sort of place had she come to, where women didn't even have the decency to cover their ankles? Perhaps such immodesty was socially appropriate within the privacy of their own home.

Dipping the sponge in the water, the gnome wiped the dirt away from Ella's wound with gentle strokes.

"So ye're name is Ella?" the gnome asked.

Ella winced at the cleaning. "Yes." After a pause, she added, "and you?"

"I'm Lexi."

"I'm glad to meet you, Lexi." Ella gritted her teeth.

"Where are ye from?" Lexi asked.

"Blisa village," said Ella. "It's in Slyzwir."

"Oh, really?" Lexi paused for a moment. "I used to live in Slyzwir."

"Did you g'ow up the'e?"

Lexi nodded, "My Father wos an aurochs rancher there. We moved when I wos six."

"Why did you move?" Ella gritted her teeth tighter.

"The aurochs caught the Death Plague. My father vened here to Llaedhwyth 'cause he heard that he'll could make a good profit sellin' mutton to the soldiers during the War—plus the Kelmarians could no tax us here."

Ella thought back to what Master Schultz had told her of

Pistosian History. "Was that the Wa' of H'ufangi-Kelma'ian Enmity?"

"No," Lexi said, "the Hrufangi Instigation from fifteen years ago."

Ella pursed her lips, trying to remember anything about this event. Master Schultz would talk about that war every now and then – since it confirmed his politics – but few other people in Blisa cared at all about the countries across the sea. Still, Ella thought she remembered the basic gist. "With Caedmon Wilkins fighting fo'h the independence of Llaedhwyth?"

Lexi nodded again.

Ella thought for a moment. "He's still the p'ime ministe'h he'e, isn't he?"

"Ay, but we call him Lord Protector," Lexi said, as she stopped scrubbing for a moment. She pulled out a pair of long tweezers and looked up at Ella. "I'm sorry. I apologize in advance."

Ella grabbed the arms of the chair firmly. Lexi held Ella's leg tightly and then picked at the most tender spot on her foot. It was all Ella could do to keep from pulling her foot back from the pain. After prodding Ella's foot several times, Lexi finally clamped down with her tweezers and pulled out a large thorn nearly an inch long.

"There we are!" Lexi flashed a triumphant smile. "Almost done then."

So saying, she scrubbed vigorously at the remaining dirt in the wound. Ella gritted her teeth until her jaw hurt, consciously holding her foot still.

Finally, Lexi stopped and dropped the sponge into the bucket. Next, she applied some ointment to Ella's foot, put a strip of bark over it, and bound it up with a long bandage.

"There ye are. It should be as good as new in a couple o' days."

Just then, the back door to the room burst open, and in

walked a rather tall, robust man with the wagon driver, Laendon, close on his heels. Ella blushed again, but had no way of hurriedly covering up her ankle.

"Well, Fawn," the older man exclaimed, "do ye tain our supper ready yet, love?"

The woman in the kitchen turned towards the man with a smile. "I do, if you'll tain my eggs?"

"Why, I think I do." So saying, the man displayed a basket filled with golden brown eggs.

"Well, then, I think we cen eat." Fawn gave a sharp whistle, and everyone in the living area jumped to their feet and rushed toward the dividing-counter. Ella limped behind them and came up last. The pain in her foot had already decreased.

"We will no be eatin' alone tonight," Mrs. Blaeith continued. "This little lady here is Miss Ella Donne."

"Aha, ay," Mr. Blaeith said. "Laendon wos jist tellin' me about her. Ye're the pirate captive?"

Mrs. Blaeith and Lexi gasped.

"Oh, no, ye were no?" Lexi asked.

Ella nodded slowly.

"Well, that is all over now. Welcome, Miss Donne, to my little house." The man gripped Ella by the hand and kissed her on the cheek.

Ella nearly fell over in shock. It had been one thing to be kissed by Mrs. Blaeith, but she felt very threatened by this burly man, especially when she wasn't wearing one of her stockings. She blushed and took a step backward. Lexi caught Ella before she fainted or did anything drastic, taking her by the arm and whispering in her ear, "Do no let the kissin' take ye by surprise. It is jist their way o' greetin' ye. It wos startlin' for me at first, too."

Mr. Blaeith continued his welcome. "I am Henri Blaeith, and I see you ha' met my wife, Fawn, and Lexi, Martyn, and Laendon. Ha' ye gotten the younkers names?" He started with the tallest of the three other boys. "Clerans, Robert, and Roland."

Ella didn't register the unfamiliar names; she was still in shock over the kiss. Mr. Blaeith smiled and removed his hat. His sons did the same. "Let us thank God fer this blessed supper." With that, he raised his hands into the air. "Lord Almighty, we thank ye extravagantly fer this meal you ha' given to us today. Ye are faithful to feed yer servants. We thank ye for bringing us Ella tonight fer us to entertain. All the glory o' heaven is yers. Amen."

Mrs. Blaeith lifted a pot from the stove and placed it on the table. Everyone took a seat on the oak benches, and then Mr. Blaeith served the food. Ella had never appreciated food so much as she did that night.

# 11

# THE BLAEITHS

*M*rs. Blaeith's soup was incredibly filling, but even so, Ella ate two full bowls before she finally felt satisfied. After that, she chewed contentedly on a small crust and took sips of the light beer Lexi had served her. The beer made her most at ease. It reminded her very much of her home; a beverage for quenching thirst—not getting drunk like that grog the pirates had given her. Ella shivered at the memory.

She sat with Lexi on her right and one of the Blaeith boys on her left. He appeared to be the oldest of the three younger boys, probably just younger than herself, maybe about sixteen summers. Ella couldn't remember his name, but he looked for all the world like a young Martyn.

"How was the factory today?" Mr. Blaeith asked.

Mrs. Blaeith shrugged. "Oh well, ye know. The factory is the factory. It's the same work day after day. There was no much o' note, really."

"So it was a good day then," Mr. Blaeith replied. "After all, we would no want anythin' excitin' happenin' at the factory, now would we?"

Mrs. Blaeith smiled broadly. "Ay, it wos a good day then."

There was a moment's pause in the conversation.

"So what wos the commotion at the docks this mornin'?" Mrs. Blaeith asked.

Laendon sighed.

"It wos a free-rider," Martyn said. "We trived that out jist as he wos leavin'. Some o' the lads were in a mind to fire up the battery, but Sheriff Laei would no let them."

Ella leaned over to Lexi. "What exactly is a f'ee-wide'h?"

"A free-rider?" It was Martyn Junior on her left who spoke.

Ella looked over at him. "Yes, I'm not familia'h with that t'em."

Martyn Junior placed his finger on the palm of his hand as if he were a politician making a grand speech before the synod. "If ye ween o' the most immoral, deceptive, disgustin' person ween-able, *that* is a free-rider. He is the sort o' person who'll would steal all o' the food from yer cupboard, prive all yer money, an' then shut down yer job so that ye cen no get any more. If ye'll ever meet a man like that, ye'll will know he is a free-rider."

Mr. Blaeith cleared his throat. "I'm no sure that ye've enlightened Miss Ella any, Clerans."

Martyn Junior—Clerans—leaned back from the table with his arms folded, eyebrows raised as if to say, "I rest my case."

Martyn leaned forward. "A free-rider is a merchant who ha' no paid the Pistosian Beacon Company fer Beacon Protection, but sails through these waters anyway."

Ella smiled nervously. "I'm af'aid I don't know any mo'e about the Pistosian Beacon Company than a little child, so you will have to explain bette'h."

Martyn thought for a moment. "Ye know what the beacons are fer, do ye no?"

"To alert ships of the cliffs and weefs?" Ella winced at her lisp, working hard to say the last word again. "I mean reefs."

Martyn nodded. "But it takes a merri o' money to fiscate

enough beacon-tenders to keep so many beacons. So the Company makes ships fiscate fer Beacon Protection in order to pass along the coast. That way, they're fiscatin' fer the service o' the beacons, since it's them that's benefitin' from them. Free-riders are ships that pass along the coast even though they ha' no paid fer Beacon Protection."

"How do you know if a ship has paid fo'h Beacon Protection?" Ella asked.

"They ha' to pay for protection every two years, an' they're given a receipt an' a colored flag to show that they paid. Ye can tell that they ha' paid if they'll tain the flag. Sometimes they'll cen fake the flag, so if ye'll suspect them, ye cen quire to gard at their receipt, an' they cen no fake the Company's signature and seal."

Ella thought for a moment. It was hard to follow Martyn's reasoning with his strange vocabulary—fiscate, gard, tain—but she thought she understood the basic gist of what he was saying. "So they'h basically thieves."

"Exactly," Mr. Blaeith said. "They steal our labor by no payin' fer it."

"A'e you beacon-tenders, then?" Ella asked.

Mr. Blaeith smiled. "Pretty much everyone in Entwerp is, or wos, or has somthin' to do with the Beacon System. I wos a beacon-tender, but now I manage a warehouse in Entwerp Proper."

*Entwerp Proper?* Ella thought. *How many Entwerps are there?*

Just then, Mrs. Blaeith spoke. "I'm sorry fer interrupting, but Martyn, ye were tellin' us about the free-rider."

Martyn nodded. "Ay, they ha' been here fer a whole week, an' we did no suspect them. But as they were pullin' out o' port, Benjamyn noticed that their flag wos fake."

"Will they be callin' up Sir Lenfellow after them?" Lexi asked.

Martyn shook his head. "The pirates saved them the trouble."

Mrs. Blaeith paused. "What are ye talking about?"

"There wos a pirate ship by the mouth o' the bay this afternoon," Laendon replied.

Clerans—on Ella's left—motioned to Ella dramatically. "Hence our company."

"But a pirate in the bay..." Mrs. Blaeith shook her head.

"Oh, do no worry, Ma," Clerans said. "We ha' driven off 'most all the other pirates that tried to get at our warehouses. Why, it wos only last May that I wos barrel monkey for Sheriff Laei when that last pirate ship vened by."

"I know we'll survive jist fine," Mrs. Blaeith said, "but these pirates still irritate me. Sometimes I remember the Singer, 'The evil men are proud, an' persecute the poor, but they will be caught in their rebellion and ensnared by their own plots.'"

"Amen," Mr. Blaeith said.

"An' on that note," Mr. Blaeith continued, "why do no we read the entire song?"

So saying, he pulled out a weighty book that bore the words "hωli scryptwr" on its cover. He flipped through the pages for a little, and when he had found the passage he was looking for, he read.

Ella didn't remember the specifics of what the Blaeiths talked about then. The soup had hit her stomach, and she had been walking all day. Her eyelids drooped, but she stayed awake. After all, it would be impolite to fall asleep in front of her hosts —particularly during vespers. But she remembered one thing about the Blaeiths' discussion of the song.

When the Blaeiths read any passage from that scripture, it was always with passionate interest. Her family had treated it like a textbook, but this family treated it like a love letter. She knew that all the words of that Book were profitable and holy, but she hadn't ever felt that truth until she saw the Blaeiths discuss that song.

After that, they sang a few hymns. Ella was more awake for

this and listened intently. Mr. Blaeith paused after they had finished one song and looked at Ella.

"Do ye know any o' these hymns?"

Ella shook her head. "I'm af'aid I don't."

"Well, then, we will teach ye one."

And slowly, he had Ella repeat after him:

> *The love of God expels the darkest places,*
> *All shadows fall before His many graces,*
> *And in His presence every fear is banished,*
> *Within His comforts, sorrows swiftly vanish.*
>
> *Then what to Him are all the worldly wiles?*
> *For He will keep you thru' your every trial.*
> *No sin or sorrow, man or devil's scheming,*
> *Can wrest you from your Father's loving keeping.*
>
> *O Lord, we look to You! Be our defender!*
> *Array yourself in Your victorious splendor!*
> *And then forever we will sing Your praises,*
> *When Your great love expels the darkest places.*

When they were done, Mrs. Blaeith stood and cleared the table. Lexi, Clerans and the other two young Blaeiths helped Mrs. Blaeith while Mr. Blaeith, Martyn, and Laendon went out by the back hallway to do chores. Later, Laendon came back in with an armload of wood and stoked the fire for the night.

Ella tried to help Mrs. Blaeith with cleaning up the meal, but Mrs. Blaeith would have none of it. "Ye jist sit back now, dear. We are yer hosts. Besides, ye ha' tained a long day. Lexi, do ye mind if she'll sleeps with you?"

"No at all," Lexi said, and with that, she took Ella by the arm and led her into the back hallway. The hall was about as long as the front room, with three doors leading to the right and two to the left. Ella guessed that both doors on the left led outside.

Lexi opened the first door on the right and led Ella in. There was a single window on the far side of the room, with a writing desk underneath it. On this, Lexi lit a small candle, illuminating the rest of the room. All there was to see was a single bed, a dresser, some paintings on the wall, and a mirror. Ella noted with delight that Lexi had several books on her desk.

"This room stays pretty warm," Lexi said. "The fireplace is jist on the other side o' the wall."

Ella sat down on the side of the bed and took off her outer clothing. At last, in a room away from the men, she took off her other stocking. She felt sure that she would fall asleep the moment she lay down.

"Thank you, Lexi, you'e so kind."

Lexi looked intently at her. "Do no go to sleep jist yet. Things are a lot different here than Slyzwir, so I'll outta-should tell ye."

Ella sat up straight to keep herself alert to what Lexi said.

"The people here are a lot more personal; an' yer space does no matter so merri much. Ye cen expect people to vene really close to ye when they'll talk with ye and touch ye a lot durin' a conversation. Ye outta-should also expect to be kissed a lot. That's the way they make greetin' and leave takin'."

Ella shifted position nervously. "*All* of them?"

Lexi pursed her lips. "Mainly jist the host and hostess, but pretty merri everyone kisses around here. So, ye outta-should learn how to do it properly."

Ella blushed.

"When ye greet someone or take yer leave o' them, ye touch yer right cheek to their right cheek and then kiss the air. If ye'll cognize them pretty well, then ye cen kiss their cheek. Now often they'll will give ye a hug too, so be prepared fer that."

Ella shifted positions again.

"Now, one more thing," Lexi said, "an' that is, ye should be prepared to hold anyone's hand. O' the men ye meet with, they will all hold yer hand when they are about town with ye, and they do no mean anythin' by it."

Ella was sure her face was bright red by now.

"Now, when ye are with any o' the women, though, they will ceive ye by the arm and no by the hand. But ye should be certain never to ceive a man by the arm unless he's yer beau, or brother, or what no."

Ella laughed nervously. "Well, at least they have some kinds of limits."

Lexi laughed. "Ye will learn them, jist ye might be surprised as ye learn."

With that, Lexi took Ella's clothes and folded them neatly. "I will wash these fer ye tonight and get a bath fer ye in the morning."

Ella looked up at Lexi. "Thank you, Lexi, thank you so much."

Lexi smiled. "Yer very welcome. Jist leave room on the bed fer me."

With that, she blew out the candle and left the room. Ella lay down on the far side of the bed and nestled into the covers. Now she could sleep without fear of Cweel and without fear of rats nesting in her hair. She was in a warm bed, with good food inside her and a wonderful family to keep watch over her.

# 12

# THE ALBINO

*E*rnest was busy filling pint jars of ale in the galley. The other pirates would be down soon enough for their food, but before that, Ernest was supposed to bring a tray of food to the captain's cabin for Holgard and Killjelly. Lewis was putting the final touches on his stew and would soon serve it up.

Ernest filled the last pint and then put them on a tray. He set the tray on the bar and looked over at Lewis, who added a pinch of some secret spice and stirred his concoction, whistling merrily. He then tasted it and stood still for a moment while he rolled it about in his mouth.

"Helen Maria! Perfection." He began ladling out two bowls for the tray. "Now, Ernest, before you take the tray, take a taste on this soup."

Ernest picked up a wooden spoon. "Be sure to put a lot of soup in there. They've been eating an awful lot lately."

Ernest tasted a bite of soup while Lewis served up the last bowl and put a few loaves of bread on the tray.

"Delicious, as usual."

"But it's different from the soup we haved this morning."

Ernest nodded.

Lewis handed him the tray. "That difference is cumin."

Ernest took the tray, stunned. Lewis had just revealed something about his cooking.

Ernest walked deftly up the stairway and out across the deck. The night was still and cool, with the coast of Llaedhwyth visible against the stars to starboard. About a hundred yards away, Longfinch's ship lay at anchor, muffled voices and laughter drifting across the water to Holgard's ship. The loose sails flapped in the slight breeze, and the ship's timbers groaned pleasantly.

As Ernest passed along the deck, he nodded to several of the pirates.

"Bill, Tell, Frank, Roe, dinner's ready below."

He came to Holgard's cabin. Balancing the tray deftly with one hand, he swung the door open. Holgard, Killjelly, and Ynwyr sat around their table. Jock lay crumpled in the corner. As Ernest entered, the three pirates stood and looked at him, breaking off their conversation. Ernest stood stock still, glancing from the pirates to Jock and then back to the pirates. Had he done something wrong by entering?

Holgard spoke. "Ernest, we've been waiting for you."

Ernest shifted his weight nervously. "Do you want me to get another bowl for Ynwyr?"

Holgard ignored the question. "Is it true that you can both read and write in Kerynian Tylwen and the common tongue?"

Ernest straightened up a little. "Yes, sir, it is true. I growed up in Keryna, and the monks teached me. I was in the monastery school, see, and—"

Holgard cut him off with a wave of his hand. "Good. Close the door and set the tray down."

Ernest obeyed and then faced Holgard, expecting some sort of explanation, but none came. Instead, Holgard pulled out a wooden bowl, filled it with a portion of soup from each of the other bowls, and then tore off a chunk of bread to dip in the soup.

Killjelly looked Ernest steadily in the face. "What you are about to see and do, you will repeat to no one, not even your messmate. Understand?"

Ernest nodded, then swallowed. What was going on?

With that, Killjelly walked to the back of the cabin and slid a carpet aside. Ernest gasped. There, hidden from view, was a trapdoor. Killjelly opened it, revealing a wooden stairway underneath.

"Ynwyr, my boy, stay here and make sure no one enters while we're gone."

Holgard walked down the stair with the extra bowl of soup, but Killjelly didn't move. Ernest hesitated. He looked at Ynwyr.

"Go on," Ynwyr said. "I don't envy you."

Ernest gulped and followed. The stair led to a small room lit by several lanterns. On one side of the room, there was a window of sorts that looked for all the world like a gun-port. On the other side was a low cot. Several desks filled the rest of the room, each littered with stone tablets, stacks of parchment, ancient arrowheads, rusted bits of armor, small metal idols, and various other trinkets. A little bookshelf stood in one corner, holding several sizable tomes.

Ernest took all of this in quickly, before his eyes strayed to the desk on the far side of the room. There, sitting on a stool with his back turned to them, was a large, motionless figure draped in a dark cloak. Ernest paused, his heart pounding.

"The gnome is here," Holgard said.

The figure stirred and slowly stood. Ernest gripped his fists tightly to keep himself from shaking as the figure turned. He was broad-shouldered and rather tall. His hair was pure white, and his skin was as pale as a newborn baby's, though wrinkled and old. His chin was long, and his nose was pointed like a hawk's. His lips were pale, almost as white as the rest of his skin.

But his eyes were bright pink, staring at Ernest from under white eyebrows.

Ernest quailed before him.

"This is Ernest," Holgard said as he set the food down on a desk.

"Thank you, Captain," the figure said in a deep and authoritative voice. Then he turned to Ernest. "So, Ernest, can you write in Tylwen?"

"Kerynian Tylwen, sir." Ernest's voice was squeaky and pitiful.

"Good." The figure turned to Holgard. "What have you told him?"

"Nothing."

The figure nodded, then took Ernest by the shoulder and sat him down at a desk. As the figure bent slightly, Ernest noticed a small amulet around his neck, with the symbol of a circle inside an upside-down triangle. Ernest thought it looked familiar, but for all the world couldn't think where he might have seen it before.

"I have no name," the figure said, "so do not ask. I am simply the Albino and the Archeomancer. I can summon power from the spirits of lost civilizations through ancient artifacts. What I am about to do requires you to write word-for-word what I dictate to you, and—as I will summon up an ancient spirit of Keryna for this work—it will be in Kerynian Tylwen. Do you understand?"

Ernest nodded and swallowed. He wasn't exactly sure what an archeomancer was, but figured that this wasn't a good time to ask. He could see several blank pieces of paper in front of him, as well as a pen and ink. Ernest picked up the pen and fumbled with it.

The Albino continued. "What I am about to do is very difficult and takes much time to prepare. Thus we must do it right the first time. Through the power of the spirit, I will delve into

Jock's mind, but I will have no memory of what I see while in his mind. I will tell you what I see, and you must write it down exactly as I give it to you. When I read what you have written, I will remember what I saw in Jock's mind."

Ernest would have doubted what the Albino said had it come from any other man, but as it was, his ominous presence kept any thought of doubt from Ernest's mind.

"Ernest," Holgard said, "you must be extremely careful. If'n you do well, then you will have my favor on this ship, but if'n you mess up..." Holgard's hands strayed to the butt of one of his pistols.

Ernest swallowed.

The Albino turned to Captain Holgard. "Your job, Captain, is to put his mind towards thoughts of the treasure. The amount of information I can glean will depend on how strong his mind is and how much we can take him by surprise."

"I will do that." Holgard then shouted up the stairway, "Killjelly, bring him down."

Killjelly tramped slowly down the stairs, holding Jock Blowhoarder before him. He closed the trapdoor behind them. Killjelly shoved Jock to his knees at the bottom of the stairs, standing behind him, with Holgard to his right and the Albino before him. Jock looked around the room but avoided looking Holgard directly in the eye. Ernest held his breath. He could see that the Albino was holding something in his hand, a tablet etched all over with letters in the Tylweni script.

Holgard snorted. "You are going to tell us all that you know about the Gwambi Treasure tonight."

Jock gave a short laugh. "Ye has not gotten inything from me yet, look ye."

"Tomorrow we will hand you over to Longfinch," Holgard said, "so it is better for both on us if'n you just talk now."

Jock laughed.

*The Albino*

Killjelly put his hooks on Jock's shoulder. "Start talking now. We know it's in Entwerp, sure..."

"No, ye do not," Jock replied. "Ye are just guessint."

Then the Albino spoke. "Look at me!"

The air seemed to become denser. Ernest could hardly breathe it—it was like breathing in water. It swarmed around in his lungs like bees. His body rejected the air. He had to force himself to breathe as he fought off the terror of suffocation. A slow and steady pulse seemed to throb through the wooden table and his very flesh, like the drumbeat of some ancient cult's summoning.

Ernest forced himself to hold the pen and keep it steady. He would write the words that came to him. He had to. His life depended on it.

Jock froze as soon as his eyes met the Albino's. The two of them stood thus for nearly a minute, and then the Albino spoke in Kerynian Tylwen. Killjelly seemed intent on every word, as if he understood everything that the Albino said, while Holgard simply watched with a blank look in his eyes.

"I see the bay of Entwerp and the town of Entwerp Coastal. Now there is another city. It's very large, full of warehouses. It is Entwerp Proper, I believe. But I am on the streets now, hurrying. We have stopped at a large house outside of town. It is made entirely of wood, with a stone foundation, large bay windows, and red gables. It is old but well kept. There is an elderly man inside with..."

The Albino paused and stared more intensely at Jock. Sweat covered Jock's face, and he clamped his jaw hard as if he were straining at a heavy weight. Ernest frantically scratched away on his paper, finally catching up with the Albino.

"He is strong-willed and now on his guard. He throws all he can in my way. I can still see the house, but it is hazy and dimming. There is a woman now, a leprechaun, with a lip split like a rabbit's. Now there is a man, a human. He has brown skin and a loud laugh. He is a gardener."

Ernest was lagging now, but still taking meticulous care with his letters. He was careful to take down the exact words that the Albino said.

"He is pulling his mind away from Entwerp now. I see an old abbey, blasted by war and fire. The nuns are all slain. He alone survives to fight another day. And fight he does, I see war all around him, I can hear the cannonade and the blast of the guns. One of his comrades is wounded in the arm; the other is blasted with a grenade. He has saved them both.

"He is on a ship, alone. Corpses of other crewmen litter the deck. They have died of thirst. He is still alive. A hope keeps him alive. He is operating the ship on his own. I see Longfinch's ship now. Pirates board him, and he swims through hell. A hope keeps him alive. Now he is in the water. He floats on a raft. Sharks circle him. He has killed one with only his hands. A hope keeps him alive.

"His hope is like a fire, like the fire in a small cottage on the top of a mountain in a little village. Inside are a woman and a young girl. The girl is blonde, with blue eyes and a speech impediment.

"There is a wall. The hope is dead. I can see only one thing now: separation."

The Albino stopped, and Ernest frantically finished writing what he had said. When the Albino did not continue, he looked up. The Albino was straining his eyes at Jock. Both were motionless. Jock's eyes brimmed with tears, and even as Ernest watched, they rolled down his cheeks.

The Albino opened his mouth one last time. "Separation."

With that, he shut his eyes and collapsed onto his stool. Jock made a strangled sound and fainted. The air suddenly cleared and Ernest could breathe properly again. Ernest finished writing and dropped his pen, staring wide-eyed from the Albino to Jock, and then at Holgard and Killjelly. Holgard didn't seem to know what was happening any more than Ernest did.

Finally, the Albino stirred. He lifted only his hand, setting the tablet he was holding back onto his desk and picking up the bowl of soup. He slowly spooned it into his mouth and then ate the bread. No one spoke as the Albino ate. When he finished, he shivered violently and then stood slowly to his feet. Without a word, he held his hand out to Ernest. Ernest handed him the paper and held his breath while the Albino read it. When the Albino finished, he laid the parchment on his desk and sank back onto his stool.

"His will was strong."

"But where is the treasure? Do'ed he tell you anything about it?" Holgard asked.

The Albino was silent, so Killjelly answered. "No, he let nothing leak. This was entirely fruitless, sure."

"You are mistaken there," the Albino said. "He was thinking about the treasure the whole time, though he told us nothing explicitly about it. Instead, he told us his story. The treasure is there, hidden in his thoughts. I will unravel it. The house and the people are all crucial to the treasure's location, of that much I am certain. I must find all. I must decipher all."

Killjelly thrust his hook at the wall angrily. "He told us nothing about the Gwambi Treasure. He only showed you a few people he knowed when he lived in Entwerp."

The Albino looked at Killjelly steadily. "I have found that most often the answer to a question is not a word, but a person."

Ernest looked from one person to another, unsure what to think of all this. Finally, the Albino spoke again.

"I will go to Entwerp and find the people he spoke of. I will also find the house."

He stood and picked up a small scrip resting against the wall. Taking the paper Ernest had written, he stuffed it into the scrip. He looked at Holgard. "I have wiped Jock's memory of this encounter; he will leak nothing to Longfinch." Then he nodded at Ernest. "Well written, gnome."

"Shall we wipe his memory as well?" Killjelly asked.

"No," Holgard said, "there is no reason. Besides, we may need him to remember later."

Killjelly lifted Jock and dragged him up the stairs. Holgard followed. Ernest jumped up from the desk and came after Holgard, and the Albino followed him, blowing out the lanterns as he left the room.

As they entered Holgard's cabin, Ynwyr turned to them, but his face turned pale as soon as he saw the Albino. Wordlessly, Holgard opened one window in the bay window that formed the back of his cabin. Holgard then pulled out a rope and tied it to a hook in the ceiling. The Albino nodded to him, took the rope, and lowered himself out the window. Ernest didn't dare come close enough to see if there was a boat waiting below.

As soon as the Albino was gone, Holgard pulled the rope back in and closed the window. He and Killjelly stared out of it for a long time.

"All on our hopes go with him," Holgard breathed.

Killjelly only let out his breath slowly.

Ernest shifted his weight nervously and then cleared his throat. Holgard turned.

"You may go now, Ernest, but not a word to anyone."

Ernest nodded and exited as quickly as he could. Finally, he was back on deck. Soon he would be back in the galley, and that albino would be far away from him—he hoped.

He never wanted to meet that dreadful archeomancer again.

## 1 3

## LEXI

*S*leep slowly left Ella—like a receding tide, so gradual that she hardly knew it was ebbing. Finally, she came completely awake as someone shook her shoulder lightly. She opened her eyes; it was Lexi. The gnome was already dressed and seemed to have been awake for some time.

"I ha' pleted a bath fer ye," Lexi said.

Ella sat up and looked around. Sunlight was peeping through the window, but the curtains were drawn. In front of Lexi's dresser sat a large trough filled with lukewarm water.

Lexi motioned to Ella's clothes, which were folded next to a towel on the dresser. "I would ha' ye put on new clothes since those are torn up so merri, but I am afraid that mine are too small, so ye will ha' to make do with yer old ones fer now. I'll will bring ye to the tailor. Now hurry if ye'll do no want to be late fer breakfast."

Ella looked at Lexi gratefully as she stood up. Her right leg was asleep and rather stiff. "Thank you so much, Lexi. I don't know how I'll eve'h wepay you."

Lexi winked. "Do no worry about that. Now is there anythin' else I'll cen help ye with?"

"I don't think so." Ella massaged her leg as the pins and needles assailed her. Her hands touched the dagger Lewis had given her. For the last several weeks, it had almost been a part of her leg. Could she actually take it off now? "Oh, I have a question."

Lexi paused at the door. "Ay?"

Ella unstrapped the dagger and held it up. "What should I do with this?"

Lexi shrugged. "Put it on the desk, I s'pose." Then she left Ella to herself.

Oh, how good it felt to have that dagger off her leg!

---

Ella entered the front room to see Mrs. Blaeith serving breakfast to the three younger Blaeith boys and Lexi. Martyn and Laendon were by the door, tying up their tall boots.

"God bless yer morning, Ella," Mrs. Blaeith said as she entered.

Ella curtsied slightly. "Thank you, ma'am."

Martyn and Laendon looked up and nodded to her. "God bless yer morning."

Ella curtsied to them and then sat down at the table next to Lexi. Lexi passed her a bowl of porridge, saying in her ear, "Fer the future, it is proper to reply with 'God return yer blessin', that's the way they give greetin's here."

Lexi's eyes twinkled as she turned back to her own food.

"Ella," Mrs. Blaeith said, "Would ye like some salt pork?"

"Yes, please, ma'am."

Mrs. Blaeith placed two thick slices on a saucer and passed it to Ella.

Just then, Martyn and Laendon stood up. "We are leavin' now, Ma. God bless yer day."

"An' may He return yer blessin'," Mrs. Blaeith replied as she walked over and kissed them both. After they had kissed her, they put on their tricorn hats and stepped out the door.

Mrs. Blaeith came back to the table and sat down. Ella waited for a moment before she spoke.

"Whe'e a'e they going?"

"To work," Mrs. Blaeith said. "They are beacon-tenders."

"Is thei'h beacon nea'h by?"

"No," Mrs. Blaeith replied. "It is about a day's journey southward."

Ella swallowed her porridge slowly. "A'e they going the'e now?"

"No," Mrs. Blaeith smiled. "They're goin' to one o' the warehouses to guard it fer the mornin', then they will cede to militia trainin' fer the afternoon."

Ella opened her mouth to ask what this had to do with tending coastal beacons, but Mrs. Blaeith answered before she could ask.

"The beacon-tendin' conditions are gruelin', so they cen no stay up in the mountains fer merri long at a time without risk o' injury or death. The Company decided that they work best when they're only up beacon-tendin' fer a week at a time, so every other week, the Company brings them back to Entwerp. They tain two days o' off time, an' then the rest o' the week the Company employs them to guard warehouses and the banks an' trains them as a militia."

"Does the Company own wa'ehouses in Entwe'p, then?" Ella asked.

Mrs. Blaeith nodded. "Ay. But the warehouses are no here; they are in Entwerp Proper."

Ella furrowed her brow. "What is the diffe'ence between Entwe'p Pwope'h and just Entwe'p?"

Clerans laughed at this question. "There is no a 'jist Entwerp,' it is a merri o' an mess, really. Where we are now is called Entwerp Coastal. Merchants will dock their ships here, and there is the battery, but really, we are pretty small. Then there is Entwerp Proper, which is jist a mile or so west o' here through the pass. It is merri bigger and the capital o' Entwerp State—oh ay, it is a merri important city too, what with the warehouses, an' the factories, and the National Banks, some say that we are the fiscal capital o' the whole nation o' Llaedhwyth!

"Ay, but then there's Entwerp Bay, an' Entwerp Valley, an' Entwerp Mountain, an' Entwerp Bog, an' Entwerp River." Clerans paused and looked at Ella like an actor about to deliver the last line of a comedy. "Knowin' that people like to name places after someone, I would guess that the first person who trived this place wos either named Entwerp, or wos in love with someone named Entwerp."

Lexi rolled her eyes. "Away with ye, Clerans. Ye should save yer lines for a stage."

"I think I jist might," Clerans replied with a mock bow.

By this time, Ella had finished her breakfast and leaned back contentedly. Lexi saw this and immediately turned to Mrs. Blaeith.

"Mrs. Blaeith, I was hopin' to take Ella out to the tailor's today. Is it possible fer Clerans to accompany us? An' is there anythin' that ye'll would need us to fiscate fer ye while we are out?"

Mrs. Blaeith thought for a moment. "Well, I believe Henri will be gettin' us our meat fer tomorrow's dinner, but then I had a few errands I wos goin' to run once I finished my shift at the factory. If ye'll would no mind runin' those fer me, that would be very helpful."

Lexi nodded. "Then I will do them."

"Right then," Mrs. Blaeith said, "I'll oughtta-might need some more spices. Then there's that axe that Henri wanted dropped off at the carpenter's fer the handle."

"Merri good," Lexi said as she stood and turned to Ella. "Would ye be ready to leave in a few minutes?"

Ella stood slowly. "I should, but..." her cheeks flushing in embarrassment. "Do you have any shoes that I could bo'ow?"

"Oh, my dear," Mrs. Blaeith said, starting up, "o' course ye cen. I tain an extra pair o' boots. Here, let me see if mine will fit ye."

She held her bare foot next to Ella's stockinged foot. They were close in size, though Mrs. Blaeith's was a little bigger.

"Well, dear, it might work, but ye'll will ha' to wear an extra pair o' socks."

"I cen get those," Lexi said as she dashed down the back hall. Clerans and the other two boys stood up. The younger two cleared the table, but Clerans winked at Ella.

"Shall I get Lexi to stop by the cobbler's as well?"

The two younger Blaeith boys gave Clerans a side-long glance.

"O' course ye'd stretch it out for the whole day, would no ye?" the older of the two said.

"Now Robert," Mrs. Blaeith replied. "I do no want to hear ye arguin'. I will be off to the factory soon, and then ye outta-should set about yer lessons. There's no reason to be jealous."

"Ay," Lexi said, emerging from the back hall with a pair of wool socks and women's boots. "If the two o' you younkers would be as diligent in yer lessons as Clerans, it might be one o' ye that I was bringin' out on the errands with me instead."

Robert and Roland sighed.

"There you are, boys," Mrs. Blaeith said with a laugh.

In a few minutes, Ella was walking down the streets of Entwerp Coastal, Lexi holding her by the arm while Clerans and Mrs. Blaeith trooped along ahead of them. Clerans held his mother by the arm and swung the broken axe handle in his free hand, whistling as he walked.

Ella's borrowed boots slipped now and then on her left foot, but the bandages on her right foot were enough to fill the extra space in Mrs. Blaeith's boot. Mrs. Blaeith had also given her a straw hat and some hem-bobs to pin to the hem of her skirts. As the wind blew off the sea and wound its way through the houses and streets, she was quite happy to have a hat rim to guard her face and the weights to keep her skirt from flapping about—though Lexi told her it would be better once she got a cornered skirt.

"How do they fit?" Mrs. Blaeith asked, turning back to Ella.

Ella took a few more steps in her borrowed boots. "Ve'y well. Thank you." She felt a lump in her throat. "Thank you so much."

Mrs. Blaeith laughed. "I am more than happy to help."

She paused for a moment and then turned back to Ella. "We would like to help ye in any way we cen, Miss Ella. Ye jist think on that. Whatever ye need, we will do our best to help ye with—food, a place to stay, a job, whatever ye need."

Ella nodded. "Thank you."

"We can," Mrs. Blaeith went on, "even pay fer yer postage, if you'll would like to send a message back to yer parents, but the postal ships will no leave for Kelmar again until the spring, so ye'll tain plenty o' time to think on that."

Ella licked her lips feeling a little embarrassed. Of course she should have tried to send a letter to her mother already. Why hadn't she thought of it sooner? Then again, if her mother knew where she was, looking for the Gwambi Treasure with pirates hunting for her, she might just die of heart-break. Still, if it was true that she couldn't even send a letter until spring, that gave her a good excuse to wait and do more investigation. "Thank you, Mrs. Blaeith."

Yet as she said this, it reminded her of something that had bothered her since the Blaeiths had introduced themselves to her.

"I do have a question, if it's not too much to ask about."

"No." Mrs. Blaeith replied without hardly thinking.

"It's just," Ella paused, articulating her 'r's as best she could. "Is 'Blaeith' really your surname?"

"Ay," Mrs. Blaeith nodded. "Should it no be?"

"I don't know." Ella blushed. "It's just that... isn't it a woman's name?"

"Ay," Mrs. Blaeith replied again, a smile playing about the corners of her mouth. "It was my grandmother's name. She and her husband were the ones who brought my family to this country."

Ella furrowed her brow. "So how did Mr. Blaeith come to be named afte'h you'h g'andmothe'h?"

Mrs. Blaeith laughed. "He ceived it when we wed. His family name was originally Godaeifa before he married me."

Ella looked at Mrs. Blaeith in alarm, hardly believing what she was hearing. She spoke now with extra clarity to ensure that she fully understood what Mrs. Blaeith was telling her. "So 'Blaeith' was your maiden name, and then your husband changed his name to 'Blaeith' when he married you?"

"That's correct," Mrs. Blaeith replied. "I assume it works the other way around where ye vene from?"

Ella nodded. "Yes. It is exactly the othe'h way a'ound."

"That's alright," Lexi broke in. "Ye'll will learn all o' the ways o' this country in time."

Ella nodded. "And I'm su'e it will take me some time to get used to."

"Ay," Mrs. Blaeith nodded, "but ye'll will trive that we do most things fer a very specific reason."

"Oh?" Ella asked.

"We do," Mrs. Blaeith went on. "In Llaedhwyth, the husbands take their wife's name because that is what the scriptures say."

"Oh?" Ella said again, drawing a blank on what Mrs. Blaeith was referring to. She wasn't super knowledgeable on the scripture, so perhaps there was an obscure passage about matrilineal naming conventions she was unfamiliar with.

"Ay," Mrs. Blaeith went on. "In the beginning it says that 'a man must leave his father an' his mother, an' cleave to his wife.'

So if he'll is goin' to leave his father an' his mother, what better way to do that, than by leavin' their family name and cleavin' to his wife's?"

Ella nodded slowly. "I neve'h thought about it that way." Truth be told, she wasn't sure what to think of this reasoning.

Just then, the street they were on ran into a much wider street. Here, Clerans let go of his mother's arm, turning to the left while she turned to the right.

"I'm off to the factory," Mrs. Blaeith said, kissing Ella on the cheek. "We cen talk more when we are all back at the house. An' again, do no hesitate to let us know how we cen help ye."

"Thank you," Ella said, again feeling the lump in her throat.

Mrs. Blaeith smiled. "But, o' course!"

And so saying, she disappeared into the crowd of people who bustled along the street.

Clerans now led the way as they turned in the opposite direction down the street. Many people bustled about here and there—into shops and stalls on the side of the street. Nearly everyone who passed them tipped their hats, and several passersby gave them a "God bless yer day." A couple even greeted Lexi and Clerans by name. Ella felt a bit overwhelmed. This town was hardly any larger than Blisa village, yet there must be twice the number of people roaming the streets. And every one of them seemed intent on greeting you.

Finally, they arrived at a small shop with a sign reading *'tnlor'* over the door. Clerans leaned up against the doorpost and winked at Lexi.

"I will jist run the axe over to the carpenter's while I wait fer you."

Lexi pushed open the door and brought Ella into the shop. Inside was a cozy room lit by a large bay window and several lanterns. A few racks along the walls displayed various pieces of clothing ranging in colors of earth-green, dusky-gray, and a million vibrant shades of brown, but all having the same firm texture—was it wool? By the bay window sat a small man stitching up a pair of trousers. In one corner, a middle-aged woman was ironing some cloth. With her was a younger woman, folding what she ironed.

As they entered, the two women looked up. "God bless yer day, Miss Lexi," the elder one said as she put her iron on the stove and walked over to them. She kissed Lexi. "What cen I do fer ye?"

"I would like to get a full set o' clothes fer this young lady here."

Ella looked at Lexi with some apprehension. Who was paying for this? Lexi seemed rather confident, though, so there was no point interrupting her.

"Well, we cen certainly do that," the woman said. "Here, Kati, get me the measurin' tape."

"Ay, Ma," the girl said as she put down a chemise she was folding and then dug around in a pile of sewing implements until she found a cloth measuring tape.

"Would ye like stockin's as well?" the older woman asked Ella as she looked her up and down with a practiced eye.

Ella looked over at Lexi, unsure what to make of this question. Was this woman actually suggesting that stockings were unnecessary? Of course, stockings were part of a full set of clothing. How could you go anywhere in public without wearing stockings? It would be the height of indecency—these boots might cover her ankles well enough, but what if she accidentally bared her knees? She wondered now if she had been naïve to think that Mrs. Blaeith and Lexi only went without stockings in the privacy of their own home. There was no telling what sort of scandalous clothing these Pistosians wore—or didn't wear, as the case may be.

"Ay," Lexi replied, "better do stockin's too, jist in case. Everything, even the hem-bobs."

The older woman nodded. "Then we'd better take ye into the back room fer measurin'."

The woman brought her into a small back room that was full of bolts of cloth. The younger woman then measured nearly every part of Ella, calling off her measurements to the older woman, who marked them down on a piece of paper.

When they finished, the older woman made a few calculations on her paper. "I will legate Kati to deliver the clothes when we'll are done with them. I expect it'll will be about thirty cubits."

"Thank ye, Mrs. Fflemins," Lexi said as she turned towards the door. The younger woman led Ella to the door by the arm; a courtesy that only embarrassed Ella. The girl was examining Ella's clothes.

"Where did ye get these?" she asked.

Ella blushed deeper. "Slyzwi'h."

"Is this what's in style there?"

Ella nodded.

"I like it," the girl finally said. "The skirt hem is especially intriguin'; it is like... circular. An' is the whole thing made o' cotton? Quite exotic."

Before Ella had to come up with a response, she reached the door, where Lexi took her arm and led her out into the street.

"Do you know those people well?" she finally asked.

"The Fflemins?" Lexi nodded. "Oh, ay. The Blaeiths ha' tained them over a few times, so I cognize them more or less. They cede to our kirk, too."

Ella furrowed her brow. "Why do you live with the Blaeiths? Are you a maid o'h something?"

Lexi laughed. "Hardly that!" Then she sighed. "They sort o' adopted me after my parents died."

Ella was silent for a moment. "I'm so'y," Ella said, then after a pause, she added, "I lost my fathe'h, too."

Lexi squeezed her hand, but quickly changed the subject. "I worked as a stevedore at first."

"A what?" Ella asked.

"A stevedore?" Lexi replied. "Do ye no know what that is? A longshoreman? We loaded an' unloaded all o' the merchant ships that vened to port."

"Oh," Ella said, a little startled. She looked at Lexi critically. "They let you do that?"

"Ay," Lexi replied. "Why would they no?"

Ella pursed her lips and looked away. "I thought that would be a man's job."

Lexi shrugged. "I did no mind the hard work. But all the sailors... it wos a lot fer a young woman like me to put up with."

Ella's stomach turned as she recalled the pirates and how they had treated her. She was pretty sure she knew what Lexi meant.

Lexi sighed. "I wos no the only woman on the docks, an' that helped. And the Pistosian men, the other stevedores, they were very good—it wos jist the sailors. You got the impression that ye were no a person to them. Ye were jist a woman."

Ella nodded. "Yes. That's it." She swallowed, and again her gut convulsed at the thought of those pirates. "It's like you a'e just a thing to be used."

"Ay," Lexi said, "but the Pistosian men—ye know, the ones from Entwerp—they are no like that. Ye'll will see what I mean. We treat ye like a person, no matter what ye are—man or woman, human, gnome, nymph, or even elf. It shouldn't matter, should it?"

"I suppose no," Ella replied, furrowing her brow. At the mention of nymphs, her mind wandered back to that little savage boy—Nōli. "What about the savages, then?"

Lexi looked alarmed. "The who?"

"The savages?" Ella replied, suddenly feeling self-conscious. "I met one in the fo'est; he helped me get he'e."

Lexi shook her head. "Ella, never call them savages. They are no savages. They are people jist like us, an' that is how our laws are."

"Oh," was all Ella could think to say.

Lexi looked at her critically. "Is that what you'll call them in Slyzwir: 'Savages?'"

Ella looked away sheepishly. "I guess."

"Oh, do no be embarrassed," Lexi said with a nervous laugh. "Ye'll will learn. I jist did no realize that Slyzwir wos still that old-fashioned."

Ella gave a nervous laugh herself. "So what am I supposed to call the not-savage people of Llaedhwyth?"

"We call them Indigies."

Ella nodded. "As in 'indiginous?' That's cleve'h."

"That is correct." Lexi let out a long sigh. "But anyway, all that is to say, I enjoyed bein' a stevedore. But I wos more than happy to move in with the Blaeiths when they invited me to tutor their boys. That wos what I wos tryin' to say."

"Befo'e the Indigies got involved?" Ella offered.

Lexi nodded. "A'fore the Indigies got involved."

Just then, Clerans came up to them from the opposite direction. "Well, I see you did no stay chattin' with the Fflemins merri long."

"As ye apparently did at the carpenter's?" Lexi replied. Then she turned to Ella. "See what I ha' to put up with now? Maybe I should go back to the docks."

Clerans laughed. "You know that ye would miss me too much."

"Ha!" Lexi replied, waving a finger at Clerans. "Maybe we should experiment, young rascal."

Clerans shrugged. "To the spice market now?"

Lexi shook her head, turning down the street. "First, the cobbler's shop."

Clerans raised an eyebrow. "An' is that where ye are tryin' to get to?"

"Ay," Lexi replied, "An' I'd get there sooner if I did no ha' ye slowin' me down."

Clerans snorted. "Well, if you want to take all day to get to the cobbler's shop, then by all means, keep cedin' down that road. Or, I cen duce ye on the *right* road."

"Rascal," Lexi replied, playfully knocking Clerans' hat off his head. "Since I trust that ye know the streets better than I do, I will follow ye. But only if ye'll promise that it does no involve saultin' over any walls, or traipsin' through anyone's garden, or walkin' along anyone's roof."

Clerans made an expression of mock horror as he put his hat on again. "What? What kind o' villain would engage in such behaviors?"

Lexi cleared her throat. "Does that mean I now tain yer permission to call ye villain?"

"Merri well," Clerans said, and the tone of his voice sounded as if he was making a life-changing concession. "I will no take you on anyone's roof, or through anyone's garden."

And with that, he marched off down an alley a little way from the tailor's shop.

"An' walls?" Lexi called out as she and Ella hurried after him. "Are ye goin' to sault over any walls?"

Clerans only flashed a mischievous grin over his shoulder. "No promises."

# 14

# THE SPICE MARKET

here were not, in fact, any walls between the tailor's shop and the cobbler's—much to Ella's relief.

After the cobbler had measured every lump of Ella's foot—cutting straps of leather and marking out the sole of her foot on another sheet—she walked out of the cobbler shop in new shoes. She, Lexi, and Clerans moved off to the spice market. This time, Clerans kept in line with the two women and even had the good manners to hold Ella's hand. Lexi nudged Ella with her elbow when she started blushing. Ella forced herself to forget how awkward she felt by talking with Clerans.

"How old a'e you Cle'ans?"

"Sixteen—fer a few more weeks, that is."

"And do you have a school he'e?"

"Only in the winter," Clerans replied. "Laendon teaches it then."

Clerans then flashed a mischievous grin back at Lexi. "For the rest o' the year I ha' to suffer through Miss Lexi."

"Away with ye, villain," Lexi replied with a shake of her head.

"But only on my off days." Clerans added quickly.

"You wo'k then?" Ella asked.

Clerans nodded. "Three days o' the week. I am a legate fer the Company."

"Clerans," Lexi said, "ye oughtta-should explain yerself. Remember that she does no know merri about the Company."

"Yes," Ella replied, "I would app'eciate that."

"Well then," Clerans said, "a legate does no tain a clearly defined job, see. We end up doin' a bunch o' odd jobs, like fixin' carts, runnin' errands, an' what no, but mostly we carry letters fer the intra-company mail."

"An' it is in that capacity," Lexi broke in, "that this villain saults over walls and traipses through gardens and walks over people's roofs."

Clerans grinned widely. "Though in all seriousness, I *do* try to keep out o' people's gardens. I respect their space, even if it is in the way o' my duties."

Ella looked at Clerans critically. "Then do you weally climb on people's woofs?"

"Roofs?" Clerans replied. "Oh, ay. Sometimes. A roof's as good as a street when ye need it—better, even."

Ella furrowed her brow, but said nothing in response to this. She'd had quite enough to think about already today.

Clerans went on. "When I'll turn eighteen, though, they will sign me on as a beacon-tender, an' then I'll hope to join Martyn and Laendon on their beacon."

"How many beacon-tende'hs a'e the'e pe' beacon?" Ella asked.

"Three," Clerans answered without hesitation, then he paused. "Well, I s'pose it depends on how dangerous the station is—they changed all o' that after the layoffs last year. Martyn an' Laendon tain three fer their beacon, so if I'll will join them, then it will be all Blaeiths."

Ella was about to ask more questions about the school when they entered the spice market. Ella had seen nothing like it before. She had often read of bazaars in the southern climates, and that was the closest thing she could compare this to—though the northern mountains, cool weather, and pale skin of the market-vendors seemed very out of place with the tropical feel.

The market was just a square filled to bursting with carts and stands. There were several narrow, crisscrossing walkways between the vendors' stalls, through which people bustled like ants. Over some booths and alleyways, vendors had thrown up thatch roofs to form shelters, but otherwise shoppers performed their business in the open air. The market was on lower ground—near the bogs that Ella had crossed to come into town, so she had a good view of the place as she entered.

The first thing that struck her was the smell of the place. Spices and perfumes wafted in the wind, mingling with the scent of garlic-fires near the bogs. Besides the smell, the noise of the market assailed her—vendors proclaimed their wares, buyers haggled for a price, women gossiped at the corner, and men laughed at the news. It was loud, though it seemed like a friendly place, nonetheless. The people in the market were also much more diverse than they had been in the rest of Entwerp, making Ella think that many of them had come from Entwerp Proper – or some other place.

Though most of the people in the market were human, Ella could also see gnomes, leprechauns, and faeriefolk walking this way and that in the same garb as the other Pistosians. Now and then, she spotted a satyr towering above the other market-goers. Then there were the nymphs—much like Nōli—in hodge-podge clothing and long hair, as if they had only just come from the savage woods to gaze at civilization for a few minutes. Once, Ella caught sight of a swarthy dwarf making his way through the crowd with an enormous bag of grain on his shoulders. However, look as she might, Ella didn't see a single elf.

"When the merchants arrive here in Entwerp," Lexi explained as they made their descent into the market, "they ha' jist vened out o' the tropical waters where they pick up a merri o' exotic foods. Most o' the food will no ship across the Great Sea to Kelmar very well, so they'll ha' to sell it here."

Lexi moved through the complicated maze of stalls with ease, ducking into various stalls to price the spices she wanted. Once, as she ducked into a stall, Ella felt a tug on her skirt. She turned to see a tall beggar sitting cross-legged by the side of a stall. His hair was whiter than any hair Ella had ever seen, and his skin was very pale. He sat wrapped in a dark cloak, with a thin cloth over his eyes.

"Alms?" He held out his hands and looked up, almost as if he could see her.

"I'm ve'y so'y, but I don't have any money with me."

The beggar continued to stare at her as if he recognized her, but he lowered his hands. "Some people have more to give than money. Thank you."

Then Lexi came out of the stall and, taking Ella by the arm, moved on.

"Do you have many begga'hs he'e?"

Clerans shrugged, "No many."

By the time they reached the market's end, Lexi appeared to have bought all the spices she wanted. They turned a corner to go back to the village when a shout arrested them.

"Clerans! Lexi!"

Clerans stood stock-still in momentary apprehension, but Lexi looked around expectantly. Just then, a girl dashed out of the crowd. She first met Clerans—and kissed him on the cheek —then she hugged Lexi and kissed her, too. She then regarded Ella. The girl looked about a year younger than Clerans, though she was nearly as tall as him. She had bright brown eyes, dark brown skin, and jet black hair. The girl stood out to Ella; her eyes seemed full of life and almost glowed. She was also dressed slightly differently from the other Pistosians. Instead of the obligatory hat, she wore a small scarf over her hair.

"I do not believe we have met before," the girl said. "They call me Haeli." She extended her hand to Ella.

Ella took the hand. "My name is Ella."

"It is a merri of pleasure to meet you, Ella." Then the girl turned to Clerans and Lexi. "And, of course, it is a pleasure to meet the two of you."

Clerans only mumbled something, but Lexi replied, "As it is to meet with ye. We tained no idea that yer family was in Entwerp."

"Just for a few days," Haeli replied. "Da and I are ordering supplies, but Ma, Dafid, and Yohni are still at the fort."

"Do ye tain a place to stay?" Lexi asked.

Haeli grinned. "We are staying with the Pickerings."

"Well then," Lexi replied, "Ma would be disappointed if you'll vened through here an' did no at least eat supper with us."

Haeli laughed. "I was expecting you to bring that up. Da has plans."

"Well, we'd love to tain you over."

Haeli grinned again. "Is Martyn off the mountain?"

"Ay," Lexi replied, "though I am surprised ye did no know."

"He does not always stop by the fort when he leaves; but I thought he was off." Haeli grinned again.

"Ay, Martyn will be here fer the rest o' the week," Lexi said.

"Good," Haeli took a few steps back. "Well, Da might be waiting for me now, so I will see you later." She waved to all three of them and then dashed back through the crowd.

Lexi then walked out of the market with Ella by the arm and Clerans loping on behind. She turned on Clerans. "Ye sure got quiet fast."

"Ha!" Clerans cried, "I'm tellin' ye, that woman is after me."

Ella laughed nervously. "I didn't get that at all."

Lexi shook her head. "Ye are bein' childish, Clerans. Ye tain no reason to treat Haeli like that."

"Ha!" Clerans cried.

"Haeli does no like ye better than any other girl in this village," Lexi replied.

Clerans grinned roguishly. "I s'pose I tain good reason to be concerned then."

Lexi rolled her eyes.

"She seemed mo'e inte'ested in Ma'tyn to me," Ella said.

"Martyn is twelve years older than her," Clerans replied, "but if he'll were closer in age, then she'll would no scare me anymore."

Lexi shook her head again. "Really, Clerans, Haeli is a merri sweet girl. In fact, she'll would prob'ly be appalled at what ye were sayin' if she'll could hear ye now."

Clerans opened his mouth to respond, but Lexi interrupted him. "But speakin' o' Martyn, ye just reminded me that we need to get the axe from his shop before we cede back."

Clerans nodded, "Right then." He turned off into an alley that soon led out of town. Ella and Lexi followed him, arm-in-arm.

The trail climbed up a little way on the mountain and then ran in a straight path along the edge about thirty feet above the level of the roofs of Entwerp Coastal. As they walked along, Ella could look off to her right and see the whole bay of Entwerp stretched out, hemmed in on both sides by straight-edged mountains. Only a small strait separated the bay from the ocean, giving Ella a narrow view of the sea.

Clerans pointed out across the bay to the narrow opening on the far end. "One o' these days, we'll will build two more batteries, one on either side o' that entrance. If we'll could put a few eighty-pounders over there, it would help to keep the pirates away, see."

Lexi laughed. "An' I s'pose ye will be the one to build those batteries?"

"I do no see why no," Clerans grinned.

*The Tower*

To her left, Ella could see the great Mountains of Pistos, with their steep sides and sheer cliffs. Far above, she could see little nooks of tall trees, which stood like sentinels on the edge of the mountains, harbingers of a larger forest behind. Yet what caught her attention most was a tall, pillar-like outcropping of mountain that stood out against the afternoon sky. From her angle, it almost looked like the outcropping had a parapet on top.

"What's that?" she asked, pointing to the outcropping.

"Oh," Lexi replied, "It is the Gwambi Tower."

Ella's heart skipped a beat. Did she say Gwambi? She tried to act casual as she furrowed her brow. "Is it actually a towe'h?"

"Ay," Clerans said, "it wos built by the Gwambi about three thousand years ago."

Ella caught her breath. "The Gwambi?"

"Ay," Lexi sighed, "Ha' ye heard o' them?"

"They a'e the ones who built a whole city out of gold?"

Clerans rolled his eyes. "That is jist a legend, an' hardly likely. About all that's left o' the Gwambi are their towers."

"A'e the'e mo'e than one?" Ella asked.

"Ay," Clerans looked over at Lexi for a certain answer, "There's somthin' like..."

"Maybe a dozen or so?" Lexi said. "I do no know—they are scattered all across the Pistosian Capes."

"But what's in the towe'hs?" Ella asked.

Clerans shrugged.

"Hasn't anyone climbed up the'e?"

"Apparently," Clerans replied, "it is a merri bit harder to scend those towers than it gards."

"Every year, dozens o' people die on that tower alone," Lexi said, "an' dozens more fail before they kill themselves."

"No one has eve'h ente'ed that towe'h befo'e?"

"No one," Clerans said. "Or a'least if someone ha', they'll did no tell anyone else what they saw."

Ella thought for a moment. "Do you know anything about the Gwambi then?"

Clerans shrugged, "There's only one or two o' their towns that ha' been trived, and there wos no merri in them."

"Entwerp Proper is built on the ruins o' one o' the Gwambi's cities," Lexi added.

"But really," Clerans replied, "the towers are a'most all that is left from the Gwambi."

Ella kicked a rock off the path, trying not to get too excited by this information. She had only been in Entwerp for one day, and she already had a lead on the Gwambi Treasure.

Soon, Clerans left the path they were on and ascended a small stairway cut into the rock face of the mountainside. From there, they wound their way upward until they reached a small terrace with a stone fence all around it. Ella could see an area of the terrace that appeared to be cultivated. A few dead plants still clung to the soil, but everything of interest must have been harvested already. Carved into the mountainside against the terrace was a shed with large wooden doors and a small hinged window.

As Clerans, Lexi, and Ella entered the terrace-yard, a hawk swooped down from a cliff above and perched on the stone wall, peering at them carefully. Ella looked at it with a mixture of shock, surprise, and fascination, noting that it had facial disks on either side of its head, like the hawk she saw on the beach. As she looked at it, the bird cocked its head and winked at her. Ella started.

"God bless yer day, Aarushi," Clerans said as he walked up to the bird, "ha' Martyn an' Laendon been by here today?"

The bird nodded.

Ella froze and looked hard at the bird. She leaned close to Lexi. "Can that hawk unde'stand you?"

The bird looked up at her as if it had heard her and gave a

shrill whistle, which might have been a laugh. Lexi laughed as well. "O' course she cen, Aarushi is no a hawk, she's a Harrier."

Ella felt this distinction had some vague importance, but she couldn't think what it might be. She furrowed her brow. "A'e Ha'ie'hs one of the talking species?"

The bird nodded.

"Ay," Clerans said. "One o' the eight species the Almighty God endowed with reason."

"Then why isn't this Ha'ie'h—Aa'ushi, I think you called he'h —why isn't she talking?"

Lexi sighed.

"Aarushi was born without a tongue," Clerans explained, "so she may be dumb, but she is no *dumb*, if you'll understand me."

"Ye mean that she cen no talk, but she is intelligent?" Lexi said.

"Exactly," Clerans replied with a bow.

Aarushi gave another tittering whistle and then hopped to the shed's door. She jumped up onto the window and, with a twist of her beak, turned the latch and flew inside. Clerans waited by the door, and after a moment, there was a sound like a lock sliding aside. Clerans then opened the door, entering with Lexi and Ella behind him.

Inside was a single room lit only by the light from that one window. The room was fairly large, with shelves on one wall and various tools lining the wall in the back. There were two tables in the room, one fairly small with only a large scale, and then an empty spot, which was just large enough for Aarushi to sit on comfortably. It was here she was sitting now, a dead rabbit beneath her feet. Various bits of metal—screws, bolts, and rivets—covered the other table. In one corner of the room, a basin of water sat.

Clerans made his way to the back of the room. "Ma sent us up here to get an axe; the carpenter is workin' on our other one."

Aarushi nodded and then looked back at Ella with interest. Ella looked back at the Harrier.

"We'e you the bi'd that found me on the beach?" Ella finally asked.

Aarushi nodded.

"Thank you."

Aarushi bowed her head demurely.

As Clerans took down an axe that hung from the wall at the back of the little room, Ella noticed several large cavities cut into the back wall, framed in at the front by wire, as if they were cages. Ella peered at these cavities closely. Yes, they must be cages, though all the doors were open, and leather harnesses hung from the wires that formed the cage door. She recognized what looked like a hood for a falcon—wasn't it called a chaperon?

Ella pointed to the cages. "That isn't fo'h Aarushi, is it?"

"Llifsa!" Lexi cried, clearly appalled at the idea. "No, we would never put Aarushi in a cage."

Aarushi whistled lightly, and Ella thought the Harrier looked as if she were laughing.

"Ay, no," Clerans said, returning with the axe. "Those cages were fer Martyn's other birds."

"Is Ma'tyn a Falcone'h then?" Ella asked.

Clerans shook his head. "He used to, but a few o' his hawks died from glwmber foot, and then the pteranodons ate the res. Martyn is a mite bit burnt out on falconry now."

Clerans walked to the door and was about to step out when Lexi turned to Aarushi. "Now, Aarushi, ye really oughtta-should vene down to the house more often. Mrs. Blaeith would love to see ye. Besides, Mr. Blysffi an' Haeli will be cedin' over tomorrow, an' I am sure we'll will tain roast moa fer dinner."

At the mention of roast moa, Aarushi perked up a good deal. She nodded solemnly and then hopped to Lexi's shoulder. She put the side of her head to Lexi's cheek and made a smacking sound that Ella supposed was a kiss. Lexi returned the kiss and then turned and left. Aarushi fluttered back to her rabbit and pulled off strips of meat.

As Clerans closed the door behind him and the two ladies, Lexi turned to Ella, "So ye ha' met Aarushi before?"

"A couple of times on the beach," Ella replied.

Just then, a shadow passed over the sun. Ella stopped in her tracks, petrified with fear as she glanced upward. A dark, winged shape had just wheeled over the peak above and was turning south. Ella threw herself up against the doors of the shed, hoping that it could not see her.

"Do no be frightened, Miss Ella," Clerans said, perplexed, "it is only a pteranodon."

Ella risked one more glance at the creature. She was certain that she could make out the outline of feathers and lizard-like tail. It was Cweel—she knew it. If only she knew whether he had seen her. Was she still safe?

# 15

## BARNACLES

*H*olgard's ship floated tranquilly outside Entwerp Bay. The anchor was down, and the sails were up. There were still plenty of rations and fresh water aboard, and they had recently careened the haul. There was no immediate need to do anything. However, any pirate that might have thought he would have a holiday was soon to be disappointed. At the crack of dawn, Quartermaster Harold's whistle had jolted Ernest awake.

"Get up right now, lazies. Orders from Captain Holgard are just in: we're to scrub the entire deck and clean the hull on barnacles."

At the mention of barnacles, a groan went up from the waking crew. Ernest heard several curses as the other pirates rolled out of their hammocks and nearly added one himself, when he remembered Lewis' discourse and muttered, "Blind prelates."

He rolled out of his hammock and looked over at Lewis. The faerie was busy in his kitchen, whistling to himself. Ernest hoped Lewis would have some use for him so he didn't have to join the other pirates. Just then, he felt a hand on his shoulder. It was the quartermaster.

"You'll be wanted, too, cook's-mate. Eat quick, and then work on the barnacles." Then the quartermaster walked on.

Ernest kicked at the wall. "Baptism!" He didn't care if Lewis heard him now.

Ernest slipped on his over-clothes and walked to the galley, where Lewis was just pulling his pot off the stove.

"Well, well, well, a good morning to you, boyo! Are you ready for a lovely day on work?"

Ernest threw himself moodily onto a stool. "You can keep all that fine wit to yourself, Lewis."

Lewis just grinned. "Blind prelates! Someone woke up on the wrong side of his hammock this morning."

"Now look here," Ernest said. "I'm on barnacle duty today. Now, if'n you were in my position, you'd be just as upset."

Lewis raised both his eyebrows. "What? You don't think *my* work is all that difficult?"

Ernest just glared at Lewis. Lewis shrugged and gave a merry whistle.

Ernest kicked the counter. "Anoint those barnacles."

"Ernest." Ernest looked up to see Lewis looking at him with concern. "Ernest, you don't have to cuss like the others. I like you better without the vulgarity."

"What's so bad about it? I'm a pirate, after all," Ernest replied moodily.

"Then there's no reason to commit any more sins against God."

Ernest laughed heartily at this. The dark humor was just what he needed at the moment. But suddenly, he realized that Lewis was looking quite serious.

"What's this now?" Ernest asked. "I thought you were joking."

Now it was Lewis' turn to be moody. "No."

Ernest studied Lewis. Finally, he said, "Lewis, you're a *pirate* ship, and you talk about God and sin? Aren't you a little late for that?"

Lewis shrugged. "We can still do the best we can with where we're at."

Ernest laughed again. "Well, someone's feeling guilty. Do you think God will forget about your life as a pirate just because you do'edn't cuss?"

Lewis thought about this for a moment, and then a roguish grin flashed across his face. "Helen Maria, Ernest! We'd best be serving out the food."

---

Ernest walked slowly up on deck, food in his belly and gloom in his heart. He was on the barnacle job. He strode moodily across the deck, fingering a dull knife in his hand. As soon as the quartermaster saw him, he motioned for Ernest to come over to the side of the ship and then handed him a rope on a harness.

"You know how it goes. Now get to it."

Ernest slipped himself into the harness and then tightened it. He looked up to see another pirate ready to lower him over the side of the galleon. The other pirate was grinning from ear to ear.

"Wipe that smile off your face, Dun," Ernest growled. "You might be next, you know."

The other pirate just shrugged. "You want to be lowered now?"

Ernest clambered over the side of the gunwale and then trusted himself to the rope as the other pirate slowly lowered him until he was halfway into the water. As he tread water easily with his long arms, the other pirate threw the rope down to him. Ernest took hold of it and tied it to his harness. Then he moved closer to the ship's side and pulled out his knife.

Several other pirates were already in the water, prying at the nasty little barnacles. Among these were the long-armed gnome, Bill, and his human messmate, Tell. Bill was just to Ernest's right, and he nodded as he started working.

"Even the cook's-mate haves to work down here."

Ernest grunted as he dug his knife underneath a barnacle and started prying it off.

"Everyone helps but the officers," Bill went on. "Isn't that how it always goes?"

"But they're officers," Tell replied with the blank look of an idiot.

Just then, Ernest slipped with his knife and gashed his knuckles on a barnacle. He inhaled sharply to keep from yelling in pain, then gripped his knife in his mouth while he pressed his knuckles with his other hand to keep the blood from flowing.

Tell continued, "It is different on Longfinch's ship, haven't you heard?"

Bill bit his tongue and groaned slightly, "No, on course not; tell me about it."

Ernest winced as he bathed his knuckles in the salt water and then resumed his work on the barnacles.

"They don't have any elections at all," Tell said, "none at all."

"What's this now?" Ernest asked.

Bill looked over at him. "You mean you haven't heared?"

Ernest shook his head.

"Well, as I was saying," Tell replied, "they don't have any elections at all."

"Who don't?" Ernest asked, popping a barnacle from the hull at that moment. His hand slipped, but he jerked it back quickly before he gashed it again.

Tell went on. "Longfinch's pirates. I can't think how they would keep the officers from lording their power."

Ernest raised his eyebrows. "They can't vote on officers?"

"All I can say is I'm glad I'm on this ship and not that one,"

Bill said as he pried another barnacle loose and dropped it into the ocean.

"I know, that's what I thought," Tell replied. "But I wonder what it's like on Captain Pennywraith's ship."

Bill rolled his eyes. "Pennywraith's crew is just like ours."

Tell nodded sagely. "Oh, right." Just then, he slipped with his knife and gashed his knuckles on another barnacle. "Anointment," he cursed, as he washed his knuckles off in the water and grit his teeth.

"Just be glad there aren't any sharks around," Bill said dryly. "We will all be bleeding by the end of this."

---

Never had Ernest been so happy to hear Lewis' voice as he was when Lewis leaned over the gunwales and said, "Alright, Ernest, Boyo, I need your help now with lunch. Quartermaster says you're done."

Ernest immediately stopped and put his knife away. Then he untied the rope from his harness and hauled himself up to the deck. Bill looked after him as he left.

"Be sure to get lunch ready for the rest on us soon. I don't wantta stay down here one moment longer than I have to."

Ernest gave him a nod. "You can count on that."

Ernest reached the deck and clambered back aboard. He wrung the cold seawater from his trousers as he climbed out of his harness. Lewis looked at him with a glimmer in his eye.

"I see you survived."

"Barely," Ernest replied as he held up his hands. Both were cut and bruised badly, and his shirt cuffs were stained red. "I don't know if'n I could take another five minutes on that."

Lewis was still smiling, though his eyes softened a little. "Do you need those bandaged before you serve out the gruel?"

"The others will want bandaging as well."

Lewis gave him a wink. "Stay here then, and I will be back."

Lewis hurried below deck. As Ernest waited, he heard a splashing sound from off deck. Perking up his large ears, he clearly made out the sound of creaking from over toward Longfinch's man-o-war. Quickly, he turned his head all the way around, looking out over the water to see a skiff being lowered from Longfinch's man-o-war. As he watched, the skiff touched the water, then the crew loosed the ropes from the boat and rowed towards the galleon. Ernest peered at the crew of the skiff, shading his eyes with his bleeding hands. There, in the prow, sat Longfinch.

"Tell the captain, Longfinch is coming over!" he cried.

Quartermaster Harold gave a few shrill pipes on his whistle, and Holgard emerged from his cabin. He turned to the quartermaster.

"Weel, what's the call for?"

The quartermaster motioned to Ernest and then at the approaching skiff. "Longfinch has been sighted."

Holgard regarded the skiff for a few moments, then snorted. "Weel then, he will be coming for Jock. Give the orders to have him bringed out on deck."

Quartermaster Harold dispatched the orders immediately.

About the time Lewis came back with the bandages, Longfinch had reached the galleon, and several pirates were hauling him aboard.

"Here you are, Ernest," the cook said as he produced a foul-smelling ointment and smeared it on Ernest's hands. Ernest gritted his teeth—the ointment stung badly. As Lewis wrapped his hands, Ernest listened to Holgard and Longfinch's conversation.

"Any new luck with Jock?" Longfinch asked as he leapt aboard.

Holgard shook his head. "I'm telling you, we need the girl before we can get any further."

Longfinch gave a slight smile. "You might be right, but until Cweel brings her back, we will have to try him. We can't delay too long, or the Llaedhwythi privateers will attack us before we can raid Entwerp."

Just then, Killjelly came across the deck, pulling Jock behind him. Jock squinted in the mid-day sun, and Ernest guessed he couldn't see Longfinch. Jock looked down at the deck while he addressed Holgard.

"I has been tortured several ways before, look ye, but niver with sun and fair weather."

Longfinch laughed. "How very witty on you, Jock. I trust you've haved a pleasant stay aboard?"

Jock froze and turned pale, looking up at Longfinch.

Longfinch smiled. "I'm sure you will enjoy the quarters I've prepared for you."

Jock let out his breath slowly. "It's a pleasure, whatever."

Longfinch laughed again. "I hear you're not cooperating with Holgard."

Some of the color returned to Jock's face as his eyes flashed. "See if ye can do better."

Longfinch stared meaningfully into Jock's eyes. "I breaked you once."

Jock laughed; it was a loud, almost maniacal laugh, full of taunting and scorn. "Ay-eigh! Ye broke yer rack on me, and ye broke yer boot on me, then *I* broke yer torturer's neck. *I* broke yer jail's door, and *I* broke Vania's sword. Ye *did not,* look ye, break me."

Longfinch's eyes narrowed. "You told me one word before you got away. Do you remember that?"

Jock was silent.

"'Silas,'" Longfinch said, "that's what you told me."

Jock shuddered and made a choking noise.

Longfinch smiled, "I breaked you."

Jock turned on Longfinch with sudden fire. With a sharp

kick, he knocked Killjelly's legs out from under him. The hooked leprechaun collapsed with a string of curses, releasing his hold on Jock. Free for a moment, Jock let out a violent yell and leapt at Longfinch. But the elf captain dashed nimbly to the side and caught Jock by the wrist. He spun Jock's arm behind his back and thrust it upwards, throwing Jock face-first to the deck.

Jock gasped in pain, but stayed still. Longfinch's large nose throbbed ever so slightly, the only evidence of his exertion in subduing Jock.

"I breaked you," Longfinch said. "I gained one piece of the Gwambi puzzle from you."

Jock grunted, "It is nothing from me ye got. Silas, look ye, has nothing to do with the Gwambi Treasure, whatever."

Longfinch laughed. "On course, that's what you say."

"Silas is not..." Jock choked there and could get no further.

Longfinch pulled him to his feet, still gripping his wrists. He nodded to one of his men who had come aboard. "Tie him up."

The pirate obeyed.

As Jock was being lowered to the skiff, Longfinch turned one last time to Holgard. "We'll have a go at him for a couple on days. He'll speak eventually. Cweel will bring the girl soon."

With that, he grabbed hold of a rope and lowered himself to the skiff.

It was then that Ernest realized Lewis had finished bandaging him and was now looking at him with a grin.

"Are you done eavesdropping yet?"

Ernest blushed.

"Well then, let's get these hungry pirates some lunch." And with that, Lewis headed below deck, whistling as he went.

# 16

# A KIRK SERVICE

*E*lla resolved to wake up early the next morning, firmly intentioned to work hard and dutifully for Mrs. Blaeith. She felt rather guilty that the Blaeiths had spent so much money on her yesterday and felt duty-bound to make up for it. No sooner had the first beam of sunlight touched her as it trickled through the window, than she snapped her eyes open and sat up in bed. Lexi was still asleep, but she stirred slightly.

Ella slipped out of bed and dressed quickly. She then set about braiding her hair. Lexi rolled over and looked up at her.

"Well, ye are up early."

Ella blushed a little. "Is Mrs. Blaeith likely to be awake? I want to help he'h with b'eakfast."

Lexi gave a little laugh. "Oh, ye'd be hard-put to get up a'fore Mrs. Blaeith—particularly this mornin'."

"Why's that?"

Lexi looked at her for a moment. "Do ye no know what day o' the week it is?"

Ella shook her head. "I lost count on the pi'ate ship."

"Well, that would explain it," Lexi said as she slipped out of bed. "It is Sabbath."

Ella paused her braiding for a moment. A mixture of joy and disappointment came over Ella—joy that it was the Sabbath, and disappointment that she wouldn't be able to work for Mrs. Blaeith. "Sabbath," she finally replied.

Lexi nodded with a wide grin on her face.

"Well, I guess I weally did lose t'ack of the days," Ella said as she continued to braid. Then she looked down at her clothes. It was one thing to run an errand around town in those travel-worn clothes, but quite another to brave the Sabbath morning in them.

Lexi seemed to read her thoughts. "Do no worry. If that ha' been a problem, I'll would ha' fiscated ye a pair o' Sabbath clothes yesterday."

Ella was a bit relieved. "Oh, Lexi, you didn't even have to get me the clothes you did. I wouldn't expect you to get me Sabbath clothes, too..."

Just then, Mrs. Blaeith came into the room. She wore a fine dress the color of goldenrod with lace around the neck and shoulders. Under her arm, she carried a roll of clothes. "Well, deary, I knew I would trive a use fer these some day, and now it's here." So saying, she handed Ella the set of clothes. "When my dear sister died, she left us these, an' since they were too tight fer me I ha' no used them, but unless I'm merri mistaken, they'll oughtta-should fit ye fairly well. An' if they'll fit, they are yers."

Ella held the dress up and had to agree. Perhaps the waist was a tad bit wide, but otherwise, it seemed perfect. The dress was a rusty-red color, with an intricately designed, earth-green trim on the waist and hems. Lace also hung from the neck and shoulders like Mrs. Blaeith's dress.

"Thank you so much," Ella gasped. "I do no know what I can do to thank you p'oper'ly." Ella could feel a lump forming in her throat and tears coming to her eyes. They were *so* kind.

Mrs. Blaeith laughed. "Do no worry about it," she said as she left the room.

Ella looked over the Sabbath dress one more time, about to put it on, when she noticed that there were no stockings with the dress. Was it not customary to wear stockings to church, either? This was getting to be too much to abide.

"Lexi," Ella said, licking her lips, "a'e stockings..." She trailed off and simply looked over at the gnome maid.

Lexi sighed. "Oh, right, I forgot about that. It took me the merriest time getting used to no wearin' stockings around town. Ay, but ye need no worry about that fer now; they all wear stockings to kirk, at least."

Not wear stockings around town? Ella let out her breath slowly. So it was true. What kind of heathen country had she landed in?

"But," Ella gasped. "But, what if...might someone see you'h knees?"

Lexi shrugged. "I'd say it's not uncommon."

Ella's stomach twisted in horror. "But if a man saw you'h knees, wouldn't he..." Ella trailed off, not even willing to finish her sentence.

"Wouldn't he what?" Lexi asked. "Unless he's a sailor, he probably wouldn't give it a second thought."

Ella's face flushed in embarrassment.

"And if he is a sailor," Lexi went on with a wide grin, "I'll will beat him red as a beet fer ye."

In a few minutes, Lexi and Ella entered the main room, arm-in-arm. Clerans and Mrs. Blaeith were the only others of the family who were in the room. They bustled about, laying the table for breakfast. Ella came up to Mrs. Blaeith.

"How can I help you?"

Mrs. Blaeith clicked her tongue humorously. "Jist sit back now, dear. It is bad enough that *I'll* ha' to set the table on the Sabbath, an' I will no let my guest do it fer me."

Ella stood back reluctantly, and Clerans winked at her. "An' it is a merri grief that ye can no work."

"But I want to help," Ella replied.

Just then, Martyn and Laendon came out of the back hallway. Martyn could almost have passed for an upper-class gentleman with his immaculate suit and dashing features. Laendon was a different matter, however. His hair—though meticulously brushed—touted a cowlick in the back, and his black boots clashed badly with his off-black trousers.

Both of the young men nodded to Ella. "God bless yer mornin', Miss Ella, Lexi."

"And may he wetu'n you'h blessing," Ella said.

Lexi frowned when she saw Laendon. "Laendon, child, ye may be merri good with yer mechanics, but ye oughtta-should learn yer combin' mechanics."

Laendon looked down at the gnome-maid. "Combin' mechanics?"

Lexi grabbed a stool, dropped it next to Laendon, and then jumped on top of it to reach Laendon's head. She licked her hand and used it to comb the cowlick until it stayed down. Laendon stood civilly and uncomfortably as if Lexi were performing surgery on him.

"An' who are ye callin' child, eh?"

Lexi finished her grooming and then hopped down from the stool. "I cen call ye child if I'll want to, now do no complain, child."

"Child?" Laendon replied, "Now really, s'ppose I wos to start callin' ye child, Lexi..."

Lexi wagged her finger up at him. "Now, who wos the one who vened out with their hair half-combed?"

Laendon turned red, but Martyn laughed. Soon enough, Mr. Blaeith and the two younger boys entered. Mr. Blaeith looked quite dignified in a golden-brown vest and deep-bay coat, but the younger boys were in a state of disorder similar to Laendon's. After Lexi had fussed over them for a moment, they all gathered around the table. Mr. Blaeith said grace, and they ate.

Breakfast comprised oat porridge and salt pork—both liberally seasoned with the exotic spices Lexi had bought yesterday —scones, and warm, pale beer. The meal was quieter than the others Ella had eaten with the Blaeiths, and everyone seemed slightly more somber.

When it was over, Mrs. Blaeith cleared the table and stacked the plates in the washbowl. She left them there for a moment to wipe the table, and Ella took her chance. She quickly stepped over to the washbasin and began to scrub the dishes. Before Mrs. Blaeith could stop her, she had filled the basin—partly with cold water from a pitcher and partly with water from the tea kettle—and scrubbed two plates clean. Then, Mrs. Blaeith caught sight of her.

She clicked her tongue. "Now, deary, ye do no ha' to do anythin'. Jist sit back an' let me an' Lexi do that."

Ella stacked the third plate to her right. "Mrs. Blaeith, I can't sit back and let you do all the wo'k."

Mrs. Blaeith smiled. "Ye cen work some other day, dearie, but today's the Sabbath, an' a day fer restin', no workin'."

"And you need a Sabbath, too, Ma'am," Ella said.

Mrs. Blaeith laughed, "Well, dearie, I ha' no seen anyone so determined to work."

Ella stacked her fourth plate. Just then, Clerans came up and began drying the plates with a hand towel before passing them off to one of his younger brothers to put on the proper shelf.

"Ye oughtta-should be careful, Miss Ella. Ma cen put ye to work merri well without yer help," he said with a wink.

"But I want to help," Ella replied as she handed Clerans plate five.

Clerans shrugged. "Ye cen take my chores fer me then."

Ella laughed.

They soon finished the dishes, and everyone prepared to

leave for the kirk. As Lexi helped the younger Blaeiths into their shoes, Ella picked up her own new shoes. They were not very dressy, but one could not be particular in such circumstances. Just then, Mrs. Blaeith emerged from the back of the house with a pair of beautiful black shoes.

"Here ye are, dear, ye can tain these fer today. They outta-should fit ye if the shoes ye wore yesterday fit."

Ella took them gratefully and thanked Mrs. Blaeith. Then she noticed that Mrs. Blaeith was wearing her normal shoes.

"Mrs. Blaeith, I can't wea'h you'h Sabbath shoes and leave you in you'h plain ones. He'e, take these back, and I'll wea'h my new shoes."

Mrs. Blaeith laughed, "I let ye wash the dishes already, dearie, now jist wear those shoes, and do no complain."

Soon afterward, the family left the house, each putting on their hat as they stepped out into the crisp morning. Ella wrapped a shawl tightly around herself to ward off the wind and—taking Lexi's arm—followed the family across town.

They made their way to a large main road and took it toward the huge, narrow valley behind Entwerp Coastal. As they reached the beginning of the valley—the end of the village —they arrived at a good-sized, rather Gothic-looking kirk on one side of a wide cobblestone square. Several wagons stood in front and to the side of the church, with many people still arriving—some from Entwerp Coastal and some from farther up the valley.

The Blaeiths started up the small flight of steps, which climbed to the door between two flying buttresses. At the door, a huge, black-skinned satyr greeted them. Ella immediately guessed he was a satyr, with his massive height, goat-like hooves, and curled horns. He wore a woolen parlor-jacket with a russet greatcoat over that and an impeccably white cravat tied around his neck.

"God bless you, Henri and all."

Mr. Blaeith tipped his hat. "An' may he return yer blessin', Reverend Daerl."

Ella jumped internally at the title 'reverend.' This couldn't be right. You couldn't actually have a satyr as a pastor, could you?

Reverend Daerl looked at Ella for a moment, but said nothing. He only smiled, showing his brilliant white teeth next to his coal-black face.

As they entered the building, Ella looked around to see if she recognized any of the people already there. Though she was certain she must have seen more people around town, she only recognized the tailor and his family sitting on a pew near the middle. She looked specifically for that dark-skinned girl she had met the day before—Haeli—but didn't see her.

The Blaeiths made their way to the pew just in front of the tailor and sat down. Mr. and Mrs. Blaeith, along with Martyn, Laendon, and Lexi, talked to some families seated nearby. They talked more solemnly and seriously than Ella had heard them speak before, almost as if they were at a funeral.

As there was no one talking with Ella, she examined the kirk. All four walls bore stained glass windows with scenes of trees, streams, and mountains. At the front of the kirk, to one side, was a pulpit carved with minutely decorated stonework. On the front wall, there was not an organ as Ella had expected, nor was there a piano in sight. Instead, on the other side of the kirk from the pulpit was a small portico where two men with fiddles and a small girl with a fife played a somber prelude while the rest of the worshipers trickled inside.

Ella studied all the people in the room. Up front, there were a few satyrs—probably Reverend Daerl's family. Ella noted several gnomes and a few leprechauns, and there were a few she couldn't readily identify. A family of dwarves sat in the pew opposite the Blaeiths, and Ella was pretty sure she could see a nymph here and there, but everyone else was human—which was the vast majority of those present.

It was then that she noticed a young woman holding her infant close in her arms. The baby was making cute swallowing noises as the mother carried on a hushed conversation with the person in the pew in front of her. Upon looking closer, Ella realized, to her horror, that the mother was actually nursing her child, openly, and in public. She glanced away, feeling embarrassed for the woman. Was it really acceptable to do such a thing so openly—and in a worship service, no less?

Clerans nudged Ella. "Are the kirks in Slyzwir at all like this?"

"Mo'e or less," Ella said. Really, this kirk was about as similar to her home church as a heathen mosque, but she thought it better to say nothing of it.

After another moment's pause, Ella leaned over to Clerans again, speaking in a low voice, and making sure to enunciate clearly. "Is your pastor really a satyr?"

Clerans nodded. "Ay, an' why should he no be?"

Ella blushed. "Bu a'en't saty'hs, you know–" Ella looked at Clerans closely, too embarrassed to say what she actually wanted to ask. "A'en't saty'hs – eh – *wild.*"

Clerans flashed a roguish smile. "No more wild than ye." Then his face turned serious as he looked around the chapel. "We do no make distinctions between the races o' mankind. You cen be a human, or a satyr, or a leprechaun, or a nymph, or even an elf – we do no discriminate. We were all made in the image o' God, so why should we be making rules about what ye can or can no do? We consider all races as equal, here in Llaedhwyth."

Just then, the musicians finished, and Reverend Daerl came inside. The huge satyr strode swiftly down the aisle between the pews and mounted the pulpit.

"Please open yer hymnals to hymn two hundred and five," he said. "We will sing the next five."

Lexi shared a hymnal with Ella, and the whole assembly began to sing. The hymnal did little to help Ella follow the song, as it was written in the Pistosian Tylwen script, which she couldn't have read at gunpoint. Instead, she simply listened as the congregation sang out the first four hymns with gusto. The musicians played along as well, but they hardly needed to. The congregation sang in four—sometimes five—part harmony, and with such strength, precision, and beauty that Ella guessed any member of her choir back in Blisa would have wept to hear it.

The last song was the same that Mr. Blaeith had taught Ella during vespers. With great pleasure, Ella sang loudly, a bit relieved to know the song, and happy to add her lisping voice to that glorious sound.

When they finished singing, they recited some liturgy. Ella knew some of it from back home, but most was new to her. After that, another man read a passage from the Scriptures, and then Reverend Daerl preached.

First, opening up a huge tome and perching a set of spectacles on his flat nose, he read. "'Are no two sparrows sold for an half cent? And yet be sure, no one of them will fall to the ground apart from the knowledge of your Father in heaven. Of how much more value are you than the sparrows?'"

He then slowly removed his glasses, prayed, and launched into his sermon. He spoke slowly and with great sincerity, but as he continued—and his excitement mounted—he would sometimes preach in a full roar, inflating his satyr throat sack and bellowing out his points until Ella's ears rang. Then he would become much softer again, reasoning sincerely with the congregation. Now he would smite the pulpit with his powerful fists, and now he would nearly choke with tears. The truth of his message had a full grip on him, and he could do nothing but convey it to all who would listen.

Ella listened with rapt attention. Never had she heard a sermon delivered with such passion, or such sincerity. Never for a moment could she doubt that Reverend Daerl believed every word he said.

Yet as Reverend Daerl continued to preach, a growing feeling came over Ella. Here was this satyr, preaching with more emotion than she had ever witnessed before, and though much of this culture was different to her, it was quite clear that they all shared the same faith. She was sitting among family.

For all the quirks of this unfamiliar country she was in, the embarrassment of being kissed all the time, and the shocking differences in modesty standards, none of it really mattered. What mattered was that she was among family.

# 17

# ELSI AND HAELI

*W*hen the service had finished, everyone stood in one great mass, and the kirk filled with the sound of merry talk. Everyone seemed to forget the sober mood from before the service, and now laughter echoed through the kirk. As Ella stood, Lexi took her by the arm, whisked her away, and introduced her to a host of Lexi's friends.

"Here, Ella, let me introduce ye to my friend Beth."

Ella curtsied and gave the proper greeting. They exchanged trivialities and then moved on.

"Ella, meet Janel, Keitlyn, an' Jenyffr."

Then in a few minutes, "Oh, Ella, let me introduce ye to my friends Sylfia an' Kati. You remember Kati do no ye? Kati Fflemins, the tailor's daughter?"

Ella did remember Kati.

Soon, Ella simply faded out of the excitement. She smiled nicely and curtsied when Lexi introduced her to three more of her friends. She was sure to respond to questions she was asked and behave herself politely, but her mind was not on it.

Ella was secretly observing the rest of the crowd; she was particularly watching Reverend Daerl. The tall satyr towered above the rest of the congregation as he talked earnestly with his parishioners. Now and then, he would burst into a hearty fit of laughter, his deep voice ringing over the rest of the talk. Ella could see that he was standing with his wife and another satyr, the spitting image of himself.

Once, when Ella stole a glance at Reverend Daerl, she saw him talking with the little fife player. The satyr was leaning over and saying something seriously, though a hint of mischief was in his eye. The fife player looked back seriously. She had a sober look in the back of her eyes. Her brown eyes were calm and assured, though solemn. Though she looked hardly old enough to be called anything else than a girl, she was regal and womanly. Ella knew for certain that she had never met this girl before, yet there was something oddly familiar about her face as if it reminded Ella of someone else she knew.

Ella immediately liked the fife-player and wished that Lexi would introduce her instead of another round, forgettable face. No sooner had she thought this than Lexi took her by the arm, saying, "Now, Ella, there's jist one more person whom ye really *must* meet."

The fife player turned to meet them as they approached, and Reverend Daerl nodded to them as well.

"Lexi, good to see ye!" the fife player said enthusiastically as they kissed on the cheek. "Who's this with ye?"

"This is Ella Donne. Ella, this is Elsi Pickering."

Ella's heart jumped and almost forgot to curtsy back. Did she say Pickering? Elsi took Ella by the hand and kissed her on the cheek. Ella was still too surprised to feel embarrassed.

"Did you say you'h name was Picke'ing?"

Elsi nodded.

"Same he'e," Ella said.

Lexi looked at her inquiringly.

"Donne is my step-fathe'h's name," Ella explained.

Elsi's brown eyes suddenly filled with compassion. "Oh, I am so sorry. I lost my mother when I wos younger."

Ella was quiet for a little. "So, who is you'h fathe'h?" she finally asked.

"Oh, Papa is Sir Saemwel Pickering," Elsi said, brightening up a little, though she still held a somber look about her eyes.

"He fought in the wars," Lexi added enthusiastically.

"Ay," Reverend Daerl said, "no one could ha' done better as a soldier than Sir Saemwel Pickering."

"Whe'e is he?" Ella asked.

"Over there," Elsi pointed to a tall gentleman leaning heavily on a cane. He had a long, careworn face, with a laborious demeanor, but twinkling, blue eyes. His frame was thickset; he must have been massive in his youth. Now his hair was bleach-white, and his entire frame hunched over with age and care. He was talking with Mr. Blaeith just then. Ella liked the look of this Sir Saemwel, as something about him reminded her of the regal town elders in Blisa.

"He wos wounded," Lexi continued, "in the Battle o' Ard-Melwyn, under Caedmon Wilkins—but he retired from the army."

Ella couldn't help but be impressed. "He looks like a very g'eat, man."

"Oh, he is!" Elsi said, "an' he's so kind, too. I could no tain a better Papa."

Ella looked down at Elsi's earnest face. She couldn't have been older than twelve, yet her demeanor and speech might have belonged to a thirty-year-old.

"The Pickerings live in Entwerp Proper," Lexi was saying. "They tain a nice manor house there—one of the oldest in town. The boys sometimes stay with them if they'll ha' to work merri late in the city."

"Is Entwe'p P'ope'h fa'h f'om he'e?"

"Oh no, it's jist up the ravine a little way," Elsi said.

Just then, Clerans ambled up to them. He nodded good-naturedly to Elsi and Reverend Daerl.

"Ma says that if we'll want roast moa fer dinner, then we'll ha' better cede home."

"Then we ha' better go," Lexi said.

Ella and Lexi both kissed Elsi in parting and then made their way back through the crowd to the door. As they came near the door, Clerans motioned over to the right.

"Martyn's over there; you cen tell him, and I'll will see if I'll cen trive up Laendon."

With that, Clerans moved along a pew in search of Laendon. Ella looked over to where Clerans had motioned. Kati Fflemins —the tailor's daughter—was passionately carrying on a one-sided conversation with Martyn. Now and again, he would say something in return—civilly—as if he were trying very hard not to be rude. Whenever he spoke, she would look up at him coyly.

"Llifsa!" Lexi said. "She's after him again."

She quickly pushed her way up to Martyn, dragging Ella with her.

"Martyn," Lexi cried, "Mrs. Blaeith wants to leave now so she cen get the moa cooked."

"Oh!" Kati said, staring sweetly up at Martyn. "I really did no mean to keep ye here so long. I do no mean to keep yer Ma waiting."

Ella was certain she saw Martyn's nostrils flare ever-so-slightly in frustration. "Ay, to be sure, ye need no worry."

He bid Kati goodbye briskly, then took Lexi by the other arm from Ella and headed towards the door. No sooner had he turned his back on Kati than he sighed deeply.

"Tar and needles," he muttered, but he said nothing else just then.

When Martyn, Lexi, and Ella reached the door, a shadow swept down from the rafters of the kirk and landed neatly on

Martyn's arm. It was Aarushi. The Harrier rubbed her head against Martyn's shoulder and made a warbling sound.

Martyn stroked her feathered head a few times. "God bless ye, Aarushi, and good to see ye. To be sure, I do no mind if *ye'll* flirt with me."

Aarushi giggled—after a fashion—and then hopped up onto Martyn's shoulder.

Martyn, Lexi, and Ella walked out the door of the kirk to see the rest of the Blaeiths waiting for them on the porch. Mr. Blaeith nodded to them and then started back toward the house.

"Whe'e was that gi'l you met in the spice ma'ket—Haeli?" Ella asked. "I thought she would be the'e."

"Oh, no," Lexi replied, "the Blysffis cede to the *other* kirk."

"What othe'h ki'k?" Ella asked.

"Oh, ye know..." Lexi trailed off.

"They are Rectificationists," Martyn said.

Ella blinked. "Whats?"

"Rectificationists," Lexi replied. "They are..." she trailed off again.

"Different?" Martyn offered with a bit of a grin.

"Ay, different. Their kirk is different from ours."

Aarushi whistled in affirmation.

The issue still wasn't very clear to Ella, and it struck her that *her* church back home was different from this Pistosian kirk, so she pressed the question further.

"They'h not teetotale's a'e they?"

"What now?" Lexi asked.

"Teetotalers," Ella repeated, careful to get her *r* right.

Lexi laughed. "Oh, no. The pump water is bad enough here. The last teetotalers died off, and no one ha' been brave enough to ceive up their cause since."

Martyn laughed.

Ella still wanted to know more about this *other* kirk. "Then in what way a'e they diffe'ent?"

Lexi looked at Martyn for help.

"Well," Martyn said with only a brief hesitation, "they do no believe in distinction in worship, so they tain no specific pastor or priests, or song leaders, or lectors; they jist take turns, men and women alike. They do tain Presbyters who oversee the kirks, though, *outside* o' worship, but that's all."

Ella looked at Martyn critically. "They don't have men and *women* Presbyters, do they?"

"Oh, ay," Martyn replied with a shrug. "They do no believe in distinctions."

Ella furrowed her brow. And she had thought the Blaeiths odd in their faith traditions!

But Martyn wasn't done. "They also do no baptize someone until they're nearly eight summers o' age."

"They don't name thei'h child'en until eight?" Ella asked in surprise.

"No, they christen them at the normal time; they jist do no baptize them."

Clerans entered the conversation then. "Are you talkin' about the other kirk?" He didn't wait for a reply. "They do no wear shoes; that is the fundamental difference."

Ella nearly tripped. "Did you say they don't wea' shoes?"

"Ay," Clerans said, apparently enjoying the surprise he had caused. "As soon as they'll enter the kirk, off go the shoes, an' they do no put them back on until they'll leave."

"The ladies also do no wear hats," Lexi added. "Jist scarves, but no hats."

"Ay," Clerans went on, "And they tain a merri o' rules about holiness, an' lovin' your neighbor. They have to share a tenth o' their income with poor or disadvantaged people, an' they must provide education fer one child who is no their own." Then Clerans seemed to rethink himself. "No that givin' money to the poor an' lovin' yer neighbor is a bad thing (we do it too at this kirk), but it is mandatory at the other kirk. They tain a merri 'o rules."

Ella raised her eyebrows. "That sounds legalistic." She was a little disappointed that they weren't more similar to her church in Blisa.

"Well, perhaps," Martyn said. "Ye may say so. They are so merri focused on 'holiness' that they'll cen sometimes cede too far. But those in the other kirk are true followers o' the Way. An' I do think they will do this country some real good. They are jist a mite different, that is all."

"An' legalistic," Clerans added. "Miss Ella wos right there."

"Perhaps..." Martyn replied. "It probably depends on the family. The Blysffis, fer instance, are no legalistic. An' after all, there are certainly families within our own kirk who are legalistic."

"Are you talking about the other kirk?" Mr. Blaeith asked as he turned slightly to face Martyn and the others.

"Ay," Martyn said.

"Ella was wantin' to know what made them different," Lexi added.

"Ah," Mr. Blaeith grinned. "Never heard o' the Rectificationists?"

"No, si'h," Ella replied.

"They are a decent kirk," Mr. Blaeith said, "an' good students o' the gospel. They are strong advocate for a holy society, and bringing justice to all, which is most commendable. My chief disagreement with them is that they are cessationists."

"They'e what?" Ella asked.

"Cessationists," Mr. Blaeith replied.

"Ay," Martyn said with a nod. "They believe in the cessation o' the supernatural."

Ella furrowed her brow in confusion. "They believe the'e is no such thing as the supe'natu'al?"

Mr. Blaeith shook his head. "No, a better way to say it is that they believe that God no longer uses supernatural means to do His work on earth."

"But they also believe in the cessation o' the supernatural works o' the powers o' darkness," Clerans said.

"But how can they believe that?" Ella asked. "That's absu'd. They can't weally believe that the'e is a natural explanation fo'h eve'ything."

Martyn nodded, "Ay, but they do!"

"If ye'll will ask me," Clerans added, "we'll live in a merri borin' world if they'll are right!"

"But," Ella said, trying to come up with the right words. "But the sc'iptu'es... the'e a'e so many mi'acles in the sc'iptu'es! Do they disbelieve the sc'iptu'es?"

Mr. Blaeith shook his head. "Oh ay, I admire their reverence for the scriptures! The Rectificationists would say that the supernatural ceased to affect our world at the Fall of Belgosse, at the beginning o' this Fourth Age."

Just then, Aarushi jumped from Martyn's shoulder with a small cry. Ella looked around in alarm, only to see Aarushi gliding towards two figures who had just turned the corner and were walking towards the Blaeiths.

As soon as the smaller one saw the Harrier, she burst out joyfully, "Aarushi! God bless you. Oh, it is merri good to see you."

Ella immediately recognized her as Haeli, the girl from the spice market. The man behind the girl gave a deep laugh. "And would you believe who is coming towards us, Haeli?"

Haeli dashed up to the Blaeiths, with Aarushi perched nicely on her arm. "And it is merri good to see all of you, too. Hello Mr. and Mrs. Blaeith. God bless you. Laendon, Clarence, Robert, Roland, and Martyn, God bless all of you, too."

She kissed each of them in greeting as she said their names. Clerans received her in a mixed state of civility and discomfort, but everyone else was just as happy to see Haeli as she was to see them.

"Hello, Lexi, and..." Haeli paused as she looked at Ella. "Llifsa, I am afraid I have forgotten your name. Emma?"

"Ella," Ella replied.

"Good to see you again, Miss Ella," and Haeli kissed her, too.

Martyn let go of Lexi's arm gently. "Lexi, ye do no mind...?"

"O' course no," Lexi said.

"Good." Martyn took Haeli by the arm and walked alongside Ella and Lexi. Aarushi now hopped back onto Martyn's shoulder with a small purr. Ella noted that Clerans had fallen back a little way and had lost his jovial mood.

About then, Haeli's father—at least, that's who Ella assumed he must be—arrived and greeted Mr. Blaeith. He was a large man with black skin—even darker than Haeli's. He wore the same style of clothing as the other Pistosian men, and tightly curled hair protruded from beneath his tricorn hat.

"Henri, God bless you; good to see you."

"An' may He return your blessin' to ye, Stifyn."

Ella thought it strange to see such strong men kiss each other on the cheek and tried hard to get over the weirdness of it.

Haeli's father looked around at the rest of the Blaeiths. "Thunder! I do believe there is a new face here, Henri." And then, as if it were a joke, the man burst into merry laughter. He laughed so earnestly that his whole body shook, and his face shone with a genuine smile. Ella couldn't help but laugh, too, though she couldn't think why she was laughing.

"And what may your name be, my dear lady?"

"They call me Ella..." she hesitated, but for only a moment, "...Donne." It was a bit of a nuisance not to be sure which of her surnames to use when introducing herself to each new person.

"God bless you, Miss Ella. They call me Stifyn Blysffi, and this is my daughter, Haeli."

"Good to meet you, Mr. Blysffi."

"I met her already, Da," Haeli said, "in the spice market—with Lexi."

"Well, then," Mr. Blysffi laughed again. "*I* have the pleasure of acquainting myself with her now." With that, he kissed Ella and turned back to Mr. and Mrs. Blaeith.

"Have you adopted her yet, or is she just a visiting relative?"

"Tar and needles, Stifyn," Mrs. Blaeith said, "do no try to be clever. Just answer me this, do ye tain anywhere to eat dinner?"

Haeli looked up at her father hopefully while she clung to Martyn's arm.

"I do believe that we do now." He laughed again and fell in next to Mr. Blaeith.

As they moved on toward the Blaeiths' house, Martyn and Haeli passed Lexi and Ella and walked a little way in front of them. Ella looked from Haeli to Martyn several times. It was quite a different picture of Martyn than the one she had seen with Kati. Now he seemed completely unreserved and informal. Gone were his civilities. Haeli leaned easily on his arm, asking him questions about how long he had been off the mountain, how his Sabbath was, and the like. Martyn answered all her questions gladly—not briskly, like he had Kati. He would laugh when Haeli made a joke, and now and then, he would tell her something confidentially.

Ella leaned closer to Lexi. "I think Cle'ans was wight about he'h and Ma'tyn."

Lexi gave a short laugh. "Clerans does no know hardly anything about Haeli. If he'll would get to cognize Haeli better, he'll would realize how childishly he treats her."

Ella gave her a sideways look. "She's awfully f'iendly with him."

"There is a merri more to them than that," Lexi replied. "Ye see, Haeli tained an older brother named Tomas. Tomas worked at the station Martyn works at now, an' if he'll were still here, I believe that he would be the same age as Martyn."

"What happened to Tomas?" Ella asked.

"He died in a logging accident," Lexi replied in a low tone. "That wos before we cognized the Blysffis well, shortly after they moved to this county. Martyn wos assigned to the station after Tomas, but the day after he left fer the station, his sister finally died."

"Ma'tyn had a siste'h?"

"Ay," Lexi said, "I ha' no told ye? She wos a sweet little girl, but merri frail. That wos about six years ago now. If she'll were alive today, I believe she would be about Haeli's age."

"I see," Ella said as she processed this new information.

"To the best o' my knowledge," Lexi continued, "neither o' them ever grieved fer their sibling's death. They replaced the other's loss, I think."

As Ella looked at Haeli and Martyn in this light, it seemed to fit. Haeli wasn't so coy and demanding of Martyn's attention as Kati had been, and neither did Martyn dote on her—as a suitor might have. For all the world, they interacted like siblings. Lexi's explanation made sense.

Just then, Ella thought she heard Mr. Blaeith say something about pirates. She strained her ear to listen but only heard Mr. Blysffi laugh and say something about an Admiral So-and-So.

"Do let that conversation wait until after dinner," Mrs. Blaeith insisted. "If ye'll do no, I'm afraid ye'll will lose interest in the moa fer all this talk o' war."

At that very moment, the party turned into the Blaeiths' street and were soon entering the merry little house.

# 18

## MOA FOR DINNER

*E*lla was slightly skeptical when Mrs. Blaeith pulled the huge moa leg from the oven. She still felt no better about it when all that Lexi could tell her was that it was from "a merri o' an bird." The leg, Ella guessed, was about four feet long and not unlike a gigantic turkey leg in shape. Once Mrs. Blaeith had garnished it with celery greens and placed the potatoes, carrots, and onions around it on the serving tray, it looked much more inviting—but Ella was still doubtful of how good the meat could be.

If it had been chicken, turkey, duck, or ptarmigan, she would have had no second thoughts. Yet even if she had seen a moa before, she would have been nervous—it was a strange, new food. But there wasn't anything for it; she wouldn't be such a terrible guest as to refuse the meal.

The Blaeiths, the Blysffis, and Aarushi gathered around the table, and Mr. Blaeith said grace. Then they all sat down, and Mrs. Blaeith served them. Even without the moa, it was a very full meal, with an egg soup, rich brown bread, roasted potatoes, a wonderful salad, and a cup of cooled stout to wash it down.

Ella took her first bite of moa slowly, ready to spit it unobtrusively onto her napkin if necessary. To her surprise and relief, the moa was actually palatable. She wasn't sure what to think of it until she was halfway through her serving, when she decided it wasn't much different from duck, though a little moister.

"Any news from yer fort?" asked Mr. Blaeith, sipping slowly at his stout.

"No, not really," Mr. Blysffi replied, "not that I have been off the mountain much longer than Martyn and Laendon. When did you leave, Martyn?"

"We ha' been down here fer two days now," Martyn replied between bites of moa.

"Ay, I have only been off that long myself," Mr. Blysffi said with a shrug. "There is not much to say. No gripping news, at least. I had to cut down my herd with the lay-offs."

"Really?" Mr. Blaeith asked. "I did no think we had laid off that many men."

Mr. Blysffi raised an eyebrow. "'We?' Come now, Henri. There's no need for you to associate yourself with those blood-sucking capitalists."

"I *do* work for them," Mr. Blaeith replied with a wry smile. "Besides, I do no see an inherent problem with a capitalistic economic system."

Stifyn Blysffi shook his head and clicked his tongue. "We must establish a holy society; and that means challenging every system that exploits one group of people for another group's benefit."

"But Stifyn," Martyn broke in, "ye cen no be so hard on the Company. Ye are a capitalist yerself, are ye no?"

Mr. Blysffi laughed heartily. "No, no, no. Are you *trying* to insult me? I do not grow wealthy by exploiting other people's labor. I work hard and benefit from my *own* work."

Martyn shrugged. "I s'pose if that is how ye'll will define things."

"Well?" Mr. Blysffi replied, still with a good-natured smile. "Is that *not* what the Company does? Exploit your labor to make the owners rich?"

Mr. Blaeith pursed his lips. "That is no entirely fair. They are providing a valuable service."

Mr. Blysffi shrugged, laughing at this last comment. "It is no wonder everyone is striking. You just better hope they do not start striking here in Entwerp. Then you will have to think about this seriously and not just jest with me about it."

Mrs. Blaeith shook his head. "Ye brought it up, Stifyn."

"Ay," Mr. Blaeith added with a smile. "If I did no know better, I'll would think ye tained a grudge against the Company or something."

Mr. Blysffi laughed his deep, contagious laugh.

"And how is Sir Saemwel doing?" Mr. Blaeith asked.

"About the same as usual, although I do think he may have another fit again soon. His wound seems to be troubling him more lately. Olyfia and Elsi do their best for him, you know, but still... I can not help but think that he will get worse. He has been through so much."

Ella leaned over to Lexi. "Is that Elsi's fathe' they'h talking about, Si'h Picke'ing?"

"Ay," Lexi replied.

"How was he wounded?"

"How wos he wounded?" Clerans asked loudly, looking up from the potato he was cutting.

"That's what I asked," Ella replied, a little unsure how Clerans had heard her.

"Well, then," Clerans winked, "I will *tell* ye."

"Now, Clerans," Mrs. Blaeith said, "do no be dramatizin' it too merri, dear."

"Oh, I will no dramatize it *too* merri," Clerans winked again, "but here is how it happened."

Clerans waited until he was certain everyone was listening and then began in a low voice.

"It wos at the Battle o' Ard-Melwyn, an' the Hrufangi had held up fer three hours straight against the bombardment o' Captain Wilkins. The cannons were firin', keepin' up a terrific fusillade o' shots. Charges were fallin' every which way, plowing up the ground, and blowing people all to bits."

"Clerans," Mrs. Blaeith broke in. "That's too graphic, no while we're eating."

Clerans nodded. "Anyway, it was all just one tremendous, ear-shattering cacophony o' noise. The enemy did no know where our army wos (because o' the thick fog), an' they were shootin' willy-nilly all over the prairie (an' makin' a merri mess o' things, I may say). Then Captain Wilkins gave the signal to charge, an' away our army flew, like Aarushi when she sees her prey."

The Harrier whistled softly at this and continued pecking at the moa.

"Well, now," Clerans continued, "when the Hrufangi saw us venin', they were right sure to pose their cannons to their proper place an' fire on us, but they did no tain much time a'fore we ran into their ranks. Oh, it was a jolly sight, that charge..."

"But how do you know, Clerans?" Haeli asked.

"What?" Clerans turned, apparently not pleased with the interruption.

"But how do you know?"

"Know what?"

"That it was a 'jolly sight'?" Haeli asked.

"That is no important," Clerans replied with a dismissive wave of his hand. "Maybe it wos a jolly sight, an' maybe it wos no, but be that as it may, it was merri terrific—*merri terrific*.

"Now, Sir Pickering—he wos *Mr.* Pickering at the time—wos

in rank with Sheriff Laei (near about four ranks in). Ye ha' seen Sheriff Laei ha' ye no?"

Ella shook her head. "No, I don't think so."

Clerans bit his lip. "Well, the story would ha' been better if ye'll ha' seen him (him and his arm), but there is no help fer it now.

"Well, as Sir Pickering an' Sheriff Laei were chargin', what should vene at them than one o' the Hrufangi explodin' shells? Well, it hit right in front o' them and exploded (like it was supposed to) and sent Sir Pickering flyin' back. The bomb had gone off nearly between his legs, an' some o' the metal had blown into him, an' pierced a hole in his lung."

"Clerans," Martyn said, "ye better no get too carried away with yer descriptions."

"I am no, *yet*, now do no interrupt," Clerans replied. "So then, Sheriff Laei saw what had happened, an' he was no hurt much himself. (Sir Pickering had ceived most o' the blow, see.) Well, Sheriff Laei stopped and lieved up Sir Pickering to carry him back to the camp. But before he could get very far, a Hrufangi soldier vened at them, a terribly bad gnome (pardon me, Lexi), and he thrust at them with his bayonet."

Clerans paused for dramatic effect. "Well now, Sheriff Laei verts himself, so that the bayonet would miss Sir Pickering, and instead, the Hrufangi thrust it all the way through Sheriff Laei's arm."

"Clerans," Mrs. Blaeith chided.

Clerans pretended not to hear. "Sheriff Laei voked a roar that would ha' lieved the dead an' broke the bayonet off from the musket (an' it still hung in his arm)."

Mrs. Blaeith cleared her throat.

"Then," Clerans went on, "Sir Pickering lashed out with his hand and broke the enemy's neck, an' that wos the last o' his strength, so he swooned then an' there in the Sheriff's arms."

"That is no how it happened," Martyn said.

"Ay, it is," Clerans replied. "The straight-up truth and nothin' else. I got it directly from Sheriff Laei myself."

"No," Martyn said, "that was anythin' *but* the straight-up truth."

Mr. Blysffi laughed heartily. "I am afraid it was embellished. I have heard Sir Saemwel tell it many times, and I think Mr. Silas was involved heavily in his rescue."

Ella perked up at the name 'Silas.' That had been her father's name.

"But (meaning no disrespect to Sir Pickering)," Clerans said, "he is far too modest to give himself the full credit fer his actions. *I* heard it from Sheriff Laei."

"And when wos this?" Martyn asked.

"Last time I wos barrel-monkey in the battery," Clerans said. "Ye remember when the last pirates were here? I cen quire Sheriff Laei about the details when I'll serve as barrel-monkey next time."

"Which might be merri soon," Haeli added.

"Oh, please do no talk about it," Mrs. Blaeith said.

"If you'll do not mind, Fawn," Mr. Blysffi replied, "I may say that Admiral Sudhrlaend, with two other frigates, is on his way to destroy the pirates. So, Clerans, you may not have to serve as barrel-monkey after all."

Ella squirmed in her seat. Any talk about the pirates made her uncomfortable. She remembered what Killjelly had done to Jock during those long, terrible nights. Those needles were still the things of her nightmares. She remembered how they had cut her, and how Cweel had interrogated her. She shuddered.

Suddenly, Lexi stood up. "Mr. Blaeith, I think I oughtta-should be collectin' the eggs. Ella, do you want to vene with me?"

"I would be glad to," Ella replied.

"Can I come, too?" Haeli asked as she jumped up from the table.

"If ye'll want to," Lexi shrugged, walking down the back hall with Ella and Haeli close behind.

They walked to the door at the very end of the hall, where Lexi slipped on a pair of boots. Ella looked around for another pair, but didn't see any.

"Is the'e…" Ella began, a little flustered.

Haeli laughed. "I'll go barefoot if you do."

Haeli took Ella by the arm and followed Lexi out the door.

The sun was just beginning to droop towards the mountains, but it was still pretty warm. Ella could see some clouds rolling in from the sea—it would probably rain soon. The dirt yard was small, with only a few sprigs of grass, and a barn at the far end. Sprouting from this barn, a wire cage covered half the yard where a few chickens hopped about lazily. It was towards this barn that Lexi was walking.

"Can I say something to you, Ella?" Haeli asked.

Ella looked over at Haeli uncertainly. "I suppose so."

Haeli sighed. "I get the idea that you have been through a lot of unpleasant situations, and you are a long way from home, but I am glad you are here right now. I do not know you merri well, but I like you."

"Thank you, Haeli, you'he so kind."

Haeli looked over at her. "What did you say?"

"I said, you'he so kind." Ella blushed when she realized what Haeli was doing. She was making fun of her missing *r*. Ella tried to draw back a little.

Haeli just kept looking at her, her face brightening. "You speak beautifully," she said. "I would have called that a lisp before I heard you say it, but it is beautiful."

Ella's blush deepened as she squeezed Haeli's arm. "Thank you, Haeli."

"Has no one told you that before?" Haeli asked sincerely.

Ella shook her head. "You'he the fi'st."

Just then, Lexi reached the barn and entered. Ella and Haeli came in behind.

"Here, Ella and Haeli," Lexi said as she handed them a basket each. "There are usually a few dozen eggs in there." So saying, she opened the door to the chicken coop.

The three girls entered and began investigating the hay and nesting boxes for eggs, placing them gently in their baskets.

"How long are you planning on staying?" Haeli asked.

Ella was at a bit of a loss for words. Should she tell Haeli what she *planned*?

"Eventually," Ella finally said, "I would like to get back to my home—ac'oss the sea in Slyzwi'h."

"Well," Lexi replied, "Ye cen no leave now or before winter is over. I do no ween any ship would risk crossin' back to Kelmar at this time o' year. The wind is all the wrong way. Ye cen sail from Kelmar to here easily enough, but until the wind changes in the spring, no even the postal ships will risk a crossin' against the wind."

"How long is that?" Ella asked.

"Oh, five months—six months if the weather is bad."

Ella thought for a long time. Six months. That should be enough time to find the Gwambi Treasure—if the pirates stayed away.

Haeli looked at Ella closely. "You are thinking hard. Do you miss Slyzwir badly, then?"

Ella wasn't sure how to answer that. "Well, yes... but..." she hesitated. "I may as well tell you; I t'ust you, and I may need you'h help."

Haeli's eyes brightened till they almost glowed, and Lexi looked hard at Ella.

"What do ye mean?" Lexi asked.

"I know why the pi'ates came he'e, and it's not just about the wa'ehouses o'h the National Banks. They'h afte'h the Gwambi t'easu'e."

Lexi laughed merrily. "Well, they will tain a hard time with that!"

"I want to find it befo'e them," Ella said.

Lexi stopped laughing and looked at Ella closely. "Ye know hundreds o' people ha' garded fer that treasure an' cen no trive it out. A lot o' them die tryin'. Most folks think it does no exist."

"I do not know about that," Haeli said.

Lexi turned and looked at her.

"I might could help you, Ella," Haeli continued, "but first, tell me why you want to find the treasure."

Ella took a deep breath. In her head, the reasons were crystal-clear, but when she tried to verbalize them, they grew vague.

"Well, you see... I have to, because..." she paused. "The pi'ates won't leave until they find the t'easu'e, and they might just dest'oy this whole town befo'e they give up."

"I do no think that likely," Lexi said. "We ha' tained plenty o' pirates try to attack this village in her day, but we ha' repelled them all, eventually."

"Did any of the othe'hs have a G'iffin?" Ella asked.

"No to the best o' my knowledge," Lexi replied.

"The pi'ates have a captive with them," Ella continued, "and they won't give him up fo'h anything but the Gwambi t'easu'e. If I can find it fi'st, then we can ba'gain fo'h him. Besides, I can keep some back to pay fo'h my wetu'n voyage to Slyzwi'h."

"Oh, Ella, ye need no worry about that!" Lexi cried. "We will be sure that ye make it back to yer home. If ye jist found a job fer the next five months, ye'd make more than enough to pay fer the voyage. Ye need no bother with trivin' the Gwambi treasure to pay fer it."

"But what about Jock?" Ella asked. "I can't be su'e I can f'ee him unless I find the t'easu'e. Besides," Ella paused, and swallowed hard before continuing. "My Papa died looking fo'h that t'easu'e. I have to find it. It's what he would have wanted."

Haeli smiled. "I think those are good reasons, Ella. I will help you."

Lexi shook her head. "Llifsa! We outta-should be gardin' fer eggs."

They finished scouring the coop in silence and then returned to the house. Just before they reached the back door, Lexi took Ella's arm.

"I will help ye, too, Ella—I will do anythin' I cen to help—but I do no want ye to get yer hopes up. Like I said, many people ha' tried to trive that treasure, and none ha' trived it yet. It might no even exist."

"Thank you, Lexi," Ella replied, "but I have to look fo'h it."

"Then I will help ye," Lexi said.

With that, all three of them marched into the house.

# 19

# EAVESDROPPING

*E*rnest couldn't sleep. Somehow, all the rest of the pirates were sleeping through the noise, but he couldn't. There it was again, a deep moan and muffled yell drifting across the waters from the other ship. Ernest shivered. He knew who made that noise. It was Jock. Longfinch had been at him all night. All night he had heard Jock groaning. Maybe it was just his sensitive gnome ears, and no one else could hear Jock's torture. Then again, none of the other gnomes seemed bothered by the sound.

Ernest swung idly in his hammock. It would be several hours yet until dawn. He suddenly realized that he was hearing voices. Now that he thought about it, he was fairly certain he had been hearing the voices for quite some time; why he hadn't registered them until now, he didn't know. He opened his eyes and noticed a dim light coming from the galley.

Silently, he rolled out of his hammock and walked over to the galley. As he peered around the corner, he could see Lewis seated on a stool with a tankard in hand, talking earnestly with Killjelly. Killjelly was grim but had a strange light in his eye, like that of a fox or a hunting cat. They were both talking in very low voices, and it seemed obvious to Ernest that they did *not* want to be overheard. This only made Ernest more interested in overhearing them.

Unfortunately, just as his head peeked around the corner, Lewis caught his eye and clicked his tongue. Killjelly stopped talking immediately, turning to see who had interrupted them.

Ernest strode into the galley, trying to look as much as possible like he hadn't been trying to eavesdrop. "Good morning to you, mates. I do'edn't hear a word you were saying, so you can just keep on talking like I amn't here. I think I'll get myself some beer."

Ernest walked over to the barrel of ale, but he could feel two pairs of eyes on him.

"How did you know we were here?" Killjelly asked in a low voice.

Ernest shrugged. "I do'edn't; I just happened to be awake and was thirsty, you know?"

"You heared us," Killjelly hissed.

Ernest quietly filled a cup with beer.

"Helen Maria, Ernest," Lewis said, "do'ed you hear anything we sayed?"

"Only something about a hmnhomn, and a whmninm," Ernest replied, trying his best to imitate their muttering.

Lewis laughed lightly.

"You're lying, sure," Killjelly said flatly.

Ernest shrugged again. "By prelates, I amn't." He took a drink of beer, satisfied to see Lewis grinning at his righteous cussing.

Lewis leaned over to Killjelly and spoke in a low voice, but loud enough for Ernest to hear what he said. "There's no harm in him knowing. He'll have to know sooner or later."

Killjelly looked at Ernest doubtfully. "Later; it will have to be later, sure." With that, the leprechaun stood. "Remember what I told you—remember."

As Killjelly stood, Ernest noticed a small amulet around the leprechaun's neck. The amulet bore the symbol of a circle inside an upside-down triangle. Now that Ernest thought about it, he had seen Killjelly wearing this amulet many times before—but hadn't he seen that amulet somewhere else?

Lewis interrupted Ernest's thoughts, saying, "I don't think I could forget it. Blind prelates! Do you really think I'd forget with so much at stake?"

Killjelly nodded, apparently satisfied, and walked up to the upper deck.

Ernest took another swig of beer and sat down opposite Lewis at the bar. "What was all that about?"

Lewis grinned. "Some secrets are better not tampered with." He stood up, drew a cup of beer, and sat down again. But Ernest could see that Lewis' hands were shaking. Underneath that enormous smile, there was something deeply disturbing Lewis.

"What were ye talking about?"

Lewis drummed his fingers idly on the bar. Finally, he said, "Ernest, do you believe in God?"

Ernest was a bit taken aback. "Well, um... I believe there's a god on some kind... I suppose..."

"Do you believe in *the God*, though?" Lewis asked as he pulled a little black book from his pocket and placed it on the bar.

Ernest thought deeply for several minutes. "Honestly?"

"Honestly." Lewis replied, and there was a hint of desperation in his voice.

"Well," Ernest scratched his head. "I can't see as it makes any difference to me if'n there is a god or isn't, but you've always been a good friend to me, and if'n you're interested in it, I'll give you a serious answer."

Ernest took a swig of his beer and thought for a moment. "When I was a little boy, this magician frequented our market square. He used to make peas disappear and then reappear from underneath shells. That man claimed there was a god."

Lewis pursed his lips. "Not much on a recommendation, seeing as he was probably cheating everyone who bet against him."

Ernest grinned. "That's true, but they still bet anyway. Then there were the monks. They teached me who to read and write. They believed in *the* God."

Here Ernest paused. Thinking of the supernatural made him think of the Albino, and the memory sent shivers down his spine. That man definitely had supernatural powers. He was surely in contact with spirits, and powerful spirits at that.

After a moment, Ernest sighed. "So I suppose there's probably something out there, but whether it's *a* god, or *the* god, or a man, or a woman, or good, or evil, I don't know. I don't know that we could ever know."

Lewis shook his head and tapped his fingers on his black book. "Oh no, no. We *can* know. God is good. God is all-powerful, and He cares about all of those He maked."

Ernest let out a short, sarcastic laugh. "Lewis, you can't be serious. You don't really believe that."

Lewis nodded firmly. "No. I do. I do believe that."

Ernest laughed again. "You say that your god is good?"

"Yes," Lewis said, and he drank some more beer.

"And he hates evil?"

Lewis nodded.

"And is he powerful?"

"All-powerful," Lewis clarified.

"But not powerful enough to destroy the evil that he hates?"

Lewis licked his lips. "You've been planning that for a while, haven't you?"

"No," Ernest replied, "I just thinked on it now."

Lewis laughed. "Well, well, well, give yourself some unction for your deep theological question, boyo!"

Lewis left his drink on the bar and stirred up the fire. Satisfied, he pulled out his big pot and put it on the stove. He didn't look back at Ernest, but he took a deep breath.

"Well, Ernest, I will be honest with you. I've never really looked for the answer to that question. But–" here he lifted his book, "the answer would be in here."

"But you don't have the answer?" Ernest asked.

Lewis thought for a very long time. After several minutes, he sighed. "Not right now, I'm afraid."

Ernest shrugged and gulped the rest of his beer.

"I'll find the answer, by prelates," Lewis said, though he seemed to be speaking more to himself than Ernest. "That I promise you, Ernest boyo; I'll find the answer for you, since you seem to care so deeply about it."

Ernest fought back another laugh. "Honestly, Lewis, I don't care."

Lewis stared at Ernest pensively. "But you asked, boyo."

Ernest looked back at his messmate for several minutes. "I don't think this is about me, Lewis. It seems to me that this is about you."

Just then, Killjelly came tramping down the stairs. Ernest perked up hopefully, but tried to cover his eagerness by taking a sip from his now-empty tankard. Unfortunately, Killjelly said nothing at all about his private conversation with Lewis.

"Surprise visitors. Captain wants a tray on scones, enough for four, maybe some cheese, too." Killjelly nodded briskly and trooped back on deck.

Lewis burst into action. He pulled out a large, circular tray and filled it with various foods he pulled from the larder. First, he piled a dozen scones in the middle, then he set a few large chunks of cheese around these. After he put several slabs of salt-pork on the side, he stepped back and scrutinized his work.

"No, no, no, it needs a little more..."

He hollowed out a nest in the middle of the scones and put a cup of lard there, with a few dull knives placed conveniently nearby. He finished these preparations by taking a handful of a spice and sprinkling it lightly over the top of the tray.

"That should do it, by prelates! There now, Ernest, take that to Captain Holgard and stay up there to wait on him."

Ernest took the tray and trudged up to the deck without a second look at Lewis.

# 20

# PIRATE COUNCIL

*I*t was a little eerie out on deck at this hour. Fog completely covered the deck, illuminated here and there by a hanging lamp. The fog was not very thick, but thick enough to make Ernest's path difficult, particularly in the dark light. Just to the east, Ernest could see the faintest hint of dawn, but other than that, it could have been midnight. Ernest passed a lone sentry as he made his way aft. It was the gnome, Bill.

"Some weather, this," Bill whispered, "it makes my job a joke, baptize it!"

"Who's the guests?" Ernest asked.

"Longfinch and that other one, Vania Bloodrummer." Bill pointed to a shadowy figure by the gunwale. "They only bringed one aide with them. He hasn't said anything since they comed; he just stands there." Bill lowered his voice to a whisper, still looking at the shadowy form of the aide. "He's bothering me."

Ernest shrugged at this observation and made his way to Holgard's cabin door. Here he stopped and (balancing the tray deftly on one hand) rapped on the door. "Scones, sir."

Holgard answered from the other side, "You may enter."

*Cweel*

Ernest opened the door and stepped into the lighted room. Around Holgard's huge table sat four other pirates. Next to Holgard was Killjelly, and opposite were Longfinch, Vania, and Cweel. They were in conversation as Ernest entered, so he padded forward and put the tray in the middle of the table. No one paid any heed to him, but Holgard took a large scone as he listened to Longfinch.

"Cweel says they could be here as soon as tomorrow evening, so we should be on our guard. We should strike before then."

"But we don't have any information from Jock," Holgard said.

Longfinch smiled patronizingly. "That's true, but we can't simply sit here and risk the Company and the Llaedhwythi government sending every privateer they have at us."

Holgard snorted, taking a huge bite of scone and quaffing it down with some ale. Longfinch leaned forward to take a scone and a piece of cheese. He then glanced up at Ernest. Ernest tried not to meet the elf's gaze.

"Cook?"

Ernest shook his head, "Cook's-mate, sir."

Longfinch touched the cheese to the end of his tapir-like nose before eating it and turning back to Holgard. Vania Blood-rummer now turned and stared at Ernest. Again, Ernest declined to make eye contact, looking straight ahead.

"What I'm saying," Longfinch said, "is that we should pretend we're only here to make a raid on the warehouses."

Killjelly thought this through briefly. "You mean, we raid them tomorrow before the privateers get here, and then we leave?"

"Which is! We pretend to leave, whatever," Vania said, finally turning away from Ernest and picking up a piece of salt-pork.

"Correct," Longfinch replied. "We would only wait in a

secluded harbor until Jock speaks or Cweel finds the girl. Then we strike again when we have more information."

"Suppose the privateers find us in that secluded harbor," Holgard asked. "Then we're just as bad off as if'n we had stayed here."

Vania laughed sarcastically, but Longfinch replied patiently, "Here we're out in the open. It's better to hide and risk being attacked in water that favors us, than to wait here where the privateers will certainly attack us in water that only favors them —when they have the battery to back them up."

Holgard snorted. "What about Pennywraith? When's he supposed to get here?"

Vania shook his head and murmured something under his breath.

Longfinch smiled cordially. "Pennywraith willn't be here for a week or two yet. Besides, his advantage is surprise. To use him and his crew as cheap reinforcements would defeat his purpose."

Holgard drummed his fingers on the table. "Weel, that makes some sense, but..."

"And we would attack tomorrow, sure?" Killjelly broke in.

"This evening," Longfinch replied.

Vania gave Ernest his tankard. "Which is, get me something good to drink, whatever."

Ernest took the cup confidently but turned hesitantly to the barrels of ale by the desk.

"*Beer*," Cweel hissed at him.

"Right," he mumbled, filling the tankard with whiskey instead. He didn't like the way Cweel had snapped at him, and he guessed that Vania wouldn't mind.

"As soon as we're through," Longfinch continued, "we'll leave this bay and travel south."

Holgard jumped slightly. "But do'edn't you say the privateers were coming *from* the south?"

"Yes, *I* did," Cweel replied.

"Exactly," Longfinch said. "That's not what they expect on us. We will put out our lanterns as soon as we leave the bay and—with Cweel's help—pass them in the dark."

Holgard snorted, drumming his fingers on the table more forcefully. Longfinch took a bite of scone as he leaned back and looked at Holgard.

Ernest handed Vania the whiskey. The swordsman smelled the drink first, then, with a shrug, downed the whole pint in one go. He set the tankard lightly on the table and nibbled at his salt-pork. Ernest backed up a little, trying his best to look helpful and capable.

Holgard snorted again, and since he didn't seem about to say anything, Killjelly turned to Cweel. "Have you made any progress with finding the girl?"

Cweel gave a low hiss. "*No.*"

"How thoroughly have you checked the mountains?"

Cweel growled. "*Thoroughly.*"

"But you haven't finded her, sure?"

Cweel stood up with his hind legs on the barrel and his front talons on the table, peering angrily at Killjelly.

"*I* think *she* has found the village."

"Have you looked there?" Killjelly asked.

"Do *you* want *me* to frighten *everyone* in the village?"

Vania laughed, "Which is! We're already doing a good job on that, whatever."

"We need to find her, sure," Killjelly stated.

"That is true," Longfinch said. "Cweel, you should probably start looking in the village now, but start from a good height."

"Why not just go over in a low scan?" Holgard asked. He seemed in a mood to quarrel over trivialities.

"There is no need to let them know we have a Griffin," Longfinch replied.

"But the girl already knows," Holgard said.

Longfinch shrugged. "Assuming she's there or has telled anyone."

Holgard snorted and resumed the drumming.

Longfinch turned to Ernest then and passed his tankard with a good-natured smile. "Could you pour me something light —beer, maybe?"

Ernest nodded, "Ay, sir."

He took the tankard and quickly filled it.

"Thank you, Mr. Cook's-mate," Longfinch said with another smile as he received it back.

Ernest nodded and stepped back again.

Longfinch sipped his beer slowly as he looked at Holgard. Vania took a scone and ate it daintily. Killjelly stuck his hook into the table absent-mindedly. Finally, Longfinch broke the silence.

"Do you have any further objections?"

Holgard still drummed his fingers on the table. "It seems a little short notice."

Vania laughed.

"Can your crew not be ready to fight in twelve hours?" Longfinch asked with a slight smile.

"No, it's not that..." Holgard trailed off and kept drumming.

"Good," Longfinch said, standing. "It's settled then—we will do it. You will attack the southern end; try to mount the dike. I will engage the battery at the docks."

With these brisk orders, Longfinch left the room with Vania Bloodrummer and Cweel following behind him. Killjelly and Holgard remained seated as they left. Ernest shifted his weight, unsure if he should clear the tray, stay a while longer, or just leave. The captain and boatswain ignored him.

Finally, Holgard spoke. "Tonight... the Albino willn't be back by then."

Ernest shivered at the mention of the man.

"He might, sure," Killjelly replied.

"Might," Holgard snorted, "but willn't. And if'n we attack the village with him in it..."

"He will take care of himself," Killjelly broke in.

"But if'n we leave here and hide in a secluded harbor, how will he tell us what he's finded? And there's no point bringing him back on deck now before he's satisfied himself with what he's finded."

"He will find us, sure," Killjelly said.

Holgard sat a long while yet. "Baptize those privateers! Baptize them all!" Suddenly, the dwarf captain looked up at Ernest. "You're still here? Weel, clear that tray and get us some real breakfast. Quickly now."

Ernest obeyed and swept out of the room. As he marched across the deck, he came to Bill again. The gnome was playing with a large coin in his hand.

Ernest nodded at him, "Bill."

Bill nodded back and flipped the coin, "You know, that Longfinch isn't half bad, really, not half bad at all."

Ernest shrugged and walked towards the stairs to the galley. As he reached them, he saw Longfinch climbing over the side of the gunwale into his boat. As he leaned over, the lantern light glanced off something around his neck. Ernest looked closer. Longfinch was wearing a small amulet which bore a symbol that appeared to be in the shape of a circle inside an upside-down triangle. Ernest caught his breath in surprise. He knew exactly where he had seen that before—Killjelly and the Albino both wore the same amulet. Where did they all get amulets like that? What did that symbol mean?

Longfinch smiled at him. "Good to see you, Mr. Cook's-mate. Give my compliments to the cook." He smiled again and disappeared over the side.

Just then, Holgard burst out of his cabin. "Who's the guard on duty!" he bellowed.

"Me, sir," Bill replied.

"Get the quartermaster. It's time to wake the crew! I want this ship perfectly clean and all the barnacles off the hull by this afternoon. Now don't just stand there—go get the quartermaster!"

Ernest walked slowly down to the galley. Maybe Bill was right; Longfinch wasn't that bad after all.

# 21

# A CARRIAGE RIDE

*B*reakfast was quite different the next day. Ella came out to find that Martyn and Laendon had not yet come out of their room.

"They will do that," Lexi explained. "It is their last day off work."

Mr. and Mrs. Blaeith apparently didn't have the day off. The family, sans Martyn and Laendon, breakfasted before Mr. Blaeith left. For most of breakfast, Mr. Blaeith was rather quiet and pensive. Clerans, on the other hand, seemed to want a lively conversation that morning.

"This porridge tastes better this mornin'; did ye do anythin' different with it, Ma?"

There was no response.

Clerans cleared his throat and twirled his spoon with his fingers. "Ma, did ye do anythin' different to the porridge this mornin'?"

Still no reply.

Ella looked over at Clerans sympathetically. Clerans caught the glance and winked at her. "Da, is there any news about the pirates?"

"Please, Clerans," Mrs. Blaeith said.

Mr. Blaeith grimaced, but tried to smile. "I am afraid there is a merri more than pirates."

Clerans sat forward in his seat. "Oh, really?"

However, Mr. Blaeith did not elaborate. Instead he cleared his throat. "Miss Ella," then he paused.

Clerans shifted positions impatiently.

"Do continue, Mr. Blaeith," Lexi said. "I am afraid that ye'll might drive poor Clerans insane if he'll ha' to wait another second to listen to another human voice."

Mr. Blaeith laughed. "Well then, Miss Ella, when Mr. Blysffi wos here yesterday, he tained an interesting proposition about ye." Mr. Blaeith cleared his throat again. "Ye see, they are stayin' at Sir Saemwel's house, an' as ye might ha' heard, Sir Saemwel is in a bit o' an bad way recently. Well, he only tains one maid, and Stifyn says he is gardin' fer another."

Mr. Blaeith paused again. "Sir Saemwel tains a merri o' an house, an' ye would tain a merri o' more privacy there than here. Now, our house is open to ye always, but I am afraid we cen no do much in the way o' gettin' ye to yer home in Slyzwir. However, Sir Saemwel would pay ye fer yer work—and no cheaply, either—which would be a merri help fer yer return voyage to Kelmar." Mr. Blaeith licked his lips.

Mrs. Blaeith quickly broke in. "An' ye do no need to feel pressure to accept a job with Sir Saemwel, if ye do no want to. We cen always help ye trive out a different job if ye'll prefer. I could ask around at the factory, or I'm sure someone else would take ye if ye like. We only want to help ye to get ye in the best place fer ye."

Lexi looked earnestly at Ella. "Sir Saemwel would pay ye merri well, Ella; ye could easily earn the money to fiscate passage in the spring."

Ella thought about this for a little. Before her mind's eye, Jock appeared. He was bleeding and bruised as he had been after the pirates' interrogations. Her earning some money would mean nothing to the pirates—only the Gwambi Treasure would have bargaining power with Killjelly and Holgard. Still, this seemed to be a very prudent thing to do in her situation.

"It sounds like a ve'y good offe'h to me," Ella finally said. "I am thankful that Mr. Blysffi thought of me fo'h it. I would only be too happy to accept."

Mr. Blaeith nodded. "Good. I'll will tell Stifyn then, and he'll will vene by later this afternoon to duce ye there."

So that was that.

---

It rained for most of the day. About an hour after Mr. Blaeith left for his work, Mrs. Blaeith headed out for the factory herself. This left Ella to her own devices with Lexi and the younger Blaeith boys. Most of the time, she helped with inside chores—sweeping floors, washing dishes, scrubbing the stove and the like.

When this was done, Lexi told her to stop cleaning and read for a bit. This was quite to Ella's liking. She perused the Blaeith's bookshelf, and to her astonishment, discovered a familiar title, *A Proposition Concerning the Gwambi* by Adicus Johnston. Her father had poured over that book for hours and filled it with hundreds of notes. Her mother said that was the book that drove him to search for the Gwambi Treasure—and never return. That book was the only book in her father's library that her mother forbade her to read. Only once had she been naughty enough to open it, and her mother had spanked her soundly for it.

Now, here she was, looking for the Gwambi Treasure herself; wouldn't it be helpful to read that book? Her mother wouldn't mind, would she? And besides, this wasn't her *father's* book. It was a different copy of the same book. She reached out, her hands trembling as she touched the binding. No, she couldn't do it. She couldn't read that book after her mother had so strictly banned it. So she sat down on a chair with a book on botany instead. She read this until Lexi needed help making dinner.

Soon after Ella cleaned up dinner, there was a knock on the door. It was Mr. Blysffi and Haeli.

Haeli greeted Ella and kissed her enthusiastically. "I am so glad you are coming up to the manor. You will just love it there, and you will have to meet Olyfia—you will have to."

Mr. Blysffi laughed heartily, so heartily that everyone else laughed—including Laendon, who by no means could have heard Haeli, as his nose and spectacles were buried in a book.

"Well now, Miss Ella, I certainly hope you did not bring much luggage? I do not tain a cart, see." Mr. Blysffi grinned.

"I do believe that all the luggage I eve'h had is back at Slyzwi'h," Ella replied, with a bit of a smile herself.

"Now, Ella," Lexi responded, "do no go thinkin' that we'll would send ye off with no necessities."

Ducking down the back hallway, Lexi reappeared with a large bag under her arm. "Here ye go, Ella. Jist some essentials." She handed Ella the bag. "Combs, ribbons, hem-bobs, an' other things. Oh, also, there is the blade ye posed on the dresser." Lexi winked.

Ella took the bag hesitantly. "Lexi, I can't take this stuff f'om you. Weally, I'm su'e I'll manage."

Lexi clicked her tongue at Ella, "Now, now, they are *yers* now, an' so I am *sure* ye will manage."

Ella took the bag.

"Well, that is not too much to carry on foot," Mr. Blysffi said. "You are a component walker, I hope? It's about three miles."

"Oh, yes," Ella replied.

"Regardless," Martyn said from the chair where he was sitting and stroking Aarushi. "I cen pull out the carriage and drive ye over there in no time. Laendon will entertain ye while ye wait."

Laendon looked up from his book in surprise. "Did someone jist say my name?"

Mr. Blysffi burst into his contagious laugh, and Martyn stepped briskly out the door.

In a few minutes, Martyn was ready with what he so generously called a 'carriage'—little more than a flat-bedded wagon, though there were some straw-stuffed sacks in the back to use as seats. Ella said her goodbyes to Lexi and the younger Blaeith boys, climbed aboard, and then they were off, trotting a quick pace through the village in the kirk's direction. Ella and Haeli sat in the back of the carriage while Mr. Blysffi and Martyn sat up front. Martyn was driving—of course—and Aarushi sat on his shoulder, now and then flying into the sky for a few minutes before returning to her perch.

"So, Ella," Haeli said, "What do you think is most different about Entwerp from Slyzwir?"

Ella hardly had to think. Two things were alarmingly different, but she was not about to mention the stocking issue in mixed company, so she said, "The kissing."

"What?"

"The kissing," Ella repeated. "In Slyzwi'h we neve'h g'eet people with a kiss."

"You do not?" Haeli's eyes grew wide.

"No, we don't."

"How do you greet each other, then?" Haeli asked.

"With a handshake," Ella replied, "sometimes a hug, but neve'h a kiss—unless you'he ma'ied."

Haeli furrowed her brow. "That is weird."

Ella felt a little slighted. "I could just as easily say that Entwe'p is wei'd, but it's not wei'd; it's just diffe'ent. You know, it's just a diffe'ent cultu'e; it's not like eithe'h one is wrong."

"I do not know," Mr. Blysffi said.

Ella looked up at him. "What do you mean?"

Martyn spoke up. "Ye know that God says in the Scriptures to 'greet one another with a holy kiss,' do no ye?"

"Well, yes," Ella replied, "but isn't that just a cultu'al command? He's not weally saying that someone f'om a non-kissing cultu'e should sta't kissing eve'yone they meet, is He?"

"Maybe God is telling us what a culture should be like," Mr. Blysffi said.

"Ay," Martyn added. "Surely the God who cares about people would care about their culture."

Ella was silent. She remembered how Mrs. Blaeith had responded similarly to Ella's question about the matrilineal surnames. There was something about this village, something about these people, that they seemed to have a scriptural basis for even these small cultural oddities.

At that moment, there was a cry just in front of the carriage.

"Martyn! Martyn Blaeith! How good to see ye out today."

Ella peered ahead to see the figure of Kati Fflemins—the tailor's daughter—coming down the street towards them with a bundle in her arms. Ella could have sworn that Martyn let out his breath slowly when he saw her.

Martyn reined in the horse slowly. "Hello, Kati; God bless ye."

"Well, imagine that I would jist happen to run into ye today of all days."

Martyn smiled civilly.

"See," Kati said, holding up her package, "I wos cedin' to yer house, anyway."

Martyn took the package. "What is this?"

"It is the suit that Lexi ordered fer your guest." She looked over at Ella. "Ella Donne, right?"

Ella nodded.

Martyn handed her the bundle. "Well, here ye are, Miss Ella, an' in perfect time."

Ella took the bundle with a nod of thanks. Trying her best to be inconspicuous, Ella checked to be sure that there were stockings for her in this bundle of clothing. Yes, Ella breathed a sigh of relief. Two stockings were folded up neatly in the middle of the bundle of clothing.

"Oh, really?" Kati asked, beaming up at Martyn.

Martyn nodded civilly. "Ay, Miss Ella is movin' in with the Pickerings fer to be their maid."

"Oh, ye will like the Pickerings. Elsi is *such* a sweetheart."

Martyn lifted the reins prominently. "Well, Miss Kati, I am afraid that we will ha' to be movin' on now..."

"Yer headed to the other side o' town?" Kati asked.

"Ay," Martyn replied.

"Do ye think ye'll could drop me off over by the kirk? It would save me from walkin' all that way."

Martyn smiled shallowly. "Ay, I think we'll could do that."

Kati offered her hand, and Martyn helped her into the carriage. The bench up front was only built for two people, but Kati sat down there anyway—next to Martyn. She was slim enough to fit just between Mr. Blysffi and Martyn, but Martyn appeared extremely uncomfortable all the same.

Aarushi looked at Kati disdainfully. As Martyn drove on, Aarushi jumped onto Martyn's tri-cornered hat and looked down at Kati's neat straw hat. She whistled sharply and then flapped into the air. Soon, she dropped back down to the wagon and perched on the floorboard by Kati's feet.

"Oh, Martyn, which o' yer birds is this one?"

"I only tain one now," Martyn replied.

"Well, which one is this? I always get them mixed up; they are so similar, ye know."

Aarushi let out a little cackle and flapped off again, striking Kati's hat with her wing as she did so. Kati caught her hat before it fell off and gave a little laugh.

"Well, Martyn, I think ye need to train him a little better."

Martyn cleared his throat slowly. "*She* is the mute one."

"Oh," Kati replied, "Squishy—wos that her name?"

Haeli broke in, "Here, *Aarushi*, you can perch with me and Ella. I would be merri glad for your company."

Aarushi flapped into the back of the wagon and perched on a bag next to Haeli. Haeli stroked her softly. Just then, Kati turned slightly so she could look back at Ella.

"Now, Miss Ella, ha' ye enjoyed yer stay with the Blaeiths?"

"Yes," Ella replied, "they've been ve'y hospitable."

"Oh, Mrs. Blaeith cen cook better than any other woman in Entwerp," Kati said.

Haeli gave a merry laugh. "And Clerans can talk longer than anyone else in Entwerp."

Mr. Blysffi laughed at this, so everyone else had to laugh as well.

"That is t'ue," Ella said. "Cle'ans has weally kept me ente'tained."

"What wos that?" Kati asked.

"I said, Cle'ans has weally kept me ente'tained."

Kati looked at Ella with a smile playing around her lips. "Well, I know ye are right, but I ha' no heard it said like that a'fore."

Ella's face turned hot at the familiar criticism. Why hadn't she thought to say her *r*'s more clearly just then? Her jaw tensed and her eyes watered.

"Oh," Kati said, "I am sorry; I did no mean to make fun o' ye. I did no mean it like that."

Ella didn't think she sounded entirely sincere. Kati turned and began talking with Martyn again, but Ella didn't hear what she said.

Haeli put her arm around Ella's shoulder. "You do not have to be upset, Ella," she whispered. "Kati meant nothing by it; she just does not think hard enough before she talks. And anyway, *I* think you sound *beautiful*."

Ella squeezed Haeli's hand gratefully. Aarushi whistled and flew over to Ella's side of the wagon. The Harrier looked up at her and nudged her slightly with her wing. Ella looked her in the eye, which seemed to speak clearly enough to Ella.

"*You* can't talk properly, but *I* can't talk at all."

Ella stroked Aarushi's head.

"I guess if you can be happy, Aa'ushi, then I can, too. And I'm so'y she called you Squishy."

Aarushi gave a low whistle.

Just then, Ella looked up to see the kirk coming up on their left. Kati hadn't seen it—she was too busy talking to Martyn. Ella thought she was uncomfortably close to Martyn's face, but Martyn seemed to handle her proximity well—though with great effort.

Mr. Blysffi cleared his throat. "Well, Miss Kati, here is the kirk right here."

Martyn reined in the horse abruptly. "Will this be a fine place fer me to drop ye at?"

Kati looked around a little. "Oh... I guess so."

Martyn helped her down from the carriage.

"Thank ye so much for the ride, Martyn."

Martyn smiled civilly as he let go of her hand. "Do no mention it."

Without waiting for a reply, Martyn urged the horses up the narrow valley just past the kirk.

# ENTWERP PROPER

*A*s soon as Kati was out of sight, Haeli looked slyly at Martyn. "Well, Martyn, Kati Fflemins seems merri comfortable with your company."

Mr. Blysffi laughed, but Martyn sighed. "Oh, that I would be saved from silly women."

Haeli laughed at this. "Silly women?"

"Ay," Martyn replied. "I cen tell ye how this started. At the last dance here, I quired her to dance with me twice. First, since she wos the nearest girl to me, and second, since she had sat out fer three dances before and would ha' sat out a fourth if I'll had no quired her."

Haeli was grinning from ear to ear.

"Well, now," Martyn continued, "she ha' taken it into her head that I am in love with her or some other sich nonsense. So, she ha' decided to return my love, maugre thinking reasonably about things."

Haeli giggled. "Well, if it is not Kati Fflemins, then it is Jenyffr Flaer or Keitlyn Dhorli..."

Martyn shook his head. "They will be the death o' me."

"Do not you mean *'they'll* will be the death o' me?'" Haeli replied, imitating Martyn's brogue as thickly as she could.

Martyn rolled his eyes. "But there is no uncertainty about it. *Ye* may no use the subjunctive *'ll*'s, Haeli, but I do, an' I use them when I mean them, an' omit them when I do no mean them. An' I mean that these silly women *will* be the death o' me—no ifs or mights."

Haeli laughed again, and Mr. Blysffi grinned broadly.

"Well, Martyn," Haeli went on, "what would you do if I sat up there next to you and cooed up at you and leaned my head sweetly on your shoulder?"

Martyn risked a quizzical look back at Haeli. "I do no think I would mind if it'll wos *ye*, Haeli, because I cognize ye would no do *that*. Ye are no a silly woman."

"So you tolerate silly girls, but not silly women?" Haeli retorted.

Mr. Blysffi laughed heartily.

"No, Haeli," Martyn replied seriously. "Ye are no silly. Ye are a good, sensible girl—I should say woman fer ye act like one. If all the women in the world were like ye, I would tain merri little reason to be concerned o' dyin' from their silliness."

Haeli laughed.

"Now wait a moment," Mr. Blysffi broke in. "What about Miss Ella? Do you think she is a silly woman?"

Martyn blushed slightly and risked another look into the back of the wagon. Ella was blushing much harder than Martyn.

"Oh, Da," Haeli said, "you need not embarrass poor Ella."

Martyn answered anyway. "As to ye, Miss Ella, I think I'll would say ye are a sensible young woman, too."

Ella blushed deeper.

"Ye quired about theology, at any rate, an' that is a good sign o' an sensible woman." Martyn suddenly flashed a mischievous grin at Haeli. "Kati, fer instance, would no know any reason no to cede to the Rectificationist kirk, an' is no concerned enough to quire."

*Pteranodon*

"What are you saying?" Haeli asked. "We are not *that* bad of a kirk."

Mr. Blysffi laughed.

Just then, Ella saw a dark shape sweeping through the sky above. She threw herself into the bottom of the cart with alarm. She was certain it was Cweel.

"Pteranodon!" Mr. Blysffi cried.

The horse gave a nervous neigh and tried to turn slightly, but Martyn held it in check and slowed its pace.

"Haeli," Martyn said, "my rifle outta-should be by ye, cen ye pass it to yer Da and see if he'll cen shoot that lizard?"

Ella risked looking up from the bottom of the wagon. What she saw was certainly not Cweel. Instead, she saw an enormous creature, scaled all over like a lizard, though it had large membranous wings—like those of a giant bat—as well as a horn-like crest on the back of its head. The flying reptile perched on one of the crags that formed the side of the narrow valley. It couldn't have been more than forty feet from the wagon, peering down at the occupants with hunched wings, like some ghastly cross between a vampire and a vulture.

"What is it?" Ella gasped.

"It is a pteranodon," Haeli replied as she passed Martyn's rifle to her father. Mr. Blysffi cocked the flint into full position. Just as he set his eye to the sight, the great lizard gave vent to a scream and launched himself from the crag, flapping his wings heavily as he flew up the side of the valley towards the mountain range. Mr. Blysffi fired the gun but must have missed, since the pteranodon flew off unharmed. Mr. Blysffi sighed and passed the rifle back to Haeli.

"Someone should really do something about those beasts."

Martyn nodded.

Haeli held the gun uncertainly. "Martyn, do you want me to reload your rifle for you?"

"No, thank ye, Haeli. I cen do that when I'll get home."

A smile crept into Haeli's eyes. "Well then, just to spite you, I will do it anyway."

Deftly, she poured the powder down the barrel and rammed down the charge and wadding. Ella watched with interest. Haeli seemed so adept at this. Was she just particularly good with a gun, or were all the other women in Entwerp so skilled?

A few minutes later, the wagon pulled onto a long, stone bridge that spanned a deep ravine. Ella looked over the side of the bridge to see a small stream far below.

"That is Entwerp River," Haeli said. "It becomes Entwerp Bog a little further on, near the spice market."

After they crossed the bridge, they passed through a narrow gorge—though it wasn't as long as the valley they had already passed through. Ella could see blast marks on the side of this gorge, and she guessed it was man-made to form a better link between the two Entwerps. The mountains stood out high and robust on either side, with the Gwambi tower just off to her right, sitting forbiddingly against the afternoon sky. She could only imagine what it must have been like to cross from the coast to Entwerp Proper before this gorge had been cut and the bridge built.

As soon as they were through the gorge, they entered a wide dale. The road before them ran down into the dale, where it met with a neat grid of streets—streets without number! All along the lengths of these rows and rows of busy streets, Ella could see crowded houses, neat shops, and enormous warehouses. Around the edges of this city lay more streets, less crowded than the streets within the city, with tidy cottages displayed at even and generous intervals along their lengths.

Ella took in this vast city at a glance, and let out her breath in wonder. It was nearly ten times larger than any city she had ever seen! There was a river running through the midst of the dale, and the greater part of the city was on this side of the river. Nestled along the river banks, Ella could see impressive brick buildings with tall smokestacks, which let out a steady trickle of steam. Those must be the factories where Mrs. Blaeith worked. A smudge of smog touched the entire city as it petered out at the foot of the mountains on the far side of the river.

Just to the south, a long dale ran between two mountain ranges. Down this valley, the city stretched, stopping abruptly several miles down. Ella could just see roads leading out of the town in that direction, and she thought she could see a few farms far away on the horizon.

The road now sloped down towards the city, switching back and forth so as not to descend too steeply. Soon, they were passing houses on the very outskirts of the city—neat and well-kept cottages mostly, with painted fences and aromatic flowers sprouting from beneath each window sill. Before long, they were in the most crowded place she had ever seen. The noise of the city was enough to drive Ella distracted in a minute.

Here a boy came past, yelling about wagers on some fight and news of company lay-offs. There a robust preacher stood, giving heated debate to a group of fuzzy-chinned students. Here was a vendor selling pears, there a vendor selling beef sides. Yet through the noise and bustle, Ella could clearly see the friendly Pistosian spirit shining. As they passed, some young woman would look up from the dirty gutter and smile at Ella as if she knew her. Or, as Martyn slowed his pace to let some pedestrians pass, a chubby toddler who could only just barely walk stumbled past the wagon and saluted her with a "God bleth ye Mith!"

Again, Ella noted this people's simple yet elegant fashion. She never grew tired of looking at the many vibrant shades of brown—here a gray-brown, there a rust-tinged russet, there a green-brown khaki. But now she noticed the sturdy and practical cut of every article of clothing. Everything was so simple, and the only materials she could see were wool and leather, yet there was a majestic beauty to this simplicity. But as Ella thought about it, this seemed to sum up the personality of this country pretty well; treating the most mundane as the most noble—just like having a scripture passage ready to defend matrilineal naming conventions.

After a little while, they passed into a large square, still overflowing with life. Yet, as Martyn started to cross over to the other side, a shout arrested him. Martyn looked around, and a sour-faced man grabbed the horse's bridle, stopping him in his tracks.

"Here, now!" Martyn cried. "What is all this fer?"

"Ye cen no pass through here," the man replied.

"An' who ha' up an' made that law?" Martyn asked.

"Ha' ye no heard?" the man responded. "It is a strike; we will no let ye past."

Martyn seemed a bit ruffled by this. "What kind o' an strike? I ha' no heard o' any sich thing—no here in Entwerp at any rate."

"It is a strike on the Company," the man replied. "They ha' up an' laid off hundreds o' us beacon-keepers from Megalytia, an' we are strikin' in protest. Would ye like to join us?"

Martyn snorted. "Most certainly no. If ye quire me what I would like, I would like to ride on in peace, an' work at my job, an' earn an honest livin' maugre complainin' about the business decision o' somebody else."

The man scowled darkly at him. "Ye would no think that way if ye'll were in our position, lad."

"I do no think so," Martyn said. "I prefer to work, no lie around."

"We tain a right to work, and they will no let us."

Martyn raised an eyebrow. "If ye'll tain a right to work, then ye'll oughtta-should be workin'."

The man growled. "But they fired us."

"Then cede to the factories," Martyn replied. "There might be an openin' there."

Ella then noticed that this side of the square was full, not of busy shoppers, but burly men lounging about on the cobblestones. Some had kindled fires, and others had set up little tents, but mostly, they weren't doing anything—just sitting and frowning.

"We do no want to work fer the factories," the man said with a dark scowl.

"You do not want to work for another massive, impersonal corporation?" Mr. Blysffi asked, glancing at Martyn with a wry smile. "Fancy that."

"It is a protest," the man growled.

"Well, I am protestin' your protest," Martyn replied. "Now let go o' my horse and let us through."

The man only tightened his grip on the reins.

"Come now, Martyn," Mr. Blaeith said with a shake of his head. Then he turned to the striker. "I feel for your plight. We all need to be looking out for the good of each other, now do not we? We can not let some rich, capitalist businessman from Kelmar get away with ruining the lives of his former employees."

The man nodded. "Ay. That's jist it. We ha' got to stand up with each other."

Mr. Blysffi nodded. "Just so. We need to show solidarity during these troubled times."

"Ye'll join us then?" the man asked eagerly.

Mr. Blysffi tilted his head to one side. "I have not decided yet. But I do tain a word of advice. If you want to gain support for your cause, you might do so in less abrasive ways than preventing men from going about their own business."

The man narrowed his eyes, looking from Martyn to Mr. Blysffi. Finally, he let out a long sigh, and let go of the horse, turning away without another word. Martyn flicked the reins, and they were moving again.

The other side of the square looked more like an army camp

than the middle of a bustling city. Every man there looked like he could throw a calf if he had a mind to, and it made Ella nervous to see such burly men sitting idly. As they passed, nearly every striker stared at them shamelessly. Ella shifted positions nervously.

Martyn shook his head slowly. "It does no seem right fer so many good, strong workers to be sittin' around with nothin' to do but cause mischief."

"Ay," Mr. Blysffi said with a nod of his head. "The Company has a lot to answer for."

Martyn raised an eyebrow. "It is no the Company's fault that they are here."

"Is it not?" Mr. Blysffi asked. "They did fire these men."

Martyn shook his head and looked away. "That was because they could no afford to pay them."

Mr. Blysffi laughed, though there was a sardonic edge to it. "You mean they can not afford to pay these men *and* own three houses and go on pleasure cruises off the coast of Erim?"

Martyn sighed. "I understand how ye feel about the owners o' the Company, an' ye may be right that they are no the best o' people. But cen ye no see the harm these strikers could cause if they'll keep loafing about and blocking people from crossin' the square?"

Haeli now broke in. "So we should be concerned about the harm these poor, unemployed men might get up to, but we can ignore the harm that the global business owners do?"

"Exactly," Mr. Blysffi smiled broadly.

Martyn only shook his head again. "Do no *ye* get into it too, Haeli. Now I am outnumbered. I'll outta-should tain Laendon to back me up with numbers and statistics."

Mr. Blysffi laughed heartily at this comment.

"But here now, Haeli," Martyn went on, "that is no entirely fair to what I am sayin'. I am no saying that we should ignore any graft or corruption or abuse from the company owners. But when they'll are makin' the best effort they cen, we cen no blame them fer layin' off a few workers."

"A few workers?" Mr. Blysffi replied, waving at the crowd of strikers crammed into the square. "Does this look like a few workers?"

"Compared to the number o' people who work fer the company, ay." Martyn replied.

Mr. Blysffi waved his hands in the air. "That's just the point. Such a large corporation does not even think before ruining the livelihood of so many men. They are not people to them, but numbers on their payrolls."

"All I am sayin'" Martyn went on, "is that I do no think these strikers are justified. What good is it goin' to do anyone to sit around an' do nothing? It is jist goin' to lead to mischief."

Mr. Blysffi then turned to look at Ella. "And what do you think, Miss Ella?"

"Me?" Ella started, not certain what to say.

"Ay," Mr. Blysffi replied. "Do you have any large companies where you come from?"

Ella pursed her lips, thinking hard for a moment. "Not that I can think of. It's mostly just logge'hs in Blisa. They probably sell the timber to bigger companies, but I don't know. We we'e always a small village. I don't think any big company would ca'e about us."

"Do they care about anyone?" Haeli asked, and she glanced pointedly at Martyn.

"Fer them it is jist business," Martyn said with a shrug. "Ye cen no hold it against them."

"I think I can," Mr. Blysffi replied, drumming his fingers on his knees. "We fought for years to gain our independence. We struggled so long to get out from under the imperial domination of Kelmar and Hrufang. And Lord Protector Caedmon Wilkins has worked tirelessly to ensure that our new government can never exploit us the same way the empires did. But as long as we allow these global corporations to operate with impunity in Llaedhwyth, we will never really be free. They are just as imperial and oppressive as any foreign government."

They were by now well out of the square where the strikers sat. Martyn turned down a large street that headed due north and followed this for a good way. After about half a mile, he turned onto another street and then again on another north-going street. Ella noted that the houses and shops by the side of the street were spacing out a little, and here and there, she could even see a little garden peeking out from between the cobblestone and brick. They didn't have to go much further before houses to their right gave way altogether to a lush, well-tended park—a common land of some sort. The houses on their left continued to space out, but they had not disappeared before the road reached the foot of the mountains and made a sharp turn to the west. Here, Martyn pulled up at a short drive in front of a large house.

The house was very old, and a bit run-down, and Ella could see that it was not at the base of just any mountain, but in the very shadow of the Gwambi Tower. A shiver ran down her spine as Martyn stopped the carriage. Unlike the other houses in Entwerp Proper, this mansion was made entirely of wood— though it had a stone foundation. It had red gables and green tiling on the roof. A long flight of stairs led to the front door, and a wide, roofless porch stretched the entire length along the front of the house. There was also a very large bay window right by the front door.

Just as Martyn helped Haeli down from the wagon and Mr. Blysffi helped Ella down, the front door opened, and a clean maid stepped out to meet them. Ella guessed she was somewhere between twenty-five and thirty-five. She was fairly short, with very curly brown hair and blue eyes. She wore a long, blue dress, bunched up around the waist with intricate red stitching.

But of all her appearance, Ella was most drawn to the maid's

face—specifically her upper-lip. She had heard about rabbit-lip
—or cleft-lip—before and had read several essays on it, but this
was her first time seeing it on another anthrogenus. The maid
really had two upper-lips that might almost have been one had
they been sewn together rather than split beneath her nose. The
split lip was just wide enough that Ella could see the flash of a
silver tooth behind the lips. Ella was so intrigued by the cleft lip
that she initially did not even think to determine what kind of
anthrogenus the maid was.

Aarushi gave a little whistle when she saw the maid, and
Haeli looked up. "Hello, Olyfia, we are back!"

"God bless ye, Haeli, Stifyn." The maid kissed Haeli in greeting, then Mr. Blysffi, then turned to Martyn. "An' God bless ye,
too, Martyn. It is good to see ye again." She kissed Martyn and
Aarushi in greeting. She then turned to Ella. "Are ye the new
maid whom Stifyn spoke of, Miss Donne?"

Ella nodded. "That would be me."

The maid took her by the hand and kissed her on the cheek.
"God bless ye, dear. My name is Olyfia. I ha' been maid here fer
nearly ten years, an' it is about time I tained some help."

"And I'm glad to be that help," Ella replied.

Olyfia nodded, "Good. Vene with me, an' I'll will show ye to
Sir Saemwel."

With that, Olyfia turned and walked up the steps to the front
door. Haeli and Mr. Blysffi followed, then Ella. Martyn took up
the rear, holding Ella's bag, with Aarushi flying at his shoulder.
As they entered the house, Olyfia took Mr. Blysffi's and
Martyn's hats and coats. Aarushi perched on Martyn's shoulder.

"Now, Mr. Martyn and Miss Aarushi," Olyfia said, "will we
tain yer company fer supper?"

Martyn shook his head. "I'm afraid that Ma will be wantin'
us back, so we cen only stay a few minutes."

Olyfia nodded. "Well, Sir Saemwel will want to see ye,
anyway. I will duce ye to him."

Olyfia led them all down a long passage well-decorated with portraits, landscapes, vases, and—in one little alcove—a suit of armor. Although the whole place was tidy, Ella noticed that some of the plaster on the ceiling was peeling. Olyfia soon reached the large oak doors of a drawing room. She opened these slowly, and they all entered.

## 23

---

# SIR SAEMWEL

The room they entered was rather large, though it still seemed homey and quaint. Windows composed the wall to Ella's right almost entirely, letting in a great deal of light and a view of the western mountains. Opposite the windows was a grand fireplace with several deer heads mounted above the mantel. Bookshelves covered nearly every other inch of wall space—from carpeted floor to vaulted ceiling—row upon row of hard-bound, linen-bound, and leather-bound books. Ella was now sure she would enjoy her stay as maid very well, particularly if she had to dust the bookshelves.

In one corner of the room stood a piano with a fife and recorder laid carefully on top of it. Next to the piano was a low table, a couch, and a few chairs. Elsi Pickering sat on the couch, sewing at something that looked like a handkerchief. Next to the fire was another chair—though this was much bigger than the others and bore more pillows. Seated there was Sir Saemwel Pickering. He held a cane in his right hand, and a small book open in his left. His feet were facing the fire, and his mouth moved slightly as he read the book through a pair of thick spectacles.

Both Elsi and Sir Saemwel looked up as Olyfia brought in Ella and company. Sir Saemwel immediately put his book down. He leaned heavily on the cane as he pulled himself up from the chair, grunting with effort and pain, but as soon as he was on his feet, he smiled graciously.

"Stifyn, I trust your excursion was successful?" Sir Saemwel spoke rather slowly but in a deep and rich voice that Ella thought very soothing, but seemed to demand the respect of a father.

Mr. Blysffi nodded, "It was, sir."

"Good, good," Sir Saemwel said, motioning with a very refined and gracious air to Ella. "I trust this beautiful young woman is Miss Donne, then?"

Ella blushed slightly as she curtsied. "Yes, si'h."

Sir Saemwel's face contoured in pain, but he recovered himself quickly and smiled. "Welcome. I see you have met Olyfia already. She will show you about the house and introduce you to your work." He turned to Elsi, "Sara, what had you said I should pay her?"

"Twenty cubits a week," Elsi replied.

Sir Saemwel turned back to Ella. "Is that satisfactory?"

Ella did not know how much a cubit was worth, but she trusted Mr. Blysffi would have objected if it were poor pay. "That will be just fine."

Sir Saemwel motioned to the other seats and the couch. "Please take a seat, all of you. I am certain Olyfia will have supper ready soon."

Olyfia nodded and left the room, while Mr. Blysffi and Martyn sat down next to Sir Saemwel. Haeli grabbed Ella by the hand and brought her over to the couch, where she sat down next to Elsi, kissing her in greeting.

"Elsi," Haeli said, "this is Ella Donne. Have you met her yet?"

"Ay," Elsi replied, setting her sewing aside. "Lexi introduced me to her at kirk yesterday."

"Oh, good," Haeli said, "that was very sensible of Lexi."

Ella laughed, and Elsi looked at Haeli with a twinkle in her large, brown eyes.

Just then, Aarushi fluttered over to their group, landing on the low table in front of Elsi. "God bless ye, Aarushi, and good greeting," Elsi kissed Aarushi, and the Harrier nodded her head and purred.

"Now, Elsi—you'h name is Elsi, wight?" Ella asked.

"Ay," Elsi replied.

"Then why did you'h fathe'h call you Sa'a?"

Elsi smiled. "My full name is Elsi Sara Pickering. Papa jist calls me by my middle name."

"That is what your mother called you, too," Haeli added. "What was the reason for that?"

Elsi nodded. "She called me by my middle name because Mr. Silas called Papa by his middle name."

At the name of Silas, Ella leaned forward with interest. That was her birth father's name. She was always interested in anyone with the name of Silas. "Mr. Silas?"

Elsi nodded. "He wos Papa's comrade when he fought under Lord Protector Caedmon Wilkins. They used to live together in the south, but moved up here together after the war."

Haeli grinned, "Clerans would have us believe that Sheriff Laei was Sir Saemwel's comrade."

Elsi smiled. "Maybe so, but Mr. Silas shared a tent with Papa. He adopted Papa as a brother—they garded enough like brothers that everyone believed they really were."

Ella licked her lips. "What do you mean he adopted you'h fathe'h as his b'othe'h?"

Elsi looked at her earnestly. "Papa did no used to tain a family. He ha' to use his middle name on his uniform since he did no tain a surname."

"That is probably why Mr. Silas called him 'Edwin' and not 'Saemwel.'" Haeli said with a grin.

"Well, he could no ha' called him *'Pickering'* because that was Mr. Silas' name."

Ella felt goosebumps rising on her arms. "Wait, a'e you saying this man gave you'h fatha'h his last name?"

Elsi nodded, "Ay. He was like a brother to Papa and Mama, and they were merri sad when he died. Papa still respects Mr. Silas. He does things because that is how Mr. Silas did them—like calling me by my middle name."

"Mr. Silas Picke'ing?" Ella asked.

"Ay."

Ella tried very hard to calm herself. *It has to be a coincidence;* she thought, *Surely there are several Silas Pickerings in the world.* "How did he die?"

Elsi grew very sober. "He wos kidnapped and killed by Longfinch, the elfin pirate."

Ella could no longer keep her hands from shaking. Longfinch? Wasn't he the one all the pirates had been talking about? Weren't they planning on meeting him here at Entwerp? "Silas Picke'ing was killed by Captain Longfinch?"

"Ay," Elsi replied, looking at her strangely.

"Why?" Ella asked.

Elsi furrowed her brow. But before she could answer, Martyn stood up from his chair by Sir Saemwel.

"I believe I will ha' to be leavin' now. Thank ye kindly fer yer hospitality, Sir Saemwel. I would best be off so Ma does no keep supper waitin' fer me."

Sir Saemwel stood and kissed him goodbye. "I am much obliged for your company, Martyn." Sir Saemwel smiled, but then burst into a fit of coughing. Ella jumped in alarm. It didn't sound like a normal cough, but much more severe—as if he were coughing out his own life. Sir Saemwel put his handkerchief to his mouth and coughed harder.

"Papa!" Elsi jumped to her feet. Sir Saemwel waved her off and gave one last cough into his handkerchief.

"I will be fine, dear. Do not trouble yourself." Sir Saemwel put his handkerchief back into his pocket, but not before Ella saw blood on it.

Martyn looked at him earnestly. "Will ye be alright, sir?"

Sir Saemwel nodded. "I should be just fine, thank you."

Martyn nodded slowly. "Well, then, I ha' best be on my way." He turned to Aarushi, "will ye be cedin' back with me, or no?"

Aarushi gave a short whistle and nodded her head. She fluttered over to Elsi and landed on her arm. Elsi kissed her, and Aarushi fluttered to Haeli. Next, the Harrier landed on Ella's arm.

Never in her life had Ella had such a large bird so close to her. Ella could feel the sharp claws uncomfortably pressing through her shirt sleeve—though Aarushi held her talons gently enough. She put her head to Ella's cheek, and Ella kissed her. Ella had never kissed a bird before—as far as she could remember. She doubted she could ever get used to it.

Aarushi flew off, kissed Sir Saemwel, and landed on Martyn's arm.

"God bless all o' you," Martyn said with a nod, and headed out the door.

Ella turned back to Elsi. "You we'e telling me how Silas Picke'ing was killed?"

Elsi furrowed her brow. "Wos I? I do no really know myself. He boarded a ship to Kelmar, and we got a privateer's report later that Longfinch had attacked Mr. Silas' ship and killed all aboard."

"That's how they knew it was Longfinch," Haeli broke in. "He is the only pirate captain that leaves no survivors."

"Why was he going to Kelma'h?" Ella asked, becoming excited again.

"That's where he came from," Elsi replied.

"Kelma'h?"

"Yes."

"A'e you su'e he didn't come from Slyzwi'h?"

Elsi thought about this for a moment. "Maybe so... but is no Slyzwir part o' Kelmar?"

"It's pa't of the continent of Kelma'h, but not the empi'e of Kelma'h."

Haeli laughed merrily. "Well, that shows how much *we* know about geography! And I should have known that, seeing as Da came from Slyzwir when he was a boy. But where is Slyzwir in relation to Kelmar? I know Slyzwir is in the mountains..."

"Yes," Ella replied, wishing she could talk more about Silas Pickering. "Kelma'h is almost all of the no'th pa't of the continent, and then Slyzwi'h is just south, and just above the easte'n boa'de'h of Ke'yna. But..."

"Is that near the Great Wall?" Haeli asked with interest.

"Yes," Ella answered, "pa't of the G'eat Wall is ou'h southe'n boa'de'h."

Elsi looked up when Ella said *our*, "Are ye from Slyzwir, then?"

"Yes."

"What is it like?" Elsi asked.

"Have you seen the Great Wall?" Haeli added eagerly.

"Yes," Ella replied, "I have seen the G'eat Wall. Slyzwi'h is a beautiful place; I love it—the mountains especially."

"Are yer mountains like the ones we tain here?" Elsi asked.

"No, ours are talle'h... and steepe'h, I think."

Just then, Sir Saemwel gave a small cough while talking to Mr. Blysffi. Elsi looked over at him worriedly.

Ella took advantage of the distraction. "But how long ago did Silas Picke'ing leave?"

"I am sorry; what wos that?" Elsi asked, turning back to Ella.

"I said, how long ago did Silas Picke'ing leave?"

Elsi thought about this for a moment. "Maybe two years ago? Why do ye quire?"

"I was just wonde'ing."

"Goodness, Ella," Haeli said with a laugh, "you have been wondering quite a lot about Mr. Silas. Why are you so interested in him?"

Ella hesitated. Should she tell Haeli?

Luckily, Olyfia entered the room at that moment, saving Ella from answering.

"Supper is ready, sir."

Sir Saemwel and Mr. Blysffi rose.

"Thank you, Olyfia," Sir Saemwel said. "Ladies, are you ready to join us?"

"Certainly, Papa," Elsi stood and made her way towards the door.

Ella was about to fall in with Elsi as they all left the parlor, but Haeli caught her by the arm and whispered earnestly in her ear, "I am going to want to talk to you for a long time tonight, anyway, but tell me this for now: why are you so interested in Mr. Silas Pickering?"

Ella bit her lip. Haeli could know; she *should* know. Haeli had said she would help find the Gwambi Treasure—there was no need to keep this a secret from her. Besides, it couldn't be the same Silas Pickering. That would be impossible.

Ella took a deep breath. "My Papa's name was Silas Pickering."

# PRIVATEERS

The mist had cleared from Entwerp Bay, and the sun was just sinking behind the mountains. The entire scene was perfect, like a landscape of paradise. A vast flock of geese took off from the water on the northern end. A piebald eagle dove into the sparkling waves to extract a fish. People bustled about the docks and dikes of Entwerp. The sea winked, just barely visible between the two outcroppings of mountains —huge ridges forming the bay's narrow mouth.

Through these two megalithic sentinels slipped two ships. Ernest stood at the front of the first, drinking in the scene of Entwerp Bay. He knew that just behind him were over two hundred guns with more than enough hands to work them. Somehow, it seemed a shame they'd have to destroy such a peaceful atmosphere. Ah, well, orders were orders.

With a stiff north wind, the two pirate ships entered the bay. Holgard's galleon turned toward the village's south side, while Longfinch's man-o-war turned slightly northwest in a close haul with the wind.

Holgard walked briskly towards the front of the ship. "Get to your fighting stations! Pull out the guns! Boarders, prepare for action! Gunners, clear out the lower deck and roll out the cannons! Load starboard side!"

The quartermaster repeated each of Holgard's orders, blowing shrilly on his whistle. Ernest felt at his breast. Yes, his pepperbox pistol was still there. He followed the general dash of boarders to the armory, where he retrieved a musket, bayonet, and rapier. As soon as he stepped back onto the deck, he thought he heard a strange noise. It was high-pitched and distant, almost like the shriek of a quartermaster's whistle, only it didn't belong to either his ship or Longfinch's.

The noise seemed to come from the entrance to the bay, so Ernest dashed to the aft deck, rushing past the sailors straining at the halyards and brace lines, and leaned over the gunwale to see if he could hear it again. Ynwyr, standing at the helm with the wheel firmly in his grasp, looked back at Ernest with a raised eyebrow.

"What are you doing back here, cook's-mate?"

"Listening," Ernest replied. "I thinked I heared a noise."

"You thinked you heared a noise?" Ynwyr asked blankly.

"Yes," Ernest said. "There it is again; do'ed you hear it?"

Ynwyr shook his head.

"It was clearer this time," Ernest pressed, "a sort on whistle."

"A sort on whistle?" Ynwyr's face was stupidly blank of any expression.

"Yes."

Ynwyr shrugged and turned back to steering the galleon. "I do'edn't hear anything."

Ernest screwed up his face in concentration. Ynwyr was a dwarf—that was all. Dwarves couldn't hear their own mother from across the ship. The noise came again, but this time it was followed by a baritone *deng* like the ship bell on one of those naval ships-of-the-line.

"Do'edn't you hear *that*?" Ernest asked.

"What?" Ynwyr turned to look back at him.

Just then, Holgard came tramping up to the deck with Killjelly close behind.

"What's going on?"

"Cook's-mate thinks he hears something, Father," Ynwyr said.

"It's a whistle, sir, and a ship's bell," Ernest added with a quick salute.

Holgard furrowed his brow. "A ship's bell?"

"Yes, sir."

Holgard snorted.

"I haven't heared anything," Ynwyr said as he turned back to steering the vessel.

Again, a little louder now, the noise sounded over the bay. *Tweew... deng!*

Killjelly flinched. "I heared it, too, sir." He strode to the gunwale and peered across the bay.

"What did it sound like?" Holgard asked, clearly anxious. "Was it a merchant ship?"

"There was a bell, sure," Killjelly replied.

"The privateers shouldn't be here yet," Holgard said. "It *must* be a merchant ship."

"There was a *bell*," Killjelly repeated.

Holgard snorted and peered out across the bay as well. Their ship was nearly half the way across Entwerp Bay now, and they would soon be within cannon shot of the battery. Just then, a sail appeared at the entrance of the bay. Holgard snorted, and Killjelly inhaled sharply. Behind the first sail pulled a second, and then a third. Holgard snapped out his telescope and closed one eye as he looked through it at the ships.

"Baptism," he hissed. "Privateers!" He slammed his telescope shut and turned back to his ship. "Privateers!" he barked. "Ship about! Prepare to fight in the water!"

The decks—already a flurry of commotion—spawned new life as more pirates leapt into action. The quartermaster repeated

Holgard's orders, piping furiously on his whistle. Ynwyr pulled hard on the wheel. The galleon turned hard to port, and the deck rolled in the turn's tightness. The sailors meanwhile scampered about the deck, hauling on the brace lines to keep the sails in the direction of the wind. Holgard remained calm in this sudden commotion, looking over at Longfinch's man-o-war. Ernest followed his gaze. He could see Cweel launch from the deck and circle over the man-o-war. Ernest could just make out some figures on deck. Holgard raised his telescope to his eye.

"What does he want me to do?" he muttered. "Do you want me to turn on the village? Baptize it! I told him we should've waited for Pennywraith."

Just then there was a sharp report from Longfinch's man-o-war, and a thick rod crashed to the galleon's deck.

"Hand it to me!" Holgard ordered the pirate who picked it up.

The pirate hurried over to the aft deck, and Holgard snatched the rod from his hand, unwrapping a piece of paper from around it. He skimmed it and then began barking orders again while Quartermaster Harold repeated each order on his whistle.

"Move in towards the front ship, there—the flagship. Load port side! Man swivel guns! Prepare to board!" Then he turned to Killjelly. "These are real fighters, here. They're used to killing our kind."

Killjelly smiled morbidly. "Then we should be ready to punish them, sure."

Holgard snorted and started towards the foredeck, but turned. "Cook's-mate, you come with me. Bring your spyglass and your big ears."

Ernest followed Killjelly and Holgard to the foredeck, running quickly below deck first to get his spyglass. When he reached Holgard, the first privateer vessel was still a way off but moving in on the port side. Ernest could see Longfinch's man-o-war closing in to attack the second ship while the third privateer ship moved around the others to get in behind the man-o-war. The wind, being such as it was, the two flotillas could sail directly at each other. At least that would make this quick. There would be no extended jockeying for positions.

Suddenly, a scream rent the air as Cweel dove towards the third vessel. The privateers stood in shock as the Eagle Griffin tore through the rigging, slicing through the shrouds and braces with meticulous care. With the braces severed, the yards of the privateer vessels swung chaotically into the wind, the sails flapping at cross purposes with one another, and the great ship floundered heavily in the water. With a mighty swoop, Cweel fell on the lookout. The crows-nest shattered, and Cweel seized the man in his talons. With a stroke of his wings, he rocketed high into the air, then struck the lookout savagely with his beak and threw him to the ship's deck.

As the privateers swarmed around the broken body of the lookout, Cweel dove again. Ernest could hear the sharp reports of several muskets, but none of them seemed to hit Cweel. The Eagle Griffin landed with all his force on the pilot. The helm fell to pieces in the impact, and again Cweel vaulted into the air, this time with the pilot in his claws.

The pilot squirmed and fought as hard as he could, but to no avail. Cweel raked his hind claws across the pilot's back and then threw him hard against the rock sentinels at the entrance of the bay. The man tumbled limply from that height and splashed into the bay.

The third privateer ship slowed; completely disabled by Cweel's vicious attack. Ernest turned away from watching Cweel's further antics as Holgard nudged him.

"What do you see about that flagship?"

Ernest peered through his eyeglass at the privateer's ship.

Holgard was looking at the ship through his telescope, too. Ernest didn't ask questions; he just obeyed orders.

"It's a man-o-war, maybe sixty guns?"

"Eighty's my guess," Holgard snorted.

"Well, the cannon ports are open on *both* sides. Can they do that?"

Holgard let out his breath and bit his lip. "You're right, so they do. It's a dual-loader."

"But *we* can't do that." Ernest had never seen a ship like this before.

"It's one on the newfangled ships, sure," Killjelly said quietly.

"Yes," Holgard said. "We'll have a time on it, that's for certain. What else do you see, cook's-mate?"

"Four masts, one gaff rigged... several decks. Three? I can't quite tell.... the hull looks thicker somehow."

Holgard nodded. "Yes, so it does. But the aft will still be weak like the rest on us."

"We'll have to get behind it," Killjelly said.

Holgard snorted. "But first we have to cross their port fire— see anything else?"

Ernest smiled thinly. "They call themselves the *Rectitude*."

Killjelly gave a short laugh.

"Baptize these christened ships," Holgard muttered. Then he bellowed, "Swivels, load with chain-shot. I want the aft and aft-port swivels loaded with heated shot. Prepare to fire on my command."

The quartermaster repeated the command by blowing on his whistle vociferously.

Just then, the voice of the privateer captain boomed out across the waves. "If ye surrender now, ye will lose yer ship and yer livelihood, but no yer life!"

"My ship *is* my life!" Holgard yelled back.

Longfinch also responded from his vessel, "Try to take them!"

No sooner had the pirates replied than the flagship hoisted a huge black flag. Ernest swallowed hard; the privateers would take no prisoners.

Holgard saw it and laughed. "You see that, mates? The black flag. No quarter to *them*, I say. Havoc! Let them hear it, mates. Havoc!"

"Havoc!" the boarders replied, beating the butts of their muskets on the decks and screaming like madmen. Ernest shuddered. He had joined in the cry but could not bear to join in the revelry. No quarter. He wondered whether Lewis needed him below deck or if he'd have to stay to see the order through.

"Fire chain-shot!" Holgard barked.

The gunners saluted and touched the swivel cannons off. There was a loud report and harsh whistle as the chain-shots tore through the air, slashing into the flagship's rigging and sails. With a loud *strachk*, one of the chain-shots hit the foremast of the privateer's ship and wound round it like a bolas. On impact, the mast cracked and sagged slightly as if struck by lightning.

"What a shot!" Ynwyr crowed with delight.

Holgard leered over the gunwales at the flagship. "Havoc, yourself, Privateer!"

Ernest felt at his breast. Yes, his pepperbox pistol was still there.

# 25

# BLOOD IN THE WATER

*T*he two ships sailed slowly toward each other.

"Swivels, fire at will!" Holgard ordered, gripping the gunwales and gritting his teeth, his cat-like eyes dilated with battle-fury.

The reports of the port swivel-guns followed the command immediately. One shot fell harmlessly into the water to the flagship's side, but most of the shells struck true. The volley was soon returned by swivels from the flagship. Ernest could feel the entire ship vibrate as the cannon balls hammered into the sides of the galleon.

"Are the port guns ready?" Holgard yelled back to the quartermaster.

"Yes, sir!"

"Tell the aft-swivels to stand by," Holgard ordered.

"Yes, sir!"

Holgard turned his attention back to the flagship and squinted his eyes at it. Ernest stood by anxiously. All they had to do now was wait. Now and then, a swivel would fire, but besides that, everyone stood at attention.

Finally, the ships came broadside of each other.

"Fire!" Holgard yelled.

And the galleon leapt to life, spewing fire and lead from its side. The flagship responded in like manner.

Ernest threw himself onto the deck and covered his head. He guessed most of the shots would be fired at the hull, not at the deck. Even so, he figured he should play it safe when his life was at stake. His heart pounded like a great drum as he listened to the cannon shells beating against the galleon's side.

The galleon reeled back, swaying back and forth as the flagship's shells poured into it. The two ships were several hundred feet apart, but still the force of the impact was enough to drive the galleon out of its course. Ynwyr hauled on the helm, trying to keep the galleon in a line as it continued to recoil under the pounding of the flagship's guns.

Holgard gripped the gunwale tighter, a murderous gleam in his eye.

"Aft swivels, stand ready! Prepare to fire on their stern."

The murderous fire continued only a few seconds longer, and then the ships passed each other.

"Now!" Holgard cried.

The aft swivels fired. Ernest peered through his spyglass.

"They're hit, sir, they're hit! We've blown two holes clear through their aft! Their rudder's an oblivion, sir."

Holgard smiled. "Load starboard side! Turn to starboard and prepare to board!"

The quartermaster whistled out the orders, and the sailors leapt to the brace lines, hauling the yards around as the great ship turned like some majestic bird of prey wheeling to attack its quarry.

The ships came broadside once more and exchanged volleys, though this time they were much closer. The yards of the two ships nearly touched. Ernest ducked down again, and none too soon, for this time the flagship sprayed grapeshot at the deck—instead of shell-shot into the hull as they had before.

Many of the boarders had not taken cover, and the murderous fire cut them to the deck. One pirate fell to the decks just in front of where Ernest crouched. Ernest gripped his musket tightly and breathed heavily. That was Iosiah, the nymph deckhand.

The pirates were back on their feet in an instant. Before Holgard could bark out the orders, many boarders had thrown grapnels across onto the flagship and were drawing the two ships together. The rigging lines and spars of the two ships now mingled as if in an embrace.

Ernest could see the privateer captain ordering some marines into a long line across the port side of the flagship, and he ducked down behind the gunwale again. He could hear the sharp crack of rifles, and many of the boarders fell dead to the decks.

"Return fire, idiots!" Holgard yelled. "Return fire! Havoc!"

"Havoc!" the pirates replied, and those able to discharged their muskets. Ernest poked his head above the gunwales, adrenaline pounding in his head. He knelt with his musket on the railing while he aimed down the barrel at the marines. The captain was an older man with a fancy hat and several bars on his uniform. Ernest aimed at him.

He pulled the trigger and watched as the man jerked and then gripped his stomach in pain. Ernest again ducked behind the gunwale as another volley from the marines peppered the deck. He loaded his musket carefully and then jumped back to a firing position.

There was that man again, still barking out orders to the other marines, though he was gripping his stomach where Ernest had shot him. Ernest's hands were shaking, but he steadied himself to aim again and fired.

The man with the fancy hat didn't even flinch, but the marine behind him dropped his gun and held his arm.

*Bother, missed completely.* What was the use of all of this careful aiming if his musket couldn't even shoot what he was aiming at? The rapier was a much better weapon.

Again, Ernest ducked behind the gunwale, loaded, and then jumped back to firing position. He aimed carefully at the captain. The man turned so that his whole body was facing Ernest. Ernest gritted his teeth and fired. The man's eyes rolled back in surprise, and he fell to the deck.

Success!

Ernest's belly lurched—whether from excitement or fear, he didn't know. Two more, and he would break his record. Something told Ernest he *would* break it this battle. He checked his breast. Yes, his pepperbox pistol was still there.

As Ernest reloaded his musket, he peeped over the side of the gunwale. The ships were very close now, their tumblehome sides nearly touching. The boarders would be across at any moment. He finished loading and then knelt again, looking down his gun at his next target. Most of the marines were fairly young (nearly as young as himself), but there were a few older men. He focused in on a leprechaun who appeared to be in his mid-thirties.

Just then, Holgard barked out commands. "Board! Send them to oblivion, mates! Havoc!"

There was a general rush towards the gunwales as the pirates threw themselves at the privateer's ship. The marines fired *en mass*, and many boarders fell back, wounded or dead. Ernest backed away from the side of the ship and stood up. Just then, Holgard caught sight of him.

"Cook's-mate, stay close to me. I'm going over."

Ernest saluted and hurried after Holgard. Just then, there was a cry and shrill whistle from the privateer's ship as the privateers surged towards the galleon, firing their guns as they came. Ernest could hardly tell what was happening. The smoke from the guns was rapidly closing his line of sight.

He was certain he could see several pirates on board the

privateers' ship, fighting for all they were worth, but he could also see several privateers on board the galleon.

Suddenly, Ernest heard a loud thud above the noise of gunfire, cannon fire, and screams of battle. He turned to see about seven marines charging down a wooden plank directly toward him. He froze. Holgard leapt forward as he drew his cutlass, a maniacal gleam in his eye. Killjelly and several other boarders followed close behind their leader.

Just before Holgard reached the gunwales, the first marine hurled a round object at his feet. Killjelly saw it coming and bowled into Holgard, shoving him aside. The other boarders were not so lucky. As soon as the grenade hit the deck, it exploded, sending shrapnel in all directions.

One of the boarders had stepped in front of Ernest just before the grenade exploded, inadvertently shielding Ernest from the shrapnel. Ernest felt a piece of metal slice his leg, but the other pirate landed limply on the deck next to Ernest. Though he was now badly mutilated, Ernest recognized him as one of the men he had served every day. George—wasn't that his name?

Ernest looked up to see the marines nearly aboard—all seven were in one line as they crossed the plank. Holgard lay on the deck with Killjelly on top of him. Both were struggling to get to their feet, but the marines would be upon them before they could. Ernest was the only one standing, and seven rifles pointed at Holgard's head.

With a tremor of terror in his stomach, Ernest whipped out his pepperbox pistol, leveled it at the charging marines, and pulled the trigger.

*All eight barrels fired simultaneously*

All eight barrels fired simultaneously, sounding more like a cannon than a pistol. Smoke and fire partially obscured Ernest's vision, and his arm hammered backward as though a falling mast had hit him. Yet he must have kept his arm steady, for all seven marines fell—either dead or wounded—some tumbling from the plank into the water, and others falling hard to the deck.

Holgard and Killjelly finally jumped to their feet. Holgard's left leg was bleeding badly from the grenade blast, but he didn't seem affected by that.

"Don't just stand there!" he barked. "We've got an open plank here. Advance! Board! Havoc!"

By now, many other boarders had come up, and they poured across to the flagship through the gap Ernest had made in the defenses. Ernest stayed back to reload his pepperbox pistol properly, and then he vaulted aboard the flagship himself.

The entire deck was full of gunpowder smoke and the noise of battle. Ernest drew his rapier. He looked around, briefly considering slipping back to see if Lewis wanted help in the kitchen. After all, he had already saved Holgard's life; that was enough for one pirate in one battle.

Just before he plunged into the fray of battle, there was a shrill scream, and a dark shape plunged through the smoke. It was Cweel. His huge wings beat back the smoke as he set a dark figure on the deck. Ernest strained his eyes to peer through the smoke—it was Vania Bloodrummer.

Vania drew his saber, looking this way and that. "Who is the leader of this ship, whatever?"

There was no response to his cry as each man continued to fight, so he let out a savage yell and threw himself into the fray. His blade slashed left and right—a swift slash here, a precise stab there. The privateers fell dead at his feet by the dozens. At every slash, Vania repeated his question. "Who is the leader of this ship?"

Ernest watched wide-eyed as privateer after privateer after marine fell under Vania's blade. He didn't treat them like men; they were dogs... rats... fleas—piling up to be burned.

"Who is the leader of this ship?"

Finally, a voice answered Vania over the noise of battle.

"Who calls fer me?"

"I do!"

Most of the pirates had stopped fighting and backed away from their opponents to see what would happen next. Ernest thought back to Vania's challenge of the merchant captain. Would he do it again?

"I do!" Vania repeated as he strode towards the man who had answered his challenge. "Which is, are you the admiral on this fleet, whatever?"

"I am. Who are ye?"

"Vania, Vania Bloodrummer."

"And why did ye ask fer me, Mr. Bloodrummer?" the admiral asked, a hint of scorn audible in his voice.

"Which is, cross swords with me," Vania replied, his saber poised at his side. "If'n you win, we will surrender to you. If'n you lose, then you must surrender to us, whatever."

The admiral sneered, "I am no in the habit o' bargainin' with pirates."

"Coward," Vania spat. "I am a swordsman. Which is, you would not refuse a fellow warrior, whatever?"

The admiral curled his lip disdainfully. "I will fight ye, pirate, but I make no promises regardin' my men."

"You lose a golden opportunity if'n you decline, whatever," Vania said.

With no warning, the admiral drew his own saber and lunged at Vania. Vania seemed to have been waiting for this. He expertly turned the admiral's blade to the side, and then, as the admiral continued to move forward, Vania drew his dirk, slashing it across the admiral's chest and then stabbing it into his side. The admiral stumbled back in shock, and Vania sneered at him.

"You're the admiral here? Which is, I've met schoolboys what can fight better than you, whatever."

The admiral growled and lunged forward again. Vania stepped smoothly to the side and slashed at the admiral's legs. He tripped and landed on his saber, driving it into the deck of his own ship. Before the admiral had time to pull his sword free, Vania fell on him. Vania's sword slashed across the admiral's wrists, and then his dirk drove into the admiral's back.

The privateers gasped in shock as their admiral fell dead to the deck. Vania turned on them, raising his saber over their heads.

"Death!"

Holgard waved his cutlass from where he stood. "No quarter. Give them the black flag. Havoc!"

"Havoc!" the pirates repeated as they fell on the privateers. Most of the privateers fell back before the onslaught, but a few hadn't lost heart yet. They hauled themselves up on the aft deck to defend against the invaders. Ernest felt himself pushed forward in the effort to overwhelm these few brave men, but before he reached the aft deck, Cweel was back.

Like a bolt of lightning from heaven, he fell on the surviving privateers and scattered them in all directions. His claws slashed easily through their uniforms, and his wings beat them to the deck. Several turned to shoot, but the pirates now swarmed up the aft deck and overwhelmed them.

Cweel snatched up the leader of the defenders. After mauling him, Cweel flung him into the rigging, where the man dangled like a fly from a spider's web.

Ernest turned away from this carnage and peered out across the bay. A light breeze had come up and was clearing much of the smoke away. Ernest could now see corpses floating in the bay where ducks had been swimming half an hour before.

Across the bay, Ernest could see that the other two ships in the privateers' fleet were in flames. Longfinch's man-o-war was turning away from the second ship and coming towards the flagship.

*We won't be needing help now,* Ernest thought. *They're as good as finished.*

Ernest looked over at the mountains. The sun was only barely visible over their peaks, casting a blood-red glow across the landscape. Was it just a trick of the sunset, or was the bay red, too?

# 26

## OLYFIA

"*This* is where ye will be stayin'," Olyfia said, holding her lantern aloft in the dark room.

The lantern provided sufficient light for Ella to see her accommodations. It was a fairly small room with bare plaster walls. There was only one—rather large—window that gave her a view of the valley and the twinkling lights of Entwerp Proper from three stories above the ground. Outside was dark, and rain drizzled across the windowsill. Inside the room, there was a low cot with clean sheets, a small dresser, and a narrow desk just in front of the window.

"We will tain breakfast an hour after sunrise, but I will need ye to do a few chores before then. Ye know where my room is, so jist knock on the door at daybreak an' I will walk ye through the mornin'. Do ye tain any quirin's?"

Ella looked around the room and put her bag on the cot. "I don't think I have any questions about the wo'k, but I—do you mind if I ask you a question about you?"

Olyfia smiled politely. "That, o' course, defends on the nature o' the question."

Ella flushed slightly. "Well...you see, I like anthrogenusology, and I was wonde'ing...a'e you a gnome o' a lep'echaun?"

Olyfia's smile lengthened. "You ha' no been out in the world much, ha' ye?"

"I can't say I have. All I weally know about othe'h anthrogenus is what I've wead in my books. I can tell between most anthrogenus, just not gnomes and lep'echauns, yet."

Olyfia was still smiling. "Well, ye'll will learn to cern between us if ye'll stay here a while. I'm Kobald, to answer ye. That's leprechaun."

"I know a Kobald is a leprechaun; my books told me that much."

"Good," Olyfia nodded and handed Ella the lamp. "Ye keep this an' I'll will see ye in the mornin'. One last thing, if ye like anthrogenusology, Sir Saemwel's library is open to all in his house." Olyfia smiled and turned to leave, but stopped as Haeli appeared in the doorway.

"Miss Haeli, is there somethin' I cen do fer ye?"

Haeli's eyes sparkled with a hint of mischief, but her demeanor also showed a sense of earnestness.

"Yes, Olyfia, there is something you can do for me. You can stay up another half hour with Ella and me."

Olyfia nodded and stepped back to let Haeli in. "I most certainly cen do that, Miss Haeli."

"Oh, Olyfia," Haeli sighed as she stepped into the room and seated herself on the dresser. "You are such a dutiful servant, but I need you to stop being a servant for now. I need you to loosen up and be a merri more casual. We all three are going to have a good, long talk, but it is strictly confidential, and will not leave this room unless we agree on it beforehand."

"I'll will agree to that, as long as this is no something naughty."

Haeli laughed heartily. "No, Olyfia, this is far too serious to be naughty."

"What's all this about, Haeli?" Ella asked.

Haeli grinned and wiggled her eyebrows. "The Gwambi treasure."

Olyfia jumped.

"I thought you might know something about that," Haeli said triumphantly.

"What do ye know about the Gwambi treasure?" Olyfia replied tensely.

"I was going to ask *you* that," Haeli grinned and tossed her hair playfully.

Olyfia studied her for a moment. "Why do ye want to know?"

Haeli motioned dramatically toward Ella. "And *that* is for *you* to answer."

Ella was silent a moment while Olyfia studied her.

"Why do ye want to know about the Gwambi treasure?" Olyfia asked almost suspiciously.

"I could answe'h that in sho't o'h in long. Which do you want?"

"Long," Olyfia replied. "Start from the beginning."

"The ve'y beginning?"

"Ay."

Ella was silent for a while. "Well, I am f'om Slyzwi'h. My fathe'h was a sailo'h who died when I was young. My mothe'h ma'ied a logge'h a few yea'hs back, and now I have two younge'h siblings."

Ella paused again. "I miss my fathe'h. I guess that's why I talk to all the sailo'hs in ou'h village."

"Why?" Olyfia interrupted.

"I just..." Ella thought for a little. "It makes me feel like I knew my fathe'h. He left us when I was ve'y young, you see." Ella paused.

"Go on, then," Olyfia said.

"Well, the'e was this one begga'h who came to ou'h village

who had lived fo'h a long time at sea. He had been lost at sea and captu'ed by pi'ates befo'e—like my fathe'h was—so I talked with him when I could and b'ought him food."

"Did yer mother or step-father accompany ye ever?" Olyfia asked.

"No," Ella replied. "I had only known him fo'h a week befo'e..." Ella paused again. "Fathe'h—I mean my step-fathe'h— had wanted to talk with him, but he didn't get a'ound to it. I went to give the begga'h b'ead one night and found some pi'ates beating him. They took me, too, and hauled both of us across the sea. They to'tu'ed Jock..." Ella broke off.

Haeli looked at her compassionately. "Did you have to see it?"

Ella nodded. "They t'ied to get me once, but I escaped, and now I'm he'e."

"An' what does this ha' to do with the Gwambi treasure?" Olyfia asked.

"The pi'ates a'e looking fo'h it. They seem to think Jock knows whe'e it is. They won't let him go until they get it."

"Has Jock ever been to Entwerp before?" Olyfia asked.

"Well, I suppose so. He was a sailo'h. He went all ove'h the place," Ella replied.

Olyfia thought this through for a while. "So ye want to know where the Gwambi Treasure is, so ye can give it to the pirates in exchange fer Jock?"

Ella nodded.

"There are other reasons, too," Haeli broke in. "Just think: if these pirates attack Entwerp, we may fight them off, but we will lose many lives in the conflict. Giving them the treasure would save those lives."

"Besides," Ella added, "my fathe'h was looking for the Gwambi t'easu'e when he died. He would want me to find it."

Olyfia was still silent.

"Please, Olyfia, help us," Haeli said.

"Do you know whe'e the Gwambi t'easu'e is?" Ella asked.

Olyfia didn't answer for a very long time. Finally, she sighed. "Very well, I will help you. I ha' thought about doin' it myself before now, anyway." She turned to Ella, "No, I do no know where the Gwambi treasure is, but I tain some idea o' where to start:

"Sir Saemwel fiscated this house twelve years ago, and he was particular about getting it. So I say the'e had to be a reason. He knew something about this house that he wos no saying and has no said since. There's also this: he wos a lowly soldier in the war. He wos honored fer his conduct on the field o' Ard-Melwyn, but still wos no a mite richer. Then, he venes here, sets his sights on a house an' suddenly finds enough money to buy it, and has been wealthy ever since."

"Are you saying we should ask Sir Saemwel about this?" Haeli asked.

"I do no think he would tell ye much," Olyfia replied.

"But all you've said is that he somehow got wich—and quick, too. That doesn't mean he knows whe'e the t'easu'e is," Ella said.

"Well, wait until I tell ye all," Olyfia answered. "When I first came to work fer Sir Saemwel, he would disappear fer hours down in the basement somewhere. I ha' ceded down there to gard fer anythin' he might ha' done, but could no trive anythin'. Ye know that this house is built on Gwambi ruins though, do no ye?"

"Is it?" Ella was suddenly much more interested.

"Ay, it is. Well, there wos one time, when Sir Saemwel was gone, that I chanced to gard up at the tower, and what do you think I saw, but a figure standing on the tower."

Haeli jumped up. "Someone *on* the Gwambi tower?"

"Ay," Olyfia said. "I watched him fer nearly half an hour, an' soon after he disappeared again, Sir Saemwel vened back from the basement. A few days later, he fiscated the plot o' land out front—which there wos no way he ha' earned enough to fiscate — and has no disappeared into the basement since."

"When was that?" Haeli asked.

"A while back," Olyfia replied, "when yer father still worked here, and Mr. Silas was around. Maybe seven years ago."

"Did he notice any of this?" Haeli asked, by this time even more excited than Ella.

"I never talked with him about it," Olyfia replied.

"Have you eve'h asked Si'h Saemwel about it?" Ella asked.

"Once," Olyfia said. "I quired him if this house was really built on Gwambi ruins, but he changed the subject merri quickly."

"So, you think the treasure is here? In this house?" Haeli pressed.

"I think that there must be a way to reach the Gwambi city from this house," Olyfia replied.

"What do you mean by that?" Ella asked. "A way to weach a Gwambi city?"

"I mean a Gwambi catacomb network," Olyfia replied, "like an ancient dwarven city."

"I thought the Gwambi we'e human, though," Ella said.

"They were," Olyfia answered, "but did yer books tell ye how the Gwambi first came here?"

Ella shook her head. Her mother had not allowed her to read the one book her father had on the Gwambi.

"They destroyed an early nation called the Sweingoli, who were both nymphs an' dwarfs. The nymphs they drove out, an' the dwarfs they enslaved—at least that is the vest we cen tell; the dwarfs did no survive."

"But haven't a'cheologists found some of the Gwambi towns?" Ella asked.

"Ay," Olyfia replied, "but those were only from their early years—presumably before they could build the underground cities."

Haeli looked at Olyfia closely. "Are you saying that most of the Gwambi cities are underground?"

Olyfia nodded.

"Whe'e did you come up with this idea?" Ella asked. "Does anyone else think these unde'g'ound cities exist?"

Olyfia smiled. "There is a fantastic book in the library named *A Proposition Concerning The Gwambi* by Dr. Adicus Johnston. I trived it soon after I saw Sir Saemwel on the tower. Dr. Johnston explained why the Gwambi must ha' lived mostly underground except at the beginning o' their reign when they built wooden structures above the ground."

"But has anyone found these unde'g'ound cities?" Ella asked.

Olyfia shook her head. "If they'll ha', everyone would know about them. Right now, they only exist in theory—though a theory I am sure is true."

"Why has not any found them?" Haeli asked.

"Well," Olyfia replied, "Dr. Johnston said that there would be only two ways to trive these underground cities. First, we'll would ha' to trive an entrance from some valley—which we ha' no trived. Second, we'll would ha' to enter through one o' the Gwambi towers, which no one ha' ever successfully climbed a'fore."

Haeli leaned back with a furrowed brow. "It is almost like some mystical force is blocking people from finding these cities."

Olyfia gave a dry laugh. "Ye would say that more emphatically if ye'll read Dr. Johnston's book."

"But someone al'eady *has* found these unde'g'ound Gwambi cities," Ella said.

"Who?" Haeli asked.

"Si'h Saemwel," Ella replied. "He's found his way up the towe'h f'om the *inside*."

"An' more exactly, from this house," Olyfia added.

All three of the girls were quiet for a long time. Finally, Olyfia opened the door.

"I had vest be gettin' to my bed. I'll will see you tomorrow mornin'." She stepped out of the room but paused in the hallway outside. Then she turned to Ella.

"Ye vened to the right house, Miss Ella. I will help ye trive the Gwambi treasure. It needs to be trived sometime, anyway, an' I may as well be one o' those to be the first to it. With these pirates gardin' fer it, too, I tain all the more reason to trive it now. The world needs to know more about the Gwambi."

She made as if to leave, but turned back to Ella again. "Ye should write a book about this when we are done." And she walked off.

Haeli laughed. "You should, Ella. It would be a tremendous benefit to the archeological community."

Ella smiled slightly as she unpacked her bags and settle into her room.

"You could name it *How To Find A Lost Civilization Cloaked by Mystical Powers*. You'd go down with James Hrunt. Think about that: Ella Pickering Donne and James Hrunt," Haeli giggled.

"You'e getting ahead of you'self," Ella said. She lifted the dagger Lewis had given her out of her bag and set it on the dresser. "We have to find the t'easu'e fi'st, and the'e's some pi'ates that might complicate that."

Haeli laughed. "They are still out in the bay. We have a long head start on them. They would need a sorcerer to catch up with us now."

## 27

## PIRATES' FEAST

*E*rnest looked uncertainly at the side of the man-o-war looming above him. He and Lewis sat in one of Holgard's skiffs. Pirates from the galleon filled the skiff, and the other skiffs were bringing the rest. Only a few pirates remained aboard the galleon to guard it.

That morning, Vania Bloodrummer had given the entire pirate crew a formal invitation to dinner aboard the man-o-war. The dinner would feature the larders of the three privateer vessels. Though everyone was invited, only Lewis seemed to know what he was invited *to*. Even now, many of the pirates shifted their weight nervously, unsure exactly what to expect.

Bill leaned over to Lewis. "Have you ever been to one of these formal dinners?"

"Yes," Lewis replied with a roguish wink.

"What is it like?"

Lewis shrugged. "It's just a fancy dinner. The same sort on food what I would serve, just more expensive, better-tasting, better-looking, and worse for the body."

"But what makes it different?" Bill asked. "Is it decorated?"

"Sometimes," Lewis said. "I don't know what Longfinch is planning."

Just then, they reached the side of the man-o-war, and a pirate tossed down a rope. "You jack-tars ready to come aboard?"

"Most certainly!" Lewis yelled back as he grabbed hold of the rope and scaled the ship's side. The other pirates followed. Soon Ernest reached the deck, too. It was much larger than the deck of the galleon. All along the length of the ship were rows of tables, each neatly laid with various gourmet dishes. Ernest had never seen the like before. A whole roast pig formed the centerpiece, surrounded and accompanied by parsley-and-apple salad, egg soup, roasted goober peas, fileted trout, warm bread, steaming-hot pudding, and a host of fried and broiled and roasted vegetables. Even as Ernest watched, several servers made their way from below deck with huge casks of ale. Ernest's mouth watered.

A burly pirate nudged Ernest's shoulder. Ernest turned in surprise. The pirate looked Ernest up and down with a critical eye. He was a hulking dwarf with a doo-rag tied tightly around his head and a squint in his left eye. He looked at Ernest's arms mockingly.

"What do you do?"

"What was that?" Ernest asked, not sure what to think.

"I said, what do you do?" the dwarf replied. "I can see you don't think, so what *do* you do?"

Ernest blinked uncertainly. "Well, I can shoot, and fight—more or less. I'm pretty decent with the rapier. I can read, and sort-of sing..."

"What's your *job*, lad?"

"Well, um," Ernest hesitated; he didn't trust this dwarf. "I'm cook's-mate."

"Oh," the pirate looked him over again, "so you're one on *those*."

Ernest looked at him closely. "What was that?"

The pirate grunted at him dismissively. "You should go talk to Bobbie over there." He motioned towards a scrawny imp carrying a tray of trout to the tables. The burly pirate turned away from Ernest as one would turn away from an oddly shaped rock that had lost its novelty.

Ernest took a few steps towards the man called Bobbie and then stopped. If Bobbie was as unpleasant as the other pirate, then maybe he wasn't worth bothering with. Ernest was just about to look around for Lewis when Bobbie looked up and saw him. Bobbie stared at Ernest as if he were a tropical toucan. Ernest waved at him casually.

"Good morning."

Bobbie continued to stare at him. After a while, he opened his mouth. "What do you do?"

"Cook's-mate," Ernest replied, trying to look smug.

Bobbie's stare changed to a look of condescension. "Oh, one on *those*."

Ernest didn't like the tone in Bobbie's voice. "And what do *you* do?"

"*I* am cook's-mate."

"Then we're the same."

Bobbie lifted his nose as he set his platter on the table. "I *suppose* you could say so."

"Well, I *am* saying so," Ernest said, feeling a need to assert himself.

Bobbie gave a slight smirk. "Well, what you do and what *I* do are rather different, cook's-mate."

Ernest narrowed his eyes. "What do you mean?"

"*You* work for some pirate cook. *I* work with Chef Euangellias."

"*I* work with Chef Lewis Sa Erinfrith." Ernest had only heard Lewis use his full name once before, but he was glad he had, as it sounded much more impressive than this other cook's one name.

Bobbie gave him a patronizing look. "Yes, but can your cook make anything like *this?*" he motioned to the tables laden with food.

Ernest hesitated. He had never *seen* Lewis make anything like that feast, though he had enough confidence in Lewis to say yes.

Bobbie didn't wait to hear an answer. He simply smirked and turned away. "That's what I thinked."

As Bobbie proceeded below deck, Ernest contemplated grabbing hold of him and giving him an earful of what an excellent cook Lewis was—and maybe even beating some tact into him with his fists—when he heard Lewis chuckling next to him.

"Well, well, well, such good manners here."

"Did you hear that?" Ernest asked. "That scrawny imp talking about you as if'n you were a blind monkey!"

Lewis laughed. "Don't let it upset you, boyo. Let's not judge these pirates until we've haved a bite on their cooking."

"Their cook could *never* beat your cooking," Ernest insisted.

Lewis grinned. "Perhaps, but he can certainly make his food *look* better than I can."

Just then, Vania Bloodrummer walked out of one of the aft cabins. He wore a new tricorn hat and his long black hair tied back with a red ribbon.

"Which is! Welcome, friends," Vania said, waving his arms expansively at Holgard's crew and bowing his head slightly. "We are glad that you have comed, whatever."

Holgard took a few steps forward. "Weel, we thank you for the invitation."

"Please, find a place to sit. We will eat when all are seated, whatever."

Holgard's crew moved forward and sat where they could find

places at the table. Longfinch's pirates followed suit. Ernest found himself with Bill and Tell on his right and one of Longfinch's pirates on his left. Tell looked up and down at the table.

"Well, are we supposed to start eating yet?" Tell asked.

"No idiot," Bill hissed. "Wait."

"Wait till what?" Tell turned to Bill with a blank look.

As if to answer the question, Longfinch suddenly appeared on deck. Twisted designs decorated both of his forearms and the right side of his face, making his tapir-like nose stand out all the more prominently. They reminded Ernest of the tribal markings of the bedouins in Keryna—maybe they were symbols of Longfinch's elfin heritage? He wore a linen shirt with the sleeves rolled up past his elbows. He also wore silk stockings, and an elaborately embroidered vest that fell well past his knees.

"I have called you all here tonight," Longfinch began, "so that you could hear straight from me what we are doing."

The pirates nodded, all turning to face Longfinch. Tell was obviously still eyeing the food, but trying to give Longfinch his attention.

Longfinch continued, "The privateers that attacked us yesterday are a warning to us. The Beacon Company doesn't want us here and will fight to get rid on us. They have many privateers they can send, and we cannot predict when they will arrive. However, as far as they know, we are just normal pirates."

Many of Holgard's pirates chuckled at this, but Longfinch's pirates gave out a round of mocking laughter.

"They expect us only to seek a quick gain—like the warehouses or the National Banks on Entwerp. We may have a few days on peace before another fleet comes. If'n we leave the harbor before then, they willn't hunt us down since we don't threaten them. On course, if'n we simply leave now after only plundering a single merchant ship, they will be suspicious and expect us to return."

Longfinch paused for a moment to make sure that all the pirates were following him. Ernest was still listening, and he could see that Killjelly, Holgard, and Lewis were as well, but Tell and many other pirates were simply staring impatiently at the food.

"So," Longfinch continued. "Tomorrow we will raid the village on Entwerp. We will carry as much plunder as we can to our ships, then retreat to the south and dock in a hidden bay. Once we've discovered the Gwambi treasure, we will return and strike this pitiful village so hard it will never recover. Then we will all share in the ancient glory of the Gwambi!"

There was a tremendous cheer from Longfinch's crew, along with a slightly less-enthusiastic cheer from Holgard's crew. Tell was still eyeing the food.

Longfinch raised his hands as if to deliver a benediction. "Let the feasting begin!"

Immediately, the pirates leapt forward and began piling their plates with the mountains of food before them. From the poop-deck, a quartet of musicians struck up a hearty reel. The servers ran this way and that with barrels of ale, filling up tankards as fast as they could. Many more streamed from below deck with platters of food to replenish the tables.

Ernest was much less enthusiastic about the food than the other pirates after his conversation with Bobbie. It was his firm intention to hate the food he was about to eat just so he could scoff at Chef Euangellias the next time he saw Bobbie. To his great relief, the first bite of salmon was terribly bland. Lewis had served roast salmon for Holgard's crew many times, and it was always juicy and full of flavor. This fish—in Ernest's opinion—was fit for nothing but sharks' bait.

Just then, Bill gagged on a bite of some strangely shaped

vegetable. "Baptism," he said to Tell in a none-too-soft voice, "what kind on food is this junk?"

"It reminds me on dirt," Tell replied with the air of someone who thinks they sound intelligent.

"It looked nice, but it isn't fit for stepping on."

"What's the matter with the food?"

Ernest heard the voice and looked up to see Bobbie standing by with a new tray of salmon. He looked rather indignant.

"What is the trouble with the food?" he repeated.

"Trouble?" Bill asked. "It's garbage; that's the trouble. You should shoot your cook and hire someone else."

Bobbie's face turned bright red, and the veins in his neck stood out.

Ernest gave a short laugh. "Oh, don't take it too hard, cook's-mate. It's nothing against old Chef Euangellias. We're just used to food from an *exceptionally* talented cook—more refined food, you know. But we can make do with *ordinary* pirate food, just this once."

Ernest turned away from Bobbie and started chewing on the flavorless salmon again. Bobbie opened his mouth and shut it, then he clenched his jaw. Finally, he turned and walked below deck without putting his platter of salmon on the table.

Bill looked over at Ernest. "I guess I do'edn't know how lucky we are to have Lewis. Anoint me! I don't know how I could put up with cooking like this."

Ernest suddenly realized that Lewis was looking at him from a table further up. Ernest met his eye. Lewis grinned and winked, then resumed eating.

## 28

## OLD WOUNDS

The sound of feet moving hurriedly beneath her room woke Ella about an hour before dawn. She lay for a while listening to it, when it suddenly occurred to her that she was now a housemaid, and it was probably her duty to see to whoever was awake.

Pulling on her over-gown, she lit her candle before stepping into the hallway outside her room. She moved slowly, with one hand on the wall so as not to miss the stairway Olyfia had pointed out to her last night. Soon she found it and followed the steep descent to the ground floor.

As she entered the main hallway, Olyfia hurried past with a large basin of warm water, nearly knocking Ella over as she passed.

"Oh, thank God ye vened down." She handed Ella the basin of water. "Sir Saemwel is in a merri bad way. Quickly bring this to his room. I will get more water."

Olyfia turned around and hurried back down the hall.

Ella made her way down the hall toward Sir Saemwel's room as quickly as she could. Olyfia had pointed the room out to her last night, and Ella thought she remembered where it was. She came to the door and pushed on it.

It was a broom closet.

Still holding the basin, Ella looked up and down the hall. There was another door on the other side of the hall, so she pushed on it. Inside was a small dark room with white sheets over all the furniture.

Ella stepped back to the middle of the hall and moved the basin to her other hip. She was fairly certain that she had not been further down the hall when Olyfia pointed out Sir Saemwel's door to her, but she could be wrong.

Ella started down the hall again when a door opened behind her. She turned—spilling water all over her skirts—to see Haeli hurrying down the hall.

"Haeli!" she called. "Is Si'h Saemwel's woom down the'e?"

"Yes," Haeli said, without turning, "the door I just left."

Ella hurried back up the hall, coming to a door just beyond the broom closet. She pushed it open and stumbled into Sir Saemwel's room. It was lit by a large chandelier, as well as several lamps. It was rather large, with its own fireplace and two easy chairs. There was also a small cot in one corner. An enormous wardrobe and several bookshelves filled the wall space, and a handful of portraits hung to the side of these bookshelves.

Directly opposite the fireplace was a gigantic bed, upon which Sir Saemwel lay, with Elsi and Mr. Blysffi leaning over him. As Ella got nearer, she could see that he was sweating all over, panting, and blood sprinkled the covers near his head. Mr. Blysffi had exposed Sir Saemwel's right thigh and chest and was soaking them in warm water. The thigh looked a bit inflamed, but Ella couldn't see much else. Elsi sat by her father's side and held his hand.

As Ella reached the bed, Sir Saemwel broke into a fit of coughing. He held his handkerchief in front of his mouth. Ella winced to see the white handkerchief stained with crimson spots.

Elsi stroked her father's hand and looked at him worriedly. "Papa, cen ye hear me?"

Sir Saemwel made as if to speak, but coughed instead. Then he lay back down, gasping for air and looking this way and that with wide, glazed eyes.

Ella put her basin down by Mr. Blysffi's basin of water. "He'e is mo'e wate'h, Mr. Blysffi."

Mr. Blysffi turned as if noticing her for the first time. "Thank you, Ella. Here," he pointed to some oak bark sitting on a desk close at hand, "soak that in the water. Then hurry and get me some more water."

"Olyfia is getting mo'e."

Mr. Blysffi grunted as he dipped his rag in the warm water and began soaking Sir Saemwel's thigh again. "Poor fellow," Mr. Blysffi murmured. "He should have told us when it first started to fester."

"Papa, cen ye hear me?" Elsi said again, still stroking Sir Saemwel's hand.

Sir Saemwel coughed, but didn't answer.

Mr. Blysffi turned slightly towards Ella. "You would not happen to know how to treat a dozen-year-old grenade wound, would you?"

Ella shook her head.

"Just as well, I suppose," Mr. Blysffi sighed. "Well, Haeli should have the horse ready soon."

Just then, Olyfia burst into the room with a third basin of warm water. "Here's more water fer ye, sir."

"Good. Ella, can you dump this out?" Mr. Blysffi pushed the basin of water he had been using over to Ella. The water was now only lukewarm and cloudy.

Ella picked up the basin and hurried from the room. She came to the back door, exited, and poured the water out on the ground behind the house. Unsure what to do with the basin, she left it on the porch by the back door and hurried back to Sir Saemwel's room.

When she entered, Olyfia was wrapping the oak bark around Sir Saemwel's thigh, and Mr. Blysffi was laying more bark on Sir Saemwel's chest. Ella walked a few paces into the room and then stopped, feeling useless.

"That should help somewhat," Mr. Blysffi said as he stood up.

Suddenly, Haeli burst through the door. "Da, the horse is ready."

"Perfect timing," Mr. Blysffi said. "You stay here, Haeli. I will be back before you know it." With that, he rushed from the room.

The four girls stood and stared at each other for a moment. Elsi touched her father's sweaty forehead. "He is burnin' up. I ha' no seen him this bad since two years ago. He does no even respond to me when I'll talk to him."

"I am sure it is jist a fever," Olyfia said. "He will be as good as new in a week or two."

"Do ye think so?" Elsi looked up.

"Ay, sure," Olyfia responded confidently.

Elsi sighed. "Well, will ye get me some cool water fer his brow?"

Olyfia nodded and—taking Ella by the arm—left the room.

"Where is the basin?" Olyfia asked.

"By the back doo'h," Ella replied. "Is that fine?"

"Ay, did ye rinse it out?"

"No."

"Ye should ha'."

They reached the back door. As they left the house, Ella picked up the basin and followed Olyfia to the water pump near the outhouse. Ella put the basin under the spigot while Olyfia pumped. Ella swirled the first few spurts of water around in the basin and then dumped them out before letting it fill all the way.

"Ay, that man worries me," Olyfia finally said.

"But you told Elsi that he'd be as good as new in a week o'h two," Ella replied.

"An' if she'll ever quires ye, ye oughtta-should say the same thing," Olyfia answered. "That poor girl cares more about her father than anything else in the entire world."

Ella thought about this for a few minutes. "Does that mean Si'h Saemwel won't be fine?"

Olyfia grunted. "I ha' no seen him that bad fer two years." She stopped pumping for a moment and looked at Ella levelly. "He almost *died* two years ago." She continued pumping. "The doctor said that if he'll ever got that sick again, he would no survive."

Ella was silent for a while. "Is it his battle wound?"

"Ay," Olyfia replied. "Doctor Heyl thinks that they never got all the pieces o' metal out o' him, and it ha' caused him no end o' trouble." Olyfia stopped pumping. "There, that should be enough."

Ella picked up the basin and started back towards the house.

"Ye do a lot o' readin'," Olyfia said. "Do ye know any reme-dies for a wound?"

"I studied scu'vy and childbi'th," Ella replied, "but I can't say I eve'h lea'ned much about t'eating wounds."

"Anythin' fer infections?" Olyfia asked.

Ella reached the door and thought for a moment. Olyfia opened the door, and they entered. "Alcohol is antibacte'ial, isn't it? That might help." Ella paused, then continued, "Fresh cinnamon and hot peppe's are antibacte'ial, too..."

Olyfia made a face. "I doubt hot peppers will do us any good."

Soon they reentered Sir Saemwel's room. Ella put the cool water down by Elsi, who bathed her father's brow with it.

Ella looked around the room. "Whe'e is Haeli?"

"Right here," said Haeli as she pushed open the door. In her right hand, she was carrying a silver tray with a teapot, cream, sugar, four teacups, and four scones. Haeli set the tray down on the low table before the fire. "I hope you were not saving the raspberry scones for anything in particular, were you, Olyfia?"

"No," Olyfia replied.

"Good," Haeli said, "we may as well sit and sip while we wait."

Haeli filled each teacup with a black tea, added cream and sugar, and then handed each girl a cup. Ella and Olyfia both took seats by the fire, but Elsi stayed with her father to drink the tea. Haeli sat on the hearth and sipped quietly at her cup. She was about as sober as everyone else, but she still seemed cheerful somehow—no, perhaps happy wasn't the right word; she looked hopeful. Haeli's eyes twinkled at Ella reassuringly as if to say, "Do not worry, Sir Saemwel will be alright."

They sat for a few minutes when Sir Saemwel coughed again. He held his handkerchief to his mouth and hacked fiercely. Elsi stroked his hand. "Papa, are ye alright? Cen ye hear me, Papa?"

Sir Saemwel lay back again, wheezing. After a few more minutes, his mouth moved. "Sara? Sara, dear, are you there?" he asked weakly.

Elsi nearly dropped her tea as she leaned close to him. "Yes, Papa, I am here."

"Olyfia?"

"I am here, too." Olyfia, Ella, and Haeli ran to his side.

Sir Saemwel breathed heavily. "I thought I saw my daughter."

"I'm here," Elsi said again, stroking his arm softly. "I'm here."

Sir Saemwel coughed slightly. "There is something I need to tell the two of you." He paused. "I should have told you this before. I should tell you now...in case. In the basement there is a door–" he broke off, coughing, but soon resumed, "–behind the empty bookshelf. The key is behind your mother." Here he broke off again, coughing up more blood.

"Oh, Papa, do no!" Elsi whispered. "Do no press yerself. Ye will be fine. Relax, do no talk."

Sir Saemwel lay back again, wheezing. He was quiet for some time, but then spoke again, more softly now. "Behind the door, you will find... it." He coughed softly. "You can sell it for a fortune if I... leave."

Ella grabbed the corner post of the bed to keep her hands from shaking with excitement. Could he be talking about...?

But Sir Saemwel wasn't done. "Do not go further. *He* might find you." His voice trailed off, and he didn't seem to see the girls anymore. His eyes darted back and forth, and he coughed heavily. "It was all for nothing, Edwin," he breathed softly. Ella had to strain herself to hear him. "I should have listened... It is my just dues."

Ella's heart pounded in her chest. If Olyfia was right about Sir Saemwel, then there was only one thing he could be talking about. He said it was in the basement?

The door burst open—interrupting her thoughts—and in strode the doctor, followed closely by Mr. Blysffi. The doctor was a rather tall and slim man, with dark hair and eyes. His brow furrowed in a perpetual look of concern. As soon as they entered, Sir Saemwel started coughing again, even worse than before.

Ella, Olyfia and Haeli retreated to the fire and nibbled at their scones while the doctor looked Sir Saemwel over. Ella's mind was hardly in the room. She was mulling over what Sir Saemwel had said. A door in the basement. Where could it lead? She had a very good guess and shivered all over at the thought of it. More than once, she nearly leapt up from her chair to run down into the basement, but before she could act on that impulse, she would see Sir Saemwel lying on his bed with the doctor and Mr. Blysffi leaning over him, and she would come back to her senses.

After several minutes, the doctor turned to Mr. Blysffi. "It gards to me like he ha' contracted some sort o' an fever, which left his body weak fer the resurgence o' his infection. It appears to be spreadin' up his leg, so I'll ha' better bleed it before it gets much farther."

At the mention of bleeding, Ella choked on her scone.

Olyfia saw her and gave a wry smile. "Ever seen a bleedin'?"

"Once," Ella replied. "I wouldn't want to see it again."

Olyfia stood. "I'll will help them do the bleedin' then. I am sure we'll will all need breakfast when it is over, though."

"I will help her," Haeli volunteered, standing and taking Ella by the arm.

The two girls left the room and headed toward the kitchen.

"Papa and Dr. Heyl will want a warm beer when they are done," Haeli said as the door closed behind them.

# 29

# IN THE SUBURB

*I*t was now about three hours after sunrise. Ella and Haeli ate together, and then—one by one—everyone else in the house had come into the kitchen for breakfast. Olyfia joined them soon after Ella finished warming the beer for Mr. Blysffi and the doctor. Haeli then left, and Olyfia quickly explained to Ella how to cook oat porridge and set a customary Pistosian breakfast.

"Ye ha' tained a rather unusual first day o' work," Olyfia said. "Usually we tain a merri big breakfast in the dinin' room with all o' us together."

Just before the doctor came in for breakfast, Olyfia ushered Ella out of the kitchen. "Cede an' get yerself ready fer the day. There is no sense in ye workin' all day in yer nightgown."

Ella obeyed. A few minutes later, she returned to the kitchen to find Elsi sitting at the small kitchen table while Olyfia served the porridge. Ella quickly grabbed the teapot and poured Elsi a cup of tea.

"Is the'e any news?" she asked.

Elsi shook her head. "Dr. Heyl wants to ceive Papa back to his house so that he cen keep a better eye on him."

Olyfia put a hand on Elsi's shoulder. "It would be fer his vest."

Elsi was silent for a very long time. She turned her porridge with her spoon absentmindedly. "I do no want to leave him."

"What does yer Da need?"

Elsi didn't reply.

Just then, Mr. Blysffi entered the room. Olyfia rushed to the cupboard to get him a bowl. "Would ye like some more porridge, sir?"

"No, thank you, Olyfia," Mr. Blysffi said as he sat down next to Elsi.

"Would you take some tea?" Ella asked.

Mr. Blysffi grinned broadly. "Well, if you force it on me."

Ella poured him a cup, and he sat for a moment in silence. "Elsi," he finally said, "with how things are shaping up, I think that if I stay here—with your Da as he is—I will be more of a burden to you than a help. I do not want you to worry about hospitality when Sir Saemwel needs you so badly. I figure I can leave this afternoon with Dr. Heyl and get back to my fort by nightfall."

"Thank ye, Mr. Blysffi. It is merri thoughtful o' ye," Elsi said.

"But," Mr. Blysffi continued, "I do not want to leave you here all alone, so I was thinking I could leave Haeli here to keep you company."

"Ye are too kind," Elsi said, "but I am sure ye will need Haeli back at yer fort."

"Do not worry about that," Mr. Blysffi replied. "If it would help you to have her here, then you need only say so. I do not want to desert you."

Elsi thought about this. "I have Olyfia, Ella, and Dr. Heyl... and Aunt Nansi, and Reverend Daerl, if it'll venes to that. No, Mr. Blysffi, take Haeli with ye."

Mr. Blysffi sat for a little while longer, as if hesitant to continue. "Dr. Heyl seems to think it would be best for your Da to stay at his house."

Elsi said nothing, but she nodded.

"I was figuring," Mr. Blysffi continued, "that I could help Dr. Heyl move your Da when I leave—to see that he is fine." Mr. Blysffi paused again. "Would you like to come, too?"

Olyfia turned and looked hard at Elsi. Elsi fidgeted with the tablecloth, avoiding eye contact with anyone. "Ella, do ye know where Dr. Heyl's house is?"

"No, ma'am," Ella replied.

Elsi stood suddenly. "I probably should no go with ye; I might no leave. Ella, ye accompany them fer me so that ye can see where Dr. Heyl lives—ye'll oughtta-should know in case I need to legate ye there." With that, Elsi left the room rather hurriedly.

———

Soon after breakfast it rained. Dr. Heyl left to get his cart, saying he would be back when the rain stopped. The drizzle lasted through dinner—which was a quiet and dismal meal. The rain stopped a few hours before sunset, and Dr. Heyl soon pulled up in his cart. It was rather large, with strong springs over each wheel, affording a very smooth ride for Sir Saemwel. Dr. Heyl and Mr. Blysffi loaded Sir Saemwel into the cart, and then they, along with Haeli and Ella, set out to Entwerp Proper.

Sir Saemwel was delirious again and fell into a violent fit of coughing when they first put him on the cart. Elsi hadn't come out to see him off, but stayed inside.

"Ye ha' better bring him back," Olyfia told Dr. Heyl. "She is in a terrible way. She will be yer next patient if ye'll cen no save Sir Saemwel."

Now they were heading across the commons to Entwerp Proper. Haeli and Ella rode in the back of the cart with Sir

Saemwel while Dr. Heyl drove, and Mr. Blysffi rode alongside on his horse.

Just before they reached the outskirts of Entwerp Proper, Haeli leaned over to Ella. "You heard what Sir Saemwel was saying to Elsi?"

Ella nodded. "How could I fo'get?"

Haeli grinned broadly. "I hoped I could be there to see what is behind the door, but I wish you a merri of luck, anyway. But–" Haeli took Ella's hand, "–do not be too eager to find the door. Give Elsi time to adjust to not having her father at home. Do not bother her about it for a week or so."

"What about Olyfia? Can I talk with he'h about it?"

"Ay," Haeli replied, "that would be fine, but don't *bother* her about it; we can afford to wait."

Dr. Heyl pulled back on the reins suddenly. Ella looked up to see a large man coming up to the cart to talk to them. She shivered at the sight of him. He was older than forty, with white hair hanging in wisps to his shoulders. His nose was hooked like a beak, and his eyes were dark and narrow like a rat's. He wore a wide belt from which hung a long-barreled pistol and a rapier. The most startling aspect of the man, however, was his right arm.

At his shoulder, three metal bars sprouted as if affixed to his bones. These then ran down his arm in a way that reminded Ella of scaffolding—or a skeleton. Hinged at his elbow, the metal bracing creaked ominously when he bent his arm. When they reached his hand, the bars wrapped around his knuckles in such a way that if he closed his fist, they protruded outwards in three spikes.

"God bless ye, Dr. Heyl," the man said, raising his left arm in greeting. He spoke in a formidable, deep voice.

"And may He return yer blessing, Sheriff Laei," Dr. Heyl replied, coming to a complete stop.

Sheriff Laei looked at each of the passengers; then his eyes lighted on Sir Saemwel. He frowned. "Llifsa! What ha' happened?"

"I am ceivin' him back to my house. It is his wound again."

Sheriff Laei nodded, a look of deep concern crossing his face. "Ye ha' best hurry, then. Be sure to avoid Nychweni Square. There are strikers there, see."

Sheriff Laei moved away from the cart to let it pass, nodding to Mr. Blysffi, Haeli, and Ella. "Sir, miss, miss," and with that, he turned a corner and was gone. Ella shuddered.

Dr. Heyl continued on his journey.

The cart wound this way and that through the crowded streets of Entwerp, sometimes waiting for another cart, sometimes slowing to accommodate pedestrians, but the crowds eventually thinned out, and they entered a part of the town— Ella guessed on the west side—that was much less crowded.

Haeli leaned over to Ella. "They just built this part of town. They call it a *sub-urban* town. Is not that a clever name?"

In a few minutes, they pulled up in front of a good-sized house, with a white picket fence and a quaint flower and herb garden. As they came up to the side of the house, a round woman came out to them.

"By the saint's beard, Charles!" she said as she came up to Sir Saemwel. "He *is* in a bad way. I ha' already got a bed made fer him; all ye ha' to do is bring him in."

"Ay, love," Dr. Heyl replied, "that is what we were plannin' to do."

The doctor jumped into the back of the cart. Mr. Blysffi handed the reins of his horse to Haeli and dismounted.

"Gently now," Mrs. Heyl said as the two men lifted Sir Saemwel's stretcher off the cart.

Sir Saemwel groaned and coughed.

"Do no hurt him now," Mrs. Heyl said.

"We jist need to get him inside," Dr. Heyl replied. "Open the door fer us, love."

Mrs. Heyl bustled back to the house, the two men following with Sir Saemwel on his stretcher.

Haeli grinned as she watched them enter the house. "Sir Saemwel should do well in there." Then she frowned. "At least he will be well cared for."

They sat in silence for a few minutes, and then Dr. Heyl and Mr. Blysffi reappeared.

"Thank ye merri much, Stifyn, fer stoppin' by and helping. I'm afraid I ha' kept ye later than ye might ha' wished. Godspeed to ye."

"Thank you," Mr. Blysffi responded with a nod. "Haeli, are you ready to leave?"

"Ay, Da," Haeli said. She turned to Ella. "Goodbye, Ella. I am glad I could meet you." She kissed Ella and slipped down from the cart. "You had better still be here next time I come up."

"I will," Ella replied.

Then Mr. Blysffi took her by the hand and kissed her as well. "Do not get into any mischief, now."

"I won't p'omise anything," Ella said with a smile.

Mr. Blysffi laughed heartily. "Do you think you can get back to the Pickerings?"

"I think so," Ella answered. "I watched the streets Dr. Heyl took."

"Good."

With that, Mr. Blysffi mounted his horse and lifted Haeli behind him.

"Tell Elsi and Olyfia that I will pray for them!" Haeli said. "Oh, and of course I will pray for you, too."

"Thank you, Haeli," Ella replied. "I'm su'e they will miss you —and I will miss you, too."

Mr. Blysffi grinned broadly. "Do not worry, Miss Ella, we Blysffis are like the measles: we stay with you through hell and high water despite your best efforts."

He and Haeli burst into a fit of laughter as they trotted away.

Ella sighed and turned around. Dr. Heyl had already moved his cart and was nowhere to be seen. She was all alone. With another sigh, she walked back down the road by which she had come. She was very certain of her way back to the Pickering's house until she left the suburb and entered the crowded streets of the city.

It was one thing for her to move through those bustling streets in a cart, but quite another to be pushed and shoved and jostled right along with all the other pedestrians. For all that, Ella felt that somehow no one bore her any ill-will. More than once, some thick-set woman, or broad-shouldered man, shoved her out of the street just as a cart came rolling by.

"Ye'll oughtta-should be more careful, ma'am," they would say with a tip of their hat and a wide grin.

Most every lady she met gave her a smile, and several even gave a "God bless ye." Several children stopped her to ask what time it was. To this question, she could only tell the child that she regrettably didn't carry a watch with her. Back in Blisa Village in Slyzwir, she had a pocket watch, but she hadn't taken it with her—which was probably a good thing, as she certainly would have lost it at sea.

She tried to keep careful count of the streets she passed in order to turn where she had seen Dr. Heyl turn, but she inevitably lost count in the bustling throng, and she soon found herself on a street she didn't recognize at all.

She turned around and went down the street she had just passed, but this was as unfamiliar as the last. She turned down an alleyway, thinking it would route her back to the first street she was on, but it led to another street altogether.

The more she tried to retrace her steps, the more she lost her way. For a moment, she gave up trying to find her way and simply let the crowd push her along. If she could just get out of the city, she would know which way to go to reach the Pickering's house.

After ambling along for several minutes, she suddenly found that the crowd had left her. She looked around and found herself in a large square filled with gruff-looking men. It only took her a moment to realize she was back in the square where the strikers had accosted Martyn the day before. Her heart beat with new confidence. She was fairly certain she could find her way back to the Pickerings from here, but she would have to cross right through the strikers' camp.

Without a further thought, she plodded through the square. Every step she took was more hesitant than the first. On all sides of her, weathered and disgruntled men peered at her, squinting their eyes and scowling. Some of them bore a strange light in their eyes that made Ella feel very uncomfortable, but still, she moved on. She wished she had thought to bring her dagger.

She passed right by a makeshift tent with a shady-looking man in front. The man looked at her closely with black, shifty eyes, like those of a rabid rat. Just as Ella passed him, he snatched at her skirt.

"Here, petticoat."

Ella dashed aside as quickly as she could, tearing the man's hand away. Losing all restraint, she ran. There was a small path of sorts through the midst of the strikers' camp; she followed this the best she could, dodging stray pots and scowling strikers.

She finally passed out of the tent-city and found herself in a small alleyway. A beggar with perfectly white hair and a cloth tied around his eyes was huddling up against one brick wall. She felt like she had seen a beggar like him before, but couldn't think of where. Ella shivered, but not from the cold. The sun was almost gone behind the mountains, and she was now just as lost as before. She felt weak and tired. She wanted nothing better than to crawl into a corner and hope that when she awoke, she would be back safe in her bed—safe at her home in Slyzwir.

But she knew giving up wouldn't help. What she desperately needed was someone to talk to; someone who knew the city's streets and could help her; someone like Clerans. She looked at the white-haired beggar. It was worth a chance.

"Excuse me, si'h," she said, stepping up to him.

The beggar looked over as if he could see her through the white cloth tied tightly over his eyes. He smiled kindly. "Yes, child?"

Ella hesitated. This man was blind. What good would it be to ask him for directions? Then again, there was no harm in asking. Surely even blind beggars have to know their way around the city. "Excuse me, si'h, but you wouldn't happen to know whe'e Si'h Saemwel Picke'ing lives, would you? I've got myself lost, you see."

"Sir Saemwel Pickering," the beggar said, as if he recognized the name. "I am afraid I do not. Which side of town is he in?"

"The no'th side," Ella replied promptly.

The beggar thought for a moment and then stood up. "Well, I might be able to point you in the right direction, but I may not be much help past that."

He moved back out through the strikers' square and turned towards a large street that exited the square to their left. Ella followed, still wary of the strikers, though more confident with the beggar guiding her.

The beggar tapped his way forward with a little cane until he reached the street. Feeling his way along the wall of a building, he came to an intersection with a much larger street. The lanterns had been lit, casting a ruddy glow over the cobblestones. Though it was late, there were several people walking this way and that. Most of these were men, and they were all rugged and shifty-looking, not at all like their bright-eyed counterparts who roamed the streets during the day.

The beggar pointed down the road. "That way is north. I

expect this road will lead you somewhere close to Sir Pickering's place."

Just then, a gruff voice called out to them. "Ho, there!"

The beggar shrank back into the shadows, and a towering figure strode up to Ella. As he walked, a creaking noise emanated from his right arm. To her horror, Ella realized this was Sheriff Laei, whom she had seen earlier that day. Ella shivered involuntarily at the sight of him.

He looked her up and down like a cat might survey a mouse just before it pounces. "Ye do no belong here," he finally said.

Ella licked her dry lips. "I'm lost."

"This is the wrong part o' town to be lost in. Nice young women do no belong here." Sheriff Laei rested his hand on a pistol butt and shifted its position on his hip. "Where are ye lost from?"

Ella hesitated. Was it safe to tell *him*?

"Sir Saemwel's place or Dr. Heyl's place?" the Sheriff pressed.

Ella could see that Sheriff Laei knew more about her than she realized. He must have recognized her from earlier. "Si'h Saemwel's place."

Sheriff Laei nodded, took hold of Ella's hand, and marched off down the street. Ella tried to pull her hand back, but the Sheriff had it in an iron grip. There was no escaping. Ella swallowed hard.

"Ye are the new housekeeper?"

Ella didn't answer. The Sheriff seemed to know too much as it was.

"Ye must be new to this city entirely," the Sheriff continued. "Ye got in no harm tonight, but if ye'll do ha' to get lost again, do no move towards the center o' the city, especially after dark. And never ask beggars fer advice. Ye do no want to know what I ha' seen them do to young women like yerself."

Ella remained completely mute as Sheriff Laei pulled her along. Soon, she recognized some buildings. Then they reached a street that Ella remembered – they weren't far from Sir Saemwel's house now. If she could just get free of the sheriff, she felt sure she could make it back.

Sheriff Laei, however, did not relinquish his hold on her hand, but kept plodding on. Soon, the houses grew farther apart and then fell away altogether. Now they were passing the moonlit common lands. Off in the distance, Ella could see the lights of Sir Saemwel's manor. If she could only get *there*—and get away from this sheriff.

She focused so much of her attention on the lights that she didn't see two figures hurrying down the road toward her.

"Sheriff Laei!"

Ella jumped; it was Elsi's voice. She looked ahead, and there were Elsi and Olyfia walking towards them.

"Sheriff Laei! Oh, I am so glad to run into ye. I ha' lost my new housekeeper..." Elsi trailed off as she saw Ella standing by the Sheriff's side. "Oh, Ella, yer safe! Thank God!"

"She still needs to learn which parts o' town *no* to wander around in," Sheriff Laei said as he released her hand.

Elsi threw her arms around Ella. "Oh, I wos worried ye ha' gotten into some harm."

Ella returned the embrace a little awkwardly. She could feel Elsi sobbing. She didn't feel like she knew Elsi that well. Why was she so upset?

Sheriff Laei nodded to them and backed away. "I am glad I wos o' service to ye." He turned and walked back towards the city.

Elsi finally let go of Ella. "Oh, I am so glad ye are back. Vene on then, we need to get back to the house. Supper is waitin' fer ye."

Elsi turned and hurried back to the manor. As Ella followed, Olyfia stepped forward and took her by the arm.

"She ha' been like that ever since Sir Saemwel left. Foor girl,

I do no know what we cen do fer her, except just weep with her."

Olyfia turned and looked Ella in the face. "Llifsa, child! Ye are as white as a sheet! Ye gard like ye ha' seen a ghost."

"I just might have," Ella replied, looking back at the retreating Sheriff Laei.

Olyfia laughed. "Ye thought he was arrestin' ye, did no ye?" Olyfia laughed again. "Ella, ye are safer with him than with me. Llifsa! Jist be glad he did no kiss ye goodby, like any well-mannered man would ha'."

Ella blushed and looked back over her shoulder. She started and furrowed her brow.

"What is the matter?" Olyfia asked, turning around as well.

Ella looked closely at the road. There was Sheriff Laei's back, almost dissolved into the moonlight, but no one else was there.

"Nothing," Ella finally said, "nothing."

*Odd,* she thought. *I was certain I saw that blind beggar a moment ago.*

# COUNTER-PLOT

*T*he cool night breeze gently brushed Ernest's face as he stepped out onto the deck. He was carrying a small tray of food for those on watch duty. The sun had set a few hours earlier, and most of the crew had gone to bed. Ernest had helped Lewis clean the galley and then brought the leftovers up to the watchers. It was a cool night, and the wind had picked up a little. Ernest wrapped his coat tightly around himself.

"Here, lads, your food's here. Come one, come all." Bill and Tell walked over from opposite sides of the ship.

"We were afraid you haved forgeted about us," Bill said as he grabbed a loaf of bread.

"I never forget about the watchers," Ernest said.

"Yes, you do," Tell replied. "You forgeted about us last time."

"Do'ed I?"

Bill shook his head. "Tell, *you're* the one what forgeted about it last time."

Tell shrugged meekly and downed a pint of ale.

Ernest set the tray down on a spare barrel and walked over to the gunwales.

"Baptism, Tell. I sometimes wonder if'n you *do* have a brain or not."

"I think I do," Tell replied.

"Then maybe you could use it," Bill said.

Tell shrugged again.

Ernest looked out over the dark water. "It's nice and calm out tonight."

"Do'edn't you ever have any schooling?" Bill asked.

"Yes," Tell said with evident pride, "I *was* in school for a year."

"And how long ago was that?"

Tell thought for a moment. "I think I was seven?"

"Do'ed you learn how to think stupidly there?"

Ernest shook his head. Let those two keep bickering; it didn't matter to him.

Just then, he heard a noise by the boat's hull, like the sound of an oar. Perking up his big ears, Ernest looked down to see a small skiff pulling up to the side of the galleon. A cloaked figure manned it. He pulled in his oars and looked up at Ernest—an old beggar wrapped in tattered clothes.

"Get out of here, old man," Ernest cried, "unless you want to feel a pirate's steel."

The man stared at Ernest. "Hand me a rope, Scribe."

Ernest shrank back at the sound of the voice. It was the Albino.

Bill and Tell both jumped when they heard the voice as well.

"Hold it right there," Bill said. "Who's that?"

"Ask your captain." The very tone of the voice made Bill and Tell freeze.

Ernest tossed a spare rope over the side. The Albino grabbed hold of it and hauled himself to the deck. Once there, he looked carefully at Bill and Tell and then examined Ernest.

"All of you, come with me."

The three pirates followed the Albino, trembling as they made their way to Holgard's cabin. Upon reaching the door, he did not knock, but simply walked in. Holgard and Killjelly froze as soon as the Albino entered. They were leaning over the table, looking at a map.

Holgard looked the Archeomancer up and down. "Weel, you're back."

"Yes," the Albino replied, "and there are two more here who have seen me." So saying, he ushered Bill, Tell, and Ernest into the room.

Both Bill's and Tell's eyes were wide with fear.

Holgard looked at them closely. "You may as well know," he finally said. "I expect we will need more on you soon, anyway. Stay here and listen, but when you go back to join your comrades—this never happened. You never speak on it outside this room. Not even to each other."

Bill and Tell nodded mutely.

Holgard turned to the Albino. "What do'ed you find?"

"I found the house, the girl, the man. Everything."

"All on *what*?" Holgard snorted.

The Albino motioned to Ernest. "Perhaps he should read the transcript to refresh your memory."

So saying, the Albino reached into his scrip and produced the parchment which Ernest had written when the Albino had delved into Jock Blowhoarder's mind. He handed it to Ernest.

"Should I read it in Tylweni?"

"No," Holgard said, "I want to understand it."

"Alright, then." Ernest cleared his throat and scanned the page, translating as he read. "He says that he seed Entwerp Coastal and then moved to a different city—Entwerp Proper. Then he seed a big house. There is an older man inside the house. Hmm, let's see. Then he seed a woman leprechaun with a rabbit-lip; then another man what's a gardener; then... well, it looks like it changes here. He says he seed a ship—"

"You can stop there," the Albino said.

Holgard thought for a little. "So, you finded this house, the old man, the gardener, and the leprechaun?"

"Yes," the Albino replied.

"But what does that *mean*?" Holgard asked. "I'm looking for the Gwambi treasure, not some random Llaedhwythi villagers."

"But they will lead you to the treasure."

Holgard was silent.

Killjelly spoke now, "How? What do these people have to do with the treasure?"

"They are the Blowhoarder's story," the Albino replied. "Jock found the treasure, and if you want to find it, too, then you must follow his story. Who did he talk to? Where did he live? What places did he frequent? To find what he found, you must become *Jock*."

There was a long silence.

"But I have found something else," the Albino continued. All the pirates looked at him with interest. "The girl, Ella, the one whom I captured with Jock."

Holgard sat straighter. "Where is she? What do'ed you do with her?"

"She is in the house, with the rabbit-lipped leprechaun."

Holgard snorted. "You should've killed her. If'n Longfinch finds her, then he may get Jock to talk. We can't let him find the treasure first."

"You miss her importance," the Albino said. "She is deeply connected to this search—deeply connected with Jock."

Holgard looked at the Albino closely. "What do you mean?"

"The house is the key to the treasure," the Albino replied, "and the gardener is the key to the house. The old man owns the house, but he is dying. The leprechaun keeps the house. Ella is another key. She was from Jock's town—a connection already. Now she works in the house, has befriended the leprechaun and the gardener, and the old man trusts her. She is a part of Jock's story. We must seek her out, learn more about her, learn what she knows."

"But we already questioned her," Holgard said. "She knows nothing about the treasure."

"Nothing consciously, but she is too interconnected with this story to be useless. She is a key link in our search. I know this. You cannot discard her so hastily. She will help us yet."

Holgard snorted. "I still don't see how this helps us."

The Albino smiled hollowly. "Longfinch wishes to raid the city?"

"Ay," Holgard nodded, "a false attack so they willn't expect us later."

"Good," the Albino said. "Give me five of your men, and we will raid the house."

Holgard considered this for a moment. "Only five?"

"The house is guarded by three women. Five should be plenty. I will question them and examine the inside of the house."

"And how will that help?"

The Albino looked Holgard hard in the eyes. "The house is built on the ruins of a Gwambi fortress. It is the gateway to the treasure."

A smile spread across Holgard's face. "Very weel, then. There are three pirates here already. I will find two more for you before tomorrow night. When Longfinch moves to raid the city, you may take them to raid the house."

The Albino nodded.

Holgard grinned savagely. "If'n one on those in the house tells you where the treasure is, kill them all. There is no need to leave someone alive to tell Longfinch."

The Albino laughed. "To be sure, but only after I have extracted everything they know."

# THE DOOR

*E*lla slept well that night. She woke before the sun with plenty of time to prepare herself for the day. She lit her lantern and took her time getting dressed, deciding to wear her dagger today after the events of the preceding evening. Next, she combed out her hair and braided it into one golden chord.

She examined herself carefully in the mirror. Her hair looked good blonde. It fit her better. Thank goodness all her wishes hadn't turned it brown. She looked closely at herself one last time. Today she would be the perfect housekeeper—on that, she was determined.

When she finished, she picked up her candle and left the room. She moved through the halls of the big house and stopped outside Olyfia's room. *Just in time,* she thought. She knocked lightly on Olyfia's door. There was no reply. Was it possible Olyfia was awake and making breakfast already? Ella knocked again, a little more firmly.

"Jist a moment," came a groggy voice from within.

Ella stepped back from the door and folded her hands together. Was she too early somehow?

Soon the door opened, and Olyfia stood before her with

frazzled hair and wrinkled night gown. Dark rings sat under her eyes. "God bless ye, Ella," Olyfia said, giving a weak smile. "I will be with ye soon. I am afraid I am a little late in startin' the day; Elsi tained a bad night o' it."

Ella looked Olyfia over. "I see."

Olyfia nodded. "Give me a moment to get ready fer the day, an' I will meet ye in the kitchen. We oughtta-should make somethin' especially nice fer Elsi's sake."

Olyfia was about to close the door when Ella replied, "Take you'h time; maybe even sleep some mo'e if ye need to. I will make b'eakfast fo'h both of you."

A look of relief spread across Olyfia's face. "Thank ye, Ella. God bless ye," and she shut the door.

Ella didn't wait to hear whether Olyfia would crawl back in bed, but turned immediately towards the kitchen.

She first stopped by the water pump and brought in two buckets of water. She stoked the stove and set a pot of water on for the oat porridge. Next, she looked around in the cupboards to see what ingredients she had to work with. Something especially nice; that was what she was supposed to make. What did her mother make for special occasions?

She finally set her mind on panned-eggs. It had been her favorite when she was younger. She used to pretend that if she ate them, they would make her hair straighter.

Ella dug around in the cabinets until she found a high-sided pan. She then put a pat of butter from the dairy into it and put it in the oven to melt. Next, she mixed up a light batter of eggs and milk with a little flour and salt. She removed the pan from the oven and poured the batter over the browned butter. Finally, she put it all back into the oven to bake.

About this time, the water came to a boil. Pouring off about half of it into a teapot, she used the rest to make oat porridge like Olyfia had shown her yesterday. About ten minutes later,

Olyfia entered the kitchen just as Ella pulled out a platter and was arranging the breakfast on it.

Olyfia looked over the whole breakfast display. "Ye are amazing, Ella. Thank God that Sir Saemwel hired ye when he did. I'll do no know what state we would be in if he'll had no."

Ella blushed. "Thank you."

Olyfia looked closely at the panned-eggs. "What is this pastry ye ha' made?"

"It's panned-eggs," Ella said. "They'h se'ved with honey."

Olyfia raised her eyebrows. "Well, they gard to be tasty."

"Shall I sea've this on the table, o'h do you think Elsi would wathe'h have it in he'h woom?"

"Vest to ha' it at the table. We oughtta-should make this day as close to normal as we cen."

Ella carried her tray out to the table, with Olyfia in front to open the door to the dining room. As soon as Ella set down the platter, she and Olyfia arranged the table to look as nice as possible. No sooner had they finished setting the third place than Elsi entered the room.

Her dress was clean and well-ironed, but askew. Her petticoats were slightly crooked, and one clasp on her bodice was loose. She had dark rings under her eyes, but she had arranged her brown hair impeccably, without a strand out of place.

She nodded to Ella and Olyfia.

"Breakfast, Miss," Olyfia said, motioning to the lovely spread, "including a specialty from Ella."

Elsi took a seat at the head of the table. "It is lovely, Ella. What do ye call it?"

"Panned-eggs," Ella replied. "It's a Slyzwi'ian staple."

"Thank ye, Ella," Elsi said, turning back to the fare. "It is beautiful. So, *so*, beautiful. Thank ye so much." Elsi took one more look at the panned eggs before bursting into tears. "Thank ye so much, Ella."

Olyfia fell to weeping as well, wrapping her arms around

Elsi. "It will be alright, Elsi, dear. We will make it fine without him."

Ella felt a lump in her throat, but she couldn't think why. She quickly served a piece of the panned-eggs and handed it to Elsi, but looking at the pitiful pair was too much for her. She threw her arms around them both and sobbed, too. Under the circumstances, it was the best thing she could have done.

Breakfast took a rather long time after that. Olyfia lost any chance of getting her "normal day." Ella didn't dare look at the clock when they finished. Still, she didn't feel like she had wasted her time, though Elsi ate hardly any of her food.

As Olyfia and Ella cleared the breakfast away, Elsi sat for a while in thought. "That door that Papa told us about..."

Ella paused. "What about the doo'h?" She knew Haeli had told her not to bring it up, but Elsi was the one who had started it.

Elsi was quiet for a while. "It must be merri important to him."

Ella clasped her hands together to keep them from shaking. She had a good guess about that door.

Olyfia put down the teapot she was about to carry into the kitchen. "Elsi, I do no want ye to exhaust yerself. Ye needn't worry yerself with the door today."

Ella looked over at Elsi. She knew Haeli had said not to press her, and she knew Olyfia was probably right, but she desperately wanted to find that door.

"It must be important to Papa," Elsi said.

"Why do you think he neve'h mentioned it until now?" Ella asked. She wasn't pressing Elsi—she had promised Haeli she wouldn't.

"He probably wanted us to trive it as soon as he wos gone," Elsi said.

Ella nodded and tried to act nonchalant.

"Do no stress yerself," Olyfia said.

Elsi stood and looked around. "Where is the basement, anyway?"

Ella let out her breath slowly—how long had she been holding it?

"The entrance is in the kitchen," Olyfia replied as she picked up the teapot again.

Ella grabbed the breakfast platter and followed Olyfia and Elsi into the kitchen. She hurriedly put the dishes into the washbasin, but left the food on a corner of the counter.

By this time, Olyfia had pushed the small kitchen table aside, revealing a trap door. "Sir Saemwel ha' me cover this over," she explained. "Are ye sure that ye want to go gardin' around down there?"

Elsi nodded. "Papa told us about the door fer a reason."

Olyfia turned to Ella. "Get a couple o' lamps from the back closet."

Ella dashed off and returned quickly with two lamps. When she returned, she found that Olyfia had opened up the trap door. Inside was utter blackness. Elsi set her face firmly, with a gleam of determination in her brown eyes.

Ella lit the lamps and handed one to Elsi.

"Thank ye," Elsi said, and then she stepped into the hole. Olyfia and Ella followed.

They were on a very large wooden staircase that descended twenty steps to a landing and then dropped in a spiral to the bottom of the basement. The basement itself was not very large —only about ten feet across and possibly twenty in length. As Elsi and Ella shined their lamps into the blackness, the light revealed several bookshelves intermittently interrupting the basement walls. Moldy volumes covered most, but one contained a strange assortment of rusted tools and sundry other bits of junk, including a broken pair of glasses, an old lamp, and a few bolts of moth-eaten cloth.

*The Door*

"He said it wos behind the empty bookshelf," Elsi said, looking at the bookshelves closer.

"There is no empty bookshelf," Olyfia added.

Ella pointed to the one void of books. "What about that one?"

"It is no empty," Olyfia replied. "It ha' got all that junk on it."

"But it's empty of books," Ella said.

Elsi looked closely at the bookshelf. "Let us jist move it an' see what is behind it."

This, of course, was much easier said than done. None of them fancied getting knocked on the head by something falling from the top shelf, so they cleaned off all the shelves and set the contents neatly in a corner of the basement—that is, as neatly as they could place such junk.

The shelf itself was built of solid oak and was immensely heavier than any of the three had expected. They put their backs against one side of the shelf and shoved with all of their might. After straining themselves to the utmost, the shelf slid about half an inch. They left off, gasping and stretching their backs.

"Again, again," Ella urged as she braced herself against the shelf, this time wedging her feet against the wall. Olyfia and Elsi joined her, and again, the shelf moved a fraction. After several more pushes, the shelf had moved just enough to see a bit of stone casing—like what might have been around a door. With the next shove, they could see part of a wooden door. Spurred on by their success, Ella, Elsi, and Olyfia threw themselves against the shelf again and again, until finally, it slid enough to reveal the entire door.

The door was a little smaller than an average door, but it looked much thicker. It was made of solid oak that bore spots of mildew here and there. Thick, black metal bands supported the door, connected to large iron hinges. On the left side of the door was a keyhole placed in the middle of one of the metal bands.

Ella, Elsi, and Olyfia stood in front of the door for a moment, panting heavily and grinning at each other.

Finally, Elsi spoke, "Does it jist open?"

"I do no see a doorknob," Olyfia replied, looking the door up and down.

Ella pushed against the door, but it didn't move. She threw her weight against it, but still, it wouldn't budge. Ella thought for a moment. "Whe'e did he say the key was?"

"Behind my mother," Elsi replied, and she turned and dashed up the stairs again. Olyfia and Ella followed. Elsi entered Sir Saemwel's room and—snatching up a stool and standing on it — removed a portrait of a regal-looking young woman from the wall. She looked carefully at the back of the frame.

Olyfia and Ella waited patiently beside her.

"I used to ha' a merri o' trouble with that picture," Olyfia said. "It would never stay balanced properly."

Elsi frowned. "I do no see anythin'."

"Was the'e a key the'e?" Ella asked. "Is that why it wouldn't balance?"

Olyfia shrugged slightly. "I gave the picture to Stifyn Blysffi once, an' he fixed it."

"What do ye mean?" Elsi asked, still looking over the picture frame.

"He took it apart, an' when he was done, it balanced right."

"Did he find a key?" Ella asked.

Olyfia shrugged. "If'll he did, he did no tell me what he did to it."

Elsi sighed and put the picture back. "We will ha' to quire Mr. Blysffi when he'll venes back into town if he'll trived any key when he fixed the frame."

Ella sighed and tapped her foot impatiently. They were too close to cracking this mystery to stop here. Besides, there were still pirates out in the bay, and Jock was still a captive. "Is the'e any othe'h place the key might be?"

Olyfia shook her head. "That's the only portrait of Mrs. Pickering. If Sir Saemwel said it was behind her, then that is the only place it would be."

Ella looked around the room distractedly, staring first at the portrait of Mr. Pickering, then back to the portrait of Mrs. Pickering. Then her eye lighted on the third portrait. The man in the portrait looked very similar to the portrait of Sir Saemwel, almost as if they had been brothers, but Ella guessed it wasn't Sir Saemwel's brother.

She pointed at the portrait. "Who is that a pictu'e of?"

Elsi looked at where she was pointing. "That is Mr. Silas Pickering."

Ella swallowed and nodded. "That was my guess."

She strained her eyes and looked at the portrait of Silas Pickering. She couldn't really remember what her father looked like, but her mother had a small picture of him in her locket. They weren't the same picture, but Ella was quite certain she could make out the resemblance between the two paintings.

She tried to think if this new bit of knowledge had any special significance to her or if it was just a strange coincidence. It only confirmed what she had suspected all along: Mr. Silas Pickering was the same Silas Pickering as her birth father; revealing the startling fact that her father had survived his trip across the sea. How her father had ended up on the coast of Pistos fighting in the Hrufang Instigation to secure the freedom of Llaedhwyth, she couldn't imagine. But one thing she knew for certain: Sir Saemwel would know more about him. Sir Saemwel had been friends with her father. To talk with him would be better than any talks she could have with Jock or any other sailor she met. Sir Saemwel had actually *known* her father. She would have to talk with him about Mr. Silas when he recovered.

If he recovered.

Ella shuddered and followed Elsi and Olyfia from the room.

## 3 2

# THE BATTERY

$\mathcal{I}$t was about midnight when Clerans Blaeith heard the bell ringing. He sat bolt upright and listened carefully. Ay, it was the large brass bell atop the battery; the pirates were finally coming. He threw his covers off onto his brother and hurriedly got dressed. His younger brother, Robert, turned over and put a pillow over his head.

"Do no make too merri o' an noise with those guns, please," he said groggily.

Clerans grinned as he belted on his skinning knife and tomahawk. "I'll will try."

Robert grunted and started snoring again. Clerans dashed into the front room to see Martyn putting on his boots. The two brothers nodded at each other.

Clerans began putting on his boots as well. "Is Laendon on duty?"

Martyn shook his head. "He and Lexi are tomorrow night."

Clerans could tie his boots just faster than Martyn (alas, one of the very few things he could beat his older brother in), so they finished about the same time, then grabbed their hats and rifles. Just before they opened the front door, Mrs. Blaeith came out of her bedroom. She took them both by the shoulders and kissed them.

"Be safe now. I love you both."

They both nodded and kissed her back, then dashed out the door with the sound of the alarm bell still in their ears.

They moved along at a quick pace through the light of the nearly full moon. Others joined them from various streets and alleyways. All headed towards the battery. In less than a minute, they had reached it.

It was a huge granite structure fashioned right against the side of the mountains. Clerans could see the waves of the bay splashing gently against the outer wall of the battery as he and Martyn came to a halt with a group of about twenty other men just before the doors.

Sheriff Laei passed in front of them, motioning towards the battery with his chin. "I need more barrel monkeys inside. Any skilled marksmen to the dike wall. I will arrange fer more powder from Entwerp Proper."

Martyn touched Clerans on the shoulder as he turned to head off down the dike. "Be safe now. I will meet up with ye when we'll are done."

Clerans nodded back to him and then dashed inside the battery.

It was rather dark inside, though several lamps hung on the walls. Clerans didn't need these, however, as he knew his way very well around the battery. Turning a wide corner, he entered the first level of guns. This level held a dozen cannons, each a huge, eighty-pound gun (meaning, of course, that it fired an eighty-pound shot, not that the gun itself weighed eighty pounds). Each cannon pointed out diagonally towards the harbor, ready to obliterate any ship that crossed into its field of fire. Men and boys scurried hither and thither through the level, bringing powder and balls to each cannon. The air was heavy with humidity and the smell of sweating bodies.

Just as Clerans spotted a cannon team that was missing a man, the battery shook and rumbled; the thirty-two-pounders on the third floor had fired.

The head gunner stormed past. "Get this level ready to fire! You tain ten seconds!"

Clerans leapt forward, pushing his way to the cannon he had spotted. He quickly dumped gunpowder down the barrel.

The gunner in charge of the cannon nodded to Clerans. "Barrel monkey?"

"Ay," Clerans said as he wiped sweat from his brow and saluted casually.

One of the other men dropped in a bit of wadding, and then Clerans threw in a shell. The other man shoved the shell down with a ramrod while the gunner pulled back the flint hammer. Once this was done, the three of them backed away.

With every gun on the level now loaded, all eyes turned to the head gunner, who was peering out of a window in the middle of the level.

"They are almost in range..." he murmured. "Ready!"

The whole level was silent. Clerans could look out of the hole his cannon pointed through and see the dim outlines of two ships coming towards the village. There was a rumble of cannons from the other side of Entwerp (somewhere farther down the dike). A few flashes of light sprung from the sides of the pirate ships, followed by another low rumble. Clerans put his hands over his ears and forced himself to yawn.

"Fire!" the head gunner bellowed.

The gunners pulled back on the firing wire to release the flintlock hammers. Clerans could *feel* the sound as all the guns fired at once. The entire building shook like a titanic hammer had hit it, and the guns jerked back, filling the level with smoke.

The other man on Clerans' cannon immediately jumped forward with a bucket of water. In his hand, he bore a rod with a rag tied to the end. Soaking the rag in the water, he plunged it down the barrel to extinguish any sparks that might still be there.

Clerans scooped more powder into the cannon while the gunner and the other man pushed the cannon forward again. As the other man shoved some wadding down the barrel and Clerans picked up another cannonball, Clerans looked out of the hole again. The level above fired, and the whole battery shook.

In the flash of light made by the cannons, Clerans could clearly see the two pirate ships. One (a galleon) was turning back towards the other side of the bay, trying to get out of range of the battery. The other (a man-o-war of the first class) was still coming towards the village. Even as Clerans dropped the shell into the cannon and the other man rammed it in tight, Clerans saw dozens of flashes of light from the side of the man-o-war.

"Return fire!" he yelled in warning as he backed away from the window. As long as he wasn't near the window, he knew he'd be in no danger. The other man backed away as well, and the gunner shoved the cannon through the window.

Just then, there was a sound like that of huge hail stones crashing against the side of the battery. Clerans could feel the battery shake slightly, but that was all. Clerans guessed that a first-class man-o-war like the one the pirates sailed must possess almost a hundred guns – a hundred guns and *no* damage to the battery.

The gunners on Clerans' deck fired back at the man-o-war. The level filled with even more smoke and shook again.

With his ears still ringing from the noise, Clerans leapt forward once more and loaded the cannon. He could see the man-o-war turning in towards the dike. One of its sails lay shattered across the deck, and Clerans thought he could see damage to the gunwales and back decks. He loaded another shell and backed away while the other man rammed the shell in tight. In about four more rounds of firing, the man-o-war would be underneath the range of eighty-pounders—too close to the dikes to shoot at safely.

A boy a few years younger than Clerans dashed by and dropped another barrel of gun-powder at his feet. The gunner fired, and the cannon lurched back. Again, Clerans loaded the cannon, and again the gunner fired. Each time Clerans loaded, he peered out the window. The galleon finally pulled out of range, all but one of its sails in shambles. The man-o-war carried on, firing now and then on the battery, but with no success.

Finally, the head gunner came striding back through the level. "They are under our range now; clear this level! Get to the dikes!"

The men fired any cannons already loaded and then dashed towards the door, leaving only the gunners to stay and clean out the barrels.

Clerans grabbed his rifle and tomahawk and headed out the door with the rest of the men. He had been working as barrel monkey for three years now, and never in that time had a pirate ship landed on the dike. Only twice had any pirates made it alive under the eighty-pounders' range.

As he passed through the door, Clerans could hear the two levels above him firing and looked out to the harbor to see if any of the shells would hit the ship, but several houses blocked his view.

He quickly made his way to a stretch of the dike near the battery. Most of the men were heading towards the section of the dike on the other side of the bay, where the man-o-war was landing. They would need more men there anyway to keep the pirates back. From his position, Clerans could better see what was happening, and besides, if any pirates tried to take a skiff to a different section of the dike, someone would need to be there to repel them.

Across the bay, Clerans could see a burst of cannon fire.

Martyn was probably down there, though more likely, he was acting as a sharpshooter, not a gunner.

The man-o-war turned to fire a broadside amidst short bursts of fire from the dike. Overhead, Clerans heard the upper levels of the battery fire again. The shells crashed in upon the pirate ship, some shots landing hard in the water to either side, but most pouring into the ship's side and across the deck.

One shell hit a mizzen mast. Groaning, the mast bowed slightly. The pirates dashed about frantically, cutting the sail from the mast so as not to strain it any more than necessary. The sail fell into the water, a mass of tattered and blood-stained cloth.

The man-o-war hovered just in range of the dike. It fired hesitantly and then waited, as if unsure whether to continue. The dike cannons fired, and Clerans could also see a line of rifles deliver a fusillade. Martyn was sure to be among those firing.

That seemed to be what the ship was waiting for. Like some wounded sea-monster, the ship turned slowly and moved back out into the bay. The battery and dike cannons fired one more round of shells and then sat silent.

Clerans strained his eyes in the moonlight. The man-o-war seemed to be heading towards the entrance to the bay, its torn sails flapping loosely in the breeze. Just ahead of it, Clerans thought he could make out the silhouette of the galleon, already passing out to the sea.

*Routed!* Clerans thought. *No pirate cen stand a'fore the guns o' Entwerp!*

Just then, he heard a weak, nasal whistle above him, accompanied by the flapping of wings. Clerans looked up to see Aarushi alight on the side of the dike parapet. She hopped about excitedly, snapping her beak and whistling.

Clerans furrowed his eyebrows. "What is it?"

Aarushi fluttered off the parapet and landed on the street a little ways off, where she turned back and bobbed her head.

"Do ye want me to follow?"

Aarushi cocked her head to one side and stamped her foot, neither nodding nor shaking her head.

Clerans looked at her closely and screwed up his mouth in thought. What *could* she want?

"Do ye want Martyn?"

Aarushi nodded her head vigorously.

"He is over on the other side o' the bay. I think he wos sharp-shootin'—by the cannons."

Aarushi nodded quickly and, with a flurry of wings, was gone.

Clerans took one last look at the retreating pirate ships, shouldered his rifle, and headed back home. Whatever Aarushi was so excited about, it was Martyn's problem now.

## 33

## A HOUSE RAID

*S*upper was just over, the sun was setting, and Ella was wiping the table of the last crumbs. Olyfia removed the last dishes and retired to the kitchen, while Elsi sat at the table pensively, her hands folded in her lap. She appeared to be deep in thought. Ella shook her rag out over the floor and then proceeded to wipe down the chairs—hers and Olyfia's; she ignored Elsi's so long as she was still sitting.

Just as Ella finished and was about to leave for the kitchen, Elsi sighed and stood up. "I am sorry, Ella. Here, ye cen wipe my chair now."

Ella nodded.

Elsi stared out the window, still apparently thinking. "We got as far as we could, I suppose."

Ella looked up. "What was that?"

"With the door," Elsi replied. "We did well today, did no we?"

"Yes," Ella replied. "We did as much as we could." Then after a pause, she added, "You'h fathe'h would be p'oud."

Elsi looked back with surprise. She smiled thankfully. "Ay, he would be, would no he?" She turned back to the window and sighed again. "We need to talk to Mr. Stifyn. I hope he'll venes back through soon."

Ella nodded and shook out her rag again. She was certain the Gwambi treasure was behind that door—and just as anxious as Elsi to get it open. She could wait, however. There was absolutely no way the pirates could figure out what she had discovered in the last few days. She could be patient. After all, a city made of gold and gowns made of diamond would probably not be going anywhere if they had already sat there for the last three thousand years.

"Olyfia," Elsi called, "two old beggars are cedin' up to the door. Do ye tain any supper left fer them?"

"Ay, ma'am," Olyfia called back, "I will attend to them."

Ella looked out the window and paused. The beggar in front was that white-haired, blind beggar she had met in town yesterday. What was he doing here? Was he tracking her?

Suddenly, she glimpsed the second beggar's face. She gasped and stumbled back against the table. In her mind, she could see Jock's tortured body lying in the hay, moaning. The pirate ship swayed beneath him, and before him were two leering figures. One—and by far the worst—Killjelly, the other, the long-armed gnome with a branding iron; the gnome who had almost caught her when she tried to escape. Now here he was again, the same long-armed gnome, helping a blind beggar onto the porch.

Elsi turned to Ella abruptly. "Whatever is the matter? Ye ha' gone pale!"

"It's one of the pi'ates," Ella gasped. "He's a to'tu'e'h."

"What?" Elsi looked at Ella blankly.

Ella bit her lip and then repeated what she had said, saying her 'r's carefully. "He's a torturer!"

Elsi gasped and looked at Ella with some concern, then looked back out the window. At that moment, the second beggar leaned forward to pull on the bell rope and as he did so, his cloak parted, and the sun glanced off a steel blade. Elsi gasped.

"Olyfia, do no answer the door! They are no beggars, but rogues!"

She must have yelled a little too loudly, for both men turned to the window at her cry. On seeing her, the blind man tore the cloth from his eyes, and the second beggar drew a cutlass from his belt.

The first man gave a cry, and four more men darted from their hiding spots at the bottom of the stairs, running up to the porch. Both girls stood breathless at the window, watching the proceedings.

The largest of the group slammed against the door with all his might, but it wouldn't open. The white-haired beggar shoved him aside and touched the door. With a groan, it burst open as if struck by lightning. The other pirates drew weapons —some swords and some pistols—and entered the house.

Elsi screamed, but stood riveted to where she was. Ella couldn't move, either. She could hear light footsteps pounding up the stairs from the kitchen. It must be Olyfia running away. Of course! That was what they needed to do—run away.

Ella grabbed Elsi by the arm and made a dash for the door to the kitchen. If they could just get out the back door, they could probably get away.

Just before she passed out of the dining room, there was a sharp report, and a bullet embedded in the door frame in front of her.

"Halt!"

She froze. She could feel Elsi trembling beside her. Ella took a deep breath and turned slowly.

Before her stood the six invaders, each one bore the unmistakable look of a sailor—with the notable exception of the white-haired beggar. Where he stood now, he no longer looked like a weak, blind man who could do naught but sit in the streets all day. He was broad of shoulder and tall. Power seemed to emanate from every part of him—most specifically, his eyes. With his cloth gone, Ella could see that his eyes were not brown, or even a pupil-less white, but a deep pink. He pulled back his thin lips and spoke in a deep voice.

"Where is the third one?"

Elsi whimpered. Ella couldn't answer; her mouth wouldn't open.

The white-haired man looked at the two girls for a moment and then turned to the pirates.

"Take care of these two. We must search the house for the rabbit-lipped one—the leprechaun."

Elsi whimpered again.

Two pirates stepped forward and grabbed the girls by their shoulders, forcing them into chairs. Ella looked at the one who held her and couldn't help but gasp. It was Ernest, the cook's-mate, the one who had been so nice to her when Killjelly first captured her. How could he have invaded this house after treating her so well? She had trusted him.

The largest of the bunch looked at the two girls dumbly, then pointed to Ella. "Hey, that one there's the one what we getted from Slyzwir."

"Obviously, stupid," the long-armed gnome said, as he nudged the large one hard in the gut. Then he turned to the white-haired man. "What do you want us to do with them? I can make them talk real quick. Let me peel them for you; you will see how I can make them talk."

The white-haired one looked at the gnome closely. "Find the rabbit-lip for me. You can do whatever you want with her. *She* must talk. She knows more than these two."

The gnome nodded. "Alright, let's find her then. Tell, you come with me. We will have fun with her when we find her, willn't we now?"

The large one nodded mutely, and the two dashed from the

room. The white-haired one watched contemptuously. He nodded to Ernest.

"Come with me, Scribe. You other two, keep the girls till we return."

"What do we do with them?" the one holding Elsi asked.

"Keep them alive, at least." The white-haired one shrugged and headed out the door with Ernest just behind.

The two remaining pirates looked at each other and then at the two girls in their care.

"What do you want to do with them?"

"What do *you* do?"

They both looked at the girls again.

The first shrugged. "There's only one thing *I* know to do with petticoats."

They both looked hard at the two girls again.

Ella sat still, but Elsi shivered.

The second pirate took a step towards Elsi and reached out his hand to touch her hair. Elsi recoiled at the touch.

"Well, that's soft now, isn't it?"

The first pirate shoved the second away. "Hands off *her*; she's the one I catched. You can have the other one what Ernest catched."

The second one shoved the first one back. "It really doesn't make a difference. They were both given to us the same."

"One's as good as another," the first shot back. "Look, the blonde's prettier, anyway."

The second one looked hard at Ella. "Holgard might want her whole, though."

The first shrugged. "Doesn't mean we can't have some fun."

Just then, Ella heard some scuffling upstairs and a sharp cry from Olyfia.

The second pirate thought for a moment. "Fine, we will peel the brunette first—together—and then we both peel the blonde."

The first one nodded and turned to Elsi. By now, poor Elsi was trembling all over.

Ella was trying to think of something she could do, but her mind simply wouldn't work. She couldn't think; she could hardly move. Her mind couldn't even make out what the pirates were talking about, though she was fairly certain she didn't *want* to know what the pirates were talking about.

The pirates each grabbed Elsi by a wrist and made as if to pull her off the chair, Elsi let out a frightened moan. The sound made Ella wince, jarring her. What was she thinking? She still had the dagger Lewis had given her. Both pirates were fully armed, but certainly she could do something with that dagger, even if they ended up killing her in the end.

As the two pirates dragged Elsi out of her chair, Ella hiked up her skirts, desperately grabbing at the dagger on her thigh.

"Here now," the first pirate sneered, still holding Elsi's wrist while he leered at Ella's legs and bare knee. Ella tried to push her skirt down with one hand while still reaching for her dagger with the other.

"Can I help you with that?" The pirate sneered again.

Suddenly, a low voice interrupted them.

"Let go o' her an' back away, an' I may no hurt you."

Ella looked at the doorway to see Sheriff Laei standing like an ill omen in the entrance. His solemn face was dark and menacing, his eyes squinted in anger. Anyone—even Sheriff Laei—was welcome at that moment.

"What's this?" the first pirate asked as he let go of Elsi and turned on Sheriff Laei with a drawn sword.

The Sheriff's hands shot out like pistons, his left catching the pirate by the wrist, while his right came forward to hit him in the temple with its metal bracing. The pirate crashed to the floor. His eyes rolled back in pain.

The second pirate snatched at his pistol, but Sheriff Laei was already on him. Punching the pirate in the stomach with his metal braces, he caught him by the hair with his left hand. The pirate made as if to yell, but he had no air left from the blow to his stomach. He took in a breath of air, but then Sheriff Laei's right hand clamped over his mouth. The Sheriff thrust the man onto the table, and then—grabbing the pirate's head firmly in both hands—he gave a sharp twist. There was a sickening crack, and Ella winced, feeling very weak in the stomach. Yet just then, she found her grip on her dagger handle and drew it out.

Elsi fell to her knees at the Sheriff's feet. "Oh, thank ye. Ye ha' saved us, sure."

"Softly now," Sheriff Laei said. "Get up on your feet. I am ceivin' you out o' here."

Elsi tried to stand, but she was trembling too badly. Sheriff Laei scooped her over his shoulder like a sack of potatoes, then turned to Ella. "Cen ye walk?"

Ella stood. Her legs were shaky, but stable enough. Her hands were sweaty as they gripped her dagger. Sheriff Laei nodded and headed out the door. Ella followed as fast as she could.

They dashed down the porch steps and moved across the common lands towards Entwerp Proper. Ella stumbled into the twilight as best she could behind the Sheriff.

"Olyfia's still in the'e," she finally gasped.

Sheriff Laei didn't even turn to look at her. "How many pirates are there with her?"

"Fou'h," Ella replied.

"Four to one are bad odds," the Sheriff replied, "especially if I'll do no know where they'll are."

He continued on in silence for a while, then said. "I'll will get her out o' there, but all the other men are hung up defending the dike."

Ella's mind tried to work through what that meant. Defending what dike from what? Come now, why couldn't she think clearly? "Why a'en't you?" It was the only half-sensible thing she could think to say.

"I wos getting' more 'munition," Sheriff Laei replied, still striding briskly towards Entwerp. "I saw the six o' them pirates when I was enterin' the city. I did no think merri o' them—I thought they wos strikers—until that hawk stopped me. What is her name? The hawk that is always hangin' around Martyn Blaeith?"

"Aa'ushi?"

"Ay, that is her. She stopped me an' made me follow her to the house. I saw the pirates talkin' in the dinin' room an' guessed what wos happenin'."

Ella's head was still spinning. "Whe'e is Aa'ushi?"

"I do no know," Sheriff Laei replied as he shifted Elsi's position on his shoulder. "Hopefully she ha' gone to get Martyn Blaeith, or someone else." Sheriff Laei then gave Ella a side-long glance. "Do ye still need that?"

"What?" Ella asked in confusion.

Sheriff Laei motioned with his eyes to her hand. Ella followed his gaze to see Lewis' dagger still clenched in her fist.

"Oh...yes."

Sheriff Laei shrugged. "You might jist put it away now."

In a few moments, they had reached a cottage on the outskirts of town. Sheriff Laei threw the picket gate open and stomped up to the porch. Ella paused for just a moment to sheath her dagger and then hurried after the sheriff. He pounded on the door loudly. There was no answer. He pounded on the door again and looked up at the moon as if to judge what time it was.

Suddenly, a light appeared in one window. There was the sound of locks being drawn back, and then the door opened slowly. A wrinkled but homey woman peered out at them.

Sheriff Laei nodded to her. "Miss Nansi."

Her eyes opened wide when she saw the Sheriff, and she

flung open the door. "Sheriff Laei! What is the matter? Is that little Elsi ye tain?"

"Oh, Aunt Nansi!" Elsi sobbed.

The woman ushered the Sheriff into the house, placing a hand on Elsi's arm. "There, there, darling, what ha' happened?"

The Sheriff laid Elsi down on a couch. "Their house ha' been invaded."

Ella sat down next to Elsi and gave a small shiver.

"Llifsa!" the woman gasped. "Wos it the strikers?"

Sheriff Laei shook his head. "Worse—pirates."

The old woman put her hands to her mouth in alarm.

"Take care o' these two fer the night, will ye, please? The housekeeper, Olyfia, is still in the house with the invaders."

"I will take good care o' them, do no worry." The old lady dashed off to the hearth to re-kindle the fire.

Sheriff Laei turned to Ella and Elsi. "I'll will be back when I'll cen. Miss Nansi will help you till my return."

Elsi nodded and licked her lips weakly. "Will Olyfia be alright?"

Sheriff Laei turned to the door and opened it. "Pray."

He touched the pistols in his belt and dashed into the night.

# DESTRUCTION

*E*lla's eyes snapped open. Had she been sleeping? She couldn't recollect anything after Sheriff Laei had left the cottage. Now she was leaning up against Elsi, who was fast asleep on the couch. It didn't seem like any time had passed since Sheriff Laei had dropped them off at the cottage, but it must have been hours ago. The sun was just flooding through the quaint windows.

Ella could hear a slight noise and looked over to see the old lady pouring three cups of tea. On a low coffee table, sat a small platter of scones and oat porridge. As she watched, Miss Nansi placed the tea cups onto the platter.

Ella stood up and stretched. She felt sore and achy all over. Her thigh, especially—where she had strapped Lewis' dagger—felt numb.

The old lady looked over in her direction. "Good mornin', dear. God bless ye."

Ella smiled. "Thank you. Thank you fo'h letting us stay in you'h house like this, with no wa'ning."

Miss Nansi smiled, showing dimples among the wrinkles on her face and slightly browned teeth. "Oh, it is no a problem. My house is always open to anyone who needs it. Especially if that someone is with my niece." She nodded to Elsi's sleeping form and then handed Ella a teacup. "Would ye like some tea?"

"Yes, thank you." Ella took the cup with a grateful nod.

The old lady watched her as she took a drink. "I am no sure we ha' met a'fore. My name is Nansi Felonica; everyone jist calls me Miss Nansi. Ye must be the new housekeeper fer my brother-in-law?"

"Si'h Saemwel? Yes," Ella replied. "I'm Ella Donne. It's a pleasu'e to meet you, Miss Nansi."

Miss Nansi gave a childish giggle. "Ye are merri proper-mannered, dear. Ye will make a merri excellent housekeeper, sure."

Ella blushed slightly and took another sip of tea to hide it. "What kind of tea is this? I don't think I've tasted it befo'e."

Miss Nansi took a teacup of her own. "It is maté. I developed a taste fer it when I lived down south, an' now I cen no get off o' it," she smiled and winked.

Just then, Elsi stirred. Miss Nansi looked over at her. "Good mornin', Elsi dear. God bless ye."

Elsi yawned and stood slowly.

"Thank ye, Aunt Nansi." Elsi walked over to the coffee table and sat down.

"Would ye like some tea?" Miss Nansi asked, holding out the last teacup.

They ate breakfast at a leisurely pace. Miss Nansi gave them each a scone and then a small bowl of oat porridge. When they had finished, she poured more maté, and they sat close by the fire. Miss Nansi carried most of the conversation, with Ella doing her best to keep up. Elsi, however, didn't seem to be in any mood for talking. She fidgeted nervously and jumped whenever there was any sound out of the ordinary.

Just as Ella reached the bottom of her third cup of tea, there was a loud knock on the door. Miss Nansi stood and opened the door. Ella swallowed the last of her tea and turned to greet visitors.

Into the house strode Sheriff Laei, followed by Martyn, Laendon, Mr. Blaeith, Clerans, and Aarushi. They all looked tired and sore. Dirt and sweat saturated their hair and clothing, and Clerans was bleeding just above his eyebrow. Each of them carried a rifle, as well as tomahawks and hunting knives in their belts. When Ella saw them, she couldn't help but think of a group of lusty hunters returning from the taming of a vast and rugged wilderness—almost like something out of the books she used to read. She had to admit that they all looked quite romantic.

"Welcome," Miss Nansi said, ushering them in. "Pull up a seat an' tain some breakfast."

"Thank ye, ma'am," Sheriff Laei said as he sat stiffly, "but we cen no stay long. We are only here to pick up the young ladies."

Miss Nansi nodded with a bit of a smile. "Would you like some tea or warm beer?"

They each said they would prefer a little beer—except Clerans. He looked at the teacups and said, "I would prefer some maté, if that was what ye meant by 'tea.'"

Miss Nansi laughed. "Ay, dear, it is maté I am talkin' about." As she poured their drinks, she looked carefully at Clerans' cut. "Did ye get into a fight? Catch any pirates?"

Clerans sighed. "I wish."

Sheriff Laei cleared his throat. "We did no fight any pirates. We ha' been trackin' them all night, though."

Ella folded her hands in her lap. "Did you find Olyfia?"

The men hesitated.

"Did you captu'e the pi'ates?"

Mr. Blaeith set his mug on the coffee table. "Jist before we reached the Pickerings' manor, we saw four pirates cedin' out o' the house an' makin' their way into the mountains."

Sheriff Laei broke in. "We tried to head them off, and

Clerans even took a shot at them, but that only made them run faster. We tracked them all night, but eventually lost their tracks somewhere in the mountains to the south along the coast."

"We would ha' lost their tracks earlier, but fer Aarushi," Martyn commented.

Aarushi looked up from where she sat beside Martyn's cup of beer and gave a nasal whistle, winking at Ella before she dipped her beak back into the beer. Ella couldn't help but smile at the bird—but it was a tired smile.

Elsi finally spoke. "Did ye trive Olyfia?"

The men were silent.

"We thought they ceived her with them at first," Sheriff Laei finally said.

"Aarushi did no see her, though," Martyn responded.

Aarushi looked up and nodded.

"There is no way they took her with them an' still outran us in the mountains," Mr. Blaeith added.

"So whe'e is she?" Ella asked.

"We assume she must still be in the house," Sheriff Laei replied.

"What do ye mean, ye assume?" Miss Nansi asked.

The men were silent.

"We cen no trive her," Sheriff Laei finally said. "We ha' garded through the house and jist cen no trive her." He paused. "We vened here to see if Miss Elsi or Miss Ella might know where she would ha' ceded."

Ella and Elsi exchanged glances, but said nothing. The events of last night flashed through Ella's mind, and she shuddered. Hadn't she heard footsteps running upstairs, and Olyfia's scream?

Sheriff Laei stood and put his empty mug down on the table. The other men followed his example, guzzling down their last swigs. Aarushi fluttered up to Martyn's shoulder.

"We should be leavin' now," Sheriff Laei said, "if the young women are ready?"

Ella stood and smoothed her skirt and petticoats. Surely there was something she needed to pack or attend to, but she couldn't think of anything.

Elsi stood as well, a bit of firmness returning to her. "We are ready."

They quickly made their way across the common lands and soon came to the Pickerings' manor. From the outside, it looked as if all was well, but when they entered the house, Elsi gasped in dismay. A detritus of wanton vandalism filled the house. Furniture lay in a jumbled, overturned disarray, and many of the pictures and tapestries had been torn from the wall and broken.

"We ha' tried to clean up a little," Mr. Blaeith said, kicking some broken glass over to the side of the room. "but we ha' been mostly gardin' fer Olyfia."

"Ay," Sheriff Laei replied, "where did you see her last? Do you tain any idea where she'll might be?"

Elsi was silent.

"I think I hea'd he'h go upstai'hs," Ella said.

"We ha' been all over the upstairs," Clerans murmured.

"Do ye tain any idea *where* upstairs she may be?" Sheriff Laei asked.

Ella thought for a moment. "I'm not su'e. She went up the stai'hs by the kitchen."

Sheriff Laei nodded. "Once more, then."

He turned, and the others followed him toward the kitchen stairway. As they entered the kitchen, both Ella and Elsi froze.

The destruction was much less in the kitchen. The cupboards seemed untouched, and even the dinner dishes sat unmoved at the edge of the washbasin. However, the small kitchen table was thrown against the wall, with the chairs in disarray nearby. The rug that had covered the trapdoor lay in a heap under the stove. Both girls stared at the trapdoor as if it were a heathen savage without the decency to clothe itself.

The men didn't seem to notice the door at all, but marched right past it to the kitchen stairway. Just as Sheriff Laei was about to lead the charge upstairs, Aarushi gave a short whistle. Martyn turned back, looked at the girls, and then followed their gaze to the floor.

"Llifsa!" he gasped. "What in the world is this?"

The others stopped and looked back. Sheriff Laei walked over to the trapdoor and scrutinized it. "I thought Saemwel had this hidden." Then he added in a voice so low that Ella could only barely make out what he said, "So, he did it. But did Edwin know?"

"Only Papa an' Olyfia knew about it," Elsi said, "until yesterday when she showed it to us."

Everyone was silent for a moment.

"Then she must be down there," Mr. Blaeith said, reaching for the latch and opening the door.

# 35

# DISCLOSED

*E*lsi grabbed Ella by the arm. "The pirates must ha' trived the door," she whispered. "They must ha' trived the door. What will Papa say?"

Ella put her hand on Elsi's shoulder comfortingly. "It's al'ight. It wasn't you'h fault." But Ella's stomach was in a knot. The pirates had found the door. What had Olyfia told them? What did they do to her to make her talk? What if they had gotten the door open? What would that mean for Jock? Her heart pounded in her chest so hard she could feel it in her throat.

Mr. Blaeith and Sheriff Laei peered down into the blackness of the basement. "It is as dark as tar down there," Mr. Blaeith said. "Do ye happen to tain a lantern sittin' around somewhere, Elsi?"

Elsi left the room and was back in a moment with a lantern. Laendon lit it and then passed it to Sheriff Laei. Just before the Sheriff descended the stairs, he looked at Ella and Elsi.

"Clerans and you ladies, do no follow us down here unless we'll call you."

Ella swallowed hard.

The Sheriff, Mr. Blaeith, Martyn, and Laendon passed through the trapdoor and were gone. Ella's heart pounded harder in her chest. She strained her ears to hear the *creak, creak, creak* of the men's boots on the stairway. Finally, the footsteps ceased. A few low words were spoken, followed by the hurried sound of feet coming back up the stair. Ella held her breath.

Martyn and Laendon stepped out of the trapdoor. Laendon's face was nearly green, and he looked like he was about to disgorge his supper. Martyn, too, looked a little sick, but he clamped his jaw tight and set his eyes narrow and sharp—like he was fighting back anger.

"Is she alive?" Elsi asked softly.

"No," Martyn replied, breathing heavily—though not from exertion.

Elsi caught her breath. "Dead?"

"Very," Laendon said, then hurried from the room.

Ella's mind was reeling. "Are you ce'tain she's dead? Did you check he'h pulse? You we'en't down the'e very long—"

Martyn cleared his throat. He spoke in a very level and controlled manner. "I did no know there wos any person on this earth who was still barbarian enough to do what those pirates did."

Laendon came back with a sheet, and they went back into the basement. All four men emerged a few moments later.

Sheriff Laei was grim. "I am sorry, Miss Pickering. Olyfia is dead."

They were all silent. Elsi let out a single sob and grabbed Ella's arm. "She cen no be dead! How cen she be dead?"

Ella could think of nothing to say. It didn't seem real. Olyfia had been alive last night; how could she not be now? *Olyfia is dead.* The words didn't have any meaning.

Everyone was silent for some time.

Clerans spoke first. "At least the pirates are gone."

"They are only gone fer now," Sheriff Laei replied. "They'll will be back. Those pirates are up to somethin'... gardin' fer somethin'..." He looked hard at Ella, but she wouldn't meet his gaze. She kept her eyes on the ground. "If this is Longfinch we are dealin' with, then you cen be certain that there is a larger plan at work here."

Elsi sobbed again and clung tighter to Ella.

The Sheriff finally spoke again, "I ha' better get the doctor to vene fer Olyfia. I am merri sorry fer yer loss, Miss Pickering, merri sorry." With that, the Sheriff walked from the room.

Mr. Blaeith picked up a chair and set it on its feet. He licked his lips slowly. "Where does that door lead?"

Elsi was silent, wiping her eyes, and Ella looked out the window.

Mr. Blaeith continued, "There were marks on the door. The pirates clearly tried to break it open. Whatever they were gardin' fer wos down there." He paused. "What is behind that door?"

Elsi took a deep breath, but didn't answer. She let her breath out and then took another one. "I am no sure. Papa said to open it. It sounded like there wos something o' great value behind it."

Ella swallowed. Mr. Blaeith may as well know. "It's the Gwambi t'easu'e."

All eyes turned to look at her. Mr. Blaeith furrowed his brow. "The Gwambi treasure?"

"Yes," Ella said. "O'h at least an ent'ance to one of thei'h cities."

Martyn raised an eyebrow. "A city?"

Laendon inhaled sharply. "Ay, I read about this! Ay, the Gwambi tained underground cities."

"Ha' anyone ever trived them?" Martyn asked, turning to his brother.

"Well, no," Laendon replied. "Ye see, they are only theoretical, but they *should* exist—to make sense o' things."

"And they do exist," Ella said. "Si'h Saemwel has been in one of them."

"How do ye know all o' this?" Elsi asked, looking up at Ella with a mixture of surprise and awe.

"Olyfia told me," Ella replied. "She said he had climbed the Gwambi towe'h f'om the inside."

No one replied to this; each person was silent, mulling over what they had learned. Elsi sobbed again, "Poor Olyfia!"

Ella spoke, "The She'iff was wight; the pi'ates a'e looking fo'h something. They'h looking fo'h the Gwambi t'easu'e. They won't stop until they find it. I've hea'd them talk. They'll lay this whole city to dust to get the t'easu'e—if that's what it takes."

"I would like to see them try! They cen no defeat the battery," Clerans said flatly.

The others were silent.

Finally, Mr. Blaeith spoke. "If what ye'll are sayin' is true—an' I am inclined to think it is—then neither o' you girls oughtta-should stay in this house. Stay with Miss Nansi, Pastor Daerl, or stay with us—Fawn and Lexi would be glad o' your company."

"We can no cede away from this house," Elsi said with a good deal of determination and decision in her voice.

Mr. Blaeith looked at her closely. "Elsi, yer in danger stayin' here. If the pirates vene back, there's no one to say that ye'll will make it out again."

"I will take that chance," Elsi replied. "Papa said fer me to keep the house fer him while he wos gone, an' I am goin' to do that fer him."

"But Elsi," Mr. Blaeith said, "yer father tained no idea that pirates would be attacking; he did no mean fer ye to stay through that."

"All the same," Elsi responded with more determination than Ella had ever heard from her before, "that is what he said, and that is what I am goin' to do, no matter the circumstances."

Mr. Blaeith was silent. He licked his lips and appeared to be thinking hard.

Aarushi whistled and preened her wing.

Finally, Mr. Blaeith spoke. "Alright then, if ye'll will no leave this house, then I will trive some folks to stay here with ye and keep ye safe. Martyn and Laendon, you cen stay here fer now, cen no you?"

"Well, ay," Martyn said. "I would need to ceive a few things from home, an' our shift on the mountain will start at the clude o' the week, but we cen stay here until then."

Mr. Blaeith nodded and turned to Elsi. "I will see if Pastor Daerl an' his wife will stay with ye, an' maybe a few others who cen stay here in shifts. We will always tain someone here who cen fight the pirates back if they'll ever come fer another gard at that door. Does that sound good?"

Elsi nodded. "Thank ye, Mr. Blaeith."

Mr. Blaeith nodded back. "It is only what yer father would want." Mr. Blaeith then turned to his sons. "We ha' best be back to the house, then. I oughtta-should pass this by Fawn first, but if she'll likes it, then Martyn and Laendon, you vene back and keep this house safe."

Martyn and Laendon nodded.

Just as they turned to go, Elsi spoke again. "Mr. Blaeith, is it possible that ye could spare Lexi as well?"

Mr. Blaeith turned back to her. "Lexi?"

"Ay," Elsi replied, "it will be hard without Olyfia, ye see. I..." Elsi trailed off as she choked up.

Mr. Blaeith smiled kindly. "Ay, Elsi, I will legate Lexi as well. I dare say she will be glad to help ye out. My boys will be back in an hour or two to help, so ye need no fret yourselves about cleanin' up much."

The Blaeith men walked from the room, but Mr. Blaeith paused as he reached the great oak doors. "Elsi," he said, "I am sorry. I am sorry all this ha' to happen to ye. With yer father gone, too."

Elsi sobbed a little.

"May God give ye strength," Mr. Blaeith continued. "We will pray fer ye. Both o' you, actually. God be with you," and they left.

Elsi buried her face in her hands and sobbed uncontrollably, sitting down in the chair Mr. Blaeith had occupied. Aarushi hopped onto the back of Elsi's chair and purred soothingly. Ella felt like crying, too—only no tears would come to her eyes. Nothing seemed real. Olyfia couldn't be dead. The pirates couldn't have found the door. This was all wrong. It couldn't be real. Perhaps she had just dreamed it all. The whole raid, breakfast with Miss Nansi...

At the thought of breakfast, she came to herself. It was a silly thought, she knew, but it was persistent.

She dashed from the room to the front door. The Blaeiths were not very far down the road yet.

"B'eakfast," she cried, "none of you have had b'eakfast yet!"

Mr. Blaeith turned back and smiled. "Thank ye fer the offer, but do no worry yerself with us. We will survive."

"Duty calls!" Clerans called back with a roguish wink. "No rest fer the weary, I am afraid."

And with that, they marched towards Entwerp Coastal.

# 36

# REPORTING BACK

As the sun reached its pinnacle in the noon sky, the Albino called a halt. The pirates had been walking all night and all morning. They hadn't stopped for anything, not even for breakfast. Ernest didn't think it was very fair, but he never said as much. He, Bill, and Tell had adopted a mute compliance to everything the Albino ordered ever since they saw what he had done to the rabbit-lipped housekeeper.

Ernest shuddered at the thought of it. *He* had just been having a bit of fun with her, but the Albino... he shivered again. Tell had been stupid enough to say something about it earlier. The Albino had just looked at Tell in his dark way.

"She talked, did she not?"

Tell nodded, too scared to say anything.

"Then it does not matter what I did."

The Albino left it at that.

Now that they had finally stopped, the three pirates sat down on the ground and panted heavily. The Albino stood a little way off, looking out at the sky. They were on a rocky ridge between two mountain peaks. Only a few scraggly bushes grew this high up, but below them, Ernest could see the tops of the enormous spruce trees that formed the forests further down. To the west was the sea, standing out like a glass mirror in the noon heat. The Albino seemed to trace a path down the ridge southwards along the coast, but Ernest didn't care enough to make much of that.

Tell lay flat on his back and gave a little groan. Ernest and Bill exchanged glances, but said nothing. Neither of them had caught their breath yet, and neither of them felt like talking, anyway.

After several minutes, Ernest reached back to his scrip. Lewis had given it to him just before they set out on the raid the afternoon before. "You may need a breakfast on the road. It might be a bit of a hike back to the ships," Lewis had said.

Ernest opened the scrip and rummaged through it. Inside were six rations of dried pork and six rations of hardtack; there was also a skin canteen of ale. Ernest smiled grimly. Six rations. Harry and Johnson would have been glad to see that Lewis had accounted for them. Still, Ernest couldn't say he was sorry they were dead. He had never liked them all that much.

Ernest tossed a ration each to Tell and Bill. "Here's a little luncheon for you."

They snatched it up eagerly and ate. Ernest chose a ration for himself and took a bite of the dried pork. "We will have two extra rations when we've had ours."

"Good," Bill said between bites of tack. "You don't think Harry and Johnson will mind?"

Ernest shrugged.

Tell gave a short giggle. "That was very funny, Bill, very funny."

Just then, the Albino approached the three pirates.

"We will reach the ship by suppertime, but we cannot approach it until nightfall—otherwise, Longfinch may see us."

Ernest nodded as he grabbed one of the remaining rations. "Would you like some luncheon, sir?"

The Albino smiled disdainfully. "No." Then he turned to Bill and Tell. "All of you, get back on your feet. You can continue to eat while you walk."

They now started the descent on the other side of the ridge, cutting ever south as they crept farther down the mountain and closer to the coast. About the time they reached the trees again, clouds rolled in, and it rained. Ernest pulled his coat tighter and kept walking. Soon, they came to a rather large stream. The water didn't look deep, but it was moving quickly.

After walking along the banks for a while with no fording point in sight, the Albino grabbed hold of a tree and muttered a few words. To Ernest's astonishment, smoke erupted from the base of the tree, and it fell across the stream with a groan.

The Albino stepped onto the log and crossed the stream easily. Bill, Tell, and Ernest just stood and watched. Had they really just seen what they thought they had? The Albino turned when he reached the other side and looked back at the pirates.

"Come on across," he said harshly.

They passed over the log and continued on. They came to a few more streams, but these they could cross with no difficulty.

The farther down the mountain they came, the thicker the forest underbrush became. Once, it was so thick that Tell—pushing ahead of the others—nearly stepped off a cliff.

The Albino pulled Tell back and pushed his way through the underbrush along the cliff's edge. When he came to a tree that jutted out nearly perpendicular to the cliff face, he turned to Ernest.

"Climb out on that tree and tell me what you see."

Ernest nodded and came up to the edge of the tree. It was a very thick spruce tree, plenty wide enough to walk across. Ernest stepped out onto it with no difficulty and walked about ten paces along its length, taking hold of the first limb from the base.

As he grabbed the limb, he glanced down. The cliff dropped

over seventy feet, and the ocean beat directly against it. The rain beat down on him in sheets, drenching Ernest and the tree trunk. Before the cliff (and directly below Ernest) was a group of razor-sharp rocks that looked almost like teeth from this vantage point. Ernest swallowed hard. Technically, this shouldn't be any more dangerous than hanging from the yard of the topgallant—yet without the foot-ropes and rigging between him and the raging ocean, Ernest felt very precarious indeed.

"What do you see to the south?" the Albino called from the cliff's edge.

Ernest looked out to the south, shielding his eyes from the rain. "I can see a bay a couple on miles further on. It looks like there's a beach there; but I can't be sure. There's a big rock face what blocks most on it from view. Wait, I think I can see a sail from here. I'm not sure, though."

"Good," the Albino said. "Come on back."

Ernest squatted down and slowly inched his way back on all fours to the cliff's edge. Every moment, he was certain he would slip and fall to his death at the bottom. He finally reached the edge, and Bill pulled him back to solid ground.

From then on, the Albino focused more on heading due south and didn't worry about moving further down the mountainside. After they spent several more hours of hacking a path through the underbrush, the ground sloped down. The forest cleared a little, and about the time the rain stopped, they reached the beach Ernest had seen from the cliff.

Opposite the beach was a huge rock ridge that jutted out of the ocean, hemming off the beach from the rest of the world. Anchored in the lee of that rock face were the galleon and the man-o-war. Tell sighed and blinked back a tear when he saw them.

Ernest looked at the two ships closely. Neither seemed to be in the best condition. The rigging on both ships was shredded, and most of the sails were torn to rags. There was clear damage and broken boards on the sides and hulls of the ships, though none of the holes appeared to be below the waterline. The man-o-war had a mast floating next to it in the water, and carpenters were erecting a new mast on the deck. The crew on board the galleon was frantically working as well. Ernest could hear the faint sounds of hammers ringing across the water.

The Albino came down close to the beach and looked along it. No one was there now, but there were keel marks in the sand and hundreds of footprints all over. Just a little way in from the beach, Ernest could see several stumps where the crew had felled trees. He guessed they must have been hard at work since dawn.

"Alright, then," the Albino said, returning from the beach. "We cannot make our way over to them until nightfall. For now, we should move back into the woods and wait for the sun to set."

"Can we sleep?" Bill asked.

"Yes—for an hour or so," the Albino replied.

The pirates moved back into the forest about a hundred yards and found comfortable places to lie down. Ernest found a little hollow where deer must have slept the night before. No sooner had he laid down than he felt the Albino shaking him by the shoulder. He opened his eyes, but couldn't see anything in the pitch-black darkness.

"Come now, I have found the boat Holgard left for us. Get down to the beach."

Ernest yawned and stood up, making his way groggily to the beach. When he got there, no one was waiting for him. The stars were bright in the sky. The moon was half full, and its glow mingled with the light of the daystar to give just enough light that Ernest thought he could see the dim outline of the ships against the black face of the rock.

Soon the Albino arrived with Bill and Tell in tow. The Albino motioned for them all to be silent, then he led the way down the beach to a dead, ivy-covered tree that had fallen half into the water. Walking into the water up to his knees, the Albino reached under the tree and pulled out a small skiff.

As soon as the pirates had crawled in, the Albino muttered a few words. Instantly, the air around the skiff grew dark and thick, as if someone had squeezed the light out of it like squeezing water from a rag. None of the pirates said anything.

The Albino gave oars to Bill and Tell while he sat in the stern and maneuvered the skiff with a short paddle. Ernest looked out from the front but could hardly see anything from where he sat. Even the daystar seemed to struggle to put out any light as if some giant titan kept snuffing it out.

"It is a cloak of darkness," the Albino said.

Ernest turned to the Albino in surprise. "What is?"

"We are in a cloak of darkness," the Albino repeated. "No one will see us approaching the ship."

Soon, a huge shape loomed before them. The Albino muttered a few more words, and the darkness cleared. They were floating right by the side of the galleon.

The Albino steered the skiff around to the aft of the boat until they were just below the window of Holgard's cabin. Taking a musket ball, the Albino threw it at the window. A moment after the ball clattered against it, the window opened, and Killjelly peered out. He only glanced at the skiff and then ducked his head back. In a moment, he reappeared to toss a rope down to the skiff. One after another, the pirates climbed the rope into Holgard's cabin, with the Albino coming last of all.

Inside, Killjelly, Holgard, and Ynwyr waited for them. Holgard drummed his fingers on the table impatiently while he waited for the Albino to reach the window. When they were all finally up, Holgard stood—so quickly that he almost knocked his chair over.

"The three on you get back to your bunks. I will need you to work hard in the morning."

*Returning to the Galleon*

The three pirates saluted. As Ernest passed last from the room, he saw Holgard take the Albino by the arm and sit him down. They would talk for a long time; that was for certain. The rabbit-lipped housekeeper told them everything she knew in a matter of minutes, but Ernest guessed Holgard would take more time than that. There was no telling what his next step would be.

Ernest made his way below deck and into the kitchen. He found all the pirates—except those on watch—asleep. But as he entered the kitchen, he saw Lewis sitting by a lantern and reading. Bill and Tell simply filed past and climbed into their hammocks, asleep in a moment.

Ernest entered quietly and sat down on a stool by the counter. Lewis looked up and grinned at him. "Hungry?"

"Very," Ernest replied.

"Good!" Lewis said as he slid his book aside and handed Ernest a bowl of stew. "I was expecting you might be. Helen Maria, Ernest, you've been gone a lot longer than I thought. I hope you finded everything you were looking for?"

"I amn't supposed to talk about it," Ernest mumbled between spoonfuls of stew.

Lewis looked at him with a merry smile. "About the raid, or the Albino?"

Ernest paused and looked at Lewis suspiciously. "How do'ed you know about the Albino?"

Lewis only winked. "I amn't supposed to talk about it."

"I see," Ernest said and continued eating.

They sat in silence for a while before Lewis reached for his book again. It was his little black scripture.

"Ernest," Lewis said, "you remember telling me that you believed there was a god?"

Ernest nodded and swallowed a bite of stew. Was this going to turn into a long conversation? It certainly sounded like it might.

"I think I should tell you about Him."

"Is he powerful?" Ernest asked, hoping that perhaps this would derail the entire conversation so that he could get to sleep sooner.

Lewis grinned. "That's what you asked last time, and now I can answer you." Lewis held up the scripture and waved it in the air.

*Baptism*, Ernest thought, *I think I just getted him started.*

"It says in here—in the very beginning—that God created everything. *Everything.* With just a few words. He spoke, and there was the world. To finish it, he made a man—which eventually led to all the rest on us. He made these brilliant stars and then the little flowers. Blind prelates, that is power! To create such huge things, and then harness beauty in such small things."

Lewis seemed to run out of words abruptly, so instead of speaking, he simply stared at Ernest intently.

Ernest licked the last bits of stew from his lips. "You should've go'ed into politics or preaching, not cooking."

Lewis didn't laugh. "Ernest, this isn't something to jest about. God is powerful, but for all that, He still wants to know us. He wants to become our intimate friend. This book talks about Him as a bridegroom—and we are the bride."

Ernest yawned, giving Lewis a critical look. "That doesn't make sense. If'n God is really that powerful, there is no way he would want to know me *personally.* Maybe he is friendly like you say, but if'n that's so, there is no way he's powerful."

"But I've just telled you," Lewis replied. "He *is* powerful!"

Ernest's mouth twitched in something approaching a sneer. "Powerful? Lewis, I've seen powerful. The Albino breaked a tree down—a full-grown, massive tree, mind you—like it was a little twig. If'n God's the maker on the tree and cared about it, then the Albino must be more powerful than God."

Lewis pursed his lips and said nothing, so Ernest went on. "The Albino maked the stars and the moon go dark. Doesn't that make the Albino more powerful than God since the Albino darkened the stars God created?"

Lewis shook his head. "I don't think that's good logic. I don't know why, but it isn't good."

Ernest snorted.

"You're missing the point," Lewis went on. "God wants to be our friend. He loves us."

Ernest's mind went back to the raid. He had done nothing to help Ella when the other pirates captured her. She had trusted him when they first brought her onto the pirate ship, but he did nothing to help her. Could God really want to befriend someone who betrayed his friends?

Then he remembered how they had cornered that rabbit-lipped housekeeper just before the Albino found them. He blushed when he thought of it. There was no reason to be ashamed; any of the other pirates would have done the same things he did. It was just a bit of fun. Still, he *was* ashamed.

Ernest took a deep breath. "Lewis, God might be friendly, but not friendly enough to worry about trash like us."

Lewis shook his head emphatically. "That can't be true. We may have evil thoughts and do evil things, but God's love is bigger than that."

Ernest held up his hands in exasperation. "Lewis, listen to yourself. For heaven's sake, we're pirates. We kill innocent people for our living. We live off the spoils on thievery. The authorities can kill us on sight." Ernest paused, looking hard at Lewis. "I don't care how powerful and friendly your God is. He doesn't care about us."

Lewis hunched his shoulders and bowed his head, like a sail losing the wind. The twinkle in his eye suddenly went out, and his face looked more like the face of a dead man. Ernest drew back in alarm. He had never seen his messmate like this.

Lewis was silent for another moment. Finally, he closed his

eyes, speaking in soft, desperate tones. "God loves us. He has to love us. He has to forgive us. I *need* Him to be like that."

Ernest took a deep breath. "Lewis, I'm sorry I said what I said. I getted carried away."

Lewis shook his head, still with that darkness in his eye. "No, it's alright."

"Look," Ernest said with a sigh. "I don't really want to talk about this anymore. I'm pretty done talking about this."

"That's fair," Lewis said simply.

Ernest turned and walked from the kitchen. He crawled into his hammock and closed his eyes, but he couldn't sleep. He opened his eyes again and looked back at Lewis. Lewis had put his book down and was now leaning on the counter with his hands lifted and his eyes closed. His lips moved slowly, as if he were talking to someone. Tears were streaming down his cheeks.

Ernest sighed and turned his face to the wall, hoping the motion of the ship would rock him to sleep.

# EPILOGUE

*J*ock lay on the floor. He was still—quite still—and pale. His hair lay matted against his head, and his face was almost blue—was that just a trick of the light? Ella looked at him in horror. Was he dead? He couldn't be dead. How had he died? Suddenly, she noticed a weight in her right hand.

She lifted her hand to her face and saw a long pistol, still smoking. She gasped and threw the pistol from her. Had she shot Jock? Why had she? She rushed to Jock's side and lifted his head, cradling it in her lap. He was limp—quite limp—and cold.

But even as she cradled Jock, his form changed. Before she knew what was happening, Jock was standing to his feet, towering over her till his head nearly brushed the high ceiling. She looked up at him, but it wasn't Jock anymore. It was her stepfather, but it wasn't his voice, it was the voice of that dreadful hook-handed leprechaun, Killjelly.

"Why do'ed you leave, sure?" he growled. "You haved no right, Ella. You have wronged the whole family, sure. You're such a waste. Such a drain. I'm dreadfully disappointed in you, sure."

Ella opened her mouth to respond and plead for pity, but her father was gone. All the lights had gone out. She was all alone.

She felt a slight draft on the back of her head and turned. As she faced the draft, it became a great gust that seemed to grasp at her hair and tear at her nightgown, penetrating her flesh and bending around her bones.

Through the gloom, Ella could see she was in the basement, facing the Gwambi door, only the door was *open*. A dull, dark light seemed to pulse from the entrance. The white-haired man with the pink eyes lay stretched out before the door, his face twisted into a grimace, but he was perfectly still.

As Ella watched, she heard a low chant. Her heart pounded in her chest, and her ears shrank with revulsion at the sound, but she could not make out what it said. Suddenly, the chanting stopped, and all was silent.

Ella took one step closer to the door when she heard a voice so close that it seemed to whisper into her ear, yet so far away that it must be screaming.

"*Ys ffayewsy ene eytacwsy ene,*
*Ys agwraswsy ene athebwsy ene,*
*Ys chreyswsy ene aeydhwffwyeyswsy ene.*"

Ella stood shuddering in terror, and her heartbeat in her throat. The voice spoke again.

"Those who make me do not need me,
Those who buy me do not want me,
Those who use me do not know me."

---

Ella sat bolt upright in her bed, sweat pouring from her body. Her heart pounded, and she gasped for air. Had it only been a dream? It was too real, too relevant. Ella shuddered again.

It was just a dream. That was it. It was only a dream.

But what if it was not? Could it be a vision? A warning? Didn't that happen in books sometimes?

Ella slid out of bed and walked to the door. She wasn't completely certain where she was going or why she was going there. Her mind was still a jumble of confusion. Was the door really open?

She soundlessly descended the stairs to the kitchen. Martyn and Laendon would be asleep in the room just down the hall, so she mustn't wake them. She came to the kitchen and stopped before the table.

All was as it should be - the rug, table, and chairs were over the trapdoor. It was concealed, as it should be.

Ella held her head in her hands and massaged her temples. What was all this about? What did it mean?

Just then, she felt a draft on her cheek. She looked up as the draft gave way to an icy blast that pierced her to the bone.

Ella faced the draft. But where was it coming from? The trapdoor was closed. It was covered. How could there be a draft coming from it? How could the wind be blowing through it?

Her heart pounded, and she couldn't move. She stood rooted to the spot, waiting for the chant to begin, but dreading it all the same.

But it never came.

The draft slowly subsided, and Ella stood all alone in the kitchen. Was she still dreaming?

Ella slowly turned and made her way back to her room. She felt drained and exhausted. What had happened down there? Had it really even happened? Or was it all just a bad dream?

Ella shuddered again. Something had been aroused; that was what happened. She was sure of it, as sure as if a trusted friend had told her—or else a feared enemy.

Something had stirred. Something had awakened from a long sleep.

It was the beginning of a summons.

# PRONUNCIATION KEY

Most of the proper nouns in this book are transliterations from Llaedhwythi Tylwen, except for a couple from Helfenic. The following is a guide to the pronunciation of Llaedhwythi Tylwen:

**Consonants** – *as in English with a few exceptions:*

- c: always hard as in *c*lub, never as in *c*ertain.
- ch: as in Ba*ch* never as in *ch*urch. Strictly not used in pure Llaedhwythi Tylwen, but often in other forms of Tylweni and foreign words.
- dh: like the *th* sound in *th*en, never as in *th*istle.
- f: v as in of.
- ff: f as in off.
- g: always hard like *g*irl, never as in *g*entle.
- ll: sounds almost like *dl*, in technical terms, a voiceless alveolar lateral fricative.
- r: flapped, as in Spanish.
- rr: trilled, as in Spanish.
- th: as in *th*istle, never as in *th*en.

*Vowels:*

- a: short as in Ell*a*. This vowel can never take the accent.
- e: short as in f*e*d.
- i: long as in sk*i*.
- o: short as in p*o*t, or long as in h*o*me.
- u: short as in p*u*t.
- y: short as in h*i*t. When followed directly by a vowel becomes a consonant, as in *y*olk.
- w: long as in pl*u*me. When followed directly by a vowel becomes a consonant as in *w*alk.

*Diphthongs:*

- ae: short as in *a*pple.
- ei: long as in h*ay*.
- aei: long as in sk*y*.
- aey: similar to *aei* but ending farther back in the mouth.

*Subjunctive:* the subjunctive case represents uncertainty or doubt, and is signified by the ending *'ll*. Example "They'll will eat," means "They might (or might not) eat."

# PISTOSIAN WORD GLOSSARY

'll – subjunctive suffix used to denote uncertainty

cede – to go, or to yield (as in con*cede*)

ceive – take, hold (as in re*ceive*)

celer – fast, quick (as in ac*celer*ate)

cern – separate (as in dis*cern*)

clude – close, shut, end (as in ex*clude*)

cognize – know in a relational sense (as in re*cognize*)

duce – to lead (as in de*duce*)

fiscate – buy

gard – look, watch (as in re*gard*)

kye – cattle

legate – send, especially as a messenger

lieve – lift, raise (as in re*lieve*)

llifsa – interjection of general surprise or consternation

merri – much, very, lot

maugre – instead of

petticoat – a crude, derogatory term for a woman

plete – fill (as in com*plete*)

pose – put (as in inter*pose*)

prehend – grasp (as in *prehen*sile)

prive – rob, steal (as in de*prive*)

priver – petty thief, pickpocket

quire – ask (as in in*quire*)

ruth – pity (as in *ruth*less)

scend – climb, rise (as in a*scend*)

spire – breathe (as in con*spire*)

sault – leap, jump (as in as*sault*)

tain – have (as in con*tain*, or ob*tain*)

trive – find (as in re*trive*)

tryst – as a verb: to have a romantic meeting. As a noun: a beau

vail – power (as in pre*vail*)

vene – to come

vert – turn (as in a*vert*)

voke – call, yell, cry (as in *vo*cal)

ween – imagine

ye – second person singular pronoun

you – second person plural pronoun

younker – youth

# ABOUT THE AUTHOR

Amos Christian Wilson is a history enthusiast, bagpipe player, fantasy cartographer, theology nerd, home-school graduate, and award-winning storyteller. His inspirations come from his love of nature and history, as well as his experience across a wide range of blue-collar trades, including carpentry and piano tuning. Amos currently lives with his wife and children in the scenic Flint Hills of Kansas.

Sign up for A. C. Wilson's newsletter to receive updates on upcoming books, and receive a free e-book prequel to *My Father's Land*!

**www.ACWilson.net**

# ALSO IN THE GWAMBI TETRALOGY

This series draws as much from J. R. R. Tolkien and Indiana Jones as it does from Charles Dickens. With a focus on immersive world-building that features fully developed fantasy races, deeply religious colonists, and labor riots, "The Gwambi Tetralogy" is black-powder, epic low fantasy, bordering on magical realism, with a faith-based, and character-driven plot.

## Book 2 - *My Father's Ghost* - Summer 2022

Her father taught Harli everything she needs to know to get along in the world, everything from breaking in stallions, to martial arts, to negotiating with the Indigenous nymphs of the coast. But then her father gives her the ancient Gwambi keys... and tells her to run.

With pirates, a sorcerer, and a griffin hunting for her and her family, Haeli must rely on all her will and wits to keep the keys safe. Is it even worth giving Ella the keys, or is she too preoccupied with the labor strikes devolving into violence, and the indigenous people taking revenge on the rural populous? Oh, and then there is the ghost...

## Book 3 - *My Father's God* - Winter 2023

Clerans must protect his village. It's the easiest thing ever. All he has to do is fire the cannons, and no one ever gets past the Entwerp battery. But now he is being sent out to board a highly explosive fireship and steer it away from the battery. How hard could that be? I mean, the only time the battery is vulnerable is during the lowest tide of the year. Oh wait, it *is* the lowest tide of the year. And if Clerans can't stop the fireship, then Longfinch's pirates will murder everyone in the village. And why doesn't he call for reinforcements? Well, the reinforcements are tied up trying to prevent the strikers from burning down the national bank.

### Book 4 - *My Father's Will* - Summer 2023

After finding God, things couldn't be better for Ernest. I mean, it would probably be better if he wasn't trapped in the ancient Gwambi catacombs, with no food or water to speak of. It would also be better if Clerans wasn't about to be skinned alive by the pirates, or if Martyn wasn't slowly bleeding to death from a traumatic head injury. But no fear, there *is* someone else trapped in the catacombs with them, someone who — if he doesn't kill them — has the medical knowledge necessary to save Martyn's life: Killjelly…

Made in the USA
Columbia, SC
23 December 2022